The
Resistance
Factor

Also by Celeste White:

Summer of Fire: A Memoir
The Last Good Fairy
Altar of Fire
Crazy Good Fortune: A Year of Adventure in Costa Rica
The Legend of the Flying Hotdog

THE
RESISTANCE
FACTOR

by

Celeste White

Keswick House Publishers

ISBN No. 978-0-9653024-9-4

Keswick House Publishers
Redding, CA

For all those on the front lines
fighting the COVID-19 pandemic

PREFACE

I wrote this novel in 1998/99, inspired by science journalist Laurie Garrett's chilling opus on emerging diseases, *The Coming Plague*. At the same time, I was enjoying books by authors who were bridging the divide between science and consciousness research, authors such as Larry Dossey, M.D., Rupert Sheldrake, and Michael Talbot. Not long before I put this book together, I published an article, "Microbes and Metaphor," in *The Noetic Sciences Review*. The philosophy underpinning that article informs this title as well.

Because this was written at the end of the 20th century, the science and medicine portrayed in this book are from that era. The diseases included are ones that were of concern at that time: Ebola, hantavirus, Mad Cow Disease, and necrotizing fasciitis (flesh-eating bacteria), to name a few. And of course, The Big One, a repeat of the Great Flu Epidemic of 1918 had been on epidemiologists' minds pretty much since 1918. The more they learned about influenza viruses, the more they worried about what the future held in store. No one was even thinking about coronaviruses. They caused the common cold; that was the sum of our experience with them, at least in recent history. SARS, MERS, and COVID-19 had yet to make an appearance on the world stage in the early 21st century.

Written at the end of the 20th century, *The Resistance Factor* also provides a snapshot of the technology and sociology of the time. Cell phones were available, but not ubiquitous. They became commonplace shortly thereafter, in 2000, 2001. Practically no one used them for international calls, and pay phones were still common. This was pre-9/11, so security at airports was far more relaxed. SUVs had yet to become popular, and car seats for children were not as widely used. The Internet was still in its infancy, and there were of course no smart phones—no connection between phones and the Internet—and no electronic tablets.

Social distancing and quarantining had not been in much use during the latter part of the 20th century; flattening the curve was not a concept. The first large scale quarantine in recent history was implemented in 2003 for the SARS outbreak, and the UK implemented a quarantine for the 2009 swine flu epidemic. Before that, flu epidemics were generally allowed to run their course, made feasible by the relatively modest mortality rate of 0.1%.

My most dramatic experience with the flu took place in 1989 in Oregon, where both my husband Richard and I were sick for two weeks with very high fever. Fortunately, we got it one right after the other, so one of us was able to care for the other. We were so sick we literally could not get out of bed. And I'll never forget the evening Richard had finally recovered and I had not yet come down with it: We had gotten dressed to go see a friend of ours perform a comedy set in a nearby small town; but on my way from the bedroom to the front door of the house, I literally collapsed. I had to crawl back to bed, it hit that hard and fast. I had a fever dream during that illness that I will never forget and that makes an appearance in this book.

When I wrote this book, I was told that "agents would run screaming out of the room" at the mention of a bio thriller, so I tucked it away in a drawer. I honestly couldn't have imagined that a pandemic in my lifetime would have made it relevant and that this book has proved more prescient than I had ever feared a harrowing work of fiction might be. That said, this is a work of fiction. It is a thriller, so it's contrived to be as dire as possible. The resolution is also fiction. But the issues raised are important and as relevant today as they were twenty-plus years ago.

We do face a great challenge, an all-too-real one, with the COVID-19 pandemic. Please listen to the experts in epidemiology and public health; they are the ones who know what we should do to lessen the catastrophic effects something like this can wreak on human civilization. One hopeful message that can be derived from this book is that several of the diseases that posed looming threats in 1999 are not of much concern now. We are capable of adapting and evolving. In fact, despite the toll that disease takes, our numbers are still putting a tremendous strain on Earth's carrying capacity and in themselves fuel pandemics.

As frightening and devastating as the current pandemic is, I believe that what will get us through is cooperation. A successful ecosystem is one in which myriad diverse species and individuals co-exist in a dynamic balance. A healthy body is one in which all tissues, organs, cells, and microbes work in harmony. Please be thoughtful of your neighbors, community members, and fellow inhabitants of this earth, whatever our differences; be kind, be generous, be strong. And most of all, be well.

~ March 2020

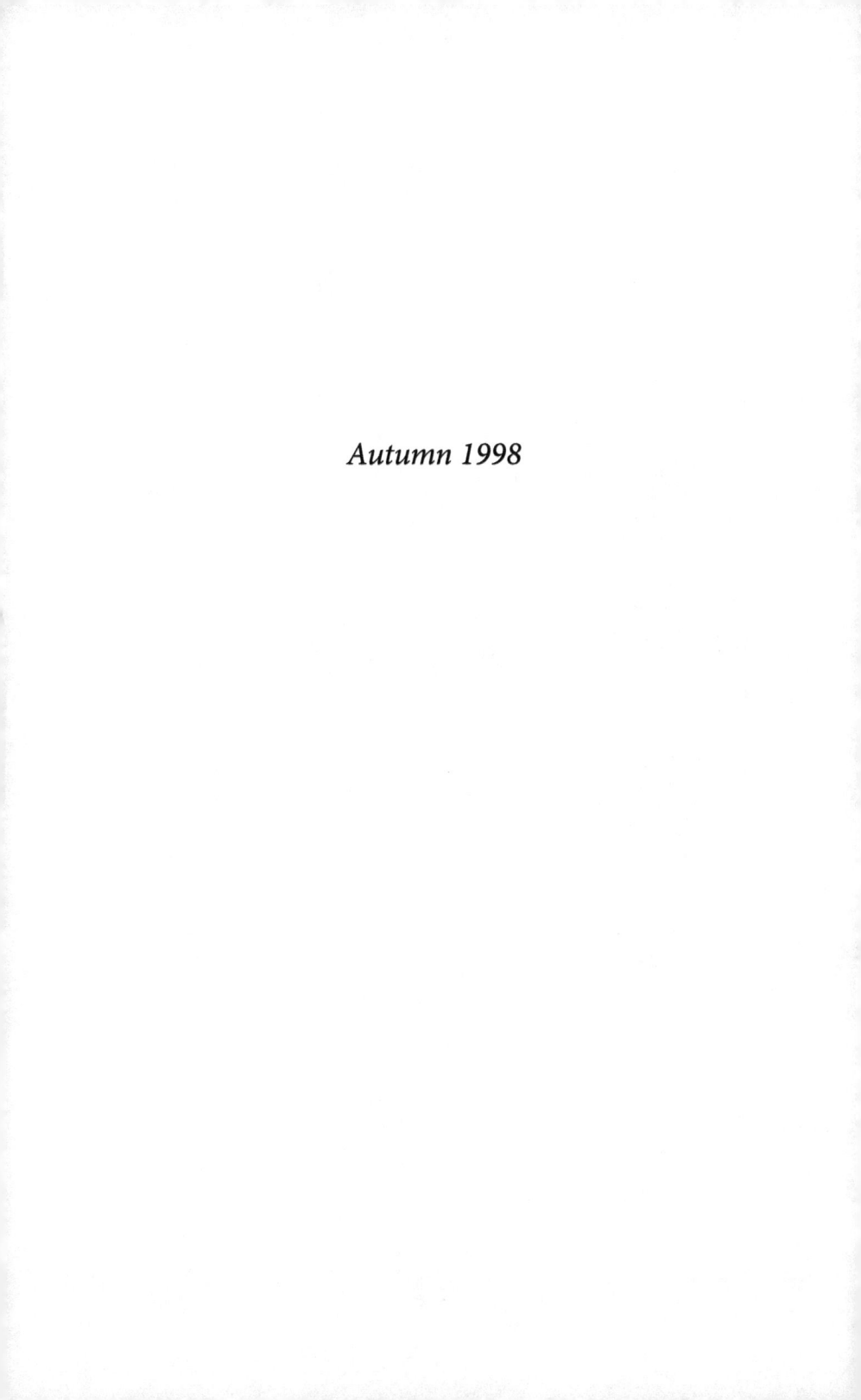

Autumn 1998

CHAPTER 1

It started with a nick that Nan got while shaving her legs in the shower. It was a tiny little nick, in fact; so tiny that Nan merely dabbed it dry with a tissue and then hastily applied a small circular Band-aid that she hoped wouldn't show. She was running late to meet Elliott for dinner at a restaurant he had spotted near their hotel, and his daughter Amber was being a bit of a pill about the fact that she hadn't been invited.

"I want to go, too!" she moaned, over and over again while Nan rushed about the suite, pulling on a dark blue silk dress and a pair of nylons, furiously brushing her hair and wishing she had time to wash it. She and Amber had returned late from their outing to Madame Tussaud's Wax Museum as Amber had resisted leaving until she had carefully inspected every single creepy, glassy-eyed figure.

Nan usually didn't wear make-up, but she applied some mascara and a little eye shadow, thinking that this might distract Elliott's attention from her hair. As she slipped on a gold necklace and pair of earrings, she felt two small, sticky hands clamp onto her leg. She looked down to see Amber's freckled little narrow face peering up at her in pain and fury.

"I don't want a babysitter! Why can't I come, too?" she whined. Nan bit her lip. She was starting to think that bringing Amber along on this trip had been a mistake. Elliott was busy all day long attending presentations at a public health symposium, so it fell to Nan to entertain her during the day. The problem was, Nan just wasn't that great with small children. She found them cute in small doses, but after a while, she wearied of playing Candyland eight times in a row and talking endlessly about the simple subjects that a six-year-old found interesting.

"Sweetie," she crooned, smoothing down the child's rambunctious orange curls and trying to sound much more patient than she felt, "sometimes grown-ups just need some time to be alone together."

"Daddy hates being away from me! He told me so!" Amber snapped, squirming away from Nan's touch. Nan crumpled into a nearby chair, feeling helpless and inept. Much to her relief, a knock sounded at the door just then, and she got up to answer it. One of Elliott's colleagues from the States had offered to babysit Amber so that Nan and Elliott could have a romantic dinner in London together. Elliott assured Nan that Amber liked this woman, and in fact, when Amber saw who it was, she yelled, "Yay!" and rushed over to her in a great display of affection. It was so dramatic that Nan figured it must be partly for her benefit, to show how unfavored she was at the moment.

She grabbed up her purse, thanked Susan for babysitting, and hurried out the door. When she reached the lobby of the hotel and looked outside, she groaned. She had forgotten her umbrella and it was pouring. The doorman seemed to be prepared for just such an eventuality, however; he graciously offered her a lovely coffee-colored one with a bamboo handle that he said she could borrow for the evening. She thanked him and dashed out into the weather, managing to keep the top of her body dry as she walked, but getting soaked from the knees down. At least the temperature was relatively warm and pleasant, for late summer in the British Isles.

Elliott was waiting for her at their table when she arrived. She gave him a kiss on the cheek as she sat down, then slipped off her wet shoes under the table. He looked handsome in a charcoal gray suit and white dress shirt; she almost never saw him in such attire at home, where he favored chinos and sport shirts from The Gap or L. L. Bean. Nan often wondered if Amber had inherited any genes from her mother whatsoever, she looked so much like a younger and more feminine version of her father. They both had red hair, although Elliott's had darkened into auburn over the years while Amber truly possessed a carrot top, and they had the same freckly skin and light green eyes. Both of them had their features centered somewhat closely in the middle of their faces, which lent them an unusual appeal somehow. They both looked inherently sweet, intelligent, and guileless, which made Amber's fractiousness hurt more than it might otherwise; it was so unexpected.

"You look great!" he exclaimed, giving her an admiring once-over as she beamed at him across the table.

"Thanks, so do you!" she replied, reaching over to give his hand a squeeze. "How were the presentations today? Anything I should know about?"

Elliott frowned. "Depressing stuff, for the most part. I had no idea, really, just how bad the drug resistance problem had gotten worldwide. I was aware that it was going on, but … it's a seriously scary situation. Some researchers are predicting that if microbes keep coming up with resistance to antibiotics and drugs as quickly as they've been able to recently, we'll be back to pre-penicillin days in less than ten years. And there's a possibility that we might start seeing malaria reappear in places like Philadelphia."

The waiter stopped by the table to ask if Nan would like a drink. She looked inquiringly at Elliott. "What do you think?

3

Should we share a bottle of wine?"

He grinned. "How about a bottle of champagne?"

"Well, aren't we the *bon vivants!*" she exclaimed. "Sure, why not?"

Elliott selected a Moët & Chandon from the wine list, then settled back in his chair, giving Nan a pleased, excited look that she didn't quite know how to interpret. Perhaps he was just feeling expansive and Continental, she mused fondly. She wanted to get back to the conversation at hand, however.

"Drug resistance has been going on for quite a while," she pointed out. "But we're coming up with new antibiotics and other drugs practically every day. We've managed to keep up so far—right?"

"True. But it might be that the microbes are finally outmaneuvering us. Mutants in a microbial population that have a selective advantage can reproduce in staggeringly short amounts of time. You know that."

Nan worked with mutations in humans but used viruses as a courier system to deliver healthy genes to individuals suffering from genetic illnesses. It was true, the brief generation times that characterized microbial reproduction comprised a great deal of the organisms' elegant adaptability. In contrast, the complexity of humans, as well as their lengthy life spans and reproductive cycles, made them rather clumsy and slow to adapt in these terms. Nan had always believed, however, that human intelligence and technological innovation put them on more or less equal footing with infectious organisms. But Elliott's information was disturbing. "It's weird, though … there've been natural antibiotics around for thousands if not millions of years, like penicillin. They've been working all this time."

"Until recently, that is."

"Right," she responded uncomfortably. "Well, I know that we've upped the ante with a certain medical and commercial practices, like feeding antibiotics to livestock to increase yield, but still, it sounds a little alarmist to me to say that we're going to be without any type of effective antibiotics in ten years. Doesn't it to you?"

Elliott spread his hands on the table and shrugged. "I don't know what to tell you. The numbers I've been seeing over the last couple of days are pretty alarming."

Nan frowned. "Any ideas as to what's going on?"

"Oh, some people think it's related to global warming. Or the breakdown of the ozone layer. Or maybe it's because of all the electromagnetic radiation we're generating these days, what with cellular phones, etc. We've altered the magnetic field of the earth as dramatically as a pole shift, which is always accompanied by increased rates of extinction, possibly due to genetic mutation from increased exposure to solar radiation."

"So, basically what you're telling me is that no one knows why this is happening."

"Just a lot of theories and speculation so far," he said.

Nan reached down absentmindedly to scratch the place where she had nicked herself with her razor. As she did so, she became uncomfortably aware of the fact that she had not swabbed the cut with alcohol or hydrogen peroxide. And now she could feel that the Band-aid was wet from the rain. Should she take it off? Or was it better to leave it on until she got back to the hotel room and had a chance to doctor it before exposing it to the air?

The only problem was, the Band-aid lay underneath her stocking. She would have to excuse herself, go to the ladies' room, and take off her nylons to remove it. Then she realized how ridiculously paranoid the discussion about drug resistance was making her. She couldn't have damaged more than a few cells, at the most. She would scrub the cut with hydrogen peroxide before she went to bed tonight and even that probably wasn't necessary.

The waiter arrived with the champagne and popped the cork with a practiced flourish. He poured a small amount in

Elliott's glass for him to sample, which Elliott did, grinning widely and proclaiming the bottle "Outstanding." After the waiter filled their glasses and left them to ponder their entree choices, Elliott held his glass aloft and said with a wink, "Here's to us." Nan smiled and raised her glass to him as well, then took a sip.

"Yum!" she exclaimed. She licked a few bubbles off her upper lip, feeling shy all of a sudden. Elliott was gazing at her once again with melting, irrepressible tenderness.

"I love you," he said.

"I love you, Elliott," she retorted playfully, twirling her champagne glass between her fingers. "You're the nicest man I've ever known."

"I am, huh? Well, that's good to hear." He cleared his throat, his expression serious. "Because I was thinking, that, uh, well ... it might be a really good idea for us to get, uh, you know ... married."

Nan's smile faded. "M–married?" she squeaked.

A look of concern began to spread over Elliott's face. "Yes, I thought ... don't you want to?"

Nan felt panicked. "Well, of course I want to," she replied hastily. "I mean, theoretically." Elliott looked baffled and hurt, which made her feel terrible. "I just mean ... I—I don't think Amber's over Lisa's death. Do you? I think it might be too soon for her."

"We can have a long engagement!"

Nan took a gulp of champagne. "We could do that," she agreed. "But aren't you forgetting something else?"

Elliott stared at her blankly. "What?"

"Muffin." Muffin was Amber's pet cat, to which Nan was violently, asthmatically allergic. Muffin also happened to be the last gift that Lisa had given her daughter shortly before she died in a horrible three-car collision two years ago. Amber absolutely adored Muffin and Nan suspected that she believed her mother's spirit continued to live on somehow in the cat's body. But Nan could not spend even a half hour in Elliott's and Amber's house without triggering a serious asthmatic episode. She had tried taking everything known to modern medicine: antihistamines, asthma medication, inhalers, shots, pills, and drops, both mainstream and alternative. Nothing worked. There was simply no way in the world that she could live in a house with a cat, no matter how much she might want to.

Elliott groaned. "I know. I haven't forgotten. I thought ... I don't know ... I thought we could figure out something. Give Muffin to a good home. Get a puppy. You're not allergic to dogs, are you?"

Nan shook her head. "Just cats." She sighed, absentmindedly rearranging her silverware.

"I think a mother is a pretty good exchange for a pet, don't you?"

"We might think so. I'm not so sure Amber would agree with you."

"Oh, come on, Nan. I think you're using this as an excuse. What's the real problem here?"

Nan hesitated, blinked back tears. "I just don't know that I'm mother material, Elliott!" she finally blurted, trying to keep her voice down. "I don't think Amber's all that enamored with me, to be honest. I don't know if she could ever accept me in her mother's place!"

Elliott rubbed the back of his neck wearily. The waiter reappeared just then, inquiring if they would like to place their order for dinner. Nan ordered the Dover sole, not feeling very hungry now. When the waiter left, Nan reached across the table and took Elliott's hand.

"You know I love you, Elliott," she told him. "I just think that Amber and I need a little more time to get to know each other. And we need to figure out what to do about Muffin. She loves that cat."

Elliott nodded and gave Nan's hand a squeeze. "Okay. I'll settle for that for now. But you haven't heard the last from me on this subject."

"I hope not!" Nan replied, laughing; but to be honest, she couldn't imagine how they were going to reconcile either one of these problems. And truthfully, Amber's rejection stung. When Nan had first met Elliott and Amber, she thought that she had never met a cuter father and daughter. Given the fact that Nan's own mother had been so emotionally distant—in fact, she made no secret of the fact that Nan had been an "accident"—she would have liked to cozy up to Amber and enjoy some mother-daughter intimacy, despite her lack of finesse with small children.

The rest of the evening passed pleasantly, and they lingered over dessert and after-dinner drinks. They arrived back at their hotel room late, where Amber was already asleep and Susan was reading a book. Elliott chatted with Susan for a bit while Nan excused herself and scooted into the bathroom to inspect her cut. To her surprise, she found a tiny speck of yellow pus occupying the center. She turned on the hot water in the tub and let it run until it was steaming, then perched on the side and ran scalding water over the cut for as long as she could stand it. She scrubbed it ferociously with soap until the wound began to bleed again, at which point she doused it liberally with hydrogen peroxide. She rummaged around in her toiletries bag for another bandage, and just as an extra precaution, she dabbed a little antibiotic ointment on the wound before applying the new Band-aid.

Susan had left by the time Nan emerged, and Elliott regarded her questioningly. "I nicked myself shaving earlier," she told him, "and hadn't had a chance to treat it properly before dinner." Elliott nodded, stretching, and said he was beat and had an early seminar to attend in the morning; so they should probably turn in. He peeked in on Amber while Nan brushed her teeth and changed into her nightgown, then they climbed into bed. Elliott curled around her tightly, falling asleep almost immediately. Nan envied him his ability to drop off so easily; she usually tossed and turned for a while. And tonight, she felt more restless than usual. Finally, she managed to drift off.

A few hours later, however, a gouging pain in her right leg awakened her. She sat up and turned on the light. When she examined her leg, it looked fine, so she took off the Band-aid to see what was happening with the cut. The wound had begun to close over, but the pain in her leg throbbed so insistently she knew that something was wrong. She shook Elliott awake.

"Mmh—what?" he mumbled.

"Elliott, something weird is going on," she said, trying to keep her voice steady.

He bolted up, turned on his light. "What do you mean?" he asked.

A sudden wave of dizziness washed over her. She closed her eyes, waiting for it to pass.

"Nan?" Elliott barked, gripping her arm. "Are you all right?"

"I've—got this intense pain in my leg. I don't really understand it. It almost feels like I've pulled a muscle, but unless I did it in my sleep, I can't figure out how I could have."

Elliott stared at her, the color draining from his face. "It feels like a pulled muscle?"

"Yeah."

He put the back of his hand against her forehead. "You're hot," he stated flatly.

"Yeah, I feel sort of hot," she mumbled. She noticed that she was feeling a little sick to her stomach, too—achy and fuzzy-headed as well. She began to shiver.

Elliott jumped out of the bed and began pulling on his trousers. "We're going to the hospital," he informed her grimly. "Can you get dressed?"

"I think so," she replied, her lips stiff.

"Good. I'll go get Amber."

Elliott dashed into the adjoining room while Nan

9

contemplated getting dressed. It sounded simple. Just get out
of the bed and put on her clothes. But she felt so incredibly
tired all she wanted to do was lie down and go back to sleep.
Elliott returned, holding Amber by the hand. He had dressed
her hastily in a cotton turtleneck and jumper, and she looked
sleepy and bewildered.

"There's no time to waste, Nan," he told her, worry making
his voice harsh.

"What's the matter?" asked Amber, sounding frightened.

"I'm sorry," said Nan, her speech slurred.

Elliott let go of Amber's hand and grabbed Nan's arm.
"Come on, sweetheart. We need to get moving." He twisted
around to address his daughter. "Amber, sweetie, could you get
a pair of slacks and some kind of top for Nan? Just give me the
first things you find, okay?"

Amber froze for a moment, but then she trotted over to
Nan's bag and dragged out a skirt and pullover. "This okay?"
she said, hurrying back over to where Elliott stood helping
Nan to pull her nightgown over her head.

"It's great," he said, not bothering to look.

Nan groaned as she stepped into the skirt, then donned a
pair of loafers Elliott found somewhere. She caught a glimpse
of Amber's terrified face and realized that she must not be in
very good shape at all.

"Shouldn't we call 911?" she mumbled, thick-tongued.
Perhaps too much champagne at dinner? she thought
confusedly.

"There's a hospital near here; we'll take a cab," Elliott told
her, wrapping her arm around his waist. "Can you walk?"

Nan nodded. She felt Amber slip her hand into hers; she
looked down to see her lips and eyebrows puckered in distress.

"I'm sorry I was mean to you today, Nan," she burst
out. Nan tried to tell her it was all right, but she was having
difficulty doing anything besides stumbling along with Elliott.
When she didn't manage to reply, Amber tightened her grip

on her hand and asked tearfully, "Daddy, is Nan going to be okay?"

"Sure she is, honey," Elliott reassured her, but all Nan heard in his voice was fear.

A doorman remained on duty, even at this hour, and he managed to procure them a taxi right away. Nan was feeling worse and worse by the minute, so when they arrived at the hospital, she whimpered in relief. Elliott threw a wad of bills at the driver and scooped Nan up in his arms. He staggered into the emergency entrance, Amber pattering behind. Everything looked far away and blurry to Nan, and sounds seemed to pummel her in odd, percussive bursts. She closed her eyes, heard Elliott say, "necrotizing fasciitis," and then she felt herself being lifted and stretched out onto a gurney. She sensed people crowding around her, smelled someone's fruity, metallic cologne and someone else's menthol-scented breath. A sharp jab in the back of her hand let her know they were starting some kind of IV, and soon after, she lost consciousness.

When she opened her eyes again, she found herself bedded down in a hospital room. Elliott sat dozing in a chair next to the bed, with Amber asleep in his lap. She looked to the other side of her where another patient presumably lay; a curtain was drawn across the room for privacy.

"Elliott?" she croaked.

His eyes jerked open immediately.

"What happened?" she asked him.

He reached over and grasped her hand tightly, so tightly it hurt. "You, my dear, have survived a brush with the infamous flesh-eating bacteria."

She shuddered. "Ew," she said, scrunching up her nose. "Seriously?"

Elliott nodded. "I just thank my lucky stars that necrotizing fasciitis was one of the topics under discussion at the symposium. It's very difficult to diagnose, but if you can catch it in time, you can escape with just a few scars. If not …"

Nan held up her hand. He didn't need to tell her. You could lose a finger, a limb, or even your life. It was a virulent, disfiguring, devastating disease. Fortunately, it was rare. "So, I guess I'll be scarred, huh?" She lifted up the sheet and looked underneath. Her leg was neatly bandaged with gauze and tape.

Elliott shrugged. "Maybe. Maybe not. We caught it very quickly. The surgeon did some intensive debriding, which was why we had to put you under."

"I see." Nan laid back against the pillow, feeling oddly euphoric from her brush with killer bacteria.

Amber stirred and opened her eyes. When she saw that Nan was awake, she shouted, "Oh, good!" and jumped on the bed to give Nan a hug.

"Hey, take it easy!" laughed Elliott. Amber ignored him, and Nan hastily returned her embrace, caught off guard by the unexpected affection. Elliott stretched his arms and legs, then stood up. "Um, by the way, Nan, I should probably go ahead and tell you something that we learned while you were in surgery."

Nan swallowed, afraid that there might be some complication or hidden health defect that no one knew about until now. "What?"

"Well, I called the hotel just to let them know what was going on, and you had received a phone call from your mother's neighbor, Ingrid. She said it was an emergency, so I called her back." He paused. "It seems that your mother almost burned her house down. She set it on fire while cooking something."

"Is she all right?" Nan asked anxiously.

"Yes, she's fine, more or less. At least, physically."

"Well, that's a relief!"

"Yeah, but ... there's something else."

Nan gave Amber an extra squeeze, then gently eased her off the bed to get a better view of Elliott. "What?"

"Well, apparently, she has multi-infarct dementia. She's

12

been experiencing a series of small strokes for some time now, apparently, but she hasn't wanted you to know."

"She's suffered some brain damage?"

Elliott nodded. "It's become fairly significant at this point. And it's only going to get worse."

Nan sat in silence, digesting this information. What was this going to mean?

A cheery knock sounded at the door just then, and a tall, gangly man with a stethoscope around his neck strode into the room.

"How's the patient?" he boomed; Nan wasn't sure whether he was asking her or Elliott. Elliott answered.

"She seems to have pulled through just fine," he said.

"Excellent!" exclaimed the doctor. "We should be able to discharge her today, in fact. We'll just need to keep an eye on things—and someone will need to take care of dressing the wound and monitoring her symptoms."

"I can do that," Elliott replied. "I'm a physician, actually. Not practicing at the moment—I work for Public Health in the States—but I can look after her."

"Brilliant," he responded. He turned his attention to Nan. "I'm going to take a look at your leg, Professor Schulte, make sure that everything's proceeding the way it should do."

"Okay," she replied. He folded back the covers and inspected her leg, both front and back. He inspected the other leg, too. "What are you looking for?" she inquired.

"Blood blisters. Purple patches. You should keep an eye out for them as well. This bacterium can get deep into your system and travel around."

Nan grimaced in distaste. "Sort of a sci-fi kind of disease, isn't it?"

"Indeed!"

"It's fortunate it's rare, isn't it? I wonder how I got it?" she mused.

"Rare until recently," the physician replied, finishing his

examination and settling the covers back over her.

"What do you mean?"

"We've had a fairly remarkable number of cases lately."

"You have? Anyone know why?"

He shook his head. "Not really. But, as you say, this is the stuff that horror films are made of. We can only hope that someone figures out what's going on before we have a real problem on our hands."

CHAPTER 2

Nan rushed around the house trying to finish up a few last minute tasks before heading off for lecture. As usual, she had too many things to take care of in too little time.

"You doing okay in there, Mom?" she shouted to her mother, who was seated in the living room with the television blaring.

"Doing okay," came the reply. Her silent strokes had continued over the last year, ravaging the part of her brain responsible for language. Often, the best she could do when replying to someone was to parrot what they had said, selectively using the phrase that would best communicate what she wanted to say. Despite the guilty resentment that her mother's new dependence elicited, Nan found this fractured ingenuity heartbreaking.

She headed into the living room, pulling on her jacket as she went. She stooped over to give her mother a quick peck on the top of her head; Myra leaned back in slow motion and smiled.

"Janice should be here any second," Nan told her, more for her own sake than her mother's. Nan would have to remain until Janice showed up as Myra couldn't be left by

herself for any length of time at all. Even if she promised to
stay seated, she wouldn't. Or couldn't. Yet if she attempted to
stand unaided, she would fall— heavily, inevitably, uncom-
prehendingly, and stubbornly. Nan found it maddening that
she couldn't stay put, and at the same time, she felt awful
whenever her mother hurt herself, which she still managed to
do even with as much supervision as she had. Luckily, several
of her students were available and willing to provide kind
and responsible eldercare. She didn't know what she would
have done otherwise. But it was true that students weren't
necessarily the most punctual employees she could have
hired. Impatiently, she glanced at her watch. Where in the
heck was Janice? Nan shifted her attention to the television,
absentmindedly stroking her mother's shoulder.

"A new outbreak of Ebola virus has been reported in
Liberia," announced the news anchor, causing Nan to stiffen.
"Apparently unrelated to other outbreaks in Zaire and Sudan,
health workers are scrambling to contain the outbreak before
it spreads. Unconfirmed reports put the death toll so far
at thirty-five, although at least twice that many have been
diagnosed with the disease. Officials have quarantined the
village of Kumba and—"

Hearing a knock at the back door, Nan hurried to answer
it. Instead of Janice, one of her undergraduate students,
Kristin, stood on the porch. "Hi, Professor Schulte," she said.
"Janice came down with some bug this morning, so she asked
me if I could fill in for her."

"Oh, okay. Come on in." Nan stepped back to let her pass.
"Thanks, Kristin. What kind of bug?"

She shrugged. "Just general yuk, I think. She told me to tell
you she was really sorry."

"No problem. I'm glad you were available." Nan grabbed
up her purse, briefcase, and keys. "I need to run—see you this
afternoon. Bye, Mom!" she called over her shoulder as she
half-ran to her car. An early cold snap had drenched the trees

in the yard various Technicolor shades of crimson, canary yellow, and pumpkin orange; a few fallen leaves swirled about her feet. She sniffed the brisk New England air, detecting a faint scent of wood smoke from a neighbor's fireplace. As she drove, she mulled over the news of the Ebola outbreak in Liberia.

It wasn't her imagination. The virulence of the microbial kingdom had increased exponentially in the last few months. But whether officials had decided that admitting this fact would only create hysteria or whether they were scrambling to figure out their strategy before addressing the problem, no one in either the media or academic circles was really talking about it. All the news stories focused on outbreaks here and there—flesh-eating bacteria in England, antibiotic-resistant pneumonia and TB in Europe, Ebola and Marburg in Africa, drug-resistant cholera and malaria in Asia: Scary for the people in these "isolated" outbreaks, but nothing for the world at large to be concerned about. Nothing that new drugs, antibiotics, and vaccines couldn't handle.

Nan used to believe this, too, but now she had her doubts. Something different was going on lately, something extremely disturbing. It wasn't just that she had experienced her own brush with a killer bacterium, although that had certainly heightened her awareness of infectious disease. It just seemed that every time she turned on the news or picked up a newspaper or even perused her academic journals, some frighteningly virulent, infectious, and resistant new strain of microbe was making an appearance. Elliott's assessment of having ten years before the world returned to a pre-penicillin Dark Age now seemed like wishful thinking. What was going on?

When she arrived at the university and was hurrying down the hall to her lecture room, she practically collided with the department head.

"Congratulations on your article in *Virology*, Nan!" he

beamed unctuously.

"Thanks, Ron," she replied. She had just published a major breakthrough she and her lab made recently in using viruses to deliver healthy genes to individuals suffering from ADA deficiency, a rare but fatal congenital blood disease.

"What's this I hear about your not wanting to patent your method?"

She stifled a groan. "Medical breakthroughs are not the kind of thing I feel comfortable profiting from," she said. "You know that. But look, I'm supposed to be lecturing in about two seconds. I'll see you later, okay?"

"Fine—but you haven't heard the last from me on this subject." He adjusted his tie, craning his neck like a rooster as he tightened the knot and smoothed it down. "You wouldn't be the only one benefiting from the patent, you know. Don't forget where the money to run your lab comes from."

Nan smiled sourly. "How could I ever forget when you're always reminding me?" She reached over and tugged on his tie to loosen it. "Later."

She shook her head in exasperation as she headed into the lecture hall. No kidding she wouldn't be the only one to benefit from the patent. The university, of course, would receive the patent, and the lucrative licensing rights would no doubt go to Ron and several of his buddies who had started a private biotech firm to take advantage of the graduating talent from the department—and the high money stakes of high tech, bioengineered medicine.

As she took her place at the podium, she felt gratified to see the hall was full. Molecular biology had become more popular in the last ten years, thanks to all the new developments in genetic engineering. When she was earning her degree, often only a handful of students attended the classes she took. Her appearance at the front of the room had the effect of quieting everyone down; notebooks flipped open, students scooted around in their seats to get comfortable, pens poised expectantly.

"Okay, class—let's get started. Last meeting we talked about molecular structure and orbital theory. Today I want to talk about molecular function. One of the most intriguing aspects of biological molecules is their multidimensionality. They are the stuff that life is made of—the building materials, if you will: the concrete, the boards, the nails, and the glue. They are also the tools that assemble the materials: the hammers, saws, nail guns, and drills. And they also serve the function of communicators. They communicate information, primarily by their shape and the patterns in which their charges are distributed throughout the molecule."

A hand shot up in the middle of the lecture hall.

"Yes?"

"Extending your analogy, does that mean molecules are the contractors and draftsmen, too?" a student with a buzz cut asked.

Nan laughed along with the class. "Hmm, I don't know about that. You might be teetering a little too far into philosophy with that analogy," she replied, smiling. "I prefer to think of them as the blueprints and walky-talkies in this context. But you're getting the idea. Molecules are amazing, miraculous entities, and their versatility is what makes life possible …"

The lecture went smoothly and well, and the intelligent and animated questions that followed pleased her a great deal. It meant that not only were the students listening, they were thinking, too. Afterward, she had a committee meeting and then she spent an hour in her office where she tried to grade some quizzes from her advanced genetics class but kept getting interrupted by visits from students and phone calls from colleagues. When the phone rang for the umpteenth time, she considered not answering it. But she finally snatched it up on the seventh ring.

"Hi, beautiful."

"Elliott! Am I glad I answered the phone."

"Me, too." He chuckled. "Hey, are you free for lunch?"

She checked her watch. "Sure, a quick lunch. Where do you want to meet?"

"How about Delancey's? I have a hankering for a big, juicy hamburger."

"Okay, I'll meet you there in … what? Fifteen minutes?"

"Fifteen minutes. See you there."

She hung up, glad for the enforced break in her day. Her work required long, hard hours, and she was still recovering from the necrotizing fasciitis that she had contracted last summer. She just didn't have as much energy as she used to, before the infection, although she was regaining her strength over time. In fact, she had finally sought out a naturopath last winter, who had prescribed a nutritional regimen, herbs, aromatherapy, and relaxation techniques. She had been worried enough that she adhered to pretty much everything her practitioner suggested, except for eliminating dairy from her diet. If she had to give up eating gorgonzola cheese and Greek yogurt, she would rather go ahead and die. Little by little, she had begun to improve.

According to Elliott, who didn't have much patience with the alternative medical movement, her improvement was gradual enough that it could have simply been due to her body's natural ability to recover. Nan didn't dispute this; he could be right. But her physical health wasn't her only concern. After her mother moved in, the stress of having her there had been so excruciating that Nan had to do something. Herbs, aromatherapy, and relaxation techniques had come in quite handy for dealing with stress; and she knew that unrelieved stress could certainly sap her strength and recuperative powers.

When Nan arrived at Delancey's, she spotted Elliott's curly hair sticking up over the top of the booth where he was seated. She slid into the seat opposite, leaning over the table to give him a kiss.

"Hey, sexy!" he greeted her, grinning.

"Hey yourself!" she retorted, smiling back. "Have you ordered yet?"

He shook his head. "I was waiting for you."

"Oh, okay. I hope you haven't been waiting long."

"Just got here," he said.

"Good." She perused the menu, deciding upon a bowl of French onion soup and a salad. After the waiter took their order, she leaned back in her seat, gazing affectionately at Elliott. He was just such a nice-looking man. His face broke easily into a lovely smile, and she could swear that his eyes actually, literally sparkled upon occasion.

"How's work?" she asked, reaching for her glass to take a sip of water.

Elliott sighed. "Fairly weird, at the moment." He pushed his menu to one side, propped his elbows on the table. "We've got a serious outbreak of hepatitis in the area right now, and it's neither type A nor type B. But it doesn't really seem to be C or D, either. In fact, it appears to be some weird hybrid of them all, but we haven't finished analyzing it yet, so we can't say for sure." The waiter came by and served them their salads, refilled their water glasses. "We're wondering if perhaps there might be a rise in the use of IV drugs. Heroin's made a comeback lately, and it could be that this is where it got started. But less than a quarter of the diagnosed cases have ever used IV drugs. It's probably being passed through touch, but again, we're having a hard time figuring out where it started. We're checking all the restaurants in the area, of course."

Nan stared at him, disquieted by this news.

"But there's more. Some reports are starting to come in from China that a very, very nasty flu is going around there." Elliott sat in silence for a few moments. "There are some indications, actually, that this might be The Big One that everyone's been waiting for."

"Christ. The superduper recombined version?" This was an ominous development. Ever since the Great Flu Epidemic of 1918, a globally devastating plague which killed twenty to forty million people—more than any other epidemic in history—virologists and public health officials waited in dread for another pandemic. They feared it was more or less inevitable, given enough time. In addition to mutating frequently in small ways, flu viruses could mix and match entire segments of their genetic structure, creating variants that no human host had ever seen before and to which they had no existing immunity.

"Quite possibly."

"Jesus, let's hope not."

"Amen," agreed Elliott, catching her eye from beneath his shaggy eyebrows.

Nan knew what he was thinking. "I know, I know. I should get a flu shot."

"Not just you, either. Myra should definitely get one."

She nodded vaguely, hoping to avoid an argument. The problem was, the flu vaccine had to be made up far enough ahead of the flu season that a fair amount of guesswork went into deciding which strains to vaccinate against. If this was indeed a new enough variant that it represented a potential pandemic, no one would have been able to guess how the genetic segments of the flu viruses would have recombined. Nan didn't see any point in getting a vaccine that probably wouldn't do much good. And Myra had the most amazing immune system of anyone she had ever encountered. She never got sick. Nan had assumed that this was just a characteristic of mothers when she was growing up, but once she left home, she began to appreciate what an amazing constitution her mom possessed.

She realized she hadn't touched her salad, so she crunched down a few bites, pondering this new information. "You know, no one seems to be really connecting all the dots here," she observed. "It seems to me that we have a really serious situation brewing."

Elliott sank back in his seat. "I'm afraid you're right."

"Not only do we have all these organisms with multiple drug resistance, their virulence and infectivity is increasing as well. We've got all these new mystery strains of diseases like hepatitis ... and I hear that certain rare infectious diseases are on the rise as well."

"All true."

Nan expelled an exasperated breath. "So why isn't Public Health addressing this? What's the CDC doing? I mean, usually whenever there's any kind of spooky outbreak at all, the CDC is all over it in ten seconds."

"Well, they have been investigating the individual outbreaks. But their funding for this sort of thing has been cut. In between pandemics, everyone thinks they're dispensable."

Nan shook her head. Shortsightedness might just be the death of the human race. "But don't you think there's more going on here? Why isn't anyone looking at the big picture? Why isn't anyone talking about why this is happening all at once?"

He shrugged, his expression grim. "I've been asking myself the same questions. I can only think that one of two things are operating. It could be the 'UFO' factor—don't let the public know because they'll only panic and make things worse. Then again, it could be that we're in a state of denial. I mean, we've had infectious disease on the run for several generations now. I think it's hard for people who have practically seen the demise of infectious disease in their lifetimes to imagine that the tide could turn."

"'On the run,'" Nan mused.

Elliott gave her a puzzled look. "Right," he said.

Nan tapped her fingers on the table. "Have you ever noticed how we always use military terminology when we're talking about disease? You know, cells are 'invaded' by viruses ... our bodies are 'attacked' by a disease ... our immune systems are our 'defense system' …"

"Uh-huh. And your point is …?"

"Well, maybe they're fighting back. We sort of assume that we can unilaterally declare war from our side and the microbes are just going to let themselves get wiped out."

Elliott gave a surprised laugh. "I wouldn't say that, exactly. They're constantly mutating ways around our defenses."

"Yes, they are. And let's not forget, a lot of our 'defenses' are really more like offenses."

"I suppose."

"So, perhaps they're launching an offensive."

The waiter came by, cleared away their salad plates and served Elliott his hamburger, Nan her soup. Elliott shook a few drops of Tabasco sauce on his fries, then blackened them with pepper. The spicy tang prickled her sinuses; she thought she might sneeze but didn't.

"No offense, sweetheart, but you're sounding a little anthropomorphic," he remarked.

Nan grimaced. "Heaven forbid! I mean, we know what it means to be anthropomorphic, right? Since we know exactly what it's like to perceive the universe from every single other creature's point of view? We can say with certainty that no other organism besides us thinks or feels or plans, right?"

"For heaven's sake, Nan!" Elliott declared, more amused than annoyed. "I'll grant you that a dog has feelings and probably thoughts, too. And cats and horses and chimps and pigs. But honestly—what would a bacterium plan or think with? They don't have a brain! They don't even have any organs at all! They're a single cell. And viruses—viruses aren't even really alive! They're opportunistic bits of protein and ribonucleic acid."

"I personally don't think we understand viruses enough to know what they are," Nan bristled.

Elliott reached over to clasp her hand. "I'm sorry. I don't mean to sound like I'm making fun of you."

"Then what are you doing?"

He gazed at her, his expression grave. "I'm trying to deal with my fear, I guess. I have no idea what's going on, Nan. These new developments—they scare the holy shit out of me. And I have no idea what to do about them."

Nan returned his gaze, unnerved by his admission. She tried to think of some reply, but couldn't. She was frightened, too. And she didn't have the slightest clue how to meet this crisis, either.

CHAPTER 3

Holding her breath, Nan carefully pipetted the solution containing her delivery viruses into the petri dish where her tissue cultures were growing—tissue cultures deficient in an important enzyme, one of the ones implicated in cystic fibrosis. She worked under the hood, which was designed to whisk away all of the air contained within its boundaries, even though her viruses were no threat to anyone. She always took precautions in her work, however. Viruses were unpredictable enough, especially when they were altered by engineering, that it made no sense to take chances. The roar of the fan under the hood effectively obscured all sound in the lab while she was working under it, so she didn't hear Ron approach until he was right behind her. Fortunately, he waited to say anything until she had finished her procedure, but he still scared the living daylights out of her when she turned around, sensing a presence.

"Oh! My God, Ron—give a person some warning, why don't you?" she exclaimed, her heart pounding.

"Sorry. I wasn't sure how to avoid startling you."

"Maybe you shouldn't sneak up on people who are working under the hood."

"You're right." He paused.

"What's up?" she asked.

"Well, we just received a notice from the administration that they're going to have to start taking a larger percentage of each grant for overhead expenses."

"Give me a break! It's already close to two-thirds!"

"I know. It's awful," he agreed. "But laboratories are very expensive to run. You know that. Reagents, equipment, utilities, liability insurance … all those things add up."

"Administrators' salaries …"

He gave a half-hearted chuckle. "Of course."

"Okay, so—great. I'll build it into my next grant. Anything else?"

"Well, I just wanted to talk to you some more about your viral delivery system. If you would patent it, the university would be able to benefit from it. We could use that money to fund more research."

Nan frowned. "But that would also make the whole procedure more expensive for those who would need to use it. And it would definitely squelch any kind of cooperation between our lab and other scientists who are working on similar systems."

"True, and that's a regrettable consequence. But if you can't do your research, that's not going to help anyone either, is it?"

"Whoa, wait a minute! What's that supposed to mean?"

"What's what supposed to mean?"

Nan leaned back against the lab bench, studying his face. "That sounded a little bit like a threat."

Ron glowered. "I think we're being just a little bit paranoid. And sanctimonious. I mean, who do you think you are, Madame Curie? Florence Nightingale? You're this pure, altruistic scientist and we're all just a bunch of money-grubbing capitalists?"

"Hey, I've never claimed to be anything but a scientist." Nan narrowed her eyes, her heart continuing to pound. "And as for the 'money-grubbing capitalist' remark, how would you characterize your interests?"

"I'm a scientist, just like you!" he snapped. "Except that I'm a realist instead of some head-in-the-clouds idealist! Labs take money to run. That's a fact. Science needs money to advance. That's another fact. Labs don't run on goodwill and high ideals! They're a business. And if you don't like that, maybe you should find something else to do."

Nan regarded him, speechless. "Look, I bring in plenty of grant money."

"And what I'm trying to tell you is that isn't going to hack it anymore." Ron's face had reddened considerably, and the veins on his neck had swollen into bulging wormlike cords. "You're going to need to cooperate in bringing other sources of money here. Big science means big bucks. If you want to play with the big boys, you have to ante up. Can I make it any clearer for you?"

"Uh, no, I think you've made yourself perfectly clear," she replied, turning away from him. "Thanks. Now, if you don't mind, I've got work to do." She picked up her pipette once more and noticed that her hands were shaking. Damn him! She would have to calm down a little before she could resume her tasks.

As soon as she was sure he was out of the room, she sank down onto a nearby desk, massaging her forehead with her fingers. One of her graduate students, Joshua, stepped out from his little cubby hole of bookshelves and lab tables that he'd erected for himself in the lab. "Uh, Nan?" he ventured.

She glanced up. "Oh, you're still here," she sighed. "Great. You got to hear that charming little interchange?"

"I'm afraid so. I—I just wanted to say that everyone else really appreciates your reluctance to cash in on your work. You shouldn't let him bully you."

"Thanks for the vote of confidence, Josh." She tried to smile. "I appreciate it."

"No problem." He hesitated, adjusted his glasses. "Um, listen, I've been wanting to ask you—what's your take on all these drug resistant outbreaks?"

Nan exhaled heavily. "I don't know what to think, to tell you the truth. It certainly seems like the process has accelerated recently."

"It seems that way to me, too. And I don't know if you noticed this or not, but the necrotizing fasciitis outbreak that you encountered in England appears to have been one of the first outbreaks in this whole wave."

"Yes, I have noticed that."

"Do you think it's significant?"

"It might be. There've been so many, though, it's hard to say."

He nodded, tugging thoughtfully at his chin. He had started to grow a goatee but he didn't quite have enough facial hair to pull it off. "What was it like? Was it scary?"

She pursed her lips, considering. Everyone in the lab usually avoided mentioning her encounter with necrotizing fasciitis, probably thinking the subject was too painful or personal. "At the time, I was really too out of it to be all that scared," she told him. "Afterward, it was scarier, thinking about what could have happened. But you know, it was interesting. I didn't necessarily react the way I thought I might. It's such a horrific disease, I thought I might end up with this fear and loathing of bacteria, despite my professional perspective on microbes."

"You didn't, though?"

He shook her head. "No, it was like ... well, this is probably going to sound crazy."

Joshua shoved his hands under his bony arms, rolled his eyes. "You're talking to someone who doesn't exactly have his finger on the pulse of mainstream America."

She chuckled. "Okay, well—it felt like something wanted to get my attention."

"Really? The bacteria?"

"I don't know. I guess so."

"For what purpose?"

Nan coughed self-consciously. It was one thing to harbor these feelings privately. It was another to actually say them out loud and hear what they sounded like. "It seemed ... like a warning, I guess."

Joshua blinked. "A warning, huh?"

"Yup." Nan stood up, brushed some nonexistent lint off her slacks. "Now, don't ask me any more questions. I've already been accused of anthropomorphism by Elliott, and I don't have any answers."

"Gotcha," he responded, holding up both hands as if to fend her off. "I hate being accused of the 'A' word." He grinned slightly and ducked back into his cubicle.

Nan remained motionless for a few minutes, trying to regain her composure. She still felt rattled by her confrontation with Ron. Unfortunately, he was right about one thing—grant money was becoming less and less important in research. Grants from the government were drying up; corporate money was taking its place. And the corporations expected a tangible return on their investment, which, in her opinion, compromised researchers' results. Patents, of course, were another source of income, especially in the area of biotechnology these days. Money generated from the licensing of rights to use the patent, however, was the most valuable of all, and Ron's lab, among others, was flush with this kind of support.

In fact, although she knew she was one of the "stars" of the department, she relied quite heavily on the loyalty and dedication of her grad students to generate her results, since she didn't have as much research income as many other faculty members. She generously shared credit on the authorship of her papers, and she never forgot who did most of the tedious, time-consuming grunt work on her experiments. It was amazing, though, that she was able to produce the science she did, considering. If she had more money, she pondered, genuinely tempted, who knew what she and her researchers could accomplish?

Still, she hated what the whole profit motive was doing to science. Despite what neo-faux-Darwinists thought, cooperation proved much more efficient and effective than competition over the long term; her study of the life sciences had reinforced that notion much more than the "red in tooth and claw" misconception. And in the olden days—that is, ten years ago—before biology had become so hot, the information that was shared between labs and the lack of duplication of effort was exactly what had led the biological sciences to make the incredible breakthroughs it had up until now. And now, with the disturbing developments in infectious disease, the thought of competitive little islands of researchers, each jealously guarding their findings in order to maximize profits, made her particularly angry.

She decided to finish up her procedures and then head home. She had invited Elliott and Amber over to dinner, and she wanted to have enough time to put together something nice. Besides, Ron and his pushy greediness had cast a pall over her work in the lab.

Janice was there, tending her mom, when she arrived. Luckily, Janice's ailment seemed to have been some very mild bug that she had already gotten over. Nan found her in the kitchen, brewing Myra a cup of tea, her thick blond hair pulled back in a ponytail.

"How's Myra today?" she asked, setting down her bag, briefcase, and wad of journals that she planned to read before going to bed.

"Mm, fine, I guess. I don't know. Today might not be one of her better days. She was having a hard time telling me what she wanted to tell me. She seems to be concerned about something, but I could never figure out what it was."

"Okay, I'll see if I can figure it out." Nan divested herself of her jacket and hat, plopping them on the counter next to her journals, and headed into the living room where her mother sat watching a figure skating competition. Myra had been a dancer when she was young, and in fact, she had been quite a figure skater, too. Nan took more after her father, a bookish botanist who taught at Boston University; but they both loved watching Myra in motion. When she became too old to perform, she had opened a studio where she taught ballet and modern dance.

"Hi, Mom!" she called, bending down to give her mother a hug and a kiss. "How's it going?"

"How's it going? Fine." She gave Nan a dazzling smiles. It was interesting, Nan mused; her mother had always had a beautiful smile—she was a striking woman with sharp, well-defined features, of which Nan had inherited only her dark, dramatic eyebrows. But her dementia seemed to have unmasked some core essence unshaped by socialization, which meant that she expressed her emotions nakedly and ingenuously. When she smiled, she seemed positively cherubic.

"Janice said you had something on your mind that you were having trouble telling her."

"Yes."

"What did it have to do with? Can you say?"

Myra gazed fixedly at Nan. She seemed to be trying to speak but couldn't. Finally, she said, "It had to do with ... " Nan waited. "It had to do with ... oh, it had to do with ... well ... nuts." Her face puckered with effort and frustration. She grasped Nan's arm with her slender, desiccated fingers.

"How about if I see Janice off and then we'll see if we can figure it out, okay?"

Her mother exhaled heavily. "Okay."

Nan returned to the kitchen, where Janice was just taking the tea bag out of Myra's cup and sweetening it with a bit of honey. "Do you want to serve this or should I?" she asked.

"Oh, I'll do it, thanks." Nan gave her a quick hug. "How are you feeling?"

"Fine—really. Whatever I had was no big deal."

"That's good." Nan felt genuinely relieved. The flu reports that continued to come out of Asia were no less than alarming. The bug over there was virulent, no doubt about it. Several elderly people and a few babies had died from it, as well as the complicating pneumonia that came after. It seemed very similar to the strain that had killed Jim Henson several years back and almost did in Elizabeth Taylor. Still, it was too soon to tell whether it was going to end up being as bad as The Great Flu Epidemic, when people would board a street car feeling perfectly fine and have expired by the time they reached their destination. But what made it all the more worrying was the increasing resistance of pneumonia germs to the few antibiotics left that had any effect on the organisms at all. Even if the flu didn't cut a large swath across the human population, the ensuing pneumonia and bronchitis certainly could.

"Why don't you head on home, okay?" she told Janice. "Be sure you're plenty rested. You don't want to risk a relapse, you know."

Janice waved her hand in dismissal. "I'm fine. But I think I will head on out. Are you sure there's nothing else you need me to do before I go?"

"Positive. Thanks."

Nan returned to the living room to see if she could guess what her mother wanted to say. Conversations with Myra had begun to resemble long, elaborate games of Twenty Questions: "Does it have anything to do with any of your caregivers?" "Does it have anything to do with me?" "Does it have anything to do with your Tai Chi class or anyone in your class?" Etc., etc. While patiently working through every possible category, Nan couldn't help but reflect upon the irony of her situation. For years, she had longed to spend more time with her mother so that they could really talk, get to know each other. When Nan was growing up, Myra had always driven herself relentlessly, arising early to limber up and work out, heading over to her studio even before Nan had eaten her breakfast. The spare time she did have she preferred to spend alone with Karl, Nan's father. Even after Karl had died—six years ago from congestive heart failure—Myra had sought solace from her friends, not her daughter. Now here they were, back living in the same house together, and Myra had become more or less unable to speak, which made her seem just as remote as she always had.

Usually Nan was able to figure out what Myra wanted to say, but this evening, she couldn't. Feeling sad and frustrated, she reassured her mom that they would figure it out eventually and then returned to the kitchen, her favorite room in the house. She had "inherited" this house from a retiring member of the molecular biology department, and it was one of the oldest houses in Amherst, a classic rambling, two-story structure with tall windows and high ceilings. The kitchen had been modernized over the years, but one of the walls was still a cozy, homey, unfinished brick where Nan hung her cast iron skillets and a photograph that a colleague had taken under the microscope of Volvox. This aquatic creature was a microscopic colonial organism, a sphere made up of hundreds of clear, orb-shaped, individual cells containing incandescent green chloroplasts that twinkled like embedded emeralds. Nan had always found the microscopic world to be exquisitely beautiful and endlessly fascinating, some of the most captivating "abstract" art that existed. Even viruses, with their vampiric implications and their unnerving ambiguity as to whether they even comprised life or not, had attracted her with their utter simplicity and their geometric perfection.

With one ear cocked toward the den for the slightest rustle or squeak that might indicate her mother was on the move, she began to put together a chicken broccoli casserole and a winter salad composed of raw spinach, Bosc pears, gorgonzola cheese, and walnuts. Janice had baked a loaf of bread in the bread maker earlier, so there was fresh bread, too.

Soon, Elliott and Amber arrived, bringing with them the smell of the crisp, cold autumn air as they swept into the kitchen. Amber was clutching Bessie, a doll that she had made herself: the body was an outgrown sleeper stuffed with out-of-favor toys, the head a small cardboard box covered with an old surgical stocking sporting two small, close-set button eyes. Bessie looked like a cross between Frankenstein and Curious George, but Amber loved her deeply. She ran to Nan and gave her a fierce hug, then dashed into the living room to kiss Myra.

Amber had warmed up to Nan since her strep infection in England—perhaps partly out of fear that she could lose the closest thing to a mother she had—but she seemed even more fond of Myra. Amber's sole surviving grandmother lived in California, and she didn't get to see her that often. The very old and the very young often forged a special bond as Myra and Amber had; and even though Nan was a little jealous of both of them, she still felt uncertain enough about her maternal prowess that she felt relieved they got along so well. It took some of the pressure off. Amber loved chattering to Myra, taking her silence as evidence of rapt attention.

When dinner was ready, Elliott helped Nan to set the table and serve the food. Amber led Myra to her chair very carefully, holding both of her hands and walking backwards so that Myra wouldn't fall. Her care touched Nan deeply, and she found herself thinking that if she could just resolve the cat situation, marrying Elliott might not be a bad idea.

They chit-chatted through most of dinner, Elliott making a good-natured and considerate effort to include Myra in the conversation, which wasn't easy. Nan could tell that it pleased her, though. Amber happily informed everyone of all that she had going on—her gymnastics, her ecology class project, her flute lessons. Nan thought about telling Elliott about her run-in with Ron but decided that it would spoil the mood;

she would tell him later. As she served brownies for dessert, however, Elliott cleared his throat and told Nan that he had more information from the CDC.

"You, uh, might want to consider stocking up on a few things," he said, trying to appear casual as he served Amber a brownie and poured her a glass of milk from the pitcher on the table.

Nan stared at him, surprised. "Really?" she exclaimed.

"Well, just as … you know, a precaution."

"Things like …?"

"Oh, rice and pasta. Canned foods and dried beans. Medical supplies."

She continued to gaze at him in consternation. These sounded like supplies for an earthquake or hurricane or other natural disaster. "Because of—of the flu?" she stammered.

He nodded, reaching over to break up Myra's brownies into pieces that she could manipulate more easily. "And … other things."

Other diseases, he meant, no doubt. She swallowed dryly, taking a brownie for herself but then leaving it untouched on her plate. "Is the CDC going to tell everyone to start stockpiling food and supplies?"

Elliott looked uncomfortable. "Probably not," he said. "Not yet. They don't want to create shortages from hoarding. You know how that goes."

In fact, she didn't. Elliott had been exposed to much more hardship than she had, serving two years in Vietnam when he got drafted as a college student, living in Zimbabwe while he worked for the Peace Corps, researching a couple of epidemics in Peru and Bolivia as a public health officer. But Nan had lived a sheltered middle-class life, obtaining her Ph.D. as soon as she graduated from college, and then joining the faculty here at the university right after she completed a post doc at Michigan State. The most exotic places she had ever visited were Scotland and England. The worst hardship she had ever experienced was the time she went backpacking with a friend in graduate school and they had realized on the first day that they hadn't brought enough food for three days in the woods; so they had had to ration their supplies. They could have come out of the woods any time they wanted, though, and when they did return to civilization, they had gorged on cheeseburgers and French fries at the first diner they had come across.

She could tell that Elliott felt loathe to go into particulars as he didn't want to frighten Amber, but she was dying to find out more about what the CDC had to say. And what about respirators and hospital beds? Was there enough capacity for a pandemic? She was pretty sure there wasn't.

Elliott promised to call her tomorrow morning and give her more details; then he glanced at his watch and announced that it was a school night and Amber needed to get to bed soon. Nan gave them a hug and a kiss as they left, thinking how good they both smelled: Elliott like a study full of books, Amber like apple juice and clean clothes dried outside in the fresh air and sun.

After everyone had left, Nan put her mother to bed, then stayed up to clean the kitchen and put away the leftovers. She watched the eleven o'clock news, hoping they would have something about the flu epidemic in Asia, but they only mentioned it in passing and didn't have anything to add to Elliott's information from yesterday.

At midnight, she climbed into bed herself with a few of her journals. One of the first articles to catch her eye was a report on the increasing antibiotic resistance of both staph and strep in Europe. Infections from the flesh-eating bacteria were no longer rare; in the last year, the number of cases had increased exponentially. As she read through the article, she noted that the first multiply drug resistant cases had occurred right around the time that she had contracted necrotizing fasciitis, just as Joshua had pointed out. She had been lucky; her infection had responded to antibiotics. But subsequent victims had not fared so well. The only treatment that had proven effective in sixty to seventy percent of the cases was to put the patient in a hyperbaric chamber. Even then, patients sometimes lost a limb in order to save their life.

Nan shivered, leafing quickly through the gruesome photos of enormous indigo blisters that looked like blood sausages and purple sacs of fluid that used to be a person's arm or leg. Something was going on; something scary. Micro-organisms all over the globe had been developing resistance to man's arsenal against them for decades, but something had shoved the process into high gear recently. What could that be?

She impatiently perused a few more journals, hoping to find some clues, but much to her frustration, she didn't really find anything. It was the same old stuff: an outbreak here, a resistant strain there. Exhausted from the day, she switched off her light and tried to go to sleep. But she had a hard time dropping off. Something was wrong. Something was terribly wrong, and if she wasn't mistaken, there was much more than simple natural selection and random mutation taking place here.

CHAPTER 4

Nan drove absentmindedly to work, preoccupied by her conversation earlier in the morning with Elliott. Both the Center for Disease Control and The World Health Organization were bracing for a pandemic, he told her. They were preparing quietly, as they feared the situation would only be made worse by panic and hoarding. Containment was impossible at this point, as it seemed that the hot spots were so numerous and ubiquitous that every location on earth was probably already exposed to something. And containment for what? he exclaimed. What was driving this insane super-resistance?

"No one has any ideas?" she had asked anxiously.

"Just the usual suspects," he replied.

"Do you have any ideas?"

He didn't answer for a moment. Then he said he had some more bad news. "Amber's come down with another ear infection," he told her, his voice strained.

Nan caught her breath. Normally, an ear infection was no big deal. Lots of children got them off and on throughout their childhoods. But with all the multiple drug resistance surfacing, any kind of bacterial infection could potentially become serious. Even fatal.

She refrained from asking him how he planned to treat it; they disagreed on this particular issue. Nan felt quite a bit of evidence existed, even in traditional medical research, that chronic ear infections in children were not necessarily benefited by antibiotics. In fact, just the opposite. Elliott, however, despite his professional concern over antibiotic resistance, felt different when it came to treating his own child.

She told him not to worry, even though they both knew he had cause for concern. She just didn't know what else to say. She told him she would stop by after work just for a quick visit, and he had said that would be nice, sounding despondent and preoccupied.

Nan switched on the car radio, wanting to distract herself from worries about Amber, but the news that came on was anything but reassuring. Health officials in Bolivia were working around the clock to contain a new outbreak of Machupo Fever, a hemorrhagic fever similar to Ebola. A virulent cholera epidemic had broken out in Bangladesh in the aftermath of widespread flooding from the most recent series of storms. An outbreak of Legionnaire's Disease had struck an entire city block of hotels in downtown Chicago. And several young people in the Four Corners area of the Southwest had died from hantavirus.

Depressing though it was, Nan continued to listen to the news in horrified fascination. As she approached the university, the streets and sidewalks became crowded with students on their way to classes; yet she had the peculiar feeling that she was viewing a scene from the past, that these students represented doppelgangers, not real flesh-and-blood. Superimposed over this academic bustle like a filmy, opaque membrane lay a chilling vision of empty streets, devoid of human life. She shuddered, turned off the radio. Perhaps the pressure of caring for her mother was getting to her more than she even realized.

Pulling into the faculty lot, she spotted a vacant parking place and nosed into it quickly, almost forgetting her briefcase in her rush to make it to the departmental meeting that Ron had called yesterday. He had an important announcement to make, he said, which she hoped didn't have anything to do with money or funding sources.

The meeting had just begun when she slipped into the back of the room, which smelled of paper and old coffee. She unintentionally caught Ron's eye as he paced in front of the assembled faculty, and she gave a little half-wave, which he ignored.

"As I was saying, the reports coming out of Asia concerning the newest flu epidemic are alarming, to say the least. It's not just killing old people and babies any more. Young, healthy people in peak condition are dying, from both the virus itself and the complications that set in afterward. It's too late to contain a flu virus at this point. We have the first reports coming in from the West Coast that the virus has made its way there now. We should have some confirmation on that later today.

"At any rate, the university wants to be proactive about this. We're going to be offering free flu shots to all faculty and students, as well as their spouses and children. We expect the president to announce a national flu vaccine campaign on television this evening, but we're not going to wait. We'd like you all to make the announcement in your classes this week. We're going to have some flyers printed up and distributed, too. Any questions?"

Nan raised her hand. "Do we know whether we have the right vaccine yet?" she asked, as soon as Ron nodded at her.

"It's the best we have given the information we had at the time the vaccines were made."

"That doesn't answer my question."

Ron sighed. Al, another virologist, turned around to reply. "The answer is no. It looks like this damn thing did its mix and match routine—the genome is all scrambled up. That's why it's so deadly. There was no way we could have predicted this."

"So, if it's not the right vaccine for this virus, why give it to everybody? What good will it do?" Nan pressed.

"Look, it'll do some good," Ron asserted. "It's better than nothing. And at the worst, it'll act as a placebo, okay? We don't want to give people the impression that we're helpless to stop this thing. It could create a panic, and that's something we definitely don't need."

"Great," muttered Nan. As the meeting broke up, Nan turned to Al and grumbled, "So we'll spend hundreds of thousands of dollars on a placebo, and unnecessarily expose others vulnerable to complications from the vaccine."

"I think you got it." He shook his head. "But what else can we do?"

"Well, for example, if we would stop our silly vendetta against homeopathic medicine—"

Al grimaced. "Please. Spare me."

"Look, just because we can't figure out how it works yet doesn't mean it doesn't work!" Nan exclaimed. "For Pete's sake, Europe is just as sophisticated medically as we are, and they're using homeopathy with all kind of success."

"Sorry. I'm not convinced." He strolled away.

She shook her head in exasperation. She found most of her colleagues' attitudes toward homeopathy to verge on religious fanaticism. No one knew exactly how aspirin worked for decades, either, but that didn't stop millions of physicians from prescribing it for headaches and pain. Health was not a competition between healing systems, damn it. It was one of those areas where you did whatever worked. She believed in high tech medicine—her work with viruses and gene splicing was just about as high tech as you could get—but that didn't mean she couldn't be receptive to other methods as well. And with all this new drug resistance, it was absolutely essential to find effective alternatives.

She headed to her class, wondering what she was going to say about the flu vaccine campaign that wouldn't compromise her own beliefs and yet wouldn't antagonize Ron even more. She still hadn't made up her mind about what she was going to do concerning the patent for her viral delivery system. She had halfheartedly obtained a patent application, but she did this more to stall Ron than for any other reason. But she couldn't stall forever, and if she made her feelings concerning the current flu vaccine public, she could alienate her allies in the department.

Quite frankly, modern technological medicine was not that well-equipped to battle the flu. A new class of drugs had appeared on the market in the last few years, which mitigated the symptoms of influenza and shortened the time during which the flu sufferer felt lousy and weak. But these drugs wouldn't necessarily prevent opportunistic infections like pneumonia from these aggressive new drug-resistant bacteria, and they had never come up against something like a virulent flu pandemic. It wasn't even known with certainty how the drugs worked, although they were believed to prevent the uncoating of the virus, a necessary preamble to injecting its nucleic acid into a host cell. Still, it remained to be seen whether they would work against this new strain. Vaccines actually comprised the best strategy modern medicine could offer against viral agents, and a good vaccine, such as the one for polio, was very effective. Did she really want to contribute to everyone feeling powerless and afraid in the face of the worst flu epidemic to come down the pike since The Big One? Perhaps the placebo effect alone was good enough reason to recommend the vaccine to her students.

So when she called the class to order, her first announcement was about the free flu vaccine being offered to all students at the infirmary. She wasn't sure whether to alert them to the fact that a potentially virulent flu was on the way or not. The cases from the West Coast had yet to be confirmed, and fear would only create stress and that alone could weaken their resistance. She certainly didn't want to communicate to them her own trepidation. However, a student raised her hand and asked about the news reports she'd heard about the Asian flu. "They're saying this might be as serious as the flu epidemic of 1918," she said. "Is there any truth to that?"

So much for avoidance. "It's really too soon to tell, Carrie," she replied, trying her best to assume a brisk, authoritative tone. "But the possibility is enough to take precautions. Wash your hands whenever you come home from being out and about, for 20 seconds. Keep your hands away from your face. And you should all take particular care to make sure that you're getting enough rest and eating properly. Do your homework and study your books throughout the semester so you won't have to pull some bone-headed maneuver like an all-nighter when a test comes along. Eat something besides coffee and pizza. And for God's sake, avoid all those over-the-counter stimulants like the plague, okay? Hand-washing, plenty of rest, low levels of stress, and a well-balanced diet are the best measures you can take to stay healthy. Okay, let's move on. Today we're going to talk about DNA ..."

The lecture went well enough, but her concern about the outbreaks of infectious disease weighed upon her mind. If the federal government was embarking upon a national flu campaign after the ill-fated Swine Flu campaign in the 1970's, particularly given the fact that they didn't even have the correct vaccine, officials must be desperate and running scared. If Elliott, who was no alarmist, was advising her to stockpile emergency supplies, the situation had to be serious.

Fear gnawed at her stomach, making her feel queasy as she made her way to her office. Everyone had known, of course, that another flu pandemic was inevitable, given enough time. But that wouldn't make it any easier to deal with once it arrived. People's children, parents, aunts, uncles, partners, and best friends would die, leaving terrible emotional vacuums in their wake. Right now, her work on viral delivery systems for genes that would help only a very small fraction of the population seemed like an insane luxury. For every person her work helped, a killer flu alone could wipe out dozens, even hundreds or thousands.

When she reached her office, she sat immobilized for several minutes, unsure what to do next. She had papers to grade, lab work to do, graduate students to check on, a couple of papers to write, etc., etc. But everything seemed absurdly frivolous compared to what was going on with the latest developments in public health. She called Elliott, but he was in a meeting—one that was probably going to last most of the day, his assistant told her. That sounded ominous, she thought grimly. When was the last time he was in an all-day meeting? She hunched over her desk, feeling both helpless and frantic. She wanted to do something, but she was a molecular biologist, not an epidemiologist. She studied genetic illnesses, not infectious ones. What could she possibly hope to accomplish?

After a while, she switched on her computer and logged onto the Internet, searching for all the news she could find about any outbreaks of infectious disease anywhere on the earth. And when she'd spent a couple of hours, working through her lunch break and ignoring her phone calls, she detected a very interesting pattern. The first outbreak of super-resistant bugs occurred with the epidemic of flesh-eating bacteria in Great Britain, as she and Joshua had already noted. After that, the outbreaks worked their way counter-clockwise around the planet. Drug-resistant necrotizing fasciitis logged sharp increases in Europe only a few days after it made its appearance in the British Isles. Soon after, the types of outbreaks began to branch out and diversify: Untreatable cases of pneumonia and Legionnaire's Disease cropped up in both Britain and Europe; then a tough, resistant strain of cholera appeared in India and parts of western Asia. It wasn't long before rates of drug- and vaccine-resistant dysentery, typhoid fever, and leprosy jumped in Africa, along with resistant strains of malaria.

At this point, bizarrely, viral diseases seemed to get into the act, too. AIDS cases had started to increase, as well as new outbreaks of Ebola. In China, hepatitis was getting entirely out of hand, and in Australia, hantaviruses were felling people in rural areas. Now, of course, there was this new killer flu strain. South America was experiencing new hot spots of Machupo Fever, hepatitis, and hantaviruses. In North America, cases of hantavirus, hepatitis, and spinal meningitis were felling victims with uncharacteristic fury. All of these diseases seemed to be in the beginning stages of an exponential rise, which meant that things were only going to get worse.

The direction of the wave of outbreaks wasn't perfectly counter-clockwise, of course. There was some zigging and zagging around, but that was only to be expected. Still, the data certainly suggested some Patient Zero, or at least some kind of Vector Zero. Somehow it seemed to start in England and spread from there, whatever "it" was. The pattern did not suggest that the problem was a diffuse, haphazard one of global warming, overpopulation, or depletion of the ozone layer. There was something far more specific going on here. But what could possibly represent the link between bacterial and viral diseases?

She leaned back in her chair, doodling on her notes for her graduate seminar this afternoon. Should she assume that some other sharp-eyed and infinitely more knowledgeable epidemiologist had discerned the same pattern? Surely someone else would have noticed, if it had jumped out at her. She checked her watch, frustrated to see that the day was still relatively young; Elliott wouldn't be out of his meeting yet. She wanted to talk to him, find out whether the CDC or WHO had addressed the issue of an index case. Since so many diseases around the globe had been affected, it was possible the idea might not have occurred to them in this context.

She turned off her computer and gathered up her materials for her graduate seminar, but she couldn't shake the foreboding feeling that her search had generated. She had a nagging feeling, too, that time was running out, that no matter what got put into place in the ensuing weeks, it was going to be too late. She toyed with the idea of getting a flu shot herself and for her mother as well. But the placebo effect wasn't going to work for her, and if it wasn't the right vaccine, that was practically all it was worth. Not only that, a flu vaccine took a few weeks to be effective, and if the flu had already arrived on the West Coast, it was too late. She swallowed uneasily, trying to block out gruesome mental images of people dropping dead in the streets. In 1918, that had literally happened. People simply collapsed on their feet, and sometimes so many people were sick and dying all at once that the bodies remained on the streets for some time. Entire households died, the bodies entombed in the victims' houses until health workers discovered them days or even weeks later.

She jumped up impatiently, feeling a desperate need to act on her information. She couldn't just keep on pursuing her usual work as if nothing else were going on. She needed to do something to try to help. The only problem was, she had no earthly idea what it should be.

CHAPTER 5

"No better at all?" Nan cradled the receiver between her shoulder and her ear, struggling to put on her jacket while she talked on the phone. She had called Elliott to let him know she was on her way over and see if there was anything she could bring him or Amber when she came. "Has she been to see her pediatrician?"

"Yeah. Romi took her since I couldn't get out of work. Danielle prescribed another round of amoxicillin, but I haven't given her the first dose yet. I'm—just not sure what the right thing to do is any more. The antibiotics haven't helped over the long term, and I'm afraid that I might be setting her up for other kinds of problems if I just keep giving them to her."

"I could bring over some essential oils," she offered tentatively. "See if they might give her a little relief."

"Could you?" he responded, sounded defeated.

"Of course! I'll be right over."

"Great," he said. "That would be great."

Nan stopped by her home to pick up her essential oil kit, told Janice that she would be coming back soon, and dashed in to give her mom a peck on the cheek. She submerged her impatience to get going as Myra grasped her arm and struggled to tell her something. Nan wasn't sure whether she really had something to say or whether she was using this as a stalling technique to keep her from leaving.

"After all …" Myra began.

Nan waited.

"Absolutely …"

"Yes?" she prompted encouragingly after several seconds had passed.

"After all, I … after all, I …" Her right hand began to shake uncontrollably, a sign that she was upset.

"Take your time, Mom," Nan told her, reaching over to quiet her hand and stroke it soothingly, wondering how many of her conflicting emotions she unintentionally communicated to her mother. On the one hand, she couldn't help but feel bitter about the fact that her mother had never been very nurturing or giving. The world had always seemed to revolve around Myra and her gift for dancing, her needs, and her desires. Her father seemed awestruck by her, amazed that a glamorous woman like Myra loved him. She was an artist, he often told Nan, and in order to be happy, she needed to feel unencumbered and free. He and Nan were more solid, more down-to-earth, he said, and they needed to be more accommodating. Nan tried her best, but often she felt as if her mother was the child and she the adult. Now she found herself in exactly the same situation; and her mother had not reached out to her until she was desperate, needy, and practically helpless.

On the other hand, she could never bear to see someone suffer. She knew that it killed her mother not to be able to walk or move on her own, when her grace and exquisite sense of balance were two of the things which characterized her the most and in which she took a great deal of pride. She not only was unable to dance, she couldn't even stand up without falling. The cruelty of this particular affliction was not lost on Nan.

Myra gazed fixedly at her. "Absolutely, I … need to know … exercise?"

Nan knew that she didn't mean exercise. Somehow, this word had become one of the catch-all words that seem to float to the surface whenever she struggled to find the word she really did want. Nan glanced at her watch, knowing that Elliott was waiting for her.

"You know what, Mom?" she said. "I'll be home a little bit later and we can figure it out then, okay?"

Myra expelled a short, frustrated breath. "Okay."

"Something will jog your memory, okay?"

"Okay."

Nan straightened up and patted Myra's shoulder to soften her departure. She felt guilty for leaving her mother without puzzling out whatever it was she was trying to say, but the fact was, it could take hours. Sometimes she wondered if her mother's neurons were firing so unpredictably and randomly that "ghost" thoughts containing no content whatsoever were zooming around in her brain, making Myra think that she had something she needed to discuss, but she didn't, really.

Nan raced up to her bedroom where she kept her essential oils, grabbed the kit, swallowed an antihistamine, took some homeopathic allergy drops, and dropped her inhaler in her purse. She wasn't looking forward to the aftermath of exposure to cat dander, but she could tell that Elliott was really worried, which made her feel concerned, too.

She drove as fast as she dared to Elliott and Amber's home, a 19th century clapboard farmhouse that now sat on the periphery of town. The twilight had dwindled to a faint, dusky, lavender welt on the horizon, casting the house in shadowy silhouette. When she parked in the driveway, she could see the light on in both upstairs bedrooms. Amber's pet sheep, Sassafras, trotted up to the gate as she approached the back door, which she knew would be open.

"Hi, Sassafras," she greeted him, giving him a rub on the

snout. He twisted his head around so that her fingers rested on top of his head. So she scratched him around the ears, thinking how much like a dog this sheep seemed to be. "Okay, off with you now," she said, giving him a light slap on the rump before heading into the house. She figured Elliott was probably in Amber's bedroom, so she made her way up the stairs, calling out to let them know she had arrived.

"Hi, you two!" she sang out, trying to sound cheerful. When she reached Amber's room and peeked inside, she found Elliott sitting on the end of Amber's bed, stroking her knee, Muffin curled up beside her on the pillow, and Amber lying still and glassy-eyed from fever. The stillness of a sick child had always pierced Nan's heart, it seemed so unnatural. The fact that this unmoving, sick child was Amber made it all the worse. As she bent over to give her a kiss and feel her forehead, her heart ached so much that she thought it might be just as well if she never had children. She probably couldn't handle the emotional demands of biological parenthood. When she turned to give Elliott a kiss, too, the panic in his eyes gave her heart another painful wrench.

He leaned over to scoop up Muffin and put her outside, but Nan caught his arm and said, "Oh, leave her there for now. I shouldn't stay all that long anyway." She set her kit on the bedside table and crouched down next to Amber. "Sweetie, I'm going to put some medicine in your ear to make you feel better, okay?"

Amber nodded, her hair making a soft skritching sound on the pillow.

Nan stood up and grasped Elliott's hand. "You've got some olive oil on hand, don't you?"

"Sure—you want me to get it for you?"

"No, that's okay; stay with Amber. Just tell me where it is. I need to warm it up a little." Because of Muffin, Nan rarely spent any time at Elliott and Amber's house, so she wasn't all that familiar with his kitchen. Fortunately, Elliott had organized everything in his usual straightforward, logical fashion, so she found the olive oil and a small pan easily. When she'd heated the oil to the right temperature, she poured it into a bowl and carried it back up to Amber's room. There she mixed in a few drops of lavender oil, filling the room with a sharp, clean, woodsy fragrance, and saturated a couple of sterile cotton plugs. Gently, she tucked the cotton plugs into Amber's ears, who remained surprisingly cooperative; then she massaged the extra oil around her ears, hairline, and throat.

"Smells nice," said Elliott.

"It does, doesn't it?"

"How long should I leave those in there?" he asked.

"Oh, overnight. I'll give you a call in the morning and see if it's helped any." She turned back to Amber, smoothing her hair back from her face. "You get a good night's sleep, honey bunch."

"'Night," she croaked.

Elliott accompanied her outside, where Sassafras stood waiting for them at the gate, his back end waggling, stubby tail twitching. "Are you sure he isn't a sheep dog? Or a dog in sheep's clothing?" Nan remarked. Her attempt at humor sounded lame, even to her, but she was feeling so anxious that she desperately needed something to lighten her mood.

Elliott chuckled charitably. "Hey there, Sass," he said, giving him a pat.

"So what kept you in a meeting all day long?" she asked.

"Oh, that. God." Elliott briefly buried his face in his hands. "The CDC is holding an emergency symposium in Atlanta day after tomorrow. Seems a whole bunch of new hot spots have developed lately. We've got epidemics coming out the wazoo, and all of the bacterial ones seem to be antibiotic-resistant."

"Jesus." Nan felt a stab of fear.

"And that's not even counting this Asian flu. More data is pouring in, despite the fact that the Chinese are trying to keep a lid on the whole situation. They don't want to be accused of starting a flu pandemic, and I can't say that I blame them. At any rate, it's looking as if this might be as virulent as the 1918 virus. This thing is scary. Really, really scary."

Nan shivered, pulled her jacket closer about her. "Are there any confirmed cases in this country yet?"

"Yeah, we just got word before I left work that there are several confirmed cases on the West Coast. It could start popping up here any minute."

Nan leaned back against the fence, fighting panic. "The university's giving out free flu shots, but according to Al, it's not the right vaccine."

Elliott shook his head wearily. "I know. We're working on a new one based on the samples we've been able to obtain from China, but it's going to be a while. I know lots of labs are working on it, though, which should help speed things up."

"That's good," Nan replied uneasily. Both of them knew a pandemic was inevitable at this point. "You know, I—I did some research on the Internet today and it looks to me like the pattern of outbreaks suggests some kind of patient zero. These hot zones and multiply-drug-resistant bugs seem to have started in Europe, then moved on to Africa, then Asia and Australia, and now the Americas."

"Interesting."

"Yeah, but the weirdest part of it is—we're talking both viruses and bacteria. I can't quite figure out what the connection could be."

Elliott remained silent for a moment, then took a deep, shuddering breath. "It's so common," he muttered. "Just an ear infection. But if we don't manage to clear it up—if it gets worse, if her fever gets much higher ..." he broke off, his voice mangled.

"We'll figure out something, Elliott, don't worry," Nan reassured him, her words sounding hopelessly false to her.

"I mean, she could end up deaf or brain damaged or—"

"Elliott, she won't! And worrying ourselves sick about it

isn't going to help her!" she insisted.

Elliott wiped his eyes. "Man, if I lost her, I don't know what I'd do," he choked.

She wrapped her arms around him and they hugged each other in a tight, frightened embrace, while Nan wondered what the world would be like without antibiotics—or one, at least, where antibiotics didn't do a damned thing. What was it like before she was born and people died from an infected cut or a strep throat or a bad ear infection? What was it like in Europe during the Plague when a full quarter of the population died? People were dying right and left, they were dying constantly, getting sick and not getting better, just inevitably, inexorably dying.

She extricated herself from Elliott and asked, "Can anyone go to this symposium?"

He shrugged. "Sure. I think so, anyway."

"Good. I'd like to go."

He nodded, looking preoccupied.

"You're probably going to stay here?"

"Yeah," he said. "I need to take care of Amber."

"I'll take notes for you," she told him, reaching over to touch his arm, wishing she could ease some of his distress.

"Thanks," he said glumly. He straightened up, gave her an appraising glance. "How are you, by the way? Any reaction to the cat?"

Nan realized that she'd been so concerned about Amber and all the other developments that she hadn't even been paying attention to her lungs. Sure enough, her chest felt tight and when she listened, she heard the telltale wheezy whistle. "It's okay. I wasn't in there all that long."

"You sure?"

"I'm fine. I'll just use my inhaler."

"So what are you waiting for?" he asked.

"Um, privacy?" Somehow she hated using her inhaler in front of anyone. It felt like dental flossing in public. She felt self-conscious and exposed.

"I see. Should I avert my eyes?"

She laughed. "Sure. You do that."

He turned his back while she took her inhaler out of her purse and took a couple of puffs. Cat dander was such an amazingly powerful allergen. She often thought that the perfect murder could be committed by locking up a feline-sensitive asthmatic in a small, windowless room with a cat.

She kissed Elliott goodbye, and he thanked her for tending to Amber. He promised to call if she got worse during the night. He looked so worried that Nan gave him another heartfelt squeeze before leaving, and as she pulled out of the driveway, she could see in the window that he had dashed back up to Amber's room.

She sighed wearily as she drove off. As scary and disturbing as Amber's ear infection was, it was only a harbinger of things to come. Right now, Earth and its human inhabitants felt like a tiny alpine village nestled at the bottom of a gargantuan avalanche chute. The avalanche had already begun its relentless, lethal descent down the mountain, and there wasn't much anyone could do to escape. There wasn't enough time. She mulled over her findings from the Internet, feeling more and more convinced that the key to this impending disaster lay with the Patient or Vector Zero. She would attend the CDC's symposium just to make sure that someone else had noted the same pattern and that someone was looking into it. Whatever happened needed to happen quickly. With a flu pandemic about to explode, every single day counted.

When she arrived home, she eased the car quietly into the garage, eager to shower and wash off any cat enzymes that clung to her hair and skin, then fix herself a simple dinner. However, Janice met her at the door, tearful and agitated.

"I'm really sorry, Nan," she gulped; "I just turned my back on Myra for a second and somehow she got up and fell."

"Is she okay?" Nan asked, alarmed.

"Pretty much, I think. You should check. She hit her eye on the corner of the coffee table, but I think she actually just hit the area around her eye. She's in bed right now."

Nan hurried into the downstairs bedroom to find her mother propped up with several pillows, her eye swelling shut, a bag of frozen peas in her hand.

"Mom! Are you okay?"

"Okay," she replied, looking guilty, frustrated, and bewildered.

"Are you sure? Let me take a look." Nan bent over her and gently probed her eye. She pulled the swollen flesh back to check the eye itself, relieved to find it unharmed. "Here, let me dab a little Arnica ointment on there," she said, "and then why don't you put that bag of peas back on there for a little while, okay? You want me to hold it for you?"

"Hold it for you? Yes."

"Okay. Lie back just a little." She positioned the bag for maximum comfort, noticed Janice hovering in the doorway.

"Is she going to be okay?" she asked anxiously.

"Oh yeah. Although, you're going to have quite a shiner, Mom," Nan remarked, shaking her head. "The people at the beauty shop are going to think you've taking up mud wrestling again."

Myra giggled.

"Either that, or they're going to think I'm involved in elder abuse," she muttered to herself. Sometimes Nan really did wonder if people secretly believed that she was using her demented, elderly mother for a punching bag, she was so often covered with bruises.

"I'm so sorry, Nan," Janice said. "I just left for a second to get her a glass of water."

"I know; don't worry. These things happen."

"These things happen," echoed Myra.

Janice gave a little hiccup of a laugh through her tears.

"Thanks, Myra. I'm sorry I wasn't there to keep you from falling."

"Okay." Myra raised her hand in a benedictory gesture. Despite her disabilities, she still managed to radiate imperiousness, which seemed especially effective with students.

Nan stayed with Myra for a while after Janice left, but her mind was elsewhere. Now that she had discovered something she thought significant, she was anxious to get moving on it. She wished that the symposium were taking place tomorrow, but realistically speaking, she was going to need tomorrow to get Myra's care in place anyway.

After Myra fell asleep, Nan got online and booked herself a ticket to Atlanta, then decided to skip dinner and go to bed herself. Lying in the darkness, worn out yet keyed up, she couldn't help but ponder the fiendish irony of Myra's condition. Her mother had never been sick from infectious illness a day in her life, but here she was now, more or less incapacitated. Watching her mother fail from nothing more than her body's own peculiar self-destruct sequence, and at the same time, waiting in dread for a possible plague the likes of which humanity had never seen, not even in the Dark Ages, Nan was realizing what an impossibly complex phenomenon disease represented.

When she first embarked upon her research in genetic illness, she had thought of herself as more or less of a gene mechanic. She found the flawed gene, she figured out how it should read, she whipped up the proper gene sequences, then she replaced the bad part with the good one. End of disease. Modern pharmaceutical medicine had more or less eradicated infectious disease, so genetic disease was really the only frontier left to conquer. The vision of a healthy, thriving humanity free from any kind of disease had beckoned to her as recently as just last year. Until now, she had thought of disease as due primarily to ignorance or lack of resources.

But now she was beginning to believe that she had oversimplified the ancient affliction known as disease. There were more players than she had originally recognized—but she still didn't know who or what they were. There was more going on, both biologically and ecologically, than she understood. And she had a feeling that a much, much bigger picture existed than she had ever comprehended or glimpsed. She felt almost as if humanity were facing a test of biological adaptability and evolutionary alacrity, yet the strategy they needed to employ was anything but clear. How they met the current crisis would undoubtedly determine their fate as a species. And the stakes, she feared, were nothing less than survival versus extinction.

CHAPTER 6

Nan grabbed up a program for the symposium and hurried to the auditorium where the presentations were being given, running late and feeling rattled. The first presentation had started by the time she eased into a seat as close to the front as she could find. The speaker, Bill Holzer, was director of the CDC and a well-respected epidemiologist who had worked in public health all his adult life. She quietly slipped out of her coat and clicked on her tape recorder, giving him her full attention.

Holzer's delivery was low-key, even bland, but as he droned on, listing the outbreaks all over the world—the new exotics, Ebola, Marburg, Machupo, and Hanta, as well as the old-timers such as influenza, pneumonia, TB, and The Plague—it became clear that he felt shaken, even dismayed. The list of drugs that had recently been demonstrated to have lost effectiveness was even more sobering. In fact, when he reached the end of his talk and mentioned the medicines that still seemed to be working, the brevity of this list was nothing short of demoralizing. It was as if the United States military, faced with a horrifyingly superior hostile force, had been stripped of every single weapon except for bayonets and hand grenades. Holzer himself framed the discussion in martial metaphor: "The war that we've been waging on disease, quite successfully over the last century, has just taken another deadly, quantum leap," he remarked gravely. "Our task now is to develop new weapons with which to fight them." To that end, he introduced the next speaker, vice-president of Cal-Martin labs, a pharmaceutical company based in California.

This speaker proceeded to describe, in glowing terms, a new antibiotic that his company had designed and which was in the final stages of FDA approval. It had shown extraordinary promise, he said, and it took advantage of a stage of bacterial metabolism that no antibiotic had ever addressed before. He briefly detailed the mechanism of the drug, using a few slides. Then he assured the assembled scientists that Cal-Martin labs could have the drug in production the minute the FDA gave the go-ahead. "This just might be the salvation of mankind," he observed, his expression grim; "and we believe that there is no time to waste in getting this drug into the hands of the people who desperately need it." He urged interested members of the audience to contact the FDA in order to speed up the approval process. Then he took questions from the audience. Nan didn't care for the opportunism that this speaker exuded while extolling the virtues of his company's new wonder drug, but she decided she should wait until everyone had spoken before bringing up her observations; so she sat tight.

After he finished speaking, another V.P. from a different drug lab, PreVentall, described a new anti-viral agent that was also mired in the FDA awaiting approval. This drug supposedly blocked assembly of viral proteins without harming the host's ability to carry out this critical metabolic step, although it carried some side-effects. Still, if the gravity of the current situation did indeed become as life-threatening as the early cases indicated, these side-effects might not matter so much in the long run. He urged the group to put pressure on the FDA to get these drugs out and available to those who needed them. "We need to kill these things," he stated flatly. "It's them or us, and we're running out of time."

This time Nan couldn't keep quiet during the question period. "Excuse me," she said, standing up to make herself heard, "how do you 'kill' a virus?"

He laughed. "I'm sorry. You're right, of course. I meant figuratively. Destroy their ability to replicate."

"This 'us vs. them' idea," she persisted. "Does this imply some sort of consciousness on the part of the virus—that you think they're out to get us?"

"Again, I was speaking metaphorically. But it does rather seem that way right now, doesn't it?"

"Well—except for the fact that they need us to survive. They can't live without a host. Killing the host is bad biology for a virus—or an infectious bacterium, for that matter."

He smiled tightly. "What is your point?"

"Just that this adversarial approach might not be the best approach, perhaps. It's the one we've taken for the last few generations, of course, and it seemed like it's been working—until now. If we declare war on these organisms, are we certain we can win? It appears that our conventional approaches aren't very effective at this point. In fact, we might have made things worse, set ourselves up for a disaster of enormous proportions. Maybe newer and 'better'" —she squiggled her fingers to put quotes around the word— "drugs aren't the answer. Maybe we need to be more creative."

"Do you have another solution?" he asked.

"Not at this exact moment. But if we put our heads together, we might be able to come up with something."

"Theoretically, I agree with you, but practically speaking, I'm afraid we might not have the time for that. Next question?"

Nan sank back down in her seat, smarting from his dismissal. She shouldn't have expected anything different, though, she chastised herself. Theoretical approaches were, in fact, more appropriate for non-crisis situations; but she just had a really bad feeling about the way things were going. None of these representatives of the pharmaceutical industry truly grasped the severity of the situation. They didn't see a crisis—they saw an opportunity, a chance to cash in on a crisis. She knew that Ron, who was on the board of directors for PreVentall, would be delighted with this new development. He owned a great deal of stock in in the company and if this anti-viral drug did get released under desperate circumstances, the stock would shoot sky high.

But the bleak fact was, the vast majority of drugs that humans had managed to develop over the last century were becoming useless—and fast. Pursuing a strategy that clearly wasn't working any more seemed not only short-sighted to her, but foolish and doomed as well. It appeared that the microbial kingdom had found a way to resist drugs as a tactic; it wasn't just a mutation here and a mutation there, a drug here and an antibiotic there. Something profoundly, terrifyingly different was occurring.

After the speaker stepped down from the podium, the assembly broke for lunch, which was served in a nearby banquet room. Nan decided to skip the meal in order to make a couple of calls and see how her mother and Amber were faring. She found a bank of pay phones near the restrooms and used her credit card to call home. To her relief, Myra was doing fine; then she checked in with Elliott. Amber was sleeping, he told her, and although she was still running a fever, she seemed to be on the mend. He sounded much calmer, which Nan found reassuring. He was eager to hear how the conference was going, so she filled him in on the morning's presentations, keeping her reservations to herself. She didn't really have much to support her misgivings except for general impressions.

"We could use a new anti-viral drug," Elliott commented. "We've got our first influenza cases in the valley."

Nan leaned against the wall of the booth. "Really? How …

many?"

"A lot, I'm afraid. In fact, I heard that the infirmary at the university is nearing capacity. The young and healthy seem to be particularly vulnerable, just like in 1918. The hospitals are filling up pretty fast, too."

Nan cringed inwardly. If this epidemic followed the pattern of the 1918 pandemic, medical and societal chaos were weeks, if not days away. "How are you feeling?" she asked him anxiously.

"Me? I'm fine."

"That's good," she replied; but she knew this didn't mean a damned thing. Influenza viruses could fell their victims with lightning rapidity.

"How about you?" he asked.

"Oh, fine. You know me. Healthy as a horse." She managed a laugh but then decided that perhaps skipping a meal wasn't such a good idea. Glancing at her watch, she saw that she could still squeeze in some lunch if she hurried. So she told Elliott she would be home tomorrow night and headed over to the dining room.

When she walked in, a bizarre scene greeted her. One of the attendees had just collapsed, face first into his plate. Those seated nearest him had jumped up in alarm. He could have had a stroke or a heart attack, but Nan knew that the fear running throughout the room was that he had collapsed from the flu. No one wanted to get near him. She rushed over to the man and pushed him back in his chair, loosened his tie and unbuttoned his top button. She felt for a pulse in his throat, both relieved and disturbed when she found one.

"Someone call 911," she shouted. And after a stupefied second, several people whipped out cell phones and started punching in the numbers.

"Could somebody help me to get this man lying down on the floor?" she asked. Again, those nearest him hesitated, but then a man and a woman at the adjoining table hurried around and helped her to get him out of his seat and lying on the floor. She used his jacket to cushion his head while waiting for the paramedics, then checked his wrists to see if he wore any kind of a medical ID bracelet that might indicate some sort of chronic or congenital health problem. She didn't find anything, so she searched for his wallet, finding it in the inside pocket of his suit coat. Looking through it gingerly, she didn't find anything there, either, that might explain what just happened. Suddenly, she became aware of someone standing over her. She glanced up.

"I'm a physician," he said. "Maybe I should take a look."

"Great," she replied, rising to her feet and moving out of the way.

When it looked as though the situation was under control, she decided to go to the restroom and wash her hands for about five minutes. Of course, if this man had the flu, then everyone who was in the auditorium was already exposed; in addition, she had probably traveled on the plane with at least one person who was infectious but asymptomatic. There was no way to avoid getting exposed to this thing, not unless everyone stayed home and/or started wearing respirator masks immediately, and even then, it might be too late—not to mention the fact that there were undoubtedly not enough masks to go around.

When the group reconvened for the afternoon presentations, an uncomfortable frisson of anxiety spritzed the air in the auditorium. Experts in disease that they were, everyone could feel fairly certain that the new deadly strain of flu virus was wafting about the room. And the main topic for the afternoon, emergency plans for the impending flu epidemic that addressed hospital bed capacity and the availability of respirators and other medical equipment, didn't assuage anyone's fears at all.

Nan felt fairly certain that most of the scientists and physicians in the room were engaged in the same process she was: half-listening, half-turned inward, suspiciously examining every physical sensation they were feeling. Were they a trifle feverish, achy? Was their throat a little sore, their lymph nodes a tiny bit swollen? Were they feeling dizzy and light-headed, or just stressed out? When the talks ended for the day, rather than linger to discuss matters with their colleagues, almost everyone made a beeline to their hotel rooms to isolate themselves as best they could. Nan decided to follow their example, since she was feeling pretty beat anyway, and she had plenty of information to mull over and digest on her own.

As she left the hall, she felt a slight tickle of observation, as if someone were staring at her intently. She turned around to see if her intuition was correct, but she didn't see anyone in particular, just a few individuals and scattered clumps of people here and there, gathering up their papers, bags, and briefcases. She shrugged and turned back around, headed out to the parking lot where she had parked her rental car. As soon as she did so, she felt it again, subtle but noticeable. This time she refused to turn around, figuring she was either an object of fear as a potential flu carrier since she had gotten so close to the man who collapsed at lunch, or someone at the conference didn't care for her comments during the morning session and was tossing little bouquets of disapproval her way.

That night, as she tried to fall asleep, she kept running all the presentations from the symposium through her mind. When she finally did drop off, her dreams were the exhausting, obsessive kind: poring through reference after reference, seemingly for hours or even days, searching for some bit of crucial information which never surfaced—that she remembered, anyway. She awoke feeling tired and groggy the next morning, and when she turned on the news, she sat in stricken silence as she listened to accounts of the first deaths from the flu that had been reported in Seattle, San Francisco, and Los Angeles. The victims were young adults, in the peak of health, and several of them had checked into the hospital, so

they had the best care available. Their bodies had simply gone
into shock and their lungs had failed, despite frantic, high tech
medical efforts on their behalf. The mortality rate was still low,
compared to number of cases, but that could—undoubtedly
would—change.

When she arrived at the symposium, wearing one of the
masks Elliott had given her, she saw that the auditorium held
quite a few less attendees and that they were all spaced as
far apart as possible. Most of them were wearing masks, too.
As she took a seat at the back of the auditorium, Bill Holzer
stepped up to the mike.

"Ladies and gentlemen," he said, "before we begin, I'd like
to make a couple of announcements. As most of you are aware,
one of the attendees collapsed at lunch yesterday. Apparently,
his collapse was related to a very sudden onset of influenza.
You'll be glad to know, however, that his condition is stable
and he does not appear to be in any danger. Three other
participants came down with the flu last night, and they are all
resting comfortably at Doctors Hospital. The virus is among
us, but there is no need to panic; the situation is currently
under control. If any of you start to feel the slightest bit ill,
you should leave the auditorium immediately. Contact Maeve
Serling, the organizer of this symposium, who will be stationed
at the back of this hall, and she'll see to it that you are properly
cared for.

"I'm sure I don't need to remind anyone to keep their
personal contact with others to a minimum—refrain
from shaking hands, for example, and if you feel a cough
or a sneeze coming on, cover your face with a tissue or
handkerchief to prevent any aerosol from being released
into the air. Try not to touch your eyes, nose, mouth, or any
other mucous membranes unless you have just washed your
hands thoroughly. A few simple precautions can make a big
difference."

Nan knew that he was trying to normalize the situation,

but his words sounded surreal in light of what humankind was facing: a pandemic of unprecedented breadth and fury. Before it was all over, no one would be left untouched. Nan decided it was finally time to introduce her findings, so when Holzer opened up the discussion to comments from the floor, she stepped up to the microphone that had been placed in the center aisle of the auditorium, feeling nervous. She knew that her data were worse than raw and that she could be mistaken in the conclusions she had drawn. But she steeled herself, removed her mask, and addressed the assembly, describing the results of her Internet survey of hot spots and the wave of resistant infectious disease that seemed to spread around the planet eastward.

"I realize that these hot zones are somewhat scattered, and that the directionality of the pattern is not entirely perfect, but you wouldn't expect to find that anyway, not with the high level of travel we have in these times. It just seems that one Vector or Patient Zero might have started this whole thing. If we can figure out who or what that was, this should give us a tremendous advantage in deciding how best to meet this crisis."

Her statements were greeted with profound silence. Finally, someone in the audience stood up and asked, "How can you explain the fact that so many different diseases—both bacterial and viral—seem to be on the increase? That doesn't make any sense in the context of a Patient Zero."

Nan nodded. "You're right. And the same thought occurred to me. All I can think is that some kind of resistance factor was introduced and now it's spreading throughout the microbial biota through some kind of powerful selective advantage. How—I don't know yet."

Bill Holzer, who stood at the podium onstage to moderate the discussion, offered a suggestion. "The agent that most readily springs to my mind if your scenario is correct, Dr. Schulte, is biological terrorism."

"That's true," Nan replied. "But who would be so insane to unleash something like this on purpose? I mean, no one group stands to gain—you couldn't possibly protect against so many different diseases. Some of the ones that are on the increase like Ebola and Marburg have no known vaccine, cure, or treatment."

"Doomsday cults have never been known for their sane, level-headed assessment of a strategy," he pointed out. "They might think that if they're 'chosen,' they'll come out of this unscathed. Maybe they're holed up somewhere. Or perhaps physical survival isn't their goal. Maybe their intention is to wipe out as many people as they can, themselves included, so they can be rid of their physical bodies and move onto some kind of cult heaven. They might be kamikaze technophobes, who want to destroy modern civilization and go down with the ship."

Another participant had come up to the microphone where Nan stood, so she stepped aside to let her speak. "This is all very titillating and dramatic," the woman said, "but so far-fetched that I don't really think it merits putting a lot of effort into pursuing it. This sounds like Hollywood to me, not science. I don't think we need to look very far from natural causes to see what's happened here. We've been polluting our air, our water, and our land for generations now. We've been pumping our livestock full of prophylactic antibiotics, and our health care system has been overprescribing them for decades. The population of humans on the planet is so burdensome and conditions of crowding so prevalent, especially in Third World urban areas, that it's no wonder infectious disease is making a comeback. What we might have experienced in the latter half of the 20th century is a rare hiatus that is a complete historical anomaly. I think what we need to do in such a crisis situation is focus on treatment. Once we have that under control, we can start looking for underlying causes."

After that, several members of the audience took a turn

at the mike. Most of them were in agreement that no matter what the cause, what needed to take place—immediately—was getting new drugs out of the development and testing phase so that patients could start using them right away. Holzer's efforts to prevent hysteria seemed to be falling flat. Everyone in attendance knew what multiple drug resistance meant in terms of human fatalities. The specter of hoards of virulent new superbugs descending ruthlessly upon mankind was as terrifying as contemplating a nuclear winter.

Much to Nan's consternation and frustration, her suggestion of tracking down the Patient or Vector Zero didn't seem to garner much support. Holzer assured the assembly that the military was already investigating the possibility of biological terrorism, but for some reason, Nan didn't take much comfort in this. Despite Holzer's arguments, she really did not believe that biological terrorism comprised the root cause of the current crisis. Her gut feeling was that something even more peculiar and unprecedented was taking place. Moreover, the combination of fear and greed seemed to be creating an atmosphere in which she doubted that any careful study or truly innovative approaches would ensue. The pharmaceutical companies would push their products with a vengeance; and the medical community, as well as the lay population, would desperately embrace their assurances, not knowing what else to do.

Nan caught an early evening flight home, feeling thwarted and deeply troubled. When she arrived home, the caregiver who was there had already put Myra to bed, so Nan just peeked in on her and saw that she was sleeping peacefully. After the young woman left, Nan settled into her mother's chair and watched the evening news for information on the flu epidemic, which had become the top news story.

On the West Coast, hundreds were coming down with the flu daily; in the South, Midwest, and East, the numbers of new victims were skyrocketing. The onset came so suddenly and violently that many people simply collapsed at work, on the bus, walking down the street, or, most dangerously, behind the wheels of their cars as they commuted to and from work. Several spectacular accidents had already been attributed to the flu and swelled the death toll. Public transportation agencies were desperately trying to figure out how to protect passengers from drivers who would come to work feeling fine, but then posed a grave danger as the day wore on and they might succumb to the flu virus; airlines were grappling with the same hypothetical problem. The number of deaths attributed to the flu, including the accidents, had climbed into the hundreds. The newscaster didn't say so, but Nan knew this was only the beginning. The epidemic had only just started in the U.S., just barely. The peak loomed several long days, weeks, or months ahead.

The president was going to address the country tomorrow, and public health officials were scrambling, but Nan could tell that no one was going to comprehend the seriousness of the situation until it was too late. It just wasn't going to sink in— very few of the people alive today had any firsthand experience with a serious epidemic. At the same time, what could be done that wouldn't crash the global economy, given the dependence of the global economy on trade?

After the news, Nan turned off the television and sat for a while, massaging her forehead. She felt worn out, but she roused herself after a few minutes and logged onto her computer to check her e-mail. She had quite a bit, she saw, so she ran through it quickly to see if anything needed her immediate attention. As she scrolled through, the subject heading of one of the messages caught her eye. "Re: Resistance Factor," it read. Curious, she opened it, unfamiliar with the sender's address and domain.

"You're on the right track, Dr. Schulte," it said.

That was all. It was unsigned.

She leaned back in her chair, wondering who the hell had

70

written it. It must have come from someone at the symposium. Hastily, she typed in a reply: "Tell me more," she wrote; "I'm listening." She sent it and then went through the rest of the mail, but none of it looked pressing. By the time she signed off, however, she saw that her reply to the cryptic e-mail had come back already. "No known addressee at that domain name," read the error message.

"Oh, that's just great," she muttered, prickly fear washing over her. Jesus, maybe Holzer was right. Maybe biological terrorism was responsible after all. But if so, why would he or she—or they—want her to know that she was on the right track? Just to taunt her? That didn't necessarily make sense. But if this person wanted to help her, why were they hiding? And why didn't they speak up at the symposium?

She glanced at her watch, wondering if perhaps she should call Elliott and tell him about this new development. She decided against it, though—it was after midnight and she didn't want to take the chance of waking up Amber. She remained in her chair, pondering, absentmindedly twisting a strand of hair around one index finger. If she was on the right track, that meant there really was a resistance factor. Something so awesomely, biologically agile, it was able to transcend not only species barriers, but kingdoms as well.

She got up and retrieved her briefcase, extracted her date book and reviewed her schedule for the next couple of weeks. If anyone was going to ferret out the index case, she was going to have to do it. Renata, another virologist in the department, would probably be willing to take over her lectures. She could keep in contact with her grad students and lab staff over the phone. Perhaps her mother could stay with Elliott and Amber; she didn't have the same allergy to cats that her daughter did. Nan could still have Janice and the other caregivers come over whenever no one else was home, and she could probably persuade them to fix meals for Amber and Elliott along with Myra.

She signed back onto the Internet and booked a flight for herself to London for tomorrow evening. There wasn't any time to lose. Travel and movement would start becoming restricted, and she would have a hard time doing the field work she needed to do. She reflected that she might possibly get stuck overseas, which wasn't something she relished— particularly if she became ill herself. In fact, she almost deleted her reservation as she contemplated all the various permutations of horrible scenarios that could conceivably take place: finding herself critically ill in a foreign country with no friends or family while an epidemic raged, hospitals bulged at the seams, and civilization teetered toward madness.

Well, whatever might happen, she felt compelled to do this. If she didn't do everything that was humanly possible and this new pandemic fulfilled all of its dire, dreadful promise, guilt and regret would plague her for the rest of her life. Seized with a sudden spasm of fear, she realized that the rest of her life might not be all that long. But she shoved this misgiving aside, feeling somewhat fatalistic.

Everyone dies, she thought defiantly—sooner or later.

CHAPTER 7

Submerging her impatience, Nan coaxed her mother out the door and down the back steps to where she had parked the car. This routine could have proceeded much more easily if she could have convinced Myra to use a wheelchair, but it seemed to represent a point of pride that she could still walk on her own two feet. She had so little left to feel proud of, Nan didn't want to take this away from her. Every few steps, however, Myra's legs froze up and refused to budge. When this happened, she often, out of desperation, tried to propel her upper body in the direction she wanted to go; but this, of course, presented a recipe for disaster.

"Feet first, Mom," Nan reminded her, her arms aching from supporting her mother's weight and trying to keep her upright; "no diving, okay?"

"Okay," replied Myra, her face pinched with exertion.

Nan steadied herself, forced herself to wait calmly until her mother could take another few steps. "You're doing great. Just a few more steps."

"Just a few more steps."

"That's right. You're almost there."

When they reached the car, Nan expelled a sigh of relief

and bundled her mother into her seat, fastened her seat belt. "You wait right here for me, okay? I'm going to get the suitcases and I'll be back in a second."

"Okay," agreed Myra, although Nan knew that if she took too long—forty-five seconds, say, as opposed to thirty—her mother would struggle out of the car and try to come looking for her.

Nan loaded the suitcases into the trunk and slid into the driver's seat, observing the time on the dashboard clock. She was already behind schedule, as she had an hour's drive to the airport after she dropped off her mother at Elliott's and she needed to check in early for her international departure. She roared out of the driveway, spraying gravel every which way, and nearly collided with a car coming down the street.

"Sorry!" she apologized, both to the driver of the car, who couldn't hear her, and her mother, who registered alarm and maintained that expression for the entire ride.

As she drove, Nan reviewed her plans for her journey in her head. She wasn't exactly trained to do fieldwork, but Elliott had had experience along these lines, and he had given her some pointers, as well as some contacts to look up once she arrived in England. She realized that she was probably looking for the proverbial needle in the haystack—and what could she hope to accomplish that public health specialists in England and Europe couldn't? —but her instincts felt so strong on this that she couldn't possibly ignore them. The cryptic e-mail message that she received last night bothered her, too. Elliott thought it might just be some crank or one of her students yanking her chain, but she didn't think so. Somehow, it felt different from that.

Ron, of course, had acted like a complete horse's ass when she called him to let him know that she was going to be taking a brief leave of absence, warning her that he couldn't be responsible for what might happen if she chose to leave at this time—whatever the hell that was supposed to mean.

Fortunately, two of her colleagues in the department had agreed to take over her lectures, and two of her graduate students would run her labs. Elliott had been surprisingly willing to look after Myra, which made her feel both grateful and guilty.

Ever mindful of the burgeoning flu epidemic, Nan switched on the radio and turned the dial, looking for news. She kept expecting international travel to become suspended in a tardy effort at a quarantine, but so far, this hadn't happened. Still, she wouldn't rest easy until she was on that plane and in the air. From morning news reports on television, she knew that hundreds of thousands of U.S. citizens were succumbing to the flu daily, and that this was starting to affect all kinds of services nationwide. The new vaccine had finally been released—some altruistic individuals had volunteered to be test subjects to speed things up—but quantities were still insufficient to inoculate the U.S. population, and given modern modes of transportation, this flu was spreading with breathtaking speed. In 1918, the flu had had to rely upon trains, ships, and pokey old cars bumping over dirt roads to reach all corners of the globe, but this flu could hitchhike on jets and highly efficient, well-maintained highways loaded with cars and trucks racing north, south, east, and west.

Soon, they had arrived at Elliott's house. He met them outside and helped escort Myra inside while Nan fetched her bag. Amber was up and about, and clearly excited about Myra's stay.

"I have a zoo!" she told Myra, dancing with impatience to show her. "And it's visiting hours!"

"Oh, my!" exclaimed Myra. Amber took over from Elliott, tugging Myra down the hall.

"How are you feeling?" Nan asked Elliott, once the two had disappeared into the den.

"Oh, fine. Amber and I have both received the new vaccine."

"That's good."

"Yeah." Elliott reached up absentmindedly to rub the back of his neck with one hand and Nan knew from this gesture that he was trying to keep himself from telling her once more that she should get one, too. Funny thing, though; even though she could feel relatively assured that this vaccine would in fact contain the correct gene sequences, she still felt reluctant to get one. She couldn't say why.

"So—I'm kind of running behind. I should probably get on the road."

"Right, right." Elliott put his arms around her and gave her a heartfelt hug. "You be careful, okay?"

"I promise."

"I mean, things could get really weird."

"I know."

He sighed. "I wish I could go with you, but with Amber in school and all this other stuff going on ..."

"I know that, Elliott," she interrupted, giving him a kiss on the cheek. "And this is probably some insane, quixotic quest driven by viral-induced dementia, but I just have this strange compulsion to go."

"Just don't get stuck over there."

"I won't." She clung to him a little longer, feeling much less confident than she was letting on. In fact, she felt suffused with dread. But the thought of staying didn't make her feel any better. "C'mon, I'll go say good-bye to my mom and Amber."

After Nan had given last-minute hugs all around, figuring they had all been exposed to one another already, she hurried out to the car and roared off. She didn't have her plane ticket, so she needed to give herself plenty of time for check-in. Traffic was light on the way to the airport, but as she approached the terminal, she ran into a traffic jam.

"Oh, great," she muttered, creeping along, trying to squeeze herself into the correct lane for long-term parking when it finally came into view—no mean feat. Over the years,

Nan had decided that changing lanes had come to be viewed as an aggressive territorial threat to other drivers in that lane.

She made it, however, and lucked out by coming upon someone exiting a parking place just as she approached. Parking hastily and grabbing up her bags—one which contained her clothes and toiletries and one which contained supplies for collecting samples—she rushed into the Logan terminal, slipping on a mask. She felt dismayed to find barely controlled pandemonium. Travelers frantic to get out of the country before the flu assailed them choked the counters. Their numbers clearly hard hit by flu cases, the staff that manned the counters looked sparse, harried, and grim. Nan knew that fleeing the country wasn't going to help in the long term—in 1918, only one tiny, remote island in the entire world had escaped that flu pandemic. Given enough time, this flu would circle the globe as well, leaving no place untouched. But panic was never known to listen to reason.

There was nothing to do but take her place at the end of a long line and wait her turn, so Nan pulled out a journal to read while she stood and waited. She couldn't quell her anxiety that air travel might get suspended at any moment. So far, the death toll had not been that high, but they were in early days. The collapsing was alarming, but not totally out of character for a virulent flu. If treated in time, lives could be saved. If the mortality rate rose above two percent, travel bans would undoubtedly be instituted.

A commotion ensued when one of the passengers standing in a nearby line collapsed; it was as if a skunk had suddenly materialized in the middle of the crowd and lifted its tail—everyone backed away in consternation. The odd thing was, the woman didn't look all that sick, if you didn't count the fact that she was unconscious. She just seemed a little pale. In this respect, influenza treated its victims a little more kindly than Ebola, say, which turned human bodies into a horror movie spectacle of leaking blood and hemorrhaging orifices.

Nan grabbed her disinfectant wipes from her purse, noticing that just about everyone in line was joining her in taking whatever small precaution they could, as useless as this particular one represented in this context. If the virus was aerosolized, which it undoubtedly was, only the proper mask would provide the requisite protection. Only a handful of people were wearing them.

Within minutes, suited-up medics seemed to appear out of nowhere and carted the victim off, probably to prevent panic as much as disease. Brave souls, Nan thought. Health care givers probably represented the highest risk population in something like a flu epidemic. There was practically no way to protect themselves or avoid exposure completely. A deadly flu was a Level 4 Biohazard, in reality; but there was no way to turn the world into a Level 4 containment facility.

Incredibly—or perhaps not so incredibly—two more people simply dropped in their tracks before Nan reached the counter, revving up her paranoia level considerably. She knew she had to have been exposed to the flu by now, but the incubation period could vary by quite a bit. She could be within hours of her own collapse, this she knew, but she steeled herself to go through with her journey. The wait between check-in and boarding seemed interminable, and she found it difficult to concentrate on her reading. Another person toppled out of his chair in the boarding area and as the ever-present medics came and scooped him up, Nan couldn't shake the feeling that an invisible sniper roamed the airport, randomly selecting victims and felling them. It was weirder than anything she had ever experienced, but, even more strangely, it was starting to seem horrifyingly normal: x number of people in any crowd were going to slump to the floor in a viremic stupor.

Once on the plane, Nan took some melatonin so that she could sleep through the flight. She would need to hit the deck running when she reached England, and she didn't want to pursue her tasks jet-lagged, sleep-deprived, and grogged out. Her sleep, however, proved fitful. The air in the cabin seemed stale and thin, at one time too hot, and then too cold. Her mask felt confining and close. The beverage cart squeaked and rattled every time it passed, and she couldn't be sure, but there seemed to be some concern about one of the passengers in the forward end of the plane. Her suspicions were confirmed when they finally landed in England in the early morning, and a long wait ensued while an ambulance pulled up to the plane, the passenger loaded into it.

So much for not feeling groggy and spaced-out, she reflected with a sigh, as she deplaned and made her way through customs. The immigrations officials wore masks and gloves, which contributed to the nightmarish feeling of the last twenty-four hours and made the airport look like some kind of operating theater. She wondered why she hadn't seen masks and gloves on personnel at the Boston airport. From reports that she had been privy to, the appearance of the flu in Great Britain was lagging behind the rest of Europe—possibly because it was an island, possibly because of public health precautions, possibly through some quirk of fate—but England was where, Nan felt, the entire recent cascade of microbial events had its genesis.

Nan hurried through the airport, glad to see that here, at least, passengers were not crumpling to the floor. She took the high speed train into London and then hailed a taxi, which whisked her through a light drizzle to her hotel, a modest, pleasant establishment on one of the quieter side streets of the city, which was kind enough to let her check in at such an early hour. Returning to the city in which she'd contracted flesh-eating bacteria felt odd, even spooky—especially since the organisms responsible had become completely resistant to antibiotics in the meantime. She half-expected to see Londoners missing hands and limbs sprinkled throughout the area as if in some freakish carnival; she spotted only one person with a prosthetic leg, however, lurching down the street near her hotel.

She intended to start phoning her contacts right away, but when she stepped into her room, the bed looked so incredibly inviting with its clean, white, plumped-up pillows and softly furrowed comforter that she couldn't resist tossing her mask onto the bedside table and sinking into it. She intended merely to "rest her eyes," but she didn't come to until four hours later. When she realized how much time had passed, a surge of adrenalin flooded her body and she frantically started calling the people on her list. To her frustration, however, most of them were out or in meetings.

Fortunately, when she called the regional public health officer for a district southwest of London a second time, she was available for a meeting later in the afternoon. Nan hung up the phone, grateful to have made some progress. She had an hour to kill before taking the train to Kingsford to meet with Marjory Binghamton, so she took a very long shower, sprayed everything she had touched with an alcohol solution, and headed to a nearby tea room where she attempted to settle her nerves by downing several cups of strong, black English tea.

When she had finished with her tea, she took another cab to the train station. Once on board, she felt tempted to take another nap on the way; but the tea did a good job of keeping her awake. As the train clicked along through the dark underground and then emerged into hazy gray neighborhoods crowded with semi-detached housing and a bristling maze of TV antennas, she noticed that the paranoia and panic that had characterized the States before she left hadn't yet arrived here; maybe it never would. Perhaps Britons would greet the flu epidemic with the same stoic, unflappable aplomb that they greeted everything. A young mother discreetly nursed her baby in the row ahead; the middle-aged couple across from her bent together over a crossword puzzle. Passengers came and went from the buffet car, carrying chocolate bars, egg salad sandwiches wrapped in cellophane, and bottles of spring water. Strangely, however, the normalcy of the atmosphere seemed contrived ... almost sinister. The fact that people were behaving in their usual fashion reminded Nan of "The Masque of the Red Death," the gruesome Edgar Allen Poe story about revelers who danced the night away at a ball while a plague raged, only to expire when the sun arose the next morning.

It wasn't long before the train pulled into Kingsford. Dr. Binghamton had sent a driver to chauffeur Nan to her offices, and he seemed to recognize Nan right away as she stepped off the train—how, she wasn't sure. Probably she looked more American than she realized, and it wasn't exactly tourist season.

The public health offices were located in a stone building with a slate roof that moss had almost entirely enveloped. The damp air here seemed chillier than in London while no difference in temperature appeared to exist between inside and outside. Dr. Binghamton, a brisk, rosy-cheeked woman shaped like the Michelin Man, invited Nan to take off her coat as she entered, but Nan decided to leave it on. One degree colder in this room, she thought, and you could see your breath. Marjory, of course, looked comfy and warm as toast in a tweed skirt, silk blouse, and cashmere cardigan.

"So," she said, once introductions had been made and Nan was seated, "you're here on an epidemiological expedition, is that correct?"

"That's correct," replied Nan. "It seems to me that the recent multiple drug resistance might have had its start here in England. I did some research on the Internet, and I found that several so-called 'killer' bacterial outbreaks occurred in this area right about the same time a year or so ago."

Marjory nodded. "Yes, you're right about that." She sighed. "And a sad thing it was, too. As perhaps you know, a dozen people in this village alone have died from staph infections, including two adorable children from a lovely family."

81

"I'm really sorry to hear that."

"Yes, it was awful. And there's no end in sight. We've had to send at least twenty people with these infections to facilities in London in the last two months because the local hospital couldn't treat them effectively." She paused. "So what are you hoping to find?"

Nan shifted in her seat. "Well, I'm looking for evidence of some kind of resistance factor. Some genetic mechanism that these organisms might have acquired somehow and are now passing around."

"Indeed."

"I realize that sounds fairly vague."

"Where do you think this resistance factor came from?"

"That—I'm not sure about." Nan shivered involuntarily, recalling the cryptic e-mail message she had received. Did the sender live in England?

"What do you propose to do?"

"Well, I'd like to collect some samples to send back to the States for analysis—water, soil, animal samples, blood samples from those infected, as well as some who haven't been. I've already cleared this with the CDC, of course." This last statement was something of a falsehood. What she was hoping was that Elliott would have wangled permission for her by the time she needed to ship her samples. Ordinarily, sending samples wouldn't be such a big deal, although any time materials that might harbor pathogens were shipped from one country to another, they had to be handled with extreme care and sent through the proper channels. But now, with a flu epidemic and new hot zones for multiple diseases popping up everywhere, officials were understandably cautious about any circulation of potential pathogens, especially something like multiply-drug-resistant killer bacteria. At the worst, however, she could have the samples analyzed here in England. She tried not to think about the fact that she would be exposing herself to these germs when she collected her samples. In fact, just coming to this part of the country could conceivably represent a risk.

She waited while Dr. Binghamton made a few phone calls on her behalf so that she could conduct interviews and obtain samples. Afterward, the doctor tapped a few commands into the computer and printed out several sheets of information for her.

"This is a summary of what we know so far about these cases," she told her, "who came down with these infections, where they live, where they work, their symptoms and lab results, all that sort of thing. I don't need to tell you, I'm sure, that this information is strictly confidential and for your research purposes only."

"Absolutely," Nan assured her. "I'm really grateful for your help."

"And we're quite appreciative of your efforts as well, Dr. Schulte." She gave Nan a smile. "You'll keep us informed of everything you find out?"

"You can count on it."

"Good." She hesitated, then rose. "If you'd like to have Benjamin drive you around, I know he'd be happy to do so."

"That would be great. Thank you so much," Nan told her fervently, rising as well.

The afternoon was waning, and Nan felt awkward about barging in on suffering families at the end of the day, but she had no time to lose, especially after that ill-timed nap she had succumbed to earlier today. She found Benjamin waiting for her in the entrance hall and asked him if he wouldn't mind taking her by one of the families' homes that she had on her list—if he didn't think she would be interrupting their dinner, she told him. Despite her haste, she knew that she needed everyone's full cooperation, and she didn't want to come on like some insensitive, overbearing American. He assured her that everyone in town wanted to get to the bottom of this horrible disease and that no one would feel inconvenienced in the least.

So they took off over a rutted, muddy road. The light rain had stopped by now and mist was rising off verdant fields and copses of autumn trees splashed with muted reds, bronzes, ochres, and golds. A few cows browsed in the pastures, looking picturesque and bucolic in the shafts of fading sunlight that pierced the tattered clouds, but Nan couldn't help but wonder if they were harboring Mad Cow Disease. Could the prion responsible for Mad Cow Disease have any relationship to this newest microbial development? she mused. Perhaps. Anything was possible, she supposed. And that made this a devil of an investigation. To find something, one usually needed to know what one was looking for. All she knew in this case was that she was looking for something terribly wrong, and terribly deadly.

CHAPTER 8

Deciding that she might as well start at the beginning, Nan requested that Benjamin take her to the house where the first index cases had lived: the two children who had died from the killer bacteria. She wasn't really looking forward to this chore—she couldn't imagine anything much more devastating than losing one child, let alone two—but she told herself that if she could help others with the information she gleaned, it would be worth it.

The family's home turned out to be a neatly kept, white-washed stucco cottage on the edge of a lovely little pond whose banks were crowded with slender reeds and supple, golden-limbed willows. A modern swing set with a slide stood in the back yard, further wrenching Nan's heart; she wondered if the family had been unable to bear removing it. Benjamin said that he would wait in the car while she conducted her interview, so she walked hesitantly up to the house, clutching her bag with her supplies in it in one hand, her purse in the other.

The door swung open almost as soon as she touched the doorbell. A pleasant young man who looked to be in his thirties invited her to come in; she introduced herself, declining his outstretched hand with an apology.

"Ah, right!" he exclaimed. "Of course. I'm Nigel. Faith!" he called into the kitchen, out of which the homey aroma of pot roast wafted. "The doctor Marjory called about is here!"

Faith emerged from the kitchen carrying a baby on her hip, which relieved Nan immeasurably. At least they still have a child, she thought, desperately trying to figure out the gentlest way to broach her topic. Both parents, though polite, seemed incapable of smiling, although the baby's cooing when Nan introduced herself once more prompted a ghost of a grin from the mother.

"I'm so sorry about your loss," she began, as Nigel invited her to sit down. "And I hope that my coming here doesn't stir up too many painful memories."

Faith shook her head, settling down on the love seat opposite Nan. The baby squirmed in her embrace so she set him down on the floor to crawl about. "Every single day brings painful memories, I'm afraid. We're just happy to do anything we can to spare other families the grief we've been through."

"Well, thank you," Nan replied. "That's a really generous attitude." She paused, gathering up her thoughts. The baby had made his way over to her feet and was curiously examining the laces on her boots. "I guess it would help if you could fill me in on your children's activities around the time that they came down with their illness. Is there anything they did, anywhere they went, that you didn't?" She realized, of course, that the parents could have had an immunity to these bugs that the children didn't, but still, it made sense to try to separate out their activities.

"No, Darryl!" admonished Nigel, darting forward to scoop up his son, who had decided to wedge the tip of Nan's boot into his mouth. He settled the boy in his lap, smoothing down his curls absentmindedly. "We've been asking ourselves the same thing, over and over again, as you might imagine," he said. "If nothing else, to protect Darryl."

Nan nodded sympathetically.

"They loved to play outside, both of them," Faith commented.

"Yes, I saw the swing set outside."

"They had a lot of fun on that swing set," Nigel agreed. "But what they really liked to do was to play in the pond. They were always bringing home turtles and frogs for pets, and Penelope loved to collect flowers and leaves, too—press them in books. Charlie was just starting to learn how to fish."

Nan took out her notebook and started scribbling notes. Turtles were known to harbor the bacterium *Salmonella*, which had caused quite a few serious infections in American households in the Fifties and Sixties, when the popularity of cute little green turtles and their accompanying plastic oases had established them as firmly as such icons as Barbie dolls. Once the source of the mysterious illnesses had been discovered, however, the turtles went the way of pogo sticks and hula hoops.

"They tramped about in the woods quite a bit, too," commented Faith.

"Did you notice any unusual bug bites around this time?" asked Nan. "Any tick bites?"

Faith shrugged. "Just the usual mosquito bites and midge bites. At least, from what we know. We weren't really paying attention to that sort of thing at the time."

"No, of course not," said Nan. She'd have to spend a fair amount of time scouring the nearby area anyway, trapping whatever insects, rodents, and water creatures she could. This wasn't exactly the most propitious time of year to do this, of course, since a lot of things weren't out and about, like the insects. Well, she'd just have to do her best. She wasn't sure what to do about investigating the possibility that a terrorist or crazy cult had released the resistance factor. But if it was something along those lines, why would anyone come here, to this sleepy little out-of-the-way hamlet, to release a bioweapon? This close to London, it would make much more sense to release it there—it would affect a lot more people, create a lot more havoc.

She learned from Faith and Nigel that Charlie was the first to develop an infection. Apparently, it had started with a mosquito bite on his leg that he scratched until it bled. Faith had washed it thoroughly with green soap and water—much to Charlie's dismay, Nigel remembered—then she had dabbed a little antibiotic cream on it and covered it up with a Band-aid. The Band-aid lasted about a day and then fell off. At that point, they could see that rather than clearing up, the spot had grown and developed a yellow, pus-filled center. Faith soaked his leg every morning and night in hot salt water for a few days, hoping to draw out the infection, but every day, the spot had grown just a little larger.

It was at this point that Penelope developed an infected spot on her arm, from a small cut she had sustained while out playing in the woods. Beginning to feel concerned, Faith took both children to their family physician, who examined their wounds and prescribed both an oral antibiotic and a topical one. She encouraged Faith to keep up the hot salt water soaks and to get in touch with her in three days if the sores had not healed.

Three days later, both sores had healed over, but they both had large blood blisters that had formed on their limbs, and they were cranky and out-of-sorts. The physician stopped by to see the children on her way home from work, and when she saw their blisters, she gasped. "Literally, audibly gasped," recalled Faith, her voice breaking. The doctor called an ambulance to take them to the hospital right away.

She warned Nigel and Faith that they might have to amputate if they couldn't get the infection under control, but after that, everything began to move at nightmarish speed. The children's fevers, which had been low-grade up until now, started to spike, even as they waited anxiously for the ambulance. By the time they were loaded into the ambulance, they were so hot the paramedics began to pack them in ice for the trip. Faith rode with them in the back, alarmed when both children became disoriented and confused. IVs flooding their systems with potent antibiotics were having no effect; nothing, in fact, that anyone was trying seemed to do the slightest bit of good. When they reached the hospital and were rushing the children to emergency surgery, first Charlie, and then Penelope began to convulse.

At this point, both Nigel and Faith fell silent as tears ran down their faces. Nan found herself crying, too.

"They—both died before the doctors could operate," choked Nigel. Darryl leaned back to regard his father in dismay, whimpering. Nigel met his eyes and forced a smile. "It's okay, sweetheart. Daddy's okay," he soothed, pressing the boy to his chest.

All three sat in silence for a moment. Finally, Nan spoke. "How—appallingly awful."

Nigel and Faith nodded, wiping their eyes.

Nan expelled a heavy breath. "Well, I think the best thing for me to do is to collect some samples for lab analysis, if you don't have any objections. I thought I'd get some soil and water samples today, pick up whatever animal samples I can, too."

"That's fine. Whatever you need to do," Faith said listlessly.

"Uh, and if you wouldn't mind," she added, "I'd like to get some blood samples. Darryl included, if that's okay."

Faith and Nigel exchanged glances. "Is that really necessary?" asked Nigel.

"Well, I think it might be. It would be really helpful anyway. I can do a tiny little stick on him. He'll barely feel it."

"All right then," Faith sighed.

Nan reached for her bag with all the vials and other paraphernalia, withdrawing her syringes, test tubes, disinfectant, and latex gloves. She stuck Nigel first, then Faith, who made a great show of acting like it was a fun thing to do for Darryl's sake. Darryl watched the proceedings with bemused interest. Hooking up a tiny butterfly needle and related apparatus to a test tube, Nan swiftly performed her procedure on him before the little guy knew what hit him. She felt glad, for probably the first time in her life, that she had taken that summer job as a pediatric blood tech after graduating from college. By the time he started to wail, it was all over, and she had the blood she needed.

Before she exited the house, Nan asked if she could take a sample from the couple's vacuum cleaner bag. Both Faith and Nigel looked at her curiously, but Faith complied by going to the hall closet and extracting her ancient vacuum cleaner. Feeling a bit silly, Nan knelt down to open it up and extract a wad of dust and lint with a pair of forceps, depositing her sample into a small, screw-capped specimen jar.

"That should do it," she said, standing up and brushing off her pants legs. "You don't have any air filters in this house associated with your heating system, do you?"

They shook their heads.

"Okay, then, I'm going to poke around outside a little, see what I can find out there, all right? I'll try to disturb as little as possible." Nan retrieved her bag, carefully sealing and storing her samples to prevent breakage or leakage, wiping everything down with disinfectant. "I can't thank you enough," she told the couple as they escorted her to the door. "You've been so kind to help me on this."

"We're happy to," Nigel replied, although true happiness seemed to be somewhat outside his emotional repertoire at the moment.

"One more question," Nan said, as she was headed out the door. "Do you eat beef?"

"Sometimes," said Faith. "We get our beef locally, from a farmer we know personally."

"Lamb?"

"Yes, lamb, too. Purchased locally." Faith paused. "Do you think that's a bad idea?"

"Oh, not necessarily," Nan told her. "I'm just gathering all the information I can. You know about Mad Cow Disease, right?"

Nigel gave a short, humorless laugh. "How could we not know?"

"That's what I thought." Nan buttoned up her coat, tucked her bags under her arm. "Thanks again."

She headed out to the car to make sure it was all right with Benjamin that she planned to gather a few more samples. He seemed quite content to sit in the car with a thermos of tea and a couple of ham and butter sandwiches, listening to the car radio. Leaving her purse in the car, she took her materials bag with her, donned another pair of gloves, and began the tedious task of sample collecting. No bugs were about—it was too late in the year—but she dug up several soil samples, some of which would, she hoped, contain the eggs of resident insects, if not larvae. She took several water samples from the pond, too, and scooped up some of the soft mud along the banks. She would probably have to set traps to get ahold of any rodents, so she made a note in her book to pick up some traps from the hardware store. Soon, it became too dark to work, so she packed up and headed to the car.

Benjamin offered her a sandwich, but she was feeling too paranoid to accept, even though she was starving. She could grab something from the buffet car on the train or wait to eat in London. She certainly didn't want to eat anything before washing her hands about eleven jillion times after gathering those samples, despite the fact that she had been wearing gloves, but she didn't want to disturb Nigel and Faith again by asking to use their bathroom. Benjamin drove her to the train station and dropped her off. She had about a half-hour wait for the next train into London, so she made a visit to the ladies' room and washed her hands and forearms carefully with soap and hot water. She was half beginning to believe that she might not come down with the flu, as she felt that she was nearing the incubation period for the influenza virus and she hadn't noticed any symptoms whatsoever. She hoped that by daring to think this, she wasn't tempting the flu gods to send a thunderbolt her way.

Once she was on the train and settled into her seat, tiredness washed over her, a combination of jet lag, she supposed, and the emotional drain of talking to Faith and Nigel. Not many people rode the train this trip; in fact, it almost seemed deserted. As Nan made her way to the buffet car to pick up a sandwich and a drink, she noticed a young man slumped in his seat, looking pale and sweating profusely. Holding her breath as she passed, as if that would do any good, she kept going until she located the train's steward, strolling through the cars, taking tickets and chatting briefly with the few passengers.

"There's a young man two cars back who looks pretty ill," Nan told him. "You might want to keep an eye on him."

"Thanks, miss. I'll do that," he replied.

Heading back to the buffet car, she picked up a curried chicken sandwich and a cup of tea. When she passed the spot where the young man had been seated, she saw that he was no longer there. Perhaps the steward had taken him to a safer or more comfortable place on the train. As Nan eased herself back into her seat and unwrapped her sandwich, she reflected on the fact that one of the creepiest things about an influenza epidemic was the invisibility and seeming innocuousness of it. If some unfortunate soul had Ebola or Marburg, he or she would look so horrifying that everyone with any sense would get the hell away. But influenza was silent, stealthy—someone could be sitting next to you shedding viruses like crazy, and you wouldn't necessarily know it. Worse, they wouldn't even need to be sitting right next to you to infect you. You could just be on the same subway car, plane, or train, or in the same office or department store with someone who was viremic, and catch the virus. It was like air or water—it traveled simply everywhere.

England felt relatively calm and quiet at the moment, but it seemed the flu had made it here, and it was only a matter of time before Britain's population became as ravaged by it as the United States. And in tiny little hamlets, shocking numbers of people were coming down with incurable diseases. Depending upon any number of factors—people's natural immunity and resistance, the virulence of the microorganisms, the synergistic interactions between various diseases, travel patterns of man and microbe—disease could carve huge swaths throughout the global population in an almost inconceivably short period of time, creating a nightmarish chain reaction of corpses piling up, breeding more disease, triggering mass panic, overwhelming even the best laid emergency plans.

Contemplating this scenario, Nan went from ravenous to not very hungry. She wrapped the second half of her sandwich back up in its cellophane and tucked it into her purse. She might want it later, and she needed to stay up and call Elliott to see how things were going—with the epidemic, with Myra, with her permission to ship samples back to the States.

She put on a mask and gazed out the window unseeing as the train hurtled along in the gathering darkness, reviewing her conversation with Faith and Nigel. She couldn't help but wonder if she had missed any essential pieces of information, neglected to ask any critical questions. It felt weird to be groping around so blindly, especially at a time when it seemed that medical science had reached such spectacular heights of prowess and efficacy. Had humans, like every other once dominant species on this planet, reached their inevitable peak? Were they biologically doomed to sink into oblivion, paving the way for another species to have their day in the sun? It was one thing to contemplate such matters for extinct creatures like the dinosaurs, to delight in their bones and fantasize about their existence in media and literature. But it was very much another to stare at the specter of your own biological inadaptability and to suffer from the toll taken by the agonized deaths of loved ones with names and faces, pets and favorite foods.

Nan shivered, pulled her coat closer about her. She did not want to observe the demise of the human race. And she was going to do everything in her power to prevent it.

CHAPTER 9

The minute Nan returned to her hotel room, she picked up the phone and called Elliott. During the taxi ride from the train station, she saw two people keel over on the sidewalk, presumably from the flu, filling her with ominous misgivings about her loved ones back home. Much to her frustration, however, she couldn't get through for a half-hour. All the circuits were busy, if she was to believe the computerized voice that kept coming through, annoying the hell out of her.

"Damn!" she exclaimed, slamming down the receiver for the tenth time. The fact that she couldn't get through didn't exactly assuage her paranoia. Finally, mercifully, she managed to put the call through. Amber answered, sounding grown-up and serious.

"Hi, sweetie; it's Nan."

"Nan!" Amber responded, sounding surprised. "Are you back?"

"I'm afraid not, pumpkin; I'm calling from England. I won't be back for a few days."

"Oh." She sounded disappointed.

"How's your dad? How's Myra?"

"They're good."

"Can I speak to your dad for a minute?"

"Sure. I'll go get him."

"I love you, sweetie—you stay well, okay?"

"Okay. Bye."

Nan heard a clunk as Amber dropped the phone to go off in search of her father. Elliott picked up soon after, sounding a little breathless.

"Hi, sweetheart," he greeted her.

"Am I interrupting anything?"

"Oh, not really. I was talking to one of the neighbors. We're organizing a neighborhood watch."

"For...?"

"The flu, of course," he sighed. "Well, and all the other diseases that are going haywire right now, too. I don't know if you've heard the news reports—"

"I've been in an out-of-the-way village most of today and I just got back to my hotel room."

"Well, it's getting bad."

Nan tensed. "How—bad?"

"We're having to use the VFW hall to house the sick—and it looks like that won't be enough for very long. All the hospitals and clinics in the entire county are full. Schools have been closed, mass gatherings have been canceled, restaurants can only serve take-out, and anyone who can is being asked to stay home. We don't have enough respirators. Emergency services are maxed out. They've stopped using sirens on ambulances because they've been running twenty-four hours a day. In fact, if you need an ambulance, you're pretty well shit out of luck."

"Jesus."

"And now food shortages have begun. There's some hoarding going on, unfortunately, of toilet paper, canned goods, and frozen foods, but fresh produce is starting to skyrocket, too. And you need to go to the store early in the day, or they'll be out. Imports have slowed to a trickle, but even the stuff from California and Florida is getting hard to come by. Farm workers have been getting sick, of course, along with everyone else—truck drivers, forklift drivers, grocery store clerks, and the list goes on and on."

"My God."

"No kidding." Elliott heaved a dispirited sigh. "So, this neighborhood watch is to help make sure that people don't get trapped in their houses and die from starvation or dehydration."

"Right."

"Or trapped in their house with a corpse that they're too weak to remove and that health officials are too busy to come and get."

Nan didn't know what to say. This all sounded too horrific to assimilate.

"How is your work going?" he asked, when she didn't reply.

"Okay, I guess. I interviewed a family today who lost two of their children to necrotizing fasciitis."

"That must have been a joy."

"Yeah. I got some samples, though. Have you heard anything about getting permission for me to ship them to the U.S.?"

"I did. That's the good news." He told her he had managed to obtain permission for her to ship samples to him at Public Health, where he would store them for her until she got back. If she wanted, he said, he could make arrangements to have her lab at the university stepped up to a Level 3 Biohazard facility so that it could be ready when she got back. "I'm assuming you don't think you need to examine these critters under Level 4 conditions, right? Because if you do, you're going to have to ship them to the CDC or the army."

"That's right." Nan didn't elaborate. Even though she didn't think the bacteria could be transmitted by air, she wasn't so certain about the resistance factor itself. If this unusual resistance was being detected in bacteria alone, she could feel reasonably certain that the factor would have to be transmitted bacterium to bacterium, through conjugation or some other bacterial method for swapping genes. But the fact that viruses seemed to have gotten in on the act complicated matters. Many viruses could travel easily through the air. Certain bacteria could, too, such as anthrax and tuberculosis, but in general, they didn't exchange genetic material with such versatility, promiscuity, and rapidity.

Viruses, however, often included extra genes from their hosts when they packaged up their new versions of themselves in their hosts, and then dragged them around with them wherever they went, often inserting these new "alien" genes into subsequent hosts. Recently, genes from an insect—a lacewing, to be exact—that had been introduced by a virus into some human genomes had been identified as the factor responsible for a rare form of cancer. Another ancient virus had inserted a gene that turned out to be essential for the development of the human placenta.

At any rate, if her hypothesis was correct, the resistance factor was already circulating in the air, all over the globe. It was too late to try to contain it. So it made no sense to try to conduct this research in a Level 4 containment facility, which would mean that she would have no access to the samples and no idea whether anyone was seriously looking at them or not. She just hoped she was making the right decision.

She spoke to Myra briefly, who couldn't say much more than a few words, and then she said good-bye to Elliott. After hanging up, Nan sat for several minutes on the edge of the bed, not exactly reassured by her conversation. She felt relieved, of course, that Elliott, Amber, and Myra seemed to be escaping the flu. But the flu wasn't the only scary bug to contend with at the moment; and it sounded like this pandemic was straining every bit of civilization's resources.

She fell asleep where she was sitting, more or less, slipping

her boots off and crawling under the comforter. She awoke
at about 4 AM and found herself unable to get back to sleep.
So she arose and switched on the television, almost afraid
to watch the news, but compelled to at the same time. The
pandemic was reminding her of a slow-motion tidal wave
that was taking weeks to strike land— except that there was
no place to escape from it. You could only stand helplessly
wherever you were and watch it approach, the embodiment of
Promethean, dispassionate, mind-numbing fury.

So many pandemic-related stories merited news coverage
that it seemed almost like a parody. An Ebola outbreak had
occurred in Brussels and claimed the lives of fifty Belgians
before it could be contained. In fact, authorities weren't
entirely sure that it was completely contained, as a few people
who might have been exposed were unaccounted for. They
could be dead—or they could be on the move, spreading the
virus wherever they went. A sudden onset of the flu was being
blamed for a tanker that ran aground in Buenos Aires; when
the captain collapsed, his body struck the throttle and shoved
it into a high speed. The ship, unfortunately, was in the process
of docking, so that by the time anyone could react and slam
the ship into reverse, the momentum carried the ship into the
port, killing 137 and wounding hundreds more. Rioting was
breaking out in some Asian cities as food shortages deepened
and health care became all but unavailable. Firefighters and
law enforcement—their ranks hard hit by the flu, cholera,
typhoid, and diphtheria, among other diseases—were unable
to quell the riots and several parts of Southeast Asia and Korea
were in flames. Stock markets were plunging worldwide, the
slowdown of traffic and commerce was creating economic
hardship all over the globe, and violent crime was on the
increase everywhere, particularly the United States.

Nan sat in stricken silence, watching horror story after
horror story before finally turning off the TV, heaving a sigh of
deep despair. She glanced at her watch and saw that it was now

five o'clock. She should probably shower and start getting ready for the day. After carefully packing up the samples that she had collected yesterday and checking to make sure that plenty of dry ice remained in the boxes to make the trip across the Atlantic, she located a nearby courier service from the phone book and map that the hotel provided. It wouldn't open for another hour, so she went to a small café down the block and ordered a light breakfast of raisin toast, tea, and a soft-boiled egg. She decided to walk to the courier service since it was on the way to the train station and she had some extra time before she needed to leave to meet the driver back in Kingsford.

As she walked, she pondered the resistance factor and all its many implications, wondered for probably the ten-thousandth time where it came from and what it represented. How and why would something like this develop? Unless a person or group engineered and released it, it had to represent an act of nature. If it were an act of nature, it really did almost seem as if the microbial kingdom had launched a counter-offensive to man's crusade against infectious disease. She knew that this sounded like science fiction, and that any self-respecting scientist would scoff at such a notion, but things were happening so quickly that mutation and natural selection simply could not account for the recent developments, not even taking into account such factors as mutagens in the environment and an increase of UV radiation striking the planet through the depleted ozone layer.

She returned to the idea of a cult or terrorist. Perhaps this was the most logical explanation, after all; but then why wasn't anyone claiming responsibility for it? Usually when ideology was involved, the person or persons responsible couldn't wait to issue some sort of proclamation. That e-mail message she received didn't really qualify, in her opinion, disturbing as it was.

It did seem interesting that the resistant streptococci first arose in the home of Mad Cow Disease. One of the people on the list that Marjory had given her worked as a chef at a restaurant, and one was a dairy farmer; Faith had said that her family ate beef and lamb. But this could just be a coincidence. That was the problem with this investigation: There were just so many damned variables and possibilities.

Traffic on both the streets and the sidewalks was light; Nan passed few other pedestrians on her way. She was so lost in thought that she didn't notice the large man in an expensive overcoat seated leaning up against a lamp post until she passed him. She flicked her gaze over towards him absentmindedly, figuring he represented another flu victim, but as he turned his head to watch her when she passed by, shockwaves of horror shot through her. Dark, oily blood trickled from his eyes, nose, and mouth.

"Oh my God!" she gasped, backing away instinctively. Then she halted, trembling. "Sir?" she called. "Can you hear me or understand me?"

He didn't reply; he merely stared at her with unnerving blankness.

"Just stay there, sir. I'm going to call someone to help you." She practically tripped over her own feet in her eagerness to alert someone to this man's presence in London. Clearly, the outbreak of Ebola in Brussels had not been contained, she thought grimly, trying desperately to squelch her rising panic.

She stumbled into the first store she came to and breathlessly asked to use the telephone. Then she realized she had no idea which agency to contact. She asked the clerk who she should call in an emergency and he reached over and punched in the numbers for her. When an operator answered, she tried to relay the information in as reasonable a voice as she could, but she knew that a note of hysteria must have crept in, as the operator kept telling her to remain calm. She could see the clerk's eyes widen while he listened to her describe what she had just seen, and he took a few steps back, practically flattening himself up against the wall. When she hung up, she told the clerk not to go outside the store, which she surmised was probably an unnecessary warning. In fact, he was eying the phone with trepidation, as if Ebola virus might be lurking on it after Nan made her call. She assured him that he was in no danger, that she had not had any physical contact with the sick man outside the store.

Once outside, Nan waited at what she thought was probably a safe distance from the stricken man. She didn't want any well-meaning passers-by to stop to help him and then put themselves at risk through contact. She couldn't be certain without getting closer, but it looked as though he might have vomited blood all down his front while she was making her phone call. Soon—quite soon, in fact—an emergency vehicle pulled up, lights and sirens blaring. A half-dozen biohazard workers in space suits erupted out of the van carrying a tented stretcher that looked like something out of a science fiction movie for transporting alien bodies. At that point, she hastened down the street as quickly as possible, fearful that the workers might quarantine the area and start rounding up everyone in sight just to be safe. Once out of sight, she slowed down a bit, feeling shaken and sick at heart. That poor man would probably die; the mortality rate for Ebola was anywhere from seventy to ninety percent. Did he have a wife? Children? A devoted pet? She couldn't bear to think about it.

She felt so rattled that she almost walked past the courier service, tucked as it was into a crease in the row of buildings that lined the street. An unconscious reminder snagged her attention, however, and she slipped into the storefront, trying to appear as normal as possible. For contents of the package, she wrote, "Medical supplies—Fragile," and hoped no questions would be asked. The courier service might not want to transport potentially biohazardous material, for which she wouldn't blame them at all, but she was extremely anxious to get these samples on their way before transportation became even more disrupted.

Fortunately, her transaction went smoothly and the clerk assured her that the package would arrive at its destination in twelve to twenty-four hours. Relieved, she went on her way, her heart still racing from her encounter with Ebola. She probably hadn't gotten close enough to the man to have sustained any risk, but at the same time, the mode of contagion had never been established with any certainty. One of the more famous CDC "cowboys" had spent an entire day in a hut filled with Ebola victims, drawing their blood and breathing the same air in close quarters, and he never did come down with it. On the other hand, veterinary researchers had evidence that a cousin of Ebola had traveled through the air from monkeys in cages that were across the room from one another.

She was starting to feel as though she walked through a mine field of deadly infectious diseases. She would need to monitor her own health even more scrupulously now. The flu was one thing—everyone was going to be exposed to it sooner or later, and if she was a carrier, she was only one of millions. Ebola, however—that was something else. Not only would she need immediate treatment if she were to come down with it, she would need to quarantine herself at the very first sign. That would certainly put a damper on her investigation. A nightmarish vision sprang into her mind of getting locked into an isolation chamber, only to have everyone outside die from infectious disease, leaving no one to get her out of there when the time came.

She shivered, drawing her coat even more closely around her. She felt certain she hadn't been exposed to Ebola, she told herself. At least 99.9 percent certain. And at any rate, there wasn't anything to do now except continue on with her plans for as long as she could. She would call Joshua when she got back to the hotel tonight and see how things were going in the lab.

She finally arrived at the train station without further

mishap, and she settled down into a seat on her train, glad for the brief respite that the trip would provide. There seemed to be even fewer passengers on the train this morning, however, than there were last night, which gave the compartments an empty, ghost-like feeling. What would Earth feel like as one enormous ghost town? she wondered: a ghost planet devoid of human life ... She rolled her eyes, scolded herself for indulging in such maudlin histrionics. But still, she couldn't shake the fear. In fact, fear seemed to be cozying up to her as a constant companion. And this is just the beginning, she thought dolefully; this is only the beginning.

CHAPTER 10

Benjamin was waiting for her when she arrived at the Kingsford station, as patient and implacable as before, his cap pulled down low, but not low enough to cover his reddened, chapped ears. Nan had noticed that certain body parts such as ears and legs seemed, in the British Isles, to be singled out to toughen up the inhabitants to their chilly climate. She had a friend who had attended a prestigious private school in England and he told her that he had suffered from chilblains as a young man, which came from exposure to constant cold. And she would never forget visiting a Scottish boys' school in the early spring a few years back; she couldn't take her eyes off the students' bare legs, raw-looking and mottled from the cold, poking out like naked little birds' legs from the shorts that constituted their school uniform. Just looking at them made her shiver.

Nan had studied Marjory's list during the train ride and decided to interview in the order that victims had come down with the killer bacteria, if possible; she hoped this would help to establish some sort of trail, which could help elucidate where the resistance factor came from originally and how it was spread—also whether it mutated along the way.

Fortunately, the next two people on this list had survived their brush with these organisms, so she could not only interview them directly as to their activities, she could obtain blood samples from them. She would check with Marjory to see if perhaps some blood samples might have been kept and stored for the two children, Charlie and Penelope.

She climbed into the car with Benjamin and asked him to take her to La Bohême, a local French restaurant, which, along with the pub, seemed to constitute the only eating establishments in Kingsford. According to the information on her sheet, the chef at La Bohême had come down with a streptococcal infection shortly after the children died. He had been treated at a hospital in London, which perhaps saved his life, she mused. As Benjamin pulled into the parking lot, she could see two cars already parked in the lot, one a well-kept Peugeot; Nan hoped that this meant the chef was on the premises. She found him in the kitchen, a stocky, dark man with moist-looking, pinkish lips hefting a pail of what looked like mussels into the sink. His helper, a slender, sandy-haired teenager with scars from acne on his face, stood at a counter, peeling a huge mound of pearly garlic cloves.

"Monsieur D'Aubec?" she inquired, stepping forward hesitantly. "My name is Nan Schulte and I'd like to ask you a few questions about the infection you had recently, if you don't mind. If you're not too busy, that is. I can come back at a more convenient time."

He shrugged, ran some water into the pail. "Now is fine," he said, turning off the faucet and wiping his hands on his apron. "Are you a doctor?"

"No, I'm a medical researcher. I'm trying to find out where this infection came from—and how it got to be so powerful."

"I see." He leaned up against the sink, his shiny lips pursed. "Would you like a cup of coffee?"

"Sure, I'd love a cup. Thanks."

"Gerard, please pour of cup of coffee for this lady," he

called to the boy at the counter. "Do you take milk or sugar?" he asked.

"Black's fine." Nan set her supplies bag on the floor, kept her purse slung over her shoulder for the time being. She took out her notebook and a pen.

"So what would you like to know?"

"Well, I guess it would help to know about your activities around the time that you came down with this infection. Did you do anything different or unusual around that time—go any place you don't normally go?"

He shook his head. "No. My routine is the same everyday: I come to the restaurant; I cook." He shrugged again.

"Okay. Maybe you could tell me a little bit about what you do here, then. Oh, thanks," she said to Gerard, as he set down a steaming cup of fragrant coffee on the counter next to her. "For example, do you do a lot of the preparation and handling of the food yourself?"

"I do."

"Okay," she murmured, jotting this down just to have something on the blank page. Clearly, Monsieur D'Aubec wasn't going to volunteer a lot of information. "And Gerard— did he come down with any infection?"

"Not yet."

A rather ominous response, she thought to herself. Of course, living in this village had to be a little scary. It wasn't a very big town to have so many people dying from staph infections. "Where do you get most of your food from? Do you buy locally?" She took a sip of the coffee and found it meltingly delicious.

"Absolutely!" he replied firmly. "As much as we can. The fresher the better, of course. Although some items we must purchase from suppliers in London. Some very special ingredients, such as my truffles, I have shipped from France."

"Mm-hmm," said Nan, setting down her cup and continuing to scribble in her notebook. "What are the products that you buy locally?"

"*Bien*, most of our meat—beef, lamb, chicken, pork. Some pheasant and quail. Frogs … snails … fresh herbs and produce in the summer and fall."

Nan considered. Any of the meat products could conceivably represent the source of the resistance factor. She would try to get samples of everything he had on hand. "Is there anything you handle that Gerard doesn't?" she inquired.

He shook his head. "No, nothing."

"What about days off? I saw from the hours you have posted that you're closed on Sundays. Do you have any hobbies, anything you like to do on your day off?"

"Sleep. Eat. Read."

"Sounds good," she commented. She looked around, wondering if there was ever any problem with rodents. She didn't want to insult him by implying that his restaurant wasn't clean, but at the same time, she needed to know. "Do you, uh, ever have a problem with mice or other pests?" she asked.

"The occasional mouse."

She smiled at his phrasing, thinking it sounded like the title of a children's story. "Seen any lately?"

"No, not lately."

"And the infection itself—where was it localized?"

"On the back of my left hand."

"How long was it before you noticed a sore and then realized it wasn't clearing up?"

He stroked his chin while he thought. "Two days, perhaps three. I scraped my knuckles with a lemon zester while preparing a sauce. I receive nicks and cuts on my hands every day, so I did not think much about it. I washed it with soap and water, then went on with my work. The following day, the cuts looked as if they had become infected, so I scrubbed them again and painted them with iodine."

"Then what happened?"

Monsieur D'Aubec whuffed air through his lips. "*Eh*

bien, it got worse. The next day, I went to see the doctor, and she sent me to a hospital in London, where they surgically removed some of the skin from my knuckles. You can see that they are scarred."

He thrust his hand forward and Nan examined it. "Whoa. Did that stop it?"

He nodded. "Fortunately."

Nan jotted down a few more remarks, then looked up. "If you don't mind, I'd like to take some blood samples from you and Gerard."

She expected him to object, but instead, he looked amused. "Certainly," he said. "Gerard?"

Gerard laid his knife down and shuffled over, his face blank. Nan quickly extracted her supplies from her equipment case, hoping to get the procedure over with before either of them changed their minds. Monsieur D'Aubec seemed less enthusiastic about giving her meat samples, but he did so. She even took a few scrapings from the cutting boards. When she had finished, she thanked them for their time and for the coffee. Monsieur D'Aubec graciously offered her a free dinner if she wanted to come back during her investigation. Nan received this invitation with mixed feelings. On the one hand, she loved French food. On the other hand, might dining at this restaurant invite another case of flesh-eating bacteria?

As she rejoined Benjamin in his car, she mulled over what she had learned so far, which wasn't that much, unfortunately. The most useful information, of course, probably resided in the samples she was acquiring. She sighed without realizing it, and Benjamin asked her if she was all right.

"I'm okay, I guess," she replied. "Thanks for asking, though. What about you? How are you doing with all this sitting in the car and waiting for me?"

"Oh, I'm fine," he assured her. "Right as rain, I am. Give me a thermos of hot tea and a nice radio, and I'm happy as can be."

"Well, that's good."

"Besides, I want you to come up with an answer to this dreadful scourge as much as anybody. I've lost two good friends to this killer bacterium."

"You have? I'm sorry," Nan told him, shaking her head in sympathy. How many friends and acquaintances might she lose before this was all over? She had often wondered in the past how people coped emotionally and psychologically during plagues and devastating epidemics. She guessed now she would get a chance to find out.

The next person on her list, William Botsford, was a dairy farmer who lived on the outskirts of town. In fact, it turned out that he owned the cows she had seen the day before looking so bucolic in the misty sunlight. As she hoped, he had finished with his morning milking, so he had some time to spare for an interview. A tall, stooped man with sparse black curls plastered on a broad forehead, he was a seventh generation diary farmer, he told Nan with pride, after they had exchanged introductions.

"Wow!" she exclaimed. "That sounds very lucky, doesn't it? The seventh son of the seventh son—isn't that a recurrent theme in fairy tales?"

"Well, except that I'm the first and only son."

"Ah."

"At any rate," he said briskly, clasping his hands together and pointing them in her direction, "what can I do for you?"

"I understand you had a brush with a killer bacterium," she replied.

He grimaced, stuck his fingers through his hair. "I did. It was the most terrifying thing that's ever happened in my life, I can tell you."

"Where did it first occur?"

"Come on in and we can sit," he told her, motioning for her to follow him as he began trudging in the direction of his house. "It began as a sore throat."

"I see," Nan took her notebook out of her purse and jotted

this down as they walked.

"It got pretty bad right away," he said. He mounted the steps to the back door and yanked it open. The hinges gave an almost human-sounding shriek. "Damn, that needs oiling again," he muttered. "Watch your step, now." Botsford held the door open for Nan after stepping inside to nudge a milk can out of the way. Nan noticed a gray-and-white striped cat slinking away into the gloom. "I'd had strep throat before, so I knew what it felt like. I went to the doctor right away, and she put me on a round of antibiotics. I had heard what had happened to those poor tots, of course, so I didn't take want to take any chances."

"Right." Nan wondered if she should suggest that they conduct the interview outside because of the cat or whether she should just keep the interview as short as possible. Of course, taking samples would be much easier inside. She decided to take the chance. Some cats, she had noticed, were better than others; Muffin, unfortunately, had to produce one of the most virulent allergens she had ever encountered.

"I guess the doctor didn't want to take any chances, either, because she put me on a combination of antibiotics—a 'cocktail,' she called it, although it didn't remind me of any cocktail I'd ever had." Botsford offered Nan a seat at his kitchen table, a clean, clay-colored linoleum table on which rested a bottle of vinegar and a wooden napkin holder carved in the shape of a frog.

"Did that beat it back?"

He shook his head. "You know, if anything, it seemed to provoke the bloody thing. The next thing I know, I've got sores breaking out over my entire body."

Nan shuddered. This investigation was starting to remind her of a horror movie, some kind of invasion of the body snatchers or Andromeda strain. "Then what happened?"

"Well, they sent me by helicopter to a hospital in London, where they put me in a hyperbaric chamber, they call it."

"Uh-huh. And that stopped it?"

"That stopped it," he replied with visible relief, even awe.

"Tell me, Mr. Botsford—have any of your cows come down with Mad Cow Disease?"

For the first time, his open, friendly expression wavered. "Do you think that has something to do with this flesh-eating bacteria?" he asked.

"I don't know. No one knows. I'm just trying to establish any kind of a link I can," Nan admitted.

He didn't respond for a moment. Finally, he said, "Well, I don't know that any of my cows have come down with Mad Cow Disease. I did have one cow that began to act rather strangely, so rather than take any chances, I had her put down."

"What did you do with the carcass?"

Botsford looked down, fidgeted. "I burned it. I figured that would be the safest thing."

"Did you … contact anyone?"

He shook his head. "I didn't really think she had Mad Cow; I just wanted to be safe and not take any chances."

"Right." Nan wished he hadn't burned the carcass—she really would have liked to get some samples from the animal—although it was probably the most sensible thing to do at the time, especially if he wanted to avoid economic ruin. Economic considerations had a nasty habit of superseding everything else, it seemed; even matters concerning life and death. She absentmindedly tapped her pencil on the table top as she reviewed her notes. "Do you ever eat out at La Bohême?" she asked.

"Oh, yes indeed," he responded, gladly seizing upon the shift in topic. "Wonderful food there. Wonderful!"

"Had you eaten there very recently before you came down with your infection?"

He frowned, considering. "Well, probably, you know. I eat there, on average, probably every two weeks or so."

"Any chance you can remember what you might have

eaten the night or nights you went there before you came down with your strep throat?"

Botsford got up and put his tea kettle on to boil. "Tea?"

"Oh no, I'm fine, thanks," Nan replied. She jumped as she felt something brush up against her ankle. Looking down, she saw the striped kitty winding around her leg. She gave it a nudge with her foot, which it interpreted, apparently, as an invitation to leap into her lap. She stood up abruptly; the cat landed on the seat of her chair and gave a sharp, scolding mew.

"Sorry about that!" Botsford exclaimed, reaching over to pick up the cat and deposit it outside. "Let's see now ... well, I'm very fond of the lamb at La Bohême. They do a very nice rack of lamb. They do a nice Beef Bourguignon, too, that I often order. Lovely snails ... frog's legs, too."

As Nan wrote this all down, she decided that she had spent enough time in a cat-saturated environment. "I have another favor to ask of you, Mr. Botsford," she said. "Could I prevail upon you to give me a blood sample?"

He chuckled. "Didn't quite fancy you as the vampire type," he observed.

"Well, we all have our favorite treats," she joked. "You like Beef Bourguignon; I like a little blood every now and then."

"I suppose I can spare a little." The kettle had reached a boil by now, so he turned it off and poured gurgling hot water into the mug he had waiting.

"Oh—one other thing. Is there a Mrs. Botsford?" Nan assumed not—she would have picked up some evidence of a Mrs. Botsford, which she hadn't really seen. Although, the napkin-holder didn't really look like a guy item.

"Used to be," he grunted, turning away. "She died five years ago."

"I'm so sorry," she murmured.

"She got breast cancer. They tried everything, but it still got her in the end."

"What a shame." Nan hesitated. "Any kids?"

He brightened. "Yes, two. The eldest is at the university—bookish lad, he is. The youngest is away today, on a field trip with his school." He plunked himself back down in his seat, rolled up his shirt sleeve. "All right, Morticia. Have a go."

Nan smiled, wrapped the rubber tourniquet around his arm and thumped his bulging vein. "Nice veins."

"Oh yeah. That's what everybody says."

Nan obtained the blood she needed, packed it into her bag, then asked if she could get some samples from the cows. Like Monsieur D'Aubec, he seemed less inclined to have her examining what constituted his livelihood, but he relented. She took blood and tissue samples from the cows and scooped up some manure as well, depositing it neatly in screw-capped jars.

When she had finished, Botsford bade her a cheery farewell and told her to be sure to let him know what she found out. She promised she would and tramped out to the car where she found Benjamin sacked out, his head tipped back, snoring softly. She checked her watch and saw that it was lunch time. She realized that she was ravenous, too. But she also realized that she had not brought a lunch with her and that her only choice was to eat in town, at restaurants that she couldn't rule out as hot spots.

She climbed into the car, and shut the door, the sound of which roused Benjamin. "Ready, are you?" he asked, blinking and sitting up.

"I am. I'm actually ready for some lunch. How's the pub?"

"Not bad," he said. "It's more of an ale pub than a food pub, but the food's not bad."

Nan thought that she could perhaps use a pint at this point; she hoped that it wouldn't make her sleepy. But after the jolt of seeing the man with Ebola on the street today, not to mention just the general level of adrenalin that seemed to be coursing through her these days, she thought she could risk it. And if she ate a vegetarian meal, she should be relatively safe from prions or Mad Cow viruses, she told herself. Assuming there was a vegetarian meal.

Of course, if she were to be perfectly honest, she would admit that a likely mode of transmission for the resistance factor was through the air, or through casual contact. She couldn't possibly protect herself against either one of these routes—not without a biohazard suit, which she couldn't imagine trying to work in. It would slow her down, alarm everyone she hoped to interview, and probably get a tear in it at some crucial, dangerous moment. No, at this point, given what was happening everywhere, precautions were probably fruitless. Trusting in God or fate seemed the only feasible strategy. She shook her head; how ironic that medical science should come to this.

Benjamin accepted her invitation for lunch at the pub, so he accompanied her into the dimly-lit, ale-scented hobbit hole proclaiming itself "The King's Arms." Pubs in England often liked to hang various paraphernalia from the open wooden beams, such as beer mugs or scotch pitchers; this pub, in a creative approach, hung assorted antique bed pans over the diners' heads. This decorating motif didn't exactly enhance Nan's appetite—she couldn't avoid a mental image of the pans dripping onto the tables below—but she was hungry enough that it didn't matter. The ale, though, tasted better than nectar to her at the moment, and she sipped it gratefully. As she drank, she contemplated microscopic reality for everyone in the room.

Every single person represented an assemblage of microscopic entities: cells, their resident mitochondria—the energy generators of the cell and body, which had probably derived from a symbiotic bacterium somewhere in the ancient, geologic past—larger bacteria inhabiting the gut and epithelial surfaces, viruses circulating throughout the body, doing God only knew what. Most people harbored some variety of herpes virus by the time they were adults and retained it for their entire life. Most people didn't even know it, either. Everyone in the room was inhaling and exhaling microscopic entities, shedding them from their skin and hair, trading them back and forth, ingesting them and expelling them.

The current scientific dogma maintained that these microorganisms performed all their helpful activities and underwent all their exquisitely choreographed movements blindly, mindlessly. But would we even know how to recognize the "mind" of a bacterium or virus? she wondered; would we even know what to look for? Of course, even thinking such thoughts constituted scientific heresy: the cardinal sin of anthropomorphism. But traditional approaches to these creatures didn't seem to be reaping many positive results at the moment. Perhaps the time had come to rethink just about everything having to do with the relationship of humans to microbes.

What do they want? she found herself thinking. And how can we find out?

CHAPTER 11

Finishing up her lunch, Nan reviewed her list once more and saw that the next three victims of the killer bacteria had not survived their bout with the microbes. She considered contacting whatever family they had remaining; however, she could probably get more useful information, not to mention blood samples, from victims who had survived their illnesses. She also wanted to talk to the local physician who had been treating all these people. Benjamin prevailed upon the barkeep to lend his phone to Nan so that she could put in a call to Dr. Oden, who agreed to meet with Nan after her last patient, around seven o'clock. Then they left the pub to check out a few more residences.

Unfortunately, just about everyone that Nan called upon this afternoon was out. She was about to despair of getting much more work done that day when they drove up to a ramshackle cottage enveloped by leafless, dormant vines. The dry sticks clacked faintly in the wind as Nan walked up the buckled sidewalk to the door. The man who answered her knock looked so wizened his face reminded her of a decaying apple or peach, while his gap-toothed smile gave the impression of a jack-o-lantern. The botanical theme extended to the interior of the cottage; inside, Nan observed great bunches of herbs drying upside-down, pegged onto cross-beams, piles of multi-shaped, multi-colored squash and bushel baskets of apples and onions sitting on the stone floor, potted plants crowding every window sill. The place emanated the earthy, musty, fruity smell of a roadside produce stand. Nan looked about cautiously for cats but didn't see any.

"So what can I do for you, miss?" he inquired, his voice surprisingly strong—at complete odds with his desiccated appearance.

Nan explained her mission and told him that she undestood he had tangled with the killer bacterium, which he confirmed. He had even lost a finger, he said, and held up his left hand as proof. A disconcerting gap existed in the space once occupied by his ring finger.

"Makes it a lot harder to do my work, that's for sure," he grumbled, gesturing for Nan to take a seat in a sagging armchair surrounded by drying gourds, books, and shoe boxes filled with seeds. He lowered himself onto a dusty wooden bench.

"What exactly is your work, Mr. Crawford?" Nan asked, settling somewhat gingerly into the chair. It looked like one of those ancient specimens that could well have a broken spring hiding in the cushion, just waiting to jab the unsuspecting.

"Oh, a little of this, a little of that," he replied. "I sell herbs to the local shops around here, some produce to the market. I sell seeds, too. Sometimes I'll gather up frogs and snails to sell to the French restaurant, although, now that I'm missing a finger, it's much harder to get ahold of frogs these days."

"I can imagine," Nan murmured sympathetically.

"I also have a few chickens, and I sell the eggs. I've got a little bit of a government pension as well, that sees me through lean times."

"That's good." Nan pondered as she scribbled all this down. She supposed that the resistance factor could have come from some organism in the soil; Mr. Crawford obviously handled a great deal of it. But there were the frogs, snails, and chickens to consider, too. She frowned. She could get samples from his chickens, no doubt, but she should probably try to get her hands on some frogs and snails, too. "Listen," she said, "I wonder if it might be possible for you to provide me with some frogs and snails. I'd pay you for them, of course. Whatever the going rate is."

He scratched his chin, the stubble on his face creating an audible sound as he did so. "I suppose that could be arranged. When would you need them?"

"As soon as possible. Now, if you'd like. I can take you wherever you need to go."

Mr. Crawford stood up with a grunt. "Let's go. I could use the pocket money."

Nan jumped to her feet as well, then waited while Crawford gathered up a pair of waders, a couple of metal buckets with lids, and a long, stout stick. "The frogs'll be harder to find this time of year, of course, but they'll be easier to catch," he told her. "They'll be quite sluggish from hibernating."

They trundled outside, Nan carrying the buckets. Benjamin saw them coming and got out to open the boot for them. After depositing the gear in the trunk, they all piled into the car and took off—as it turned out, to the pond that bordered Faith and Nigel's place.

Benjamin decided to accompany Nan and Crawford on this expedition; he had heard about Crawford's frog gigging skills and wanted to see the master at work, he said. This pleased Crawford immensely. When they reached the pond, he donned his hip boots and rubber gloves— "The gloves make me a bit clumsy," he commented, "but this time of year the water is absolutely freezing!"—and then plunged bravely into the frigid waters. He used his stick to poke about here and there, moving carefully so as not to stir up too much mud, he told them. "They like to hide under rocks and such when they hibernate for the winter," he added. Soon his search was rewarded. He bent down and reached under a rock that neither Nan nor Benjamin could see from their vantage point and then held up a large brownish green frog. It remained so immobile it almost looked like a fake rubber frog. Crawford sloshed to the shore and dropped the frog in one of the buckets and secured the lid. "Need any more?" he asked.

Nan considered. "A couple more probably wouldn't hurt," she replied.

So Crawford waded back in and poked around some more and eventually produced two other frogs, about half the size of the first one. Then he scooped up some mud to cover them with. "That'll keep them happy," he remarked with satisfaction. "All right, now, let's get you some snails."

They tramped into the nearby forest where Crawford again used his stick to rummage about in piles of fallen leaves and duff, unearthing about a dozen snails. Nan felt that this was probably plenty, and besides, dusk was starting to fall. Benjamin drove Crawford back to his house where Nan obtained blood from him and a few samples from his chickens. After she paid him for the frogs and snails and he had transferred them into plastic containers, she packed everything up and checked her watch. She saw that it was just about time to meet with Dr. Oden, so she and Benjamin headed over to her office.

The doctor was finishing up with her last patient, the receptionist told them, so they seated themselves in the waiting room where Benjamin picked up a *People* magazine and began leafing through it, shaking his head occasionally in either disbelief or disapproval, Nan couldn't tell which. Soon, Dr. Oden, a lean, red-haired, bespectacled woman, appeared at the door that led to the examining rooms and her office, inviting Nan to come in.

"Hello, Benjamin," she added. "I take it you're not here as a patient, are you?"

"Oh, no. I'm just driving Dr. Schulte around while she conducts her investigation."

"I see. Well, if you'd like a cup of tea, just ask Marsha."

"Will do. Thanks, doctor."

Dr. Oden smiled at Nan as she closed the door behind them, refraining from shaking hands. She held up her index finger in explanation, which she had swathed in a bandage. "Occupational hazard," she remarked.

"Is that—strep?" Nan asked.

"Afraid so. I suppose it was only a matter of time before I contracted it, with all that I've been exposed to."

"Is it under control?"

Dr. Oden gave a slight shrug. "I certainly hope so," she said. "Come on into my office and have a seat. I'll be happy to share any information that I have."

Dr. Oden's office exuded a smell of alcohol, despite the vases of fresh flowers that adorned the bookshelves and corners of the desk. Overall her office looked neat and tidy, except for the center of the desk, which had papers spread all over it in a seemingly haphazard fashion. Her eyes followed Nan's and she groaned, "Paperwork. I think that might be the death of us, don't you?"

"That's for sure," Nan agreed, settling into one of the sleekly upholstered leather chairs that faced Dr. Oden's desk, trying not to feel completely paranoid that flesh-eating bacteria were perched on every surface, ready to transfer themselves onto her skin the minute she made contact. She questioned the doctor about the patients she had seen that had staph and strep infections, learning that a shocking forty percent of the village population had contracted a bacterial infection in the last year or so.

"And it hasn't peaked yet," the doctor commented grimly. "I see more cases every day. I'm thinking I might need to get another doctor in here to help me with the case load. And that isn't all—we're seeing a jump in all kinds of infectious diseases: pneumonia, hepatitis, *E. coli* poisoning, *Salmonella* ... you name it, it's on the rise. And then there's the flu, of course. We haven't received the brunt of it yet, but I imagine it's only a matter of time. I saw my first cases yesterday, and today, I had twice as many." She shook her head wearily. "Antibiotics seem to have become useless practically overnight. If anything, they seem to inflame these germs. I've been using herbal and homeopathic remedies for the milder cases. The more serious ones, I'm simply shipping off to London where they have more sophisticated facilities to care for these people. I don't mind telling you, I'm frightened." Her gaze fastened on her infected index finger before she could tear it away.

I bet she's frightened, Nan thought, unable to keep from staring at the finger as well. She started to ask Dr. Oden if she'd noticed any trends—whether any particular age group, for example, seemed more susceptible to acquiring one of these infections—when the phone rang.

"Excuse me, will you?" Dr. Oden said, reaching for the receiver. "It might be an emergency."

Nan murmured a polite response, trying to appear as if she weren't listening to the conversation, but then Dr. Oden sat bolt upright.

"You have got to be kidding me!" she exclaimed.

Nan jerked her head up, dropping all pretense.

Dr. Oden listened for a few moments, then said, "Well, we can only hope that it's not too late. What a nightmare." She paused while the speaker on the other end babbled something tinny-sounding and undecipherable from where Nan sat. "All right, well, thanks for calling. I'll let everyone know." She replaced the receiver and covered her face with her hands for a moment before meeting Nan's questioning gaze. "They've quarantined London," she said finally. "They've got an Ebola outbreak."

Nan sat in stunned silence for a few moments before she

could reply. "Quarantined London?" she finally croaked.

"It seems impossible, doesn't it? And, I daresay, it may be impossible." She expelled a heavy breath and slumped back in her chair. "The microbial world has gone insane," she murmured.

"It certainly seems that way," Nan agreed, wondering what this would mean in terms of her own movements. If London was quarantined, she wouldn't be able to return to her hotel for days, possibly weeks. And what did this mean for Heathrow? Would she be able to leave the country?

Dr. Oden gripped both arms of her chair as if to stand, then met Nan's eyes. "I'm sorry," she said, "I don't think I can continue this interview."

"I understand completely," Nan responded, scrambling to her feet. "I actually need to make some plans myself. Did the caller happen to say what was going on with the airports?"

She shook her head. "I'm sorry, he didn't."

"That's fine." Nan retrieved her purse from the floor, glad, at least, that she always carried her passport and plane ticket with her when she traveled abroad. Out of habit, she started to offer her hand to the doctor, then checked herself. "I appreciate your time, Dr. Oden."

"Oh, don't mention it," she replied, getting up to see Nan out. "Good luck with your investigation. It sounds as if you've got your work cut out for you."

"It sure does, doesn't it?" Entering the waiting room, she found Benjamin leaning up against Marsha's desk, sipping a cup of tea.

"All done, are you?" he asked, straightening up and setting down his cup.

Nan nodded.

"By the way, I'm getting the word out," announced Dr. Oden; "I just received a phone call; London has been quarantined. There's no travel in or out of the city."

Both Benjamin and Marsha looked stricken. "Is this

because of the flu, then?" asked Marsha.

Oden shook her head. "No, it's Ebola."

Their faces turned ashen. Benjamin wiped a trembling hand across his mouth. "Excuse me, did you say Ebola?"

"Yes, I'm afraid I did."

No one spoke for a moment. Finally, Nan said, "I, uh, was wondering if I might be able to make a few phone calls? Do you have more than one line here?"

"Absolutely," the doctor replied. "You can use the phone on Marsha's desk."

First Nan tried calling the airport, but she found it impossible to get through. Then she called her airline; again, all circuits were busy. She tried making a call to Elliott's, which miraculously went through, but she got his machine, which seemed a little odd. If Myra was staying there, someone should be there to answer the phone. She left a message saying that she would call back later, then decided to call her own number and retrieve her messages. After several tries, she finally got through. Most of the messages weren't pressing, and Elliott hadn't called, but the message Joshua left got her attention: "Hi, Dr. Schulte," it said; "I've been thinking about this mystery e-mailer of yours. Why don't you try posting some more information on some UseGroups and see if you can't draw the person out again? If you get another message, he or she might reveal a little more about themselves. Oh, and by the way, Dr. Holt came by the lab today with a bunch of suits. I don't know what they were up to or what they wanted, but I thought you might like to know. Hope things are going well for you wherever you are." She hung up, eager to follow through on his suggestion; then she realized that her laptop was at the hotel back in London. Not only that, she had no place to stay the night.

"Are there any hotels in town where I could stay overnight?" Nan asked the room at large. Everyone shook their heads in unison.

"There's a place two towns over, in Faulkingham," said Marsha.

"It's quite a drive, though," Benjamin remarked. "I've got a better idea. Let's give Marjory a call. She's got a big old house and it's just her and her dogs that live there."

Nan protested that she didn't want to impose, but Benjamin insisted upon making the call. Apparently, Marjory was adamant about putting Nan up at her place, so she acquiesced, glad, in fact, to have a place to stay, and one that didn't involve any more travel. She felt beat.

Benjamin stopped by the pharmacy on the way over to Marjory's so that Nan could pick up a toothbrush and some deodorant. Marjory lived in a beautiful old stone house graced with slate-roofed gables and an imposing entrance covered by an old-fashioned portico. Benjamin declined to come in, saying he was ready to head home himself, and Marjory met her at the door with her two Airedales. The dogs crowded around Nan to sniff and nudge her in a friendly way, but a heavy drizzle had begun to fall, accentuating the despair that Nan was beginning to feel surrounding not only her immediate plight, but the fate of mankind.

Naturally, Marjory's house was as cold as a crypt, but she did have a cheery fire blazing in her fireplace, a warm, comfy chair with a soft wool lap robe to wrap herself in, and not only a steaming hot Gloucester pie to eat, but a nice, big glass of claret to wash it down with. By the end of her meal, Nan was starting to feel better.

It turned out that Marjory had more information about the situation in and around London. The army had been called out to enforce the quarantine, and they took their duties very seriously. So far, only one victim with Ebola had been identified (Nan guiltily withheld the information that she had in fact crossed paths with this man), but it was possible that this man had infected others. Authorities were taking no chances. And the number of flu victims had also begun to rise rather precipitously, so this was an additional reason to restrict travel. Apparently, travelers were allowed to leave England, but at this time, no one was being allowed in. She wasn't sure what the situation was with any other countries, however, so she offered to turn on the news at eleven.

Nan said that this sounded good to her, although she didn't know if she would be able to stay up that late. She really wanted to talk to Elliott and find out how everything was going back home, so she asked if she could use the telephone. Marjory brought her a mobile phone and graciously left her alone in the room so that she could have some privacy. Again, when Nan managed to put her call through to Elliott's number, she received no answer, just the machine. She tried calling Joshua—the thought of Ron Holt prowling around her lab with a bunch of "suits" sounded ominous—but the phone gods didn't seem to be cooperating and she never could get through. With a sigh, she got up to look for Marjory. She found her in the kitchen, washing up the dinner dishes.

"Any luck?" asked Marjory.

Nan shook her head. "No, unfortunately. I'm having a hell of a time getting a line, and the one time I did get through to my party, he wasn't there. I just got his machine."

"Frustrating."

"Yeah, no kidding. I'm kind of worried, actually. My mother, who has pretty advanced dementia, is staying there. Someone should be there to answer the phone. It doesn't make any sense."

"Hmmm." Marjory placed a handful of silverware in the drying rack, wiped her hands on a dish towel, and turned around to lean against the sink facing Nan.

"I left the number here—I hope you don't mind. I suppose he could call at an inconvenient time."

Marjory waved a hand in dismissal. "Oh, don't worry about that."

Nan stood with her arms folded, thinking. "I wonder—do

you have a computer at home?"

"Of course!"

"What about ... access to the Internet?"

Marjory gave her a sly smile. "I confess I'm an addict."

"Really? Well, great! I'd like to make a few posts on some UseGroups, if you don't mind."

"Come along, my girl," said Marjory, folding Nan's arm over her own to walk her down the hall, gliding like some sort of regal Tall Ship.

"I really appreciate this—"

"It's my pleasure, truly." Marjory halted, then turned. "Heathcliff! Rochester! Come!" she commanded. "They love it, too," she confided.

"Do they," murmured Nan, fighting down a giggle. For the first time in several days, she felt somewhat optimistic. This e-mailer might hold some key to this whole nightmare. Thoughts of Elliott, Amber, and Myra intruded, however, and sent a wave of anxiety through her. Where would they be on a Saturday afternoon?

Perhaps they went out for a drive or something, she speculated, to get Myra out of the house. With all the chaos surrounding the flu, however, she wouldn't think they would leave on some trivial mission. Perhaps one of them needed to go to the hospital. Except that Elliott had said the hospitals were worse than useless right now. She chewed her lower lip nervously, feeling light years away. Maybe a neighbor needed their help and they decided to all go, stick together or something. Elliott would undoubtedly call later, she told herself, trying to feel satisfied with this reasonable-sounding, probable scenario.

Her intuition was sounding an alarm, however, persistent and shrill. I'll head for home first thing in the morning, she decided suddenly; before it's too late to leave. That is, if it wasn't too late already. She shook her head stubbornly, trying to focus on the issue at hand: setting a snare for the mystery e-mailer. They had arrived at the computer, and Marjory switched it on, standing before the monitor with visible pleasure.

Soon, Nan was posting a message to all the UseGroups she could find having to do with epidemics, the current flu, infectious disease, and global disasters: "I wonder if anyone can help me with my research to find a resistance factor that's responsible for the recent pandemic of drug-resistant diseases," she typed. "I'm in England, where the first cases seem to have appeared, and I've obtained quite a few samples. If anyone can give me any information that might give me an idea of what to start looking for first, you will have my —and the world's—undying gratitude. This is urgent. If you have ANY INFORMATION AT ALL, please (!!) contact me as soon as possible. We could conceivably be facing extinction. Sincerely, Professor Nan Schulte."

Marjory stood behind her, watching as her fingers clicked rapidly over the keys. "My, my," she commented. "I would certainly think that will get somebody's attention."

CHAPTER 12

Nan awoke from a troubled sleep the next morning, uneasily aware of the fact that Elliott had not phoned during the night. He could have been waiting to call at a reasonable hour—or he might be having the same problem getting through that she was—but she couldn't shake a terrible feeling of foreboding. She tried calling him again, but the phone lines seemed even more jammed up today than they were yesterday. That settled it. She needed to get home. She pulled on the same clothes she wore yesterday, resigned to the fact that she would just have to forsake her laptop and all of her other belongings that she had left at the hotel in London. Perhaps they wouldn't mind shipping them to her. Fortunately, she had backed up all the information on her laptop before coming here, so there wasn't anything on there that she didn't have in the States.

Marjory was already up, brewing a pot of coffee, when Nan strolled into the cold, drafty kitchen. "Did you ever get ahold of your party?" she asked, setting a cup on the table for her.

Nan shook her head. "No, and I'm getting really worried. I think I'm going to try to get a flight home today. Heathrow will probably be a madhouse, but I don't know what else to do."

Marjory turned off the flame under the coffee pot, then

filled Nan's cup. "How do you plan to get there?"

"I don't know. Maybe I could rent a car. Is there a car rental agency in town?"

"I'm afraid not. But look, it's Sunday—I don't have any plans that I can't put off. How about if I take you?"

"That's an awful lot to ask," she protested. "You've been so kind already—I hate to inconvenience you like this."

"Don't be ridiculous! It's not all that far away, and I like to drive."

"Really? Well …"

"It's settled then. We'll have a nice breakfast and then be off."

Tears welled up in Nan's eyes, she felt so grateful. She also felt antsy enough to get going that she would have been happy to skip breakfast, but Marjory insisted, since, she said, there was no telling what they would find at the airport.

"The news was not very encouraging last night," she said primly, without elaborating.

So Nan joined Marjory in a plate of scrambled eggs, toast, and kippers, eating as much as her anxiety would allow. She also accepted a couple of raisin buns wrapped in waxed paper to stash in her purse for an emergency. What to do with her samples posed a problem, since she didn't want to try to get them through customs; but Marjory once again came to her rescue and said that she would pack them up for her and ship them to the States. This time, Nan didn't argue. It was probably the only chance for those samples to make it to her lab.

The ride to the airport seemed to take forever, what with flocks of sheep standing obdurately in the middle of the twisty roads, a dozen little congested hamlets to pass through, and horrendous traffic clogging the approach to Heathrow. Marjory dropped Nan off at the terminal but told her that she would try to find a place to park so that she could come in and find her in case any problems arose with obtaining a flight.

Her heart sinking, Nan slipped on a mask and made her

way to the Delta counter where an absurdly long line of restive passengers snaked along the cordons that designated the queue. She took her place at the end, trying to remain calm when the line moved along at a glacial pace. Soon, Marjory appeared to keep her company, and, she said, use whatever influence, authority, and fear tactics she could muster to get Nan a seat on a plane. Two hours later, they had reached the counter. The agent at the counter looked haggard and exhausted, and when she found that Nan had no reservation, she shook her head pessimistically.

"All flights out today are filled," she told her. "Overbooked, in fact. There's not a single seat to any destination in the U.S. that I can offer you. I'm sorry."

Panic gripped Nan. "But it's an emergency. A serious emergency. I have to be able to get out today!"

The agent smiled at her sadly. "Everyone's got an emergency, I'm afraid. I'm sorry. I wish I could help you. I might be able to book you a flight for tomorrow or the next day."

"But that could be too late!" wailed Nan. Marjory laid a restraining hand on her arm.

"Now see here," she said to the agent. "This woman is involved in extremely important medical research related to the outbreaks. It is absolutely imperative that she get back to the States as soon as possible. Thousands, if not millions of lives depend on it."

"Excuse me, who might you be?" asked the agent.

"I'm the director of the Kingsford branch of public health." Marjory dug in her purse and produced an ID card that she flashed at the agent. The agent took it, frowned.

"Let me speak to my supervisor," she said. She stepped away from the counter and conferred with a mustachioed gentleman, pointing Nan and Marjory out to him, gesticulating and showing him Marjory's ID. He accompanied the agent back to the counter.

"What is your position?" he asked Nan.

"I'm a molecular biology professor at Stafford University. I'm studying multiple drug resistance, and I've obtained some crucial information that I need to analyze at my lab back home."

"I see." He massaged his chin, scrutinizing her carefully. Then he tapped some commands into the computer, gazing at it poker-faced. "I can offer you stand-by on a flight to Kennedy," he said finally.

"Stand-by?" she echoed. With such a mad crush of people, getting on anything as a stand-by seemed hopeless.

"It's the best I can do."

Nan turned to Marjory, who shrugged. "Might as well take it," she advised. "Sounds like your best shot."

Nan waited while the agent printed out her ticket; she tried not to give into despair. With all the chaos that ruled at the airport, however, Marjory wasn't allowed to accompany Nan to the gate; she could only go so far as the security checkpoint. Given her distress, Nan found this monumentally discouraging. Every single one of her muscles felt taut and tense as they walked to the entrance of the concourse and her breakfast of kippers and eggs weighed in her stomach like hardened cement. Stuttering through a profuse thank-you, she was surprised when Marjory halted in mid-stride and seized Nan by the shoulders.

"Look, I think the reason that fellow gave you a stand-by was to prevent a riot back there," she asserted. "He couldn't very well assign you a reservation on an overbooked flight with all those other desperate people out there trying to do the same thing, could he? My guess is, he'll put in a call to your gate and get you on that flight somehow."

"I sure hope you're right," Nan replied, trying to rise to Marjory's no-nonsense optimism but failing miserably.

"Of course I am," she retorted. "Now, go on!" She spun Nan around and gave her a little push. "Oh—and you'll let me know your findings, won't you?"

"You'll be one of the first," Nan promised over her shoulder. She took a deep breath, placed her purse on the conveyer belt and stepped through the metal detector. "Thanks again!" she called from the other side. Marjory gave her a cheery, maternal wave. As she made her way to the gate, however, Nan wondered if she would have any findings to share. She hadn't been able to collect nearly as many samples as she wanted.

The flight wasn't leaving for another two hours, but the waiting area around the gate was packed. The agents appeared at the gate an hour before the departure time, when Nan joined another long line of desperate-looking people to see if she could possibly score a boarding pass. She really didn't have much hope when she finally made it to the counter, but it appeared that Marjory had assessed the situation correctly: she was given a seat assignment and told that boarding had already begun. Greatly relieved, Nan shuffled onto the plane with the other passengers and settled in. Ten minutes before take-off, a steward carrying a kennel hurried down the aisle behind an elderly woman, passing Nan on the way. Looking inside the kennel, she saw, to her dismay, that a fluffy, blue-eyed cat peeked out. Two seats in front of her, the woman stopped, took her seat, and the steward carefully placed the kennel under her seat. "There you go, kitty," he said.

Nan groaned. She couldn't believe it: trapped inside a closed compartment for six hours with a cat. As the steward passed back in her direction, she caught his arm. "Excuse me," she said, "but I have asthma, and I'm violently allergic to cats."

He shrugged. "What do you want us to do?"

"Well, isn't there some place else the cat can go?"

He shook his head. "I'm sorry, but our policies allow passengers to bring small pets on board with them if they pay for it."

"I don't think you understand—I could have a really

serious asthma attack."

He regarded her blank-faced. "Well then, I'm afraid your only option is to de-plane and try to get another flight."

"Oh, that should be easy!" she exclaimed.

"There's nothing else we can do," he said, with maddening implacability. "It's our policy. I can see if someone in the back wants to trade places with you."

"Why don't you do that?" Nan snapped, trying not to hate him. She fervently wished that airlines had a better system for safely transporting pets that would take serious allergies into account.

He disappeared into the back, then returned with another passenger who was willing to trade seats with her. Panicked and fuming, Nan retreated to the rear of the plane and squeezed into her new seat. Fortunately, she had her inhaler in her purse. Unfortunately, she had left her antihistamines in her bag back at the hotel. She tried to calm herself, since she knew that getting upset would only make things worse.

Four hours into the flight, however, she was in trouble. She tried to delay using her inhaler, since she knew, given the source of the allergen, that it would wear off in a fraction of the time allotted before she could safely take another dose without risking a rebound effect, closing up her lungs even more. But finally she was gasping so ineffectually for air, she went ahead and used it, then tried breathing through a tissue for the rest of the flight. She arrived in New York exhausted, her back muscles absolutely killing her from struggling to breathe. And as she deplaned, she contemplated the unpleasant fact that she still had to make her way to Hartford where her car was waiting for her.

All of these thoughts, however, went scattering once she entered the terminal.

It looked and felt like a post-holocaust scene. No one was waiting to greet their loved ones coming off the flight. Only a handful of flights were operating, judging from the empty gates and skeleton crew that appeared here and there. So few people roamed this enormous building that their footsteps actually echoed in the vast stillness, sounding ominous and doomed. Even the PA system remained silent; no one was paging anyone, no flights were leaving at this time, absolutely nothing was going on in one of the world's busiest airports.

Along the way, Nan tried calling Elliott's number once again, but she kept getting the message that all circuits were busy. She almost felt surprised when she found someone manning one of the rental car booths. She made arrangements for a rental, then waited an agonizingly long time for a bus to come along to take her to the rental station. Eerily, the afternoon traffic was lighter than she had ever experienced on the congested East Coast. It was as if she were living in a Stephen King novel, where some nameless monster had risen up from the sewers and devoured two-thirds of the population. She was beginning to feel so creeped-out that she practically expected to find a skeleton driving the van that would take her to her car.

Instead, a burly, middle-aged man drove the van. Nan turned out to be the only passenger on the bus, so he struck up a brief conversation with her on the way, asking her where she was coming from, what it was like in England, whether the flu epidemic was hitting as hard there as it was here.

"No, not yet," she told him, speaking in short bursts from breathlessness. "But it was accelerating ... as I was leaving. What's been going on here?"

He gave a grunt of consternation. "It's been freaky as hell, I don't mind telling ya. That vaccine they tried to give everybody isn't working or something. Seems like everybody's coming down with it sooner or later."

This piece of information caused a spasm of fear to grip Nan's heart. "You mean the new vaccine?"

"The new vaccine ... the old vaccine, nothing's working. Things are getting tough. A lot of people are moving out of the city. I mean, food's getting scarce—they can't find enough drivers to deliver it. Everybody's sick, for Chrissake."

"What about you? Have you been ill?"

He shook his head. "Not yet. But that doesn't mean I won't. By the way, you doing all right?"

"What do you mean?"

"Seems like you're having trouble breathing."

Nan checked her watch and saw that she still had an hour to wait before she could safely use her inhaler again. "I'm okay," she wheezed, hating the whistling sound that emanated from her lungs; "it's just asthma."

A Ford Taurus was waiting for Nan at the rental car parking lot, and since no one else was there to rent a vehicle, her check-out went quickly and smoothly. An hour down the road, she used her inhaler again. She considered stopping to pick up some over-the-counter antihistamines, but then rejected the idea, as they could make her sleepy while she was driving.

Again, traffic along the way was so sparse that it seemed surreal. It made getting to her destination much easier, especially since she hit Hartford right around rush hour, but at the same time, she kept feeling disoriented, as if she were in the land of the midnight sun and it was actually two in the morning, not five in the afternoon.

She dropped off the rental at the airport office, then took the shuttle bus to the parking lot where she had left her car. She made it to Amherst in record time, but the ghostly emptiness of the interstate filled her with apprehension. She switched on the radio for awhile, hoping for news of the epidemic. A couple of stations actually seemed to have gone off the air, although she had a hard time believing that this could be true. The one station she did tune into produced nothing but a list of closures and cancellations of schools, meetings, theaters, galleries, and public events, curtailed hours at banks, grocery stores, drug stores, and clinics. Chillingly, the announcer listed hospitals that were closed, too, due to overcrowded conditions and staff shortages.

She passed the scene of a spectacular accident on her way, which, she supposed, could have been much worse if the traffic had been heavier. As it was, it involved only two cars, but they both looked totaled. One appeared to have rolled, as the roof was crushed flat and the side that Nan could see was all bashed in; the other looked as if some malevolent force had come along and pummeled every square inch into the metal equivalent of hamburger. Only one ambulance had made it to the scene, and it looked as if the crew was trying to squeeze more victims into the interior than could reasonably fit. Two lifeless bodies lay on the shoulder, covered from head to toe with dark blankets.

Shuddering, Nan continued on her way, her anxiety increasing the closer she drew to home. She drove straight to Elliott's house, barreling up the driveway and coming to a screeching halt in front of the back door. She saw Elliott's car in the drive, which did nothing to assuage her fears, and when she burst into the house, she found her mother lying in the middle of the kitchen floor, her right leg twisted into such an impossible, freakish angle that Nan felt nauseated just looking at it.

Crying out, Nan rushed to her mother's side, feeling close to hysteria. "Mom!" she shrieked. "Mom, can you hear me?"

Myra opened her eyes. "Hear me?" she croaked softly.

"Oh, God," wailed Nan. "Where's Elliott? Where are Amber and your caregivers?"

"Elliott?"

"Yes, is he here?"

Myra closed her eyes again, apparently unable to answer. Nan didn't know what to do first—call 911 or go looking for Elliott and Amber. She decided to phone 911. The call miraculously went through, but the operator didn't sound too optimistic about how soon anyone would be able to respond to her call. "But my mother's leg is broken! She could be bleeding internally! And she's in terrible pain!!" Nan shouted, frantic.

"I'm sorry ma'am. We're doing our best. We'll send someone out as soon as possible."

Nan slammed down the receiver, shaking.

"Absolutely ... they won't come," said Myra, surprisingly lucid.

"Who won't, Mom?"

"The ... the ..." She halted, frustrated.

"The people from 911?"

"The people from 911."

"Okay, well, I'm—I'm going to go look for Elliott and Amber, okay?" she replied, unsure whether to try to straighten out her mother's leg or whether to leave it alone, for fear of causing more damage.

"Okay."

Somehow her stoic little "okay" was almost more than Nan could bear. She had never felt so unbelievably helpless in her entire life. Desperately, she searched every room in the house, finally finding both Amber and Elliott in the den, Amber curled up on the sofa with Muffin crouched on top of her as if guarding her, Elliott crumpled on the floor. Neither of them moved or even twitched. Neither of them responded to her calling their names. They looked, in fact, dead.

"No!!" Nan screamed. "Goddamn it, no!!!" She threw herself on top of Elliott, crying and sobbing and clutching at him. His body stiffened, which scared the hell out of her until she realized that he was actually alive. She fumbled for his wrist and took his pulse, vastly relieved to find a weak, but steady heartbeat. She turned her attention to Amber and realized that she was still breathing—softly and shallowly, but she was breathing. Both of them felt terribly hot, and some sort of yellowish white discharge caked the corners of their mouths. Amber's eyelids seemed glued shut with a dried, sticky fluid.

Nan flopped onto the floor, trying to formulate a plan. She didn't know how long Elliott and Amber had been like this, and she didn't know how recently her mother had broken her leg; but she assumed that it could have been at least thirty-six hours ago, when she had left her first message on Elliott's phone machine. They were probably dangerously dehydrated, all of them, so while she waited for the EMTs to show up, Nan raced between the den and the kitchen giving water to everyone. Her mother was able to sit up a bit and drink, but with both Amber and Elliott, she had to trickle water into their slack mouths. When an ambulance didn't show up within a half-hour, she dragged first Amber and then Elliott into the downstairs bathroom and into the tub, where she ran cold water over them to reduce their fevers. Exhausted and panicked, she paid little attention to her own physical condition until she was having so much trouble breathing that she began to feel light-headed.

"Come on, come on," she muttered to the emergency crew she assumed was on the way. Elliott, who was in the tub, began to shiver violently, so she hauled him out and dried him off, wrapping him up in a towel. "Hang in there, Elliott," she murmured, smoothing back his hair and kissing his limp hands. She made him as comfortable as she could on the floor of the bathroom, next to Amber, deciding to leave them there since she didn't have the strength to drag them back out again.

She staggered back into the kitchen to check on her mother and watch out the window for the ambulance, but once she got there, strange black spiders began to crowd into her vision. Her bronchioles felt as if they had shrunk to the diameter of the filament in a light bulb. When she made a herculean effort to draw in some air, her airways simply collapsed on her. Lunging for her purse to grab her inhaler, she stumbled and smacked her head on the counter. And then the black spiders all oozed together and totally blotted out everything else.

The last thing she heard was her mother insisting in an anguished, agitated voice, "After all, they won't come! They won't come …"

CHAPTER 13

Nan awoke to find herself in the interior of an ambulance, screaming its way through the streets of Amherst. Her left arm ached where she assumed she had received a shot of some kind, epinephrine, no doubt; and she wore a nasal prong that was delivering an extremely revivifying dose of oxygen. Wedged beside her in the cramped space was an extra gurney bearing her mother; the EMT's crouched against the walls, making space for themselves as best they could.

"Where's Amber and Elliott?" she gasped, trying to get the technicians' attention over the sound of the siren.

"Hmm?" one of them asked, bending toward her.

"There were two other people in the house who needed emergency care."

"We got 'em," he assured her. "They're in another vehicle."

"Thank God," she sighed, reveling in breathing again. Nothing in the world felt better than being able to breathe, even though her back muscles felt studded with a thousand metal splinters from her previous futile efforts.

The ride to the hospital passed in a high-pitched, noisy blur. So much for Elliott's report that they weren't using sirens on ambulances any more. Perhaps this driver was particularly fond of the drama of the siren; personally, she could have done without it. Her head felt as if it were splitting open.

Once at the hospital, she found herself parked in a corridor with at least a dozen other patients. Utter pandemonium reigned. Medical personnel rushed up and down the hallway. Some of the patients lined up along the walls were groaning, some weeping, some screaming; some seemed ominously still and those were the ones doctors and nurses were working on the most frantically. Carts rattled with bottles, medications, and syringes, oxygen tanks were wheeled through, hooked up, and slapped on gray-blue patients, who wheezed and gasped for air with the hardened leather that the flu virus made of their lungs. Broken bones from accidents were roughly splinted, physicians roared for nonexistent assistance, orderlies were literally running from place to place, technicians hastily plied their craft on those who were still living. Those who were not were wheeled out the back door, covered with a sheet, while still more sick and dying people spilled through the front door like swarms of broken, frantic insects.

Several times in the two hours that Nan spent in this corridor, some of the medical workers themselves simply dropped wherever they were standing, as if in a ghoulish parody of the illness they strove to treat. Those left standing hefted the fallen onto collapsible cots that had appeared and seemed to be replacing the gurneys, which presumably had run out.

When Nan felt strong enough to get up, she slipped off her nasal prongs and vacated her bed so that someone who really needed it could use it. Normally, she would be kept for observation and additional medication, but she actually felt okay, and she needed to find out what was going on with Myra, Elliott, and Amber.

Normally, too, she probably wouldn't have been allowed to wander so obviously all through the hospital, but everyone was too busy to stop her or ask her what she was doing; so she roamed through choked corridor after choked corridor, taking care to stay out of everyone's way, helping to lift the occasional downed nurse or orderly onto a cot where they could be tended to. She saw that several people had died in their beds but that everyone was too busy to do anything about them.

Finally, she came upon Elliott and Amber, both hooked up to oxygen and IVs. Elliott was semi-conscious, it seemed, although he was in no condition to talk, and Amber was still pretty well out of it. She felt their foreheads, relieved to note that their fevers had lowered somewhat. She found a sink and a paper towel dispenser and spent some time sponging off both of their faces with cool, soothing water.

Continuing on her search, she finally found Myra in the recovery room from surgery where an intern was fitting a cast onto her leg. He looked up when she came in.

"Are you next of kin?" he asked.

Nan nodded.

"Well, she is one tough old bird."

Myra laughed loudly.

"Lucky as hell, too," he said. "She could have bled to death from this fracture, but she's going to be okay."

This news came as such a welcome relief that Nan sat down abruptly in the chair next to the door. "I am so glad to hear that, I can't even tell you," she said, tears brimming her eyes. She hoped, irrationally, that this meant Amber and Elliott would pull through, too.

Myra needed to stay for a blood transfusion and some fluid replacement, but afterward, the intern told her, the hospital would appreciate it if Nan could take her home.

"Under usual circumstances," he said, "we'd keep her here for a few days, but as you can see, we just don't have the space or the personnel to care for her properly. She'd probably fare better with family."

"Sure, I understand," Nan replied, her heart sinking. What would this mean in terms of her work? The fact that no caregivers were at Elliott's when she arrived didn't bode well for finding someone to look after Myra while she worked in the lab. With Elliott out of commission for a while, she didn't even have his help to count on. And—she shivered, trying not to linger on the idea for fear of making it come true—what would happen if she herself was to come down with the flu? Elliott's neighborhood watch clearly didn't help Elliott, Amber, and Myra.

Nan stood beside her mother for awhile, stroking and patting her hand, then realized that her car was still back at Elliott's. She told Myra that she needed to retrieve the car and that she would be back shortly. Before she left, she stopped by to check up on Elliott and Amber once more. They seemed to be resting peacefully so she didn't disturb them. She then headed to the lobby where she called a cab, which took over an hour to arrive.

Once at Elliott's house, she decided to make sure that everything was locked up in his absence. At this point, most people were probably too sick to engage in much looting and theft—a low crime rate was one of the few blessings of the 1918 epidemic, despite the shortage of police—but she figured, no point in tempting fate. The back door was locked, so she used her key to let herself in, and when she did so, Muffin came tearing out of the house as if her tail was on fire.

"Muffin!" she called. "Come back!"

But she had already disappeared around the corner. Nan noticed Sassafras standing disconsolately in his pen, so before she went inside the house, she opened the gate and went over to give the little sheep some attention.

"Hey there, Sassafras," she crooned, scratching him behind his ears. He perked up and leaned into her. She decided to give him an entire body rub, so she massaged his neck and back and chest and tummy. By the time she was through, he was wiggling with pleasure and wanting to play. He lowered his head in butting position and pushed up against her hands.

"Sorry, guy, that's enough for now," she said, giving him a final pat. "I'll be back, though." She refilled his water trough and made sure that he had plenty to eat, then she held her breath and quickly went through the house to make sure all the doors and windows were secure. She started to get in her car and leave, but she remembered Muffin was outside. There wasn't a pet door that she could use to get back inside, either. Tramping around the yard, she called for her several more times, but the cat never appeared. So Nan went back in and brought out her food and water dish, both filled to the brim. She set them on the steps, hoping that Muffin would fare all right until Amber returned.

Back at the hospital, she had to search a little to find her mother once more; she had been moved from the recovery room to an examining room that housed two other accident victims. Myra's transfusion was finished, and she just had one more bag of fluid and electrolytes to go through. So Nan returned to the hall where Elliott and Amber were parked, and this time, she found Elliott awake. His face brightened considerably when he saw her; she grabbed him up in a bone-crushing hug.

"Oh, Elliott, I am so glad to see you!" she cried.

"Likewise," he responded weakly, grasping her hand and giving it a feeble squeeze. "How's Amber?"

"She's on the gurney right behind you. I think she's okay." She hoped and prayed that this was true. She still seemed deeply unconscious, and her breathing sounded labored. A passing nurse stopped to check Amber's IV and Nan asked her if she could give them any information on Amber's condition. She shook her head and hurried on to check on the next patient.

"Can you wheel me around so that I can keep an eye on her?" Elliott asked.

"Sure!" Nan grabbed his gurney to spin it around, waiting for several medical personnel to rush by so that she didn't trip them up in doing so. Elliott's face became quite still when he saw his daughter.

"So, what happened, Elliott?" she asked, hoping this might help to distract him from morbid fears involving Amber. "Why weren't there any caregivers at the house when I got there?"

He sighed deeply. "Teresa was there for awhile, but then she starting feeling ill—so I told her to go home, that we could take care of Myra. And for the next few hours, everything was just fine. But then Amber collapsed on the sofa, saying she felt really bad. Within a half-hour, she was running a temperature of 102. I wasn't feeling great, but I thought I was okay, until all of a sudden, I got so weak I couldn't stand. It was bizarre! It was as if someone had snatched a plug or stopper out of my body and all my strength just ran out all at once. I couldn't even make it to a chair or anything. I had to lie down right where I was, mid-step."

"How awful!"

"Yeah. Myra was in the den with us at the time, which seemed like as good a place for her to be as any, so I told her just to stay put. I thought I'd gain enough strength to call someone to come help us if I just rested for awhile, but it just got worse and worse until I must have become unconscious. I've never, ever experienced anything like this! It was like my entire body was paralyzed. No matter how much I wanted to move or get up, I just couldn't. I couldn't even crawl over to the phone."

"But what about your neighborhood watch? What about your neighbors?"

Elliott shook his head gloomily. "I can only think that everybody ended up in the same boat. In fact, we need someone to check on all those houses."

God, what a nightmare, Nan thought morosely. Everything was breaking down, coming apart at the seams.

"So where is Myra? Is she okay?" Elliott asked.

"She's here," Nan said. "I found her in your kitchen.

Somehow, she broke her leg. I don't know how."

Elliott blanched. "I am so sorry, Nan."

"Oh hey, it wasn't your fault. This has been coming for a long time, actually. I mean, it's a miracle that she hasn't broken anything before." This time, of course, she was probably trying to do something to help Elliott and Amber, but Nan didn't voice this thought. Elliott clearly felt bad enough about the whole thing as it was.

"So, how did we get here? Did you bring us?"

"No, as a matter of fact, I ended up here myself with a massive asthma attack."

"Jesus, Nan!" Elliott exclaimed.

"It wasn't just Muffin—it's a long story … somebody brought a cat on the plane I took back from England. I'm okay now, though. I'm going to be taking Myra home soon, as a matter of fact. But I'll be checking in on you and Amber. If they decide to kick your ass out, too, it would probably be a good idea for you two to come stay at my house."

Elliott nodded, his eyes straying to his daughter.

"You should try to get some rest for now, okay?"

"Yeah."

"I love you," she murmured, leaning over to kiss him on the forehead.

"I love you, too," he replied, tears trickling from the corners of his eyes.

Nan bit her lip. She knew he was worried about Amber. Stepping over to smooth the child's hair back from her face, she bent down and whispered in her ear. "You get well, sweetie," she said. "Your dad needs you and so do I. Not to mention Myra! We're counting on you to pull through, okay?"

And although Amber didn't respond, Nan could swear that she saw her eyelashes flicker just a little, which gave her a shred of hope.

"I'll be back," she told Elliott, then left to fetch Myra.

An orderly helped her to load Myra into the car, and

fortunately, the hospital was able to loan her a wheelchair until she could rent one. Unfortunately, Nan was on her own when she arrived back at her house and had to unload her mother. Myra wasn't able to help much at all, given the fact that she couldn't put any weight on her broken leg. Getting her out of the car and into the wheelchair ended up being a half-hour burlesque show that had Nan exhausted by the time she finally wheeled her mother into the house. Nan hadn't eaten anything for hours, so she heated up a couple of microwave dinners, gobbled hers down, then spent another half hour getting her mother into bed. She knew she should check her phone messages, knew she should check her e-mail, especially to see if her posts had generated any results, but a tidal wave of fatigue seemed to be rolling over her. It was all she could do to stagger up to her own bedroom and collapse onto the bed where she fell asleep in her clothes.

She awoke at 3 AM, short of breath and jittery. Taking a shot from her inhaler, she felt more wakeful still, so she decided to get up and check her messages. She ran through the phone messages, but she hadn't received anything new since she checked from England. Booting up her computer, she logged onto the Internet, then scrolled anxiously through her messages. She had generated quite a few responses to her post, "Virologist seeks info on drug resistance epidemic," she saw with interest; she hoped the mystery e-mailer was among them. She needed to call Joshua first thing in the morning; Janice, too. She absolutely had to get to work on her samples, which she assumed would be waiting for her at the public health office.

Her heart nearly stopped when she saw the subject heading "Re: Resistance Factor," the same heading the mystery e-mailer had used before. Hands shaking, she clicked open the message, flabbergasted when a long block of triplet codons filled the screen like some sort of alien script or sentient machine language. At the bottom, in place of a signature, it read, "Ribbit. Ribbit."

She reeled back in her chair, as if a physical blast had erupted from the screen. Jesus, she thought. Who is this?

Quickly she typed back a reply, but she wasn't surprised when it came back to her as undeliverable before she logged off. She checked through all the rest of the messages, which contained some interesting information about hot spots, outbreaks, and the diseases that seemed to be affected, as well as some theories about chemical dumping, nuclear fall-out, terrorism, disruption of the earth's electromagnetic field, pole reversal, aliens from outer space, karma, the wrath of God, Revelations, cults, nation states conducting research that went awry, Nostradamus, and Armageddon.

"What about Bigfoot?" she muttered to herself, frustrated that she wouldn't be able to get her hands on her samples for at least another three hours. She logged off, printed out the gene sequences in the e-mail message and puzzled over the signature. She guessed from this that she should start with the frog samples, although those wouldn't be arriving for at least another day, maybe two. Or was this person just being cute, toying with her?

She reached for the phone and dialed up Joshua, who answered so quickly and briskly she knew he hadn't been sleeping.

"Joshua, hi, it's Nan Schulte."

"Hey, what's up?"

"I'm back home now ..."

"That was quick!"

"Yeah, I'll tell you about it later. But listen, I took your advice before leaving England and I made some posts on the Internet about the resistance factor. It looks like the ploy worked."

"Heh heh hehhhhhh ..." he chortled gleefully, rubbing his hands together so noisily she could hear it over the phone. "What did you find out?"

She hesitated. She thought about telling him what the message contained, but decided she'd rather show him. She was feeling the need for some support and company, too. "Well, I'd kind of like you to look at it. Would you mind coming over?"

"Hell, no. I can't sleep, as usual. I might as well make myself useful. "

"Great!" she replied, relieved. After hanging up the phone, she took a shower and changed clothes, then paced around the house until Joshua drove up. She hurried to let him in so that he wouldn't ring the bell and awaken Myra.

"This must be pretty good if you're dragging my sorry ass over here in the middle of the night," Joshua remarked.

"Wait'll you see."

He raised his eyebrows curiously.

"Want any coffee?" she asked.

He shook his head. "No, thanks, I'm wide awake."

Ushering Joshua into the library, Nan wordlessly handed him the print-out. His eyes literally bugged out of his head when he saw it.

"Holy shit!" he exclaimed.

"No kidding."

"Well, Christ—do you think this is for real? Or do you think it's meant to throw you off?"

"I have no idea. I think it's worth checking out, though. It at least gives me a place to start."

He nodded. "True. True." His eyes kept scanning the codons; then he reached the end. "Ribbit ribbit?" he said. "Is that supposed to be a hint? Or a joke?"

"I have some frog samples. Or I will, in a couple of days."

"Uh-huh. Well. I take it you tried replying to this message."

"Yup. No dice."

Joshua handed Nan the print-out, bent down to squint at the computer screen. "Unfortunately, I don't see anything here that would give away the guy's whereabouts."

Nan dropped into the nearest chair, heaving a sigh. "I was

afraid you were going to say that."

They both sat in glum silence.

"Well, at least you've got these gene sequences to check out," he said finally. "And classes have been suspended for the time being, so you'll have plenty of time to work on them."

"Right." Nan tugged on her lower lip. She wanted to race to the lab this instant and get started. But she couldn't leave Myra alone.

"Can you do me a favor, Josh?"

"Sure!"

"Would you mind staying here with my mom for a few hours while I go to the lab? I would really like to get started on assembling these sequences to see if I can match anything in the samples I obtained in England. I'll pay you, of course."

Joshua swiped his hand through the air in deprecation. "Don't worry about it!" he said. "I'm happy to help."

"Thanks," Nan replied gratefully. "The sooner I can get started, the sooner, hopefully, we can put the brakes on this whole catastrophe."

"No kidding," Joshua agreed. "Before it's too late."

CHAPTER 14

Nan took a short break in her office cubicle while the DNA fragments she'd obtained from her gene library were separating on her gels. If she was going to be able to look for the resistance factor in frogs or anything else, she needed to have a template with which to match it; and even though it helped considerably to have the gene sequences, there was still a great deal of work involved in creating the template. Since classes were suspended anyway, she would enlist as much help from her lab staff as possible—assuming everyone besides Joshua wasn't ill. And of course, right now, Joshua was tending her mother. She sighed dispiritedly, wondering if she should just give up—start stockpiling food and seeds, buy a couple of rifles to hunt small game with, and dig in, hope the flu virus or some other bug didn't kill her.

She reached for the phone to call the agency she used to provide care for her mother, even though she didn't feel very optimistic about her chances of getting coverage with the flu outbreak in full swing. Before she could dial, however, the door to her lab opened and Janice strolled in, her hair lank and unwashed.

"Janice!" she exclaimed, replacing the receiver. "How are

you doing?"

Janice pulled off her mittens and stashed them in her pockets, hung her coat on one of the pegs on the back of the door. "So far so good," she replied cautiously. "Three of my house mates are sick, but all of them seem to be pulling through."

"That's good."

Janice nodded grimly. "Our next door neighbors weren't so lucky, though," she said. "Two of them died from the flu."

Nan caught her breath. "How awful!"

"Yeah, and at least four of my friends have developed secondary infections with bronchitis or pneumonia."

"How—how are they doing?"

"Not good." Janice hastily wiped a tear from her eye.

Nan got up and put her arms around her. "I'm sorry," she murmured.

"I guess there's not much to do except just try to get through this," Janice responded, her voice wavering.

"Well, I have some information that might do some good."

"Really?" Janice's head shot up. "What?"

Nan retrieved the e-mail that contained the triplet codons and showed it to her, filling her in briefly on the events of the last few days.

Janice stared at the print-out as Nan talked, her expression a mixture of disbelief and outrage. "Do you mean to tell me that someone engineered this resistance factor?" she blurted.

"It—looks that way."

"Jesus, who would do such a thing?" she cried. "Why? Why would they do this?"

"Who knows?" Nan replied wearily. "And maybe it wasn't engineered. Maybe someone just figured out what the resistance factor was comprised of."

"Then why are they being so sneaky?"

"That's what I can't figure out, either," Nan admitted. "But then, why are they giving me this information if they don't want me to do something about it?"

Janice sank down onto a lab table, hugging her arms. "God, this is so sinister and creepy. Like some sick, evil mastermind."

Nan walked over to her gels to see how they were coming along. "Well, I don't know that it'll do much good to think about it that way," she said. "What we need to do is use this information to our advantage. I should be getting at least some of my samples from England today, and I've already started the process of putting together this template. We can use it to search for the factor in my samples, and also translate the proteins it codes for, see if we can figure out what the hell these genes are doing to make everything so resistant and virulent."

Janice groaned. "That should only take about five years."

Nan didn't reply for a moment. She was right, of course. "Maybe not," she said finally. "I was hoping we could stop everything else we're working on and focus on this."

"Even so ... God, Nan ..."

"I know. I know. I just don't know what else to do. Do you?"

Janice shook her head.

"Okay, so—look, I need to go home and check on my mom. I also need to go over to the hospital and check on Elliott and Amber. Could you finish up these gels for me?"

"Sure, I'd be happy to."

"I'll probably also need you to do some elder care, too."

"Okay."

"And the other thing we need to do is start cloning this template once we've gotten it. If you could start preparing some *E. coli* for me..."

"Sure." Janice sounded so defeated and despairing that Nan reached over and gave her a little shake.

"Don't give up yet. We've just gotten started. And this is an incredible break we have here."

Janice nodded, blinking back more tears.

"Who else has been in the lab this last week? Who's been out sick?"

"Well, Teresa's sick, but you know that. Connor and Felix seem to be doing okay so far, but I was gone over the weekend, helping to take care of my housemates."

"Okay, give them a call when you get a spare minute, will you? Tell them what's going on and what we need to do."

"All right."

"Now, the other thing we should do is—" The door opened once again and Nan halted, tensing when Ron entered, followed by two maintenance men.

"Ah, Nan!" he exclaimed, looking startled.

"What's up?" she asked.

"Well, er, ah, I've come to, uh, partition off part of your lab."

Nan shook her head to clear it, thinking she must have misunderstood. "I'm sorry—you've come to what?"

He handed her a memo. "Under orders from the Chancellor's office. We've got an emergency, as you must know, and we're having to use all nonessential laboratory space in order to beef up production of a new antiviral drug that's showing a lot of promise."

She gaped at him, open-mouthed. "You have got to be kidding."

"Sorry."

She continued staring at him for so long that he began to squirm. "Look, I know your work is important, but right now, this other just takes priority. I'm sure that once things calm down a little—"

"Look, asshole," she practically spit, "there is no way in hell that I'm going to let you take over my lab! No way! I've obtained some absolutely crucial information concerning the current pandemic—information that has far more applications than merely treating this flu, do you understand me?"

"I have no doubt that you think it's crucial, Nan, but the

fact is, I have the legal right to do this," Ron sputtered angrily. "You try to stand in my way and you'll find your ass out of here so fast you won't know what hit you."

"Keep threatening me, Ron, and—" The door opened once more and Felix walked in. He had recently shaved off his dreads and the nappy growth coming back reminded Nan of velvet. He took a quick look around at everyone's faces and ducked into the back of the lab where his desk was stationed. "I'm calling the Chancellor's office," she announced, making eye contact with the maintenance men. "Don't anybody move until I've had a chance to talk to him."

Ron rolled his eyes, folded his arms. "Go right ahead. It won't do a bit of good."

The chancellor was in a meeting when she called, but Nan managed to convince his secretary to pull him out of the meeting, that he—and she—would be sorry if she didn't. When the chancellor got on the phone, his inclination was clearly to put Nan off, reinforce to her that his decision had been made, but she managed to keep him on the phone long enough that he began to listen to her.

"There is a resistance factor that's become unleashed in the microbial population," she argued. "It's affecting everything, not just the influenza virus. Our biggest threat isn't from the flu right now—or from any virus, in fact. It's everything, particularly bacteria, that we've got to worry about the most. Antibiotics are worse than useless right now. And I think you'll find that this antiviral drug is merely wishful thinking. No one's come up with a decent antiviral drug for decades and I seriously doubt that they've come up with one now. I have the actual gene sequences of this resistance factor, and if you will let me keep working on this, I promise you, I'll come up with something much better than this antiviral drug. It'll work on everything! If you've got to commandeer some lab space, commandeer someone else's."

She stopped, waited for him to respond, but there was only

silence.

"Sir?"

"You say you actually have the genes for this resistance factor?"

"I do! I'm right in the middle of making a template so that we can start coming up with a defense against it!"

He gave a skeptical grunt. "How can you be so sure that you have the right genes?"

"I've just come back from England where the first outbreaks began. I've obtained incontrovertible evidence." She knew better than to reveal the source of her information. The sequences she received could be discounted as the work of a madman or villain, a wild goose chase at best, sabotage at worst.

He heaved a long, heartfelt sigh. "Okay. Put Ron on the phone."

Flashing him a wicked smile, Nan handed the receiver to Ron. She savored the look of fury on his face as he listened to the chancellor, enjoyed his clipped responses. When he hung up, he didn't even glance at her. He merely turned and gestured for the maintenance men to follow him out the door.

"Thanks for stopping by, Ron!" she called after him. When the door closed, she grinned at Janice, allowing herself to wallow in her triumph for a few moments. But then she collected herself, calling for Felix to come join her and Janice in a brief huddle. She knew that she hadn't necessarily put a stop to Ron's machinations. She might have merely delayed him, and they needed to work as quickly and efficiently as possible just in case. She outlined the research tasks that she had in mind and divvied them up between them. She put in a call to Connor as well, telling him what had transpired and to get into the lab as soon as he could. Then she put her call through to the elder care agency, which, as she feared, did not have any extra staff to spare. Half of their employees were out sick, and the rest were already scheduled to work at other places. She would have to figure out what to do about Myra in more creative ways.

On her way home, she stopped by the hospital where Elliott was now feeling better and apparently through the worst of the flu. Amber, however, remained very sick. And although she had regained consciousness during the night, her fever was running high, and she muttered deliriously now as she slept. Elliott was beside himself with worry. They had both been moved into a crowded room, and his bed was pushed up against hers so that he could reach over and hold her hand. He looked so gray and drawn that Nan could hardly bear to look at him.

"I'm so glad you're here, Nan," he rasped.

"Me, too, Elliott—me, too," she said soothingly. She leaned over Amber and gave her a kiss on the forehead, startled by how hot her skin felt. She looked as if she'd shrunk since the last time Nan saw her. God, what to do—what to do? she thought mournfully.

She stayed for a while and clasped Elliott's free hand while he clutched his daughter's limp little paw, as if trying to beam his life energy into her. While Nan waited, a nurse came into the room and stopped by each bed, checking on the patients. When she saw Amber, her face creased into a troubled pucker.

"Sweet baby," she crooned, smoothing back her damp curls. Elliott swallowed a sob as she did so, making an odd, strangled sound. She looked over at him.

"Do you mind if I try some Therapeutic Touch on your little girl?" she asked.

"By all means," he choked. Nan nodded her agreement as well, knowing that the nurse probably assumed that she was Amber's mother.

The woman began to weave her hands through the air around Amber, coming close to, but never touching her, caressing and smoothing, flicking and pushing invisible currents. As she worked, Amber stopped mumbling and began to breathe more easily. Nan stayed as still as possible, not wanting to interfere with whatever energy fields this woman was creating. Finally, the nurse stopped and gazed intently at Amber, who stirred and gave a gasping sigh, snuggling down deeper into the covers.

"Let's see if that helps the little angel," she whispered, moving on to the next patient before Nan or Elliott could even thank her.

Nan had heard about Therapeutic Touch but never seen it performed. If she considered it in a strictly scientific manner, she had to admit that it certainly looked bogus—just a well-meaning woman waving her arms over a sick child. But she knew enough about the power and subtlety of biophysics not to discount it on appearances alone; besides, she seemed to remember some fairly well-controlled studies that validated the effectiveness of Therapeutic Touch. It certainly seemed to have given Amber some temporary comfort, if nothing else.

Glancing at her watch, she saw that much more time had passed than she realized; she needed to relieve Joshua and check on her mother. So she gave Elliott a hug, told him she would be checking on him and Amber later, and reminded him that they were coming to stay with her when they were discharged from the hospital. She refused to consider any other possibility than their getting well enough to leave.

On her way home, she stopped to pick up some groceries, sobered by the emptiness of the shelves and the skimpiness of fresh produce. She selected some carrots, onions, garlic, and cabbage, frozen orange juice, several packages of different kinds of beans, and a large ham. All of these items would keep well, and they were nutritious, too. She could make some batches of soup and freeze them, in case she got too sick for food preparation.

When she got to her house, she found Joshua and her mother in the library where Joshua had moved the television and was working on the computer. Myra was sitting in her wheelchair, a plate with a few bites of uneaten toast in her lap, an unhappy expression on her face. Nan glanced at the TV set where a World Federation Wrestling match was playing on the screen. Picking up the remote, she surfed through several channels until she found an old black-and-white movie and left it there.

"How are you doing, Mom?" she asked.

"Okay."

"Are you hurting?"

"Hurting," she echoed, glaring at Nan for emphasis.

"I asked her if she wanted to take some of the Darvocet you've got in the medicine cabinet, but she said no," Joshua commented, swiveling around in the computer chair.

"Are you sure about that, Mom? It would help ease the pain."

Myra's right arm began to shake violently. "Ease the pain?"

"Right. I know you don't like to take pills, but this might be time to make an exception."

"Make an exception."

"Yeah, let me go get you one, okay?"

"Okay."

Nan left to fetch the Darvocet with a heavy heart. Her mother had an incredibly high pain threshold; if she was willing to take pain medication, that meant she was really suffering. When Nan came back with a caplet and glass of water, she told Joshua that he could leave if he wanted, but that she could really use his help in the lab.

"Janice and Felix are there right now, and they can show you what we've gotten started. I'll go by Public Health later and see if my samples from England arrived."

"Sounds good. I'm on my way," Joshua told her. He sauntered over to where Myra sat, bent over and took both of her hands, catching her droopy gaze. "It's been a pleasure, Mrs. Schulte," he said, giving her a wink.

"It's been a pleasure," she repeated, with a ghost of a smile.

After Joshua left, Nan finished up the toast on Myra's plate and made herself an extra slice. She watched the movie with her mother while she ate, her mind in overdrive, trying to figure out how she was going to do the research she needed to do and care for her mother at the same time—not to mention Amber and Elliott. If Teresa had the flu, she was going to be out of commission for at least two weeks. Janice, Connor, Felix, and Joshua were healthy for the time being, but that could—and undoubtedly would—change at any moment. And she was depending on them for not only lab assistance but elder care. One backhanded blessing of Myra's broken leg was that this immobilized her more than usual, so the chances of her getting up and falling were much less; but Nan couldn't count on the fact that her mother would stay put despite her injury. If left unsupervised, she could still do even more damage to herself.

She excused herself and went into the kitchen to call the assisted living centers in town, see if they had a spare room where she could place Myra temporarily. Unfortunately, they told her, they hadn't a spare room anywhere. And they were shorthanded as it was. Feeling utterly overwhelmed with no one to turn to for help, Nan laid her head on the table and started sobbing silently. When she felt a light touch on her shoulder, she jumped, surprised to find that Myra had managed to wheel herself into the room.

"What's wrong?" she asked.

"Oh—everything," Nan replied, trying to laugh. Instead, more tears ran down her cheeks.

"Everything?"

"Yes, everything. Elliott's sick, Amber's sick, you've broken your leg, it looks as if infectious disease has launched the mother of all plagues upon humanity, all of our tools to fight this are useless, I can't find anyone to help me take care of you, I need to get to work at my lab so I can figure out what the hell is going on with all of these microbes, and the head of the department is trying to take my lab away from me."

Myra didn't respond for a moment. Then she declared, "I'm fine."

"No, you're not!" Nan cried. "You're not fine! You've broken your leg, for God's sake."

"I'm okay," her mother insisted, her arm starting to shake once again.

"Mom, I appreciate your moral support, but you are not okay. Even if you hadn't broken your leg, you still have all the other problems associated with your dementia."

Myra stared defiantly at Nan. "It doesn't matter—" she gasped, as if getting these few words out cost her a tremendous effort.

"What doesn't matter?"

"It doesn't matter if … It doesn't matter if …" Her arm continued to wobble, causing Nan's heart to ache even more. She reached over to grasp her hand and quiet the motion.

Waiting a few moments, she then prompted, "It doesn't matter if …"

"If … if … I die."

Nan couldn't reply. Tears started streaming down her face.

"It doesn't matter …" Myra said once again, plaintively.

Nan leaned over and grabbed her mother up in a fierce hug. "It matters to me, Mom," she wept. "Are you telling me you're not having much fun these days?"

"Not having much fun."

Nan bit her lip, trying to keep from losing all emotional control. She didn't know what to say. If she were in her mother's position, she would feel desperate for a way out, too; but there was no way Nan could do anything but protect her mother, even if she wanted to die, no matter how much she empathized. And frankly, she wasn't ready to let her go yet. As limited and difficult as their relationship might be, it was better than nothing. The irony was, lots of people who didn't want to die, young people in the prime of their lives, were expiring from this flu. And her mother, who was ready to quit this life, would probably never catch this damned influenza—and if she did, she would undoubtedly sail through it with the same remarkable resilience she had always shown.

In the end, Nan didn't say anything, merely kissed her mom on the forehead and wheeled her back into the library to finish watching the movie. She stayed with her for an hour, working out the details of some of the experiments she would want to run on her samples from England, then called over to the lab and asked who wanted to come help out with Myra. Janice volunteered, as she was quite fond of her, and Nan got started on making some soup while waiting for her to show up.

Before Janice arrived, Nan went back into the library and sat in the chair next to her mother. She squeezed her hand, stroked her arm. "We'll make it through this," she said, not knowing for whose sake she was saying it.

"We'll make it through."

"Yes we will, Mom. We will. We will."

CHAPTER 15

Nan sat slumped at her desk, reviewing the results of the experiments she and her lab staff had performed over the last two weeks. Alarmingly, though perhaps not surprisingly, the group of proteins they were calling "the resistance factor" was present in just about every single biological sample they'd examined. However, the factor they'd been turning up was not the exact same one as the mystery e-mailer had sent. Either it had mutated since it made its first appearance, or the author of the e-mail hadn't gotten all the sequences right. Additional efforts to draw this person out on the Internet had produced nothing. Apparently, whoever it was had gone back into hiding. Or perhaps they had shared everything they knew, although Nan thought this highly unlikely.

She and her staff had managed to translate the proteins that the resistance factor coded for, but frustratingly, several of them were proteins no one had ever encountered before. No one had a clue what they might do, how they might work, or where they plugged into the metabolic machinery of the cell. And Janice was right; this was the really hard part, figuring this out. It was like looking for someone in a huge crowd, but she didn't even know what the person looked like or what his or her name was. Just coming up with the x-ray crystallography was difficult, and the results were not necessarily unambiguous. Since these were unfamiliar proteins, it was hard to know whether the crystallized versions took the same shapes they assumed in a living cell, and the shape was what determined their biological activity. Even if they had the right shape to work with, interpreting an x-ray crystallograph was not only a science, it was an art, which meant that a certain subjectivity was involved.

Nan sighed heavily, shuffling through her papers, hoping some detail might catch her eye, give her some insight. She would give anything to get her hands on the person who sent the triplet codons. Instead of working backwards on this thing, she could work with the knowledge of what these proteins were designed to do. The situation was getting more desperate by the day, even though the first wave of influenza had peaked on both coasts of the U.S. Now everyone was dealing with secondary infections, bacterial infections, ones that were proving stubbornly, universally, and virulently resistant to every antibiotic known to man—including the highly touted one that she had heard about at the symposium. Nothing in the conventional arsenal was working. Nothing. And other, more exotic diseases were continuing their upward climb as well. Ebola hadn't made it to the United States yet, but hantaviruses and other hemorrhagic viruses were spreading like wildfire. And given the fact that Ebola was making appearances all over Africa, Asia, and Europe, it was probably only a matter of time before it reached the States.

A soft knock on the door broke her reverie, and she looked up to see Teresa peering down at her through her glasses. "Are you okay?" she asked.

"As okay as I can be, I guess," Nan replied wearily. "How about you?"

"Feeling stronger by the day."

Nan smiled. "That's good."

"Listen, I'm headed home for lunch—do you want me to check on Myra and Amber? It's right on my way."

"That would be fantastic—thanks," Nan said, grateful for her thoughtfulness.

In fact, all of her students had been terrific, even though every member of her lab staff except Janice had succumbed to the flu at some point during the past two weeks. Joshua, fortunately, got a very mild case and was only out for a few days, but Connor and Felix were still recuperating, spending just a few hours a day in the lab. Thanks to her student Kristin, Nan had managed to find a group of undergraduates who were sharing a house, the majority of whom had recovered from the flu and managed to avoid complications. Kristin and her roommates were keeping Myra for her full-time for the time-being, as well as babysitting Amber during the day while Elliott went to work. Schools were still closed, and the students were glad not only for the money but for something to do. A couple of them had gone home to be with their parents until classes started up again, so this freed up some space for Myra. Nan felt very lucky to have managed this care situation, and Myra was being reasonably cooperative. In fact, Nan suspected that she might be a little sweet on one of the young men in the house, a rather hunky young track star at the university.

Laying her papers aside for the moment, she dialed up Elliott's number at Public Health, anxious to make sure he wasn't working too hard. Ever since he had recovered, he'd been working like a demon to come up with a solution to the public health crisis. He answered after several rings, sounding tired and discouraged.

"Hey, sweet thang," she greeted him.

"Hey yourself," he responded, his tone brightening.

"You're not working too hard, are you?"

"Probably."

She growled at him.

"I know, I know." He paused. "Look who's talking."

"Yeah, you're right." She sighed.

"How's it going?"

"Oh, reasonably well, I guess, at least with the experiments we've run so far. The only problem is, it's the experiments I don't even know to run that I need."

"Sounds familiar," Elliott concurred gloomily.

"How's your work coming?"

"Not well. Like you, we just don't have any clue how to tackle this thing. There's no point in making a vaccine for the resistance factor, because everyone's been exposed to it already. In a normal situation, as you know, the exposure itself should confer immunity on the survivors, but that's just not happening. There are too many different bugs with this resistance factor, too many variables."

They both sat in dejected silence for a moment.

"And there's another problem," he said.

"What's that?"

"We're starting to have a problem with corpses building up. There are pockets where entire neighborhoods got hit with the flu at the same time—well, like my neighborhood—and there aren't enough hale and hearty public health officers to search out all the bodies. We've been going into households where every single person has died. And their bodies have been lying there for days."

Nan shuddered. "What about the armed forces? I heard they were being employed to help out with things like that."

"They are. There just aren't enough of them, either. I mean, they've been drafted into helping with food production and distribution, helping to maintain essential lines of communication, all that kind of thing, too. And unfortunately, their numbers were particularly hard hit during this wave of influenza."

"Yeah, I heard that."

"So. We're pretty much up shit creek."

"Sure looks that way. Although, Christ—there's got to be

some kind of makeshift paddle we can come up with." Nan mashed her lips together in frustration, twiddled her pencil between her fingers. "Any, uh, sign of Muffin at the house when you went by there this morning?"

"No."

"Oh," Nan sighed. "Well, I just wanted to check in, make sure you weren't risking a relapse. What time do you think you'll be home?"

"Not too late. Probably before you get there. I'll swing by and pick up Amber. You want me to start dinner?"

"Sure—if you're not too tired. I'll probably stop by and visit my mom before I come home. If you're feeling pooped, though, you can always heat up some of that frozen stew or soup."

"Okay. Thanks for calling, sweetheart."

"I love you, guy. See you tonight."

Even after Elliott and Amber had gotten over the worst of their bout with the flu, they remained at Nan's house. It made no sense to have two households, especially now that Muffin had disappeared. Nan felt awful about Amber losing her beloved pet, but she also had to admit that she felt guiltily glad as well. It meant that they could all be together, and she hadn't had to play the part of the bad guy cat banisher. Unfortunately, she didn't have any place for Sassafras to live, either, so he was currently boarding at a nearby farmer's. He seemed happy enough, though, the time that she stopped by to check in on him.

She returned to contemplating her research results, pulling her lunch out of her drawer and munching on a peanut butter sandwich while she did so. Somehow she felt that something important, something key, was dangling there right underneath her nose but she just couldn't see it. What on Earth could it be?

She had a little bit of a breather in that Ron had come down with a bad case of the flu over a week ago and had been

bedridden since then. She certainly didn't hate him enough
to wish him dead, but again, she took a secret satisfaction
in the fact that he was out of commission for a while so
that she could work in peace. The pandemic itself, however,
represented a far worse taskmaster than Ron could ever
be. Everyone was still shell-shocked from the worst of the
influenza epidemic, but the worst was far from over. People
might not be falling ill and dying in such spectacularly sudden
ways now—bacterial illnesses tended to linger much longer—
but in fact, even more people were going to be losing their lives
in the coming months if something didn't happen to change
the course of this plague. As it was, the current death toll in
the United States alone stood at a sobering two million. And
if this influenza epidemic followed the pattern of the 1918 flu
epidemic, there could be a second wave as deadly as the first.

Nan spent the rest of the afternoon in the lab, along with
Teresa and Connor. Janice was working on the department's
electron microscope, examining slices of different sample
tissue from England, looking for anything anomalous or
out-of-the-ordinary. Part of the "good" that the winds of the
current epidemic had blown their way was a department
sparsely occupied by even faculty and researchers; so it was
relatively easy to get time on instruments such as the electron
microscope.

Nan and crew were running a battery of tests to
characterize the activity of one of the new proteins they'd
translated. As the tests were tedious and time-consuming, Nan
felt relieved when Janice showed up with her micrographs.
Janice wore a very peculiar expression on her face which
piqued Nan's curiosity immediately.

"What?" she asked.

Janice shook her head, seeming a little dazed. "I don't
know what to think."

This got Teresa's and Connor's attention as well. They both
stopped what they were doing and all three of them crowded

around Janice to take a look at her prints. She held them up for viewing on the palms of both hands, as if she were offering a tray of cookies or surgical instruments. A shocked silence ensued.

"This can't be what I think it is," said Connor.

"Well, what else looks like that?" demanded Teresa.

"What do you think, Nan?" asked Janice.

Nan couldn't speak for a moment. All she could think was that she was a carrier and she had contaminated the samples. She was carrying Ebola virus right now. Shedding it. Spreading it. Her heart started pounding so hard she had to sit down. When she glanced up, everyone was looking at her with various degrees of panic on their faces.

"Which—which sample is that, Janice?" Nan stammered.

Janice frowned, consulted the code on the bottom of the print. "Ummm, Faith Burnham."

Adrenalin was pumping through her so intensely that it took Nan a moment for this information to register. But then she realized: she couldn't have contaminated that sample with Ebola from the man she passed on the street. That sample was completely sealed up and ready to ship when she encountered the man. Moreover, Faith hadn't seemed sick in any way. What the hell was going on here?

"But there's more," Janice was saying. "I found the same virus in some of the pond water, and I found it in one of the tissue samples from the cows."

Nan received this information in silence. Was this the resistance factor? Some bizarre form of Ebola? The sequence of codons that they had received, though, didn't code for an entire virus, just several proteins. And it wasn't just Ebola that was creating havoc, it was everything. But perhaps this was the vector, the transmitter of the resistance factor.

"Nan?" prompted Connor, his voice sounding higher than usual. "Shouldn't we be, like, working under Level Four conditions if we've got Ebola in our lab?"

"Well, possibly, if we actually had Ebola Zaire or Sudan," Nan managed to reply, wanting to keep everyone calm. "But my guess is that this must be more akin to the Reston version, the simian strain that doesn't cause disease in humans."

Everyone relaxed visibly.

"This woman, Faith Burnham, wasn't even sick."

They relaxed even more.

"And no one in this town I visited had any symptoms that even slightly resembled infection from Ebola."

"Whew, that's a relief!" exclaimed Teresa.

"And we need to make sure that this isn't some sort of artefact."

"Right," replied Janice, looking the most relieved of all.

"Okay, so look," Nan announced briskly, "everyone's put in a good day's work here. Maybe we should finish up these tests and then go home, think about what we've discovered so far."

No one argued.

"And don't worry about this virus. The fact that Janice found it in all three of the samples she mentioned could mean that it's somewhat universal, something we might even be harboring already. No one has gotten anything but the flu in this lab and we've been working with these samples for two weeks."

Everyone dispersed to finish up their work, while Nan did the same. No one spoke much for the rest of the afternoon. It was easy, of course, to say that there was no reason to panic, but with all the epidemiological weirdness going on, such a finding as Janice's was bound to scare the hell out of anyone.

Nan herself felt glad when she had shut down her experiments for the day and was headed home. She stopped by the undergraduates' house, an old Victorian on a street near the university, to check up on Myra and found her with a bowl of popcorn in her lap, her broken leg propped up on a pillow on the coffee table, watching a rerun of a football game that had taken place last year. The toll of illness taken on the athletes themselves, not to mention all the ancillary positions involved in running media-oriented sports events, had shut down the current professional and college football season, so the networks had resorted to airing reruns. Myra's "boyfriend" was on the couch next to her, manning the remote control, tossing off the occasional comment that made her howl with laughter. Clearly, Myra was not suffering any hardship by staying with this group, which helped to ease Nan's feeling that she had abandoned her mother by lodging her here.

When she got home, Elliott and Amber were already there, making a batch of macaroni and cheese for dinner. She gave them both a hug and a kiss, then joined in the dinner preparations, pouring both herself and Elliott a glass of red wine to sip on while they cooked. Elliott had lost a lot of weight during his bout with the flu, so Nan figured he could use all the calories he could get. Amber was thinner than normal, too, and the dark circles under her eyes still hadn't gone away, but Nan comforted herself with the conviction that she looked a little better every day. She was giving everyone Astragalus supplements, since this herb boosted and balanced immune function. But she was going to run out soon and she wasn't sure if she would be able to get any more when these were gone. When traditional medicine failed to work, everyone had rushed onto the alternative medical bandwagon, and now these remedies were not only scarce, they had become exorbitantly expensive.

Guiltily, she refrained from sharing Janice's findings with Elliott. She knew that he would want to know and that if he found out she had withheld this from him, he would be not only angry, but hurt. But she feared that if she told him, the public health official in him would have to insist that she hand the project over to the CDC or the military. And she just wasn't willing to do that. She would tell him soon, she rationalized—as soon as she had something concrete and certain to tell him.

After dinner, they played a few hands of Go Fish! before Nan retired to the sofa with a larger pile of journals than usual. She had made it her habit lately to comb through every single article she could, trying to find some lead for the current disaster. When the phone rang, she let Amber answer it, since Amber delighted in picking up the handset and saying slowly and distinctly, "Professor Schulte's residence." She listened to the speaker on the other end, her gaze traveling around the room before lighting upon Nan.

"It's for you," she said, holding out the phone. "It's Joshua."

Nan got up, gave Amber a little pat on the back as she put the receiver to her ear. "What's up?" she asked.

"Well, I'm not entirely sure. It might be nothing."

"Okay. But why did you call?

He cleared his throat. "Well, I'm in the lab right now, and I've been doing some stuff on the Internet."

"And?"

"The thing is, I can't be sure until I run some more tests …" He paused.

"Right, right …" Nan prodded him impatiently.

"But it looks like someone has been hacking into the lab computer from outside."

Nan gave an exclamation of surprise. "Hacking into our computer? How weird. Who would do that?"

"Exactly," Joshua responded, unable to keep the excitement out of his voice. "Exactly."

CHAPTER 16

Bathed in the glow from the screen of the electron microscope, Nan scanned her sample in the otherwise darkened room, looking for the telltale shape of the virus her lab had discovered: a filovirus which looked very much like Ebola but which differed in several key respects. Once they started looking for it, they had found it just about everywhere, using every kind of test they could think of to run. Moreover, it appeared as if her hunch was correct—the resistance factor had been found associated with this virus in all the specimens they had examined.

Disconcertingly, every single one of their own blood samples had revealed the presence of this new virus, along with the resistance factor; so it wasn't just in the samples Nan had brought back from England. Of course, this had made everyone feel extremely strange, as if they had a time-bomb inside of them, ticking away. But evidently, just the presence of this virus and the associated resistance factor wasn't fatal in and of itself. Something else had to act in concert with this virus, Nan surmised, in order for it to start wreaking havoc.

Just to make sure that she was arriving at the correct assumptions, she had decided to check some stored cell cultures that Elliott had been able to procure for her, ones that had been taken over three years ago, before any of the most recent drug resistance had reared its ugly head. If her hypothesis was correct, then she shouldn't find any of this filovirus, dubbed the Doomsday Virus by Felix, in samples obtained before the current wave of multiple drug resistance. She had Teresa running some fluorescent antibody tests on these samples as well, which she hoped would come up negative, but she also wanted to look for the virus with the electron microscope in case Teresa ended up with ambiguous results.

So far, so good—she had scanned a large number of cells in these older samples yesterday and today and not found any of these Doomsday Viruses. Of course, it was harder to prove that these viruses hadn't been around in the past than it would be to establish their presence; there was always the chance that they had been around, just in sufficiently small titer that they wouldn't register in any of the tests and scarce enough that they wouldn't show up in any of the cells that she happened to look at. Once you got to the level of magnification that an electron microscope was capable of elucidating, there were vast reaches of space to cover, even in a microscopic sample. Still, the longer she looked without finding anything, the more optimistic she began to feel.

She twirled the dial that moved her sample under the beam of electrons, skimming past some mitochondria, a few ribosomes, and copious ribbons of endoplasmic reticula. Nothing ... nothing ... she passed the nucleus and it looked just fine, the granular, seemingly disorganized, unraveled ball of yarn that characterized interphase ... more endoplasmic reticulum—wait a minute! She halted. What in the hell was that? She backed up.

She sat and stared at the screen. There it was. It was unmistakable, that funky, J-shaped tangle of a filovirus. What was it doing there? And why hadn't anyone ever noticed it before? Granted, this was the first cell she had found to contain this virus before the pandemic, and she had looked at thousands, if not tens of thousands of cells herself. With millions of cells in one human body alone, that didn't really add up to all that many. And if no one was looking for it, it could conceivably go unnoticed, particularly if the preparation of the microscope sample had sliced through it in such a way that its characteristic shape became obscured. Nan glanced at her watch. She had only a few more minutes to go before Renata was scheduled to use the electron microscope, so she made a print of her screen and logged off the scope.

One virus in one cell didn't necessarily mean anything, but she couldn't help but wonder if the index cases existed much farther back in time than she had thought. This virus might behave like HIV in that respect—stay quiet and hidden for years before exploding inside a person like a molecular Trojan horse. She removed her sample from the scope, gathered up her notebook and purse, and practically collided with Renata on her way out the door. She was anxious to know if Teresa had finished her fluorescent antibody tests, and if so, what she had found.

In addition, Joshua was engaged in some sort of hush-hush collaboration with an old high school friend of his, a hacker extraordinaire, he claimed proudly when presenting his plan to track down the mystery e-mailer. Joshua and "Wormy," as he was known in hacking circles, had been at work on the lab computer for the last week, doing God-only-knew-what to trace the person who was hacking into their computer. Joshua was convinced that it had to be the mystery e-mailer, and Nan couldn't think of who else would want to do such a thing— who would even know that prying into this computer might yield some pay-off. So far, they hadn't gotten anywhere, but Wormy was extremely patient and dogged, and once he caught the scent on a cybertrail, he apparently pursued it obsessively. It was a matter of personal honor, Joshua explained.

Nan hurried to her lab with her print, figuring she would share it with the staff, as inconclusive as it was. But when she entered, she seemed to have walked into some kind of surprise party. Everyone was standing around in a circle drinking some sort of beverage out of laboratory glassware, huge grins on their faces.

"What's—this all about?" she asked.

"Tell her, man," Wormy said, nudging Joshua, who looked as if he'd just been awarded the Nobel Peace Prize for Medicine.

"We found him."

Nan's jaw dropped. "You did? Seriously?"

"Yup." He and Wormy turned to one another and gleefully slapped their hands in a high five.

"How—how did you locate him?"

Wormy became serious. "Well, it's sort of complicated. And I guess, probably, it's sort of, kind of, well, like, maybe quasi-legal, but there's this software—"

"You know what?" Nan interrupted. "I don't really need to know. I think maybe this should fall into the category of 'don't ask, don't tell.'" She snatched a beaker from the nearest lab bench and held it up in a toast. "You guys are princes," she crowed. "Congratulations!"

Connor grabbed a bottle of Southern Comfort from under his desk and poured a couple of fingers' worth into Nan's beaker, then clinked it with his Ehrlenmeyer flask. They drank and heaped praises on Wormy and Joshua; then Nan decided it was time to get back to work.

"Okay, so, when you say you found him, what exactly does that mean? A person's name? An address? A phone number?"

"Well, an address and a phone number," said Joshua. "We got the address from the phone number."

"So, you don't know which person at this particular address might be the hacker, right? If there's more than one person living at this address?"

"Yeah, I guess that's right," Joshua assented.

"Where does this person live?"

"In Berkeley."

"Oh, great." It had already occurred to her that the best way to interact with this person would be in person. That way, he couldn't hang up on her. And she would need to surprise him, too.

"Do you think this person had any idea you were checking on him?" she asked.

"Nah," Wormy responded. "No way."

"Well, it's possible, I suppose," Joshua countered. "But I'd be surprised. They don't get much better than Wormy when it comes to sneaking around undetected. You know those hackers who broke into the—" Joshua broke off as Wormy dug an elbow into his ribs. "Uh, never mind."

"Okay." Nan sat pondering for a moment. "By the way, Teresa, what kind of results did you get on those antibody tests?"

Teresa shook her head. "I'm not sure, actually. The results weren't really very conclusive. I'm afraid I'm going to have to run them over again—I might have done something wrong or contaminated the samples."

"I see. Felix, how are you coming along with crystallizing those proteins?"

He, too, looked frustrated. "A couple of them I've managed pretty well—well enough to get a decent-sized, consistent sample. But there's one, with a pretty large molecular weight, that's acting really, really strange. I get a different crystal each time."

"Hmm." Nan set her beaker down, picked up her print and handed it to Janice. "This came from one of the old cell cultures that Elliott got for us."

Janice's eyebrows shot up. "You're kidding!"

"Nope. What this means, I have no idea. But I'll tell you what—if I can get my hands on this e-mailer and find out what he or she knows, I think this should speed up our progress considerably. You guys might have to work on your own for a bit while I go find this bozo."

Everyone regarded her dubiously as Janice passed around the micrograph.

"What if this person is dangerous, Nan?" asked Connor. "You're not thinking about going alone, are you?"

"Yeah, some of us should go. In fact, I know Berkeley," said Joshua.

"Thanks, guys," Nan told him, smiling at them. "But you know, I don't think I want to answer to any of your parents or partners if anything should go wrong. I mean, anything could happen. And I probably don't need to remind you that California's struggling with a pretty serious outbreak of Bubonic Plague at the moment."

This had a chilling effect, as Nan hoped it would. Although she appreciated her young staff's valor, she really didn't want to put any of them in any more danger than she already had. And she needed as many bodies in this lab as possible to fend off any further attempts by Ron to take over the space. He had recovered from the flu and was back at the department, casting murderous glances her way whenever they passed each other in the halls.

Having decided that she would make the trip West, she conferred briefly with each member of the lab staff, outlining the experiments that she wanted them to undertake in her absence. Then she left to go by the house where Myra was staying to let her know that she would be leaving in the morning.

As she trudged up the walk to the front door, it gave her a weird feeling to contemplate the possibility that this could be their last meeting if something happened to Myra while she was gone, or if she herself didn't make it back from her journey. She had brushed off Connor's and Joshua's concerns about her safety, but in fact, she knew that this was going to be a dangerous quest. The hacker that Wormy and Joshua had found could be dangerously unpredictable, and she knew, from news reports, that traveling had become much more hazardous than in the past. Flights were scarce enough and unpredictable enough that she planned to drive to California, but not only were there food shortages, there were gas shortages, too, the flu epidemic was peaking in the Midwestern states, and after enjoying a brief disease-induced lull, violent crime was once again on a precipitous increase.

Myra was snoozing in her wheelchair with the television on when Nan stepped inside, while two of the residents played Foosball on a nearby set. Nan sat down next to her mother on the sagging sofa and took one of her twisted hands in both of her own. Myra's eyes opened slowly and she turned her head toward Nan with stately implacability. When she saw who was sitting beside her, an enormous grin lit up her face.

"Hi," she said, in a soft, surprisingly husky voice, sounding almost seductive.

"Hi, Mom." Nan smiled back at her. "How've these kids been treating you?"

Myra struggled to answer. "Fine," she finally said.

"Hey, we've been treating you like a queen!" shouted one of the Foosball players. "Tell her!"

"Like a queen," Myra echoed, chuckling.

"Well, that's good. It's what you deserve," Nan replied. She cleared her throat, certain that her news was going to cause her mother consternation. "So, Mom, I came by to tell you that I'm going on a trip tomorrow."

"A trip?"

"Yeah, there's someone I have to find out in California, someone really important to my research."

"California?"

"Yes, I'm going to be away for several days, maybe ten or so. Maybe two weeks."

"Two weeks?" Myra's right arm began to shake. Nan

reached over and smoothed it down.

"I know, it's sort of a long time. But I'll be back before you know it, especially now that you've got all these young hunks to wait on you hand and foot."

Myra cackled. "Waiting on me hand and foot!"

"That's not so bad, is it?"

"Not so bad."

"I didn't think so." Nan turned to address the students. "Think you guys can handle her on your own for a couple of weeks?"

They assured her it was no problem and that they'd let everyone in the household know that she was going to be out of town for a while. Nan brushed her mother's hair back from her face, cupped her cheek in her hand. "I love you, Mom," she said. "And I'll call whenever I can, all right? You be good while I'm gone. No standing up and diving."

"No standing up and diving."

"Right." Nan leaned over and gave her mother a hug, then blew her a kiss as she left the room. Myra slowly raised her hand and blew a kiss to Nan, which Nan pretended smacked her on the side of the face, eliciting another grin from her mother.

To avoid dwelling on her misgivings, Nan trotted to her car and roared off to her house, making a mental list of all the things she needed to take with her on her trip. She hated the thought of leaving Elliott and Amber once again, too, but finding the person who provided the triplet codons took precedence over everything else at the moment. She did not feel she was being hysterical when she considered that the future of the human race could be at stake.

When she arrived home, Elliott and Amber were already there, enjoying an afternoon snack of crackers, cheese, and apple juice. "You're home early!" Elliott exclaimed, rising to plant a big smooch on her lips while Amber giggled at this display of passion.

"Mmm, yum," responded Nan, ruffling his hair, then reaching over to do the same to Amber. "Hey, cutie," she greeted her.

"So, to what do we owe this unexpected pleasure?" asked Elliott, sitting back down and offering her a cheese-and-cracker. "A big breakthrough? Or total frustration?"

Nan joined them at the kitchen table, pouring herself a glass of juice. "A breakthrough, actually," she began tentatively.

Elliott's face became animated. "Really? What?"

"Well, it looks like Joshua and his friend have traced the person who was hacking into our computer. And as you know, we think this is the same person who sent us the triplet codons for the resistance factor."

"No kidding!" Elliott popped a slice of cheddar in his mouth enthusiastically. "That's great! Who on Earth is it?"

"They don't quite know that exactly. They just have a phone number and an address in Berkeley, California."

"So—what, you're going to have the authorities contact the person?"

"No, actually … I was thinking of going out there."

Elliott stared at her. "You were what?"

"You know, drive out there … confront the person. Make sure he doesn't get away and take everything he knows with them."

Elliott scooted his chair back, continuing to regard Nan with an incredulous expression. "Nan, this is an extremely dangerous undertaking you're talking about here. Haven't you been listening to the news? We're dealing with barely controlled chaos in this country."

"I know, I know, believe me."

"And this weirdo, this possible cult member terrorist wacko—do you really think it's smart to just waltz in on this person?"

Nan set her jaw stubbornly. "Maybe it's not 'smart.' But I think it's what has to be done."

"Look, I admire your courage and your willingness to sacrifice yourself for humanity, but honestly—this kind of thing is better left to people who know how to handle it. I mean, Jesus, Nan! You're not some hardboiled gumshoe!"

Amber had been looking anxiously back and forth between her father and Nan. Now she broke out in a wail. Elliott picked her up and pulled her into his lap, while Nan stroked her arm. "I don't want anyone to hurt Nan!" she sobbed.

Elliott shot Nan an exasperated look. "No one's going to hurt Nan, sweetheart," he reassured her.

"But—but you said—"

"I know, shh, I know. I was speaking ... hypothetically."

"No one's going to hurt me, pumpkin," Nan repeated, feeling absolutely awful. Still, nothing was going to change her mind.

"What does 'hypotestically' mean?" she whimpered.

"Nothing. It doesn't really mean anything," Elliott muttered through clenched teeth. No one spoke for a moment.

Finally, Nan said, "Look, I just can't trust the authorities not to come on too heavy-handed and blow this whole thing. Obviously, this person is terrified of being found out. If he's arrested, he—or she—might clam up and we might never find out what he knows. I'm the person he contacted in the first place—it seems he might trust me to a certain extent. There's just too much at stake here, Elliott. Thousands of people are dying every day!"

Elliott stared straight ahead, his jaw muscles flexing. "Okay," he said slowly, "if you insist upon going, let Amber and me come along. That way, you won't be alone, and we won't have to be separated again. Schools are closed, so Amber won't be missing any classes, and I know that I would feel much, much better if we were together in this."

Nan swallowed. "But, I don't want to put you and Amber in da—uh, I mean, you know ..."

"Yes, I do know," Elliott snapped. "And this is your choice. You can stay here with us. Or you can go with us."

"Elliott, no! I can't let you do this!"

He glared at her, tight-lipped. "Would you stop being so goddamned stubborn and listen for a minute?" he barked. "You've never been west of Michigan. Do you even have any idea what it's like to drive over one of those mountain passes out West?"

"Oh, come on, Elliott—I've driven on snow my whole life!"

He shook his head. "It's not the same, believe me. And it would be a hell of lot safer if we shared the driving—we could make much better time. And surely you've heard about the car-jackings that have been taking place on the highways. You're going to need to take a gun, and you're going to need to know how to shoot it. You've never even held a gun!"

"Jesus, a gun?" Nan gave a small laugh. "I don't think that's really necessary."

"Think again, Nan. Civilization is unraveling out there. As for Amber's safety, she'll be safe with us, safer than she will be with anyone else. And if you don't agree to go together, I'll just follow you. You can't stop me."

"You can't stop us," Amber piped up in a determined little voice.

Nan expelled a heavy sigh. Their loyalty made her heart ache with love and gratitude, but she couldn't shake the feeling that this could turn out to be a disaster. Elliott was right, though. She couldn't stop them. "All right," she said reluctantly. "You win."

"Okay, it's settled then. When were you planning on leaving?"

"Tomorrow, actually."

"Well, then, we should start getting ready now."

"Yeah, we should."

Elliott kissed Amber on the top of the head and gave her a squeeze. "Looks like we're going on a trip, sweetie."

"Yay!" she shouted. "Where?"

"California," said Nan.

"Oh, goody!" she exulted. "We can go to Disneyland!"

Elliott and Nan exchanged glances, but neither one of them had the heart to disillusion her yet. And when Nan left the room to begin packing her things, she wasn't sure whether she felt relieved or terrified.

CHAPTER 17

Nan and Elliott stood beside Elliott's van, reviewing their travel list with a flashlight in the frosty morning darkness. Amber sat cozied down on a mattress that Elliott had placed in the back, snuggled up with several stuffed animals and a sleeping bag.

"Okay, we've got food for two weeks, just in case, we've got extra water, medical supplies—you have your kit, right?" Elliott asked Nan, glancing up at her.

She nodded, nervousness gripping her stomach.

"Gas can ... flares, camping gear, just in case, cell phone ..." Neither one of them mentioned the gun, but they both knew that it was nestled in the glove compartment. "Road atlas ... okay, I think we're all set."

"Great," Nan replied faintly. Despite her bravado from the night before, she had serious misgivings about the journey they were about to make. She wasn't sure if it was because she felt responsible for Amber and worried that something might happen to her, whether it was because she was operating outside of her element, or whether it was because of the ominous reports Elliott had obtained from colleagues at other public health agencies along the route that they had planned late last night. Perhaps she feared that she was going off on a wild goose chase, that the hacker wasn't the mystery e-mailer, and that her time would be much better served by doing what she did best: working in the lab. Still, her conviction remained. She wasn't going to back out now. And thankfully, once Elliott had decided that he and Amber should accompany her, he was taking charge of logistics in a way that she appreciated. She needed his help and strength.

They both climbed into the van and buckled their seatbelts. Elliott took the driver's seat, as he would drive the first two hours, at which point they would switch off. Nan glanced into the back at Amber, who looked like a fluffy little fox kit peering out from her covers and pillows.

A lurid dawn was breaking as they pulled onto the highway south; oily fingers of dark red and indigo streaked the bottom of a gray cloud bank, while the lightening space beneath it looked like a chasm plunging into a lost world. Practically no other cars occupied the road at this time, which oddly, made Nan feel light-headed. She couldn't count the number of times she had cursed the traffic and overpopulation on the East Coast; but she took no satisfaction in the still emptiness they drove through now. A disconcerting number of abandoned vehicles were strewn along the shoulders, some bashed-in from accidents, some not, while crumpled newspapers and Styrofoam containers tumbled across their path in fitful gusts.

"Jesus, I feel like Mad Max," Nan muttered.

"Ain't that the truth," Elliott replied, with a humorless bark of a laugh.

"Who's Mad Max?" asked Amber.

"Just a guy in a movie," Nan told her.

"Oh." Amber sighed. "Daddy?"

"Yes, sweetheart?"

"Do you think Muffin might try to follow us out to California?"

Elliott gripped the steering wheel, craning his neck to look at Amber in the rear view mirror. "I doubt it, honey. Why do you ask?"

"Well, I heard that sometimes pets do that. They follow their owners when they move."

Nan bit her lip. She was aware that Amber had been checking outside the back door every day, in hopes that Muffin might show up at her house.

"Sometimes they do, but I think it's pretty rare," Elliott said.

"I just don't want her to get lost."

"Well, Muffin's an awfully smart cat. I'm sure she'll be fine, sweetie."

Amber sighed again. "That's good."

They drove along in silence for a while as the skies grew lighter and a few cars and tractor trailer rigs began to appear here and there. Nan obsessively reviewed the experiments that she had left for her lab staff to work on while she was gone, hoping that she had thought of everything. Now that she had discovered the filovirus in the older cell cultures Elliott had given her, she needed to find out if the resistance factor had also been present. To do that, they still needed to finishing translating and interpreting the proteins from the triplet codons the mystery e-mailer had sent, see if they could get any clues to the function and purpose of the new, unusual proteins that Felix was crystallizing. Acutely aware that she still had not told Elliott about the filovirus, she decided that she needed to tell him. She shouldn't keep something like this from him. Especially when she had discovered the virus in public health cell cultures.

"By the way, uh, we, uh, came up with some rather odd findings in the lab yesterday," she said. "I've been meaning to talk to you about them, but everything's been so crazy, I haven't really had a chance."

Elliott threw her a sideways glance. "What's that?"

"Well, it looks as if a filovirus might be associated with the resistance factor."

"A filovirus?!" Elliott hit the brakes out of shock, causing the van to swerve.

"Careful!" Nan admonished, touching his shoulder and looking back to make sure Amber hadn't tumbled off the mattress. She seemed to have fallen back asleep, though, and hadn't budged.

"Sorry!" He regained control, driving more slowly now.

"So—yeah, that was our reaction, too. But it must be different from Ebola, even though it sort of looks like it. Because it turned up in all of our blood samples, and none of us, obviously, has Ebola."

"Jesus." Elliott shook his head in disbelief. "Unless it's some sort of Ebola with a really long latency period, like AIDS."

"Well, I suppose that's a possibility," Nan replied uncomfortably. "But we, uh, also found it in one of the cell cultures that you gave us from three years ago."

"What?!!!"

"I know. It seems impossible. But you know, there've been no recorded cases of Ebola in this country at all. So I really don't think that this virus acts like Ebola. Unless, of course, as you say, the latency period is extremely long … more than three years. Which I guess is a possibility."

Elliott swallowed dryly, making a clicking noise in his throat. "So. You were too busy to tell me this, huh?"

"All right. I didn't want you to take the project away from me," she admitted. "Which I was afraid you might do if you knew."

"You're damn right I would!" he exclaimed. "Christ, Nan, you've got something that looks like Ebola in your lab? It's essential that Public Health know about this! The CDC needs to know about this!"

"See? This is exactly why I didn't tell you!"

Elliott put on his blinker, prepared to pull over. "We've got to go back. We need to assess this. This is not okay!"

Nan folded her arms angrily. "I knew this was how you were going to react. Damn it, Elliott, whatever it is, it's everywhere! We can't stop it now. If we were going to stop it, we would have had to start years ago. It's too late now!"

Amber stirred, made a whimpering sound in her sleep.

Elliott pulled to a stop on the shoulder, rested his head on the steering wheel. "God, will this nightmare never end?" he groaned.

Nan exhaled heavily, reached over to massage his neck. "I don't know, sweetheart. All I know is, we've got to find this person we're looking for. I just can't help but feel he's the key to the whole thing."

Elliott didn't respond for a moment. Finally he muttered, "And if he's not? What then?"

"Then … we'll figure out what to do from there. I can only take it one step at a time. If I try to think about too much all at once, I get so overwhelmed I can't do anything. And that certainly won't help to solve the problem."

Elliott leaned back, looking more haggard than Nan had ever seen him. He reached for Nan's hand, held it tight. "I suppose you have a point. Everything is so upside-down right now, I feel pretty paralyzed myself. Actually, I … haven't told you everything, either."

Nan waited.

"It appears—and we can't be sure, of course—but it appears that using drugs and vaccines to combat these resistant organisms makes everything worse. The people who seem to be faring the best and surviving in the greatest numbers are the people who are using alternative methods, like herbal medicine and homeopathy. Or, even weirder, those who aren't doing anything at all."

"You can't be serious!"

Elliott nodded glumly. "Oh, but I am."

"Well, why aren't you letting people know about this? This

is certainly the first I've heard about it!"

He held up his hands, let them drop helplessly. "Well, as I say, we can't be sure. We don't want to contribute to panic or the rumor mill. And as I'm sure you are aware, every single holistic health huckster is out there preying on people, promising them everything under the sun. And the numbers are not that significant."

"I know, but still!" Nan exclaimed.

Elliott gave her a pained look. "The pharmaceutical companies have been asking us to sit on these findings. And I mean, they're right, too ... these are only preliminary findings. But I—I have to say that I agree with you. People need to know. They need to be able to make up their own minds as to what they want to do."

They both sat in silence. Finally, Elliott took off the brake, pulled back onto the highway.

"So—what are you going to do?" asked Nan.

"Drive you to California, what do you think?"

She heaved a grateful sigh of relief. "Thanks," she said.

"Hey, don't thank me," he countered. "One thing I have learned over the years is to listen to a woman's intuition."

"Oh, right," Nan responded dryly.

Soon it was time to switch drivers, so they pulled into a rest stop, Elliott checking the premises warily before turning off the engine. Only one other lone car, a dilapidated old Plymouth sedan, sat in the parking lot, the driver apparently snoozing in his seat. At least, Nan hoped that's what he was doing. She took Amber by the hand and accompanied her to the restroom, which turned out not to have any toilet paper in any of the stalls. In fact, it appeared the facility hadn't been cleaned in days and it smelled rank and sour. Fortunately, Nan had come prepared and brought their own toilet paper, which she carefully covered the seat with since no seat covers were in evidence, either. They didn't wash their hands until they returned to the van and used their own filtered water;

Elliott had heard that typhoid and vaccine-resistant polio
were starting to make appearances in different parts of the
country, apparently unaffected by the chemicals used by water
treatment plants.

Back on the road, they passed the time by singing songs
and playing "Animal, Vegetable, or Mineral?" Amber stumped
both Nan and Elliott for a long time by coming up with the
"mineral" false teeth, giggling herself silly when her father
asked, "Is it something you hang on the wall?" One of her
favorite games, spotting out-of-state license plates, didn't get
very far, as the traffic was so sparse. And almost no one was
roaming very far from home, it seemed.

When lunch came around, they once again stopped at a
rest area near Wilkes-Barre. Even if some restaurants and fast
food joints were open, they felt safer eating food that they had
prepared themselves. According to Elliott's sources, hepatitis
was running rampant everywhere. Apparently, too, many of
the recent spate of car-jackings had taken place when travelers
exited to avail themselves of services off the highway. As Nan
set out plates and cups on the picnic table, turning up the
collar of her coat against the stiff, raw wind that blew out of
the north, she couldn't help but reflect how much everything
in her day-to-day life had changed—and how quickly. She felt
as if she had stumbled into some alternate reality or fallen into
a coma herself and this was what she dreamed. The world not
only seemed deserted and spooky, it gave the weird impression
of having turned black-and-white.

They munched on tuna fish sandwiches and tortilla chips
and drank grape juice from cartons, hurrying to finish so
that they could get out of the wind. They could have eaten
inside the van, but all of them were eager to get outside in the
fresh air and move around a little bit. A few cars and a semi
straggled through the rest area while they ate, their occupants
looking shell-shocked and stooped as they trekked to the
restrooms and back. The one lively traveler turned out to be a

bushy black dog with a beautiful plume of a tail, who chased a Frisbee for a few throws, which the owner threw joylessly. Amber ran over to pet the dog, which Elliott didn't try to prevent. Amber had a way with animals and the dog looked friendly enough, Nan thought. When it was time to go, Elliott called Amber back over to the table where they carefully washed their hands again before climbing back into the van. Then they headed back onto the interstate after making a stop for gas at the next exit with services, Elliott once more in the driver's seat. Thankfully, they ran into no problems.

Once they were underway, Amber settled herself happily on the mattress with her sketch pad and some crayons, humming to herself as she worked. She had a sweet, soft little voice that soothed Nan's nerves. When she finished her picture, she duckwalked up to the front of the van and slipped into the seat behind Elliott, handing Nan her picture.

Nan turned the picture around to get a good look at it, a bit taken aback when she saw what Amber had drawn: two snakes twisted around one another like the medical profession's caduceus, practically pulsing in vivid purple, orange, red, and green.

"Well, that's a very interesting picture, honey," she told her. "Very nicely drawn!" She angled the picture so that Elliott could see it.

"Look, Dad!" Amber told him excitedly.

Elliott appeared disconcerted as well when he realized what she had depicted. "That's terrific, sweetie." He took a second look. "Where, uh, did you get the idea for that drawing?"

"I dreamed it."

"You dreamed it? Last night? Or this morning while you were napping in the van?"

Amber shook her head. "No, when I was sick. These snakes came and visited me. They were nice. They licked me with their tongues—like this." She leaned forward and darted a pointy little tongue onto her father's cheek. He chuckled, reached around behind him to pinch her on the ribs, causing her to shriek and scamper back onto the mattress.

Elliott cleared his throat. "You know, while I was recuperating at your house, I read that book you had in the stack next to your bed, *The Cosmic Serpent*. Have you read it?"

Nan shook her head. "No, I haven't had a chance. It sounded interesting, though. Why?"

"Well, the author is an anthropologist, from Switzerland, I think, although he received his PhD from Stanford."

"Uh-huh. Good book?"

"Very intriguing. He believes that humans are able to access molecular levels of information in altered states, and that this is how ancient and tribal cultures access the herbal wisdom that they use in their healing systems."

"Not through trial and error, huh?"

"No, he thinks the lore is too specific, complicated, and sophisticated for that. I'm not sure I'm completely convinced, but he made a pretty good argument, I thought. At any rate, apparently a lot of tribal cultures use hallucinogenic plants and states to obtain this information, and one of the most common images that appears to their shamen is that of a snake."

She nodded, stretched in her seat. "Yes, you see a lot of snake imagery in tribal art."

"But not just snakes. Often twin snakes. Twin, intertwined snakes."

"Like the caduceus."

"Yes. Like Amber's picture." He paused. "Remind you of anything?"

"Well, sure. DNA, of course."

"Exactly. That's what this author thinks, too."

"Very interesting. I'll have to read that book," Nan said.

"But it's not just snakes that make appearances. It's ladders, too, which also evoke DNA. And vines wrapped around one another." Elliott tapped his thumbs absentmindedly on the steering wheel.

"Weird."

"You know, August Kekulé, the German scientist who discovered the cyclical structure of benzene, first came up with the idea for the benzene ring when he dreamed of a snake whirling in front of him, biting its tail."

Nan reached for the water bottle and took a swig. "Yes, I remember hearing that story in graduate school. Actually, I get a lot of good inspiration for my experiments from my dreams. Not that I want this to get around, mind you."

Elliott grinned. "Of course not."

Nan turned to check on Amber. She was now leafing through a picture book, her doll Bessie propped on her lap, apparently sharing the book with her. "I've always liked snakes," she mused.

"So cuddly," Elliott teased.

"That's true."

Then Elliott turned serious once more. "So, Nan ..."

"Yeah?"

"How do you think you've managed to avoid this flu?"

She turned to him in mock horror. "Bite your tongue!" she scolded him. "What are you trying to do, hex me?"

"Hardly!" he replied, laughing. "I'm just curious."

She laced her fingers together in her lap, stared at them without seeing them. "I don't know. Just lucky, I guess. Knock on wood." She twisted in her seat, looking for some wood, but couldn't find anything and settled for gently rapping Elliott on the side of the head. "I'm keeping my fingers crossed. You know, if this flu follows the pattern of the 1918 epidemic, we could have a second wave."

"I'm aware of that."

"Yeah. So."

"So what?"

"So ... nothing, I guess." She smiled at him, then fell silent. She had found herself getting rather superstitious lately and

didn't want to talk about this any more. She just felt glad that
the trip had gone as uneventfully as it had so far. She hoped
they could keep it up. But then, they'd only gone a short
distance, and according to news reports, the flu epidemic,
while subsiding on either coast, was raging in the Midwest,
where they would be traveling for the next couple of days.
She hoped all that meant was that they wouldn't have much
traffic to contend with. Yet, the anxious feeling in the pit of her
stomach would not go away.

CHAPTER 18

Nan stamped her feet while waiting to use the pay phone; the sun had barely broken over the horizon, sending weak, watery rays that did nothing to warm the chill, overcast morning. The person in front of her seemed in no hurry whatsoever to relinquish the phone, which irked her. Even more irritating, the woman was obviously ignoring the pleas of the government and utility companies to restrict phone conversations to essential matters, since they were working with skeletal crews and couldn't handle normal demands on the system. Nan had tried using the cell phone, but for some reason, it wasn't working at all.

"That's right," the woman was saying. "If we act now, we can scoop up a lot of properties for practically nothing … I've got my eye on several cabins on the lake. You know a lot of them are going to be hitting the market as soon as the dust settles …"

Nan heaved an exasperated sigh, glanced behind her to see how Elliott was faring in making his way to the gas pump. Only one gas station in Salina was open, and every person in town healthy enough to be driving, as well as all the interstate traffic, had crowded into it. Fortunately, a jeep full of camouflage-clad army personnel had parked over by the convenience market, helping to maintain order, she supposed. One shouting match had already occurred while she waited, over who had gotten to a particular pump first.

"And you know that last litter of Chihuahuas we had?" the woman chattered on. "Well, two of 'em didn't make it, and the rest was all sickly. I don't know if they had the flu or what, but it sure seemed strange …"

Nan indulged in a brief fantasy of jerking the phone out of the woman's hands and smacking her on the head with it. Didn't she have a telephone at home? Finally, after what seemed like an eternity, the woman hung up and gave Nan a pinched smile before exiting the booth. Nan slipped into the cramped space, waving her arms to clear out some of the cloying perfume left behind, and dialed up the number where her mother was staying. Kristin answered. She assured her that Myra was doing just fine. She put Myra on the phone, who mainly just echoed Nan's statements but managed to gasp out that she missed her near the end of the conversation.

Touched and surprised, Nan told her that she missed her, too. She said that everything was going fine and that they hadn't run into any problems.

"Well, good," Myra said, booming out the second word.

"You stay healthy, okay? I—love you, Mom." Nan waited. She could hear her mother struggling to reply.

"I … love you," she finally burst out. As Nan depressed the lever to break the connection, she shook her head, her heart aching. Every word seemed to be such an effort for her poor mom, as if she had to use every single muscle in her body to force it out. She often wondered what would be worse: to have your mind so destroyed that you really didn't know much of what went on around you, or to have your mental faculties more or less intact, yet be unable to communicate or do anything on your own. Personally, she thought the latter might be more unbearable, but she couldn't stand to dwell on this for very long.

She then dialed the lab, anxious to know what information her staff had managed to obtain over the last couple of days. She hadn't been able to get through yesterday, when she called from their stopover in Columbus, Ohio. Columbus had been particularly hard hit with the influenza epidemic, and they had been lucky to find a motel open. They were prepared to camp, of course, but it was cold enough at night that a motel was definitely preferable, especially with Elliott and Amber still recovering from the flu. It had a tendency to linger, and lots of people had experienced relapses.

Much to her relief, this time her call went through and Joshua answered the phone. He didn't have a whole lot to report, however, which was actually unsurprising, considering not much time had passed since she left. It just felt like forever. So far, they hadn't located the resistance factor in any of the older cell cultures, but that didn't mean, of course, that it wasn't there. They had translated some of the proteins from the resistance factor genes relayed to them by the mystery e-mailer, and one of them appeared to code for a fairly common sequence that conferred bacterial resistance to erythromycin. They were double-checking these results. Apart from that, Ron had stayed away, although he had extended his bad vibe campaign to all of Nan's lab staff whenever they ran into him in the department.

"I'm starting to think his face is going to freeze into a permanent scowl," Joshua said. "In fact, I'm thinking about sneaking up on him in his sleep and getting a plaster cast for my Halloween mask this year. Only problem is, I don't really want to frighten small children. Too much, anyway."

Nan gave a hollow laugh. "If you find any nasty little dolls with pins stuck in them, let me know," she told him, wondering if she really had managed to fend Ron off or whether he was just doing his plotting more privately now. Unfortunately, his ill will seemed to have gone beyond mere greed and opportunism at this point and become more of a personal vendetta. And she didn't have the time to figure out the best way to placate him.

She returned to the van, which had finally reached an open gas pump, where Elliott stood filling the tank. She started to help him by washing the windshield, but apparently, someone had made off with the squeegee and no liquid remained in the dispenser anyway. So she settled into the driver's seat for her stretch of driving. They wanted to time their shifts so that Elliott would be driving over the Front Range in Colorado, as he had experience driving in these mountains. In fact, Elliott had an aunt and an uncle in Denver, whom they would have loved to visit if they hadn't been in such a rush to get to California. Amber had fallen back asleep after leaving the motel, which Nan was glad to see. She needed all the rest and sleep she could get. She still hadn't gained back the weight she lost during the flu. Nor had Elliott, for that matter.

Once on the road, Nan fought to stay awake herself, as the flatness and featurelessness of the landscape, relieved only occasionally by a massive silver water tower mushrooming up from the ground, proved intensely hypnotic. Elliott did his best to keep her alert, chatting about the geology of the area, which turned out to be more interesting than Nan had realized. Apparently, most of western Kansas and all of eastern Colorado represented an enormous, gargantuan, alluvial fan from the ancestral Rockies. In fact, they were driving on the remnants of the ancestral Rockies, the ancient mountain range that once rode atop the contemporary Rocky Mountains. Little by little, it had been pulverized into dust by wind and rain and washed onto the plains to the east. This was why, despite the fact that the terrain seemed utterly and monotonously flat, Denver's elevation rose to a mile above sea level from the low-lying, primordial ocean beds of eastern Kansas.

They switched off at a rest area, then drove for another two mind-numbing hours, made another switch, and then Elliott took the wheel for the ascent into the mountains. They tried to find a radio station that might give them some idea of what kind of weather to expect going over the passes, but many of them appeared to be off the air, and the ones they did manage to tune into either relied upon canned programming or merely listed closures of schools and businesses and cancellations of events.

When they first spotted the Rockies—a tantalizing smudge upon the horizon that looked more like foam than mountains—everyone perked up, glad for something to occupy their attention. But as they drew closer, it became clear that the reason for the frothy appearance of the Front Range was a huge bank of clouds that hugged the mountaintops. They debated whether they should stop in Denver and see if they could stay with Elliott's aunt and uncle; but they would reach Denver by two o'clock or earlier, and they had hoped to make it as far as Grand Junction by evening.

"We could stop today, but there's really no way of knowing whether the weather will improve tomorrow," Elliott observed. "This time of year, the mountain passes are always unpredictable. In fact, I've run into snow squalls in August going over Vail pass."

"People drive in these mountains in the snow year round, don't they?" Nan asked.

"Sure! How do you think the ski industry stays alive?"

"That's what I thought."

"We'll just take it easy. No need to rush."

Amber leaned forward in her seat. "There's going to be snow?" she exclaimed delightedly.

"Quite possibly," Elliott replied.

Amber gave a squeal of excitement. "Maybe we can stop and build a snowman!"

"We'll see," said Elliott.

"Or at least, a snow baby," she amended, making Nan smile.

"Surely we can scrape together a snowball, if nothing else," she promised, giving her a squeeze on the knee.

They stopped at a park outside of Denver for lunch: cream cheese and olive sandwiches, one of Amber's favorites, and apples they had brought with them from home. The weather in Denver was sunny and somewhat mild, but the gusts of wind that blew from the mountains felt and smelled wintry. Elliott claimed he could taste snow in the wind, which Nan seriously doubted but didn't contest. Before they took off, he sat Amber down and told her that as much fun as snow could be to play in, driving in snow was a completely different matter. She needed to be quiet and stay still in her seat if they ran into a storm.

"If we have a chance to stop and play a little, we will," he said; "but we might not be able to. We might need to keep driving to stay safe. Is that clear?"

She nodded solemnly. In fact, she seemed subdued as they began their ascent. A couple of does standing on the side of the road got her excited again, however, and when a coyote dashed across the highway, she was back to her bubbly self. When the first flakes of snow began to sift down upon them from the clouds, she plastered her face against her window, then rolled it down and attempted to catch some on her tongue.

"Brrrr, sweetie—could you please roll your window up?" Nan asked her.

Obligingly, she complied. Nan could tell she was having hard time remaining still, though. She twisted around in her seat, scooted forward and back, looking for more animals.

It wasn't long before the flakes got bigger, falling in soft, moisture-laden clumps that hit the windshield with an icy splat. Elliott geared down and turned up the windshield wipers.

"You have your seatbelt on nice and snug, don't you, sweetheart?" he inquired.

"Yup," Amber answered, sliding back and tugging on her

belt.

"That's good." He tightened his grip on the steering wheel. Snow began falling harder; he turned on his lights.

"Man, it's really coming down, isn't it?" Nan commented— uselessly, she knew, but she was started to feel nervous herself.

Elliott didn't respond. He eased off even more on his speed, until they were driving little more than twenty-five miles an hour. Soon, the snow had thickened to near white-out conditions. It reflected the headlights so blindingly that Elliott tried turning them off at one point, but then they were engulfed in a well of snow-induced darkness. Drifts began piling up across the road and before long, snow was blowing sideways with a disconcerting ferocity.

"I'm getting off at the next exit," Elliott informed them tersely.

"That's a good idea," Nan concurred, trying to sound calm. She couldn't keep from clutching the dashboard, though. She glanced back at Amber and saw that she was staring out the windows, her eyes round with either wonder or fear, Nan couldn't be sure which. When she turned back around and looked ahead, she realized that she could no longer see the road. She hoped Elliott knew where he was going. It would have been nice to have some tail lights in front of them to follow, but if any other vehicles occupied the road, the snow had effectively swallowed them up.

"Maybe—we should just pull over until the snow lets up," Nan gulped.

Elliott flicked a glance at the shoulder, and at that precise moment, a large buck bolted from the opposite side of the road, directly in front of them. Instinctively, he slammed on the brakes, but it was too late. They plowed into the deer, which flew into the air, causing Amber to scream. Then they began fishtailing.

"Hold on!" Elliott yelled, trying to get the van under control. It was no use. They slid helplessly sideways down the road, then careened into a gully. Snow flew everywhere, rushing past the windows like the wake of a huge ship.

When they finally came to a halt, after several long, agonizing minutes, no one moved or spoke. Then Elliott tore off his seat belt and whipped around to face Amber.

"Are you okay, honey?" he demanded, his voice shaking.

Amber burst into tears.

He squeezed himself into the space next to her seat, anxiously running his hands over her arms and legs. "Can you breathe? Does anything hurt? Can you speak?"

An incoherent rush of words tumbled out in between sobs, but the general gist seemed to be that she was okay. Elliott unbuckled her seatbelt and crushed her to his chest.

"It's okay, sweetheart, we're okay. We just slid off the road. Nobody's hurt, so we're okay."

"What about the deer?" she bawled.

"I think he ran off, sweetie," Nan said, trembling violently from adrenalin. "We weren't really going all that fast when we hit him."

"Are you sure?" she wailed.

"Yes, I'll—I'll get out and look," she said, unfastening her own seatbelt and reaching for the door. Elliott seized her arm.

"Wait!" he warned. "Let's make sure we know where we've stopped before anyone gets out."

"Right, right." Nan ran a hand over her face, trying to steady her nerves. Elliott peered out the windows, but unfortunately, he said, he couldn't really see much. "Well, I'll just open the door and look out," she told him.

"Okay. Just be careful."

"I will." Cautiously, she opened the door as far as she could, which turned out to be a couple of inches. "That won't work," she commented crisply.

Climbing into the driver's seat, she opened that door. It swung open all the way, so she stuck her head out to make sure they weren't on the highway or teetering on the edge of a cliff.

"We, uh, appear to be wedged firmly in a snow bank at the bottom of a ditch," she reported.

"Great," Elliott muttered.

"Hey, it could be worse." Nan had glimpsed some pretty spectacular drop-offs before the snow had become so heavy. Just thinking about them caused her bones to tingle in a strange and painful way.

Amber's sobs had subsided and she was now breathing in hiccups and gasps while Elliott stroked her back, making comforting noises. Nan shut the door and sat staring into the snow for a few moments. Then she roused herself. The van was tipped at a little bit of an angle, but it really wasn't too bad. She rolled down her window, lit the heater they'd brought, then set up the cook stove. It was too early for dinner, but she heated up some water for chamomile tea, thinking everyone's nerves could use some soothing. Elliott dug around in their stores and produced a bottle of Jack Daniels, from which he took a couple of slugs, then offered it to Nan, who accepted. Elliott tried calling out on the cell phone, without much hope because of the storm and the mountains; his instincts proved correct.

"I guess we might as well just relax," he observed morosely; "looks like we're spending the night here."

"If the snow lets up, maybe some emergency vehicles will come through. If we're not too far off the road, maybe they'll see us," Nan said.

"Yeah, maybe."

Amber looked up at her dad, his dejected tone not lost on her. "Are we going to be okay, Dad?" she asked in a small, pitiful voice.

Elliott closed his eyes, put his arm around her and hugged her to his side. "Sure we are, honey. We'll just be camping out."

"That's fun, right?"

"Sure is!" he declared, making a valiant effort to sound hearty.

"I'll bet Bessie could use some tea," Nan offered.

"Yeah! Poor Bessie, she was really scared!"

Amber clambered into the back of the van to fetch
Bessie and pretended to share her cup with her doll. Nan
and Elliott decided to fix an early dinner and then they all
played Old Maid around the heater, which also functioned
as a lantern. When it came time to go to bed, however, they
turned the heater off, to protect against both fire danger and
carbon monoxide poisoning. They rolled up the windows
and snuggled up close in their sleeping bags, Amber in the
middle. The van felt fairly cozy when they drifted off to sleep.
Their sleeping bags were designed to keep them warm down to
twenty degrees Fahrenheit; but in the middle of the night, the
storm blew past and the temperature plummeted. Nan awoke
from the cold, her feet and ears absolutely freezing. Amber
seemed to be shivering in her sleep. She shook Elliott by the
shoulder.

"Elliott, wake up," she said.

"Mmh, what?"

"Wake up, Elliott. It's freezing in here."

He bolted upright, looking confused and disoriented.
"What?"

"I'm going to turn the heater on for a little while. You
might want to rub Amber's arms, warm her up a little."

Elliott pulled his daughter close and began chafing her
arms, which awakened her.

"Where are we?" she mumbled plaintively.

"We're camping out, remember?"

She whimpered. "I'm cold," she said.

"I know, honey," Nan replied. "I'm putting the heater back
on to warm things up."

"My ears hurt."

Elliott and Nan exchanged stricken glances. Nan reached
into a pile of hats and coats and grabbed a wool watch cap.
"Here, put this on."

Elliott took the cap and snugged it down over her ears,

breathing on them through the yarn to warm them up even faster. Tears trickled down Amber's cheeks.

"I'm scared, Daddy," she wept.

"We're okay, sweetheart. We're just fine."

"I'm cold. I want to go home," she responded, her voice quivering.

Elliott squeezed her tight. "We can't go home right now, baby. I'm afraid we're stuck, at least for the night."

Amber began to sob. "I want to go home!" she repeated.

"Shhh, we can't go home right now. But as soon as you warm up, you'll feel better."

"I miss Muffin!" she cried.

Tears crowded into Nan's eyes. This scenario was exactly why she had feared bringing Elliott and Amber along. She should have listened to her instincts, she thought wearily. On the other hand, she certainly was glad that she hadn't been the one driving in this storm and that she wasn't by herself right now. Still, she felt so guilty and responsible, she could hardly bear it.

"Sh-sh-shh," Elliott murmured. "It's okay. We'll be okay. And when we get back, if you want, maybe we could get a puppy."

"I want Muffinnnnnnnnnn," she moaned.

Nan hunched in her seat, blowing on her hands to warm them, feeling absolutely miserable. Morning couldn't come fast enough, but she didn't want to look at her watch, for fear that day break was hours away. She just hoped that the van was okay, that they would be able to get out of this ditch tomorrow, and that they could continue their journey.

As a fierce wind howled and skirled around the van, however, causing it to buck and shudder, she fought to maintain her emotional equilibrium. Amber continued to cry in her father's arms, and it was so damned cold, the heater seemed hardly to make a dent, as if they were huddled around a single lit match. If ever there was a time in her life to believe in prayer, this was it. So she prayed. But she couldn't help feeling that, like the faint warmth in their small enclosure, her prayers were evaporating into the vast, frigid, impersonal darkness.

CHAPTER 19

When the sun finally rose the next morning, it illumined
a world of heart-stopping beauty. Massive, impossibly high
peaks stretched away from them in every direction, peaks
clearly sculpted, gouged out, even tortured by glaciers, the
brutal edges softened by vast amounts of billowing, dazzling
white snow. The pine trees which surrounded the van bore so
much snow Nan couldn't believe that they were able to stand
under the weight; they looked almost like a confection instead
of a forest. And the inside of the van's windows had frosted
over during the night, creating a lovely abstract, etched-glass
appearance and reminding Amber of the windowpanes made
of sugar in the wicked old witch's gingerbread house.

Their spirits rose, too, the brighter and warmer it became,
and Elliott decided that perhaps now was the time to build a
snowman. The engine had started just fine when he had tried
it, but they weren't going anywhere until someone came along
to pull them out of the ditch. Nan used the small shovel that
they had brought with them to start digging the van out of
the snow bank they'd wedged themselves into—perhaps even
helped create with their out-of-control slide last night—while
Elliott and Amber staggered around in the deep snow, rolling

up balls of it to serve as the head, thorax, and bottom of the snowman.

It wasn't long, though, before she heard the welcome scraping roar of a large snowplow coming down the highway. She struggled up to the shoulder of the road, waving her arms to get the driver to stop. When he rounded the curve and spotted her, he geared down and then came to a gradual stop beside her, leaving his engine running. Nan stepped up onto the running board.

"What can I do for you, ma'am?" the driver asked.

"Well, I'm afraid that my family and I ran off the road last night and our van is stuck in the ditch." She pointed down the side of the hill.

The driver peered in the direction she was pointing and clucked his tongue. "Man, are you ever lucky," he said, not exactly what she was expecting to hear. Still, looking around at the various possibilities of where they could have ended up, she knew he was right.

"Is there any way you can get ahold of someone who can help us get out?"

He nodded. "When I get off at Vail, I'll send a tow truck out for you. It'll probably be a little while, though."

"I understand," said Nan. "Thanks."

He saluted and put the snowplow into gear while Nan jumped back onto the shoulder and floundered down the hillside to where Elliott and Amber had stopped work to observe her conversation. She let them know that help was on the way and then went back to digging. By the time she was finished, Elliott and Amber had completed their snowman, creating a fellow who resembled the Green Man of Celtic folklore, with brilliant emerald tree moss for hair, dark gray rocks for eyes, a roguishly crooked stick for his mouth, and a bulbous, bristling pine cone for his nose.

They had already munched down a light breakfast by the time the tow truck arrived to haul them out of the gully, but when they drove into Vail for gas, they decided that they would stop for a meal, too. Elliott reasoned that such an upscale community would have the hepatitis threat well under hand, and besides, after such a cold and arduous night, he thought they could all use a boost. Spookily, however, most of the restaurants were closed, due to influenza, said signs on the doors which had notices, and very few people walked or even drove on the streets. But they managed to find a nice, cozy cafe that served delicious waffles and omelets, as well as steaming, fragrant cups of hot chocolate and strong coffee. And as Elliott predicted, they did feel much better when they got back on the road, all toasty and warmed up, inside and out.

Fortunately, the weather remained clear and sunny as they continued on their drive, and after Vail summit, they didn't encounter any passes nearly as high. Soon, the alpine winter wonderland gave way to a drier, lower, more exotic frontier landscape, at least as far as Nan was concerned, since she had never been west of the Mississippi. The terrain began to resemble the settings for the classic Westerns that she had watched as a child: sage brush and chaparral, intriguing rock formations starkly exposed, as their strata bore practically no vegetative cover whatsoever. The only thing that masked the colorful cakelike layers of rock were unstable shale layers that disintegrated and slid down the sides of ridges.

When they pulled into the Grand Junction area, Nan felt a strange discomfort, as the sterile, foreboding Book Cliffs preceded them into town. Somber slate gray buttes extended broodingly into the far distance, their slopes so friable and crumbly that they resembled colossal piles of dark sand with a flat, impassive cap on top. No plant could manage to establish a foothold on such a substrate, so nothing grew there. Nan shivered, trying to ward off the premonition that someday the entire planet might feel that empty and indifferent toward life.

Putting the area behind them cheered her up considerably, even though once they passed into Utah, they drove through

equally inhospitable badlands. The colors became more varied
and striking, however, the formations more unusual and
enchanting; to her, this scenery seemed filled with grandeur
rather than menace. Obviously the surrounding mountains
had received quite a bit of snow from the same storm system
that had clobbered them in the Rockies, but the roads on the
basin floor were plowed and clear, and only a few high cirrus
clouds washed across the deepening indigo sky.

They decided to stop for the night once they reached
Interstate 15, which ran north/south from Arizona to Utah.
Finding an open motel proved more difficult than they had
anticipated, but finally they located a Motel Six with its lights
on and its "Vacancy" sign glowing. The diminishment of night
lighting in settled areas because of the need to save power was
turning out to be one of the most unnerving aspects of the
flu epidemic. Nan had always thought that the modern world
had far too many bright lights burning into the night, but now
the subdued flicker of urban centers seemed to symbolize the
flagging, precarious health of the human race.

Exhausted from the events of the night before, they ate
a simple dinner in their room and turned in early. Everyone
slept like the dead until early morning, when the first rays of
light awakened Nan and Elliott and prodded them to get up
and keep moving. They had already lost a day by running off
the road in Colorado. After breakfast, they began their search
for an open gas station. To their consternation, they discovered
that gas was being rationed in this part of Utah.

Nervously assuring themselves that they would find more
gas along the way, they took a place in line and waited for their
turn at a gas pump. Nan tried once more to use the phone to
call her mother and the lab, but she kept getting a busy signal
on her cell phone, and several people waited in line for the pay
phone. So instead, she paced outside the van while Elliott crept
forward. Finally, they reached the pump where they could
obtain their allotment. A tall, weathered young man wearing a

cowboy hat, boots, and rodeo championship belt buckle stood filling his tank across from them. He tipped his hat at Nan while she attempted to use the credit card machine.

"I don't think that works, ma'am," he told her.

"Oh, thanks," she said, peering into her purse to see how much cash she had on hand.

"You heading up north?"

"Well, west, actually."

"I hope you're not planning on going on I-80," he said.

"We—were thinking about it. Is something going on up there?"

He nodded. His dispenser clicked off, so he replaced the nozzle then screwed down his gas cap. "Bad outbreak of The Plague. They've cordoned off parts of I-80."

"Bubonic Plague?"

"One and the same."

Elliott climbed out of the car to help with the gas. "Everything okay?" he asked.

Nan turned to him. "This man says that parts of I-80 are closed. Bubonic Plague. I guess they're attempting a quarantine."

The car behind the man began to honk. Elliott whipped around and glared at the driver, held up his hand to plead for patience. "I'd better go pay for the gas," he said. "You stay here to pump, okay?"

"Sure." Nan returned her attention to the cowboy, who had gotten into his car to move his vehicle out of the way. "This is kind of late in the year for Plague to be spreading. Do they know where it's coming from?"

"California, they think," he said, starting up the engine with a roar.

"Oh, great," she muttered, her heart sinking.

When they got back in the van, Nan and Elliott conferred briefly on the best route to take west. I-80 had been their preferred itinerary, as it was an interstate and it took them more or less directly to the Bay Area in California. Going south on I-15 through Las Vegas would take them out of their way and add considerably more miles to their trip. They finally decided on Highway 50, as it cut directly across Nevada, and Elliott felt confident that they would find the gas they needed somewhere along the way.

"Highway 50 is well traveled, I'm sure of it," he said. "It's probably practically an interstate itself. And if I-80 is closed, a lot of people are going to be driving on 50. It's actually even less mileage from here than taking 80."

Nan felt apprehensive about taking 50, but she didn't have any better ideas. Besides, Elliott was the one who had experience out West, even though he had never driven from Colorado to California himself. He had always flown when he traveled to the West Coast from Massachusetts.

They picked up the highway a few exits north and once again headed west across high, mountainous desert. Nan thought that she had never, ever seen such lonely country as that in western Utah, but that was before they entered Nevada. The colors became darker and more muted, and the massive basin-and-range loomed silently in front of them, seemingly endless. The mountains here seemed to be slowly swallowing themselves up with their own run-off; in some places, only the very tip-top peeked out of a powdery, lunar-looking basin. Nan's heart went out to the pioneers who traversed this alien environment on foot or in wagons; it frightened her now, racing across it at eighty miles an hour. The landscape represented the very antithesis of homey New England, where humans nestled their houses up against one another in populous neighborhoods and clumped together in the shaggy, sheltering forests like hamsters.

Half of the settlements they passed—comprised mainly of a truck stop and a handful of slumping shacks—looked like ghost towns, appearing as if they had been abandoned way before the epidemic. And despite the closure of Interstate 80, they drove two hours before they saw another car, coming the other direction. They saw no open gas stations, not even in Ely, a good-sized town. Elliott thought that they could make it to Austin, where he figured at least one gas station would be operating, but forty miles outside of Austin, the van used up the last dregs of gas and quit running. Coasting over to the shoulder, Elliott guided the van to a safe place and then parked.

Everyone sat for a moment, staring straight ahead as if they were still driving. Nan cleared her throat and said, "I guess this is why there's no one on this road."

Elliott didn't reply. He reached for the cell phone, took out his AAA card and punched in the 800 number listed; but apparently, no one answered. Furiously, he yanked the door open and walked over to the brush at the side of the road. Before Nan realized what he was doing, he had thrown the cell phone as far as he could. She unbuckled her seat belt and scrambled out of the van.

"For Christ's sake, Elliott!" she yelled. "What did you do that for?"

He turned, his eyes smoldering in a way that scared her. "Because it gives us false hope, that's why!" he shouted back, gesturing violently, choppily. "It makes us think that we might, just might be able to get ourselves out of this mess. Which we won't! This whole, goddamned, stupid trip is fucking pointless! We're never going to figure this thing out! The earth has turned against us, and we might as well accept it—we're the goddamned dinosaurs and dodos of the 21st Century and we should just go down gracefully, goddamn it!"

Nan glanced back at the van, hoping that Amber couldn't hear what her father was saying, but pretty sure that she could. "This is not the time to give up, Elliott," she replied quietly. "We're this close to California." She pinched a small increment of air between her thumb and finger. "We'll just wait until a car comes by. We'll flag them down and get them to call AAA for us when they get into the next town."

"Right," he snapped. "One of the thousands of cars that we've passed on this road."

"Well, I'm sure at least one car will come by sometime in the next day or so."

"I'm glad you're so sure. Because I'm not."

Nan sighed, leaned against the door of the van. "Come on, Elliott. This is a major east-west thoroughfare. 80's closed. Someone is bound to come this way. If nothing else, we can send up a flare."

"Oh, good. The coyote brigade ought to be a lot of help. They can piss into the gas tank and we can drive the rest of the way to California on coyote pee."

Nan folded her arms, unsure what to say next. The back door to the van opened then and Amber climbed out. Both adults stared at her awkwardly. Clutching Bessie under one arm, she walked over to her dad and pressed her head against his hip.

"Don't be scared, Daddy," she said.

His face contorted with emotion, Elliott reached down to squeeze her shoulder. "I'm sorry, sweetheart. You're right," he choked.

Amber leaned back to look up at him. "Bessie said she would help."

"That's—great, honey. Bessie's—always been a big help."

Amber's expression contained such a heart-wrenching mixture of fear, courage, concern, sorrow, and earnestness that Nan found herself blinking back tears. She stepped forward and snatched up both Amber and Elliott in an embrace. They stood holding one another for quite some time.

Wiping her eyes, Nan finally disentangled herself and said, "I don't know about anyone else, but I'm starving. It's way past lunch time according to my stomach clock."

Elliott and Amber both seized gladly upon this suggestion, so they put together a picnic on the side of the road, the sharp smell of sagebrush filling the air. Afterward, they all fanned out into the brush to see if they could locate the cell phone. Amber's sharp eyes finally detected it sticking halfway out of a hole dug in the ground by some kind of creature. It almost looked as if whatever animal it was had tried to drag the phone down into its burrow; she called for them to come look before she picked it up.

"Maybe a pack rat," suggested Elliott, amused. He fished it out with a stick, then wiped it down with a paper towel and some alcohol back at the van.

Two more hours passed, and still there was no sign of any cars coming in either direction. Neither Nan nor Elliott voiced their fears, but they both knew that several remote communities had been entirely wiped out in the 1918 influenza epidemic, once the flu had finally reached them. Nan wasn't sure that even if they could get to Austin whether they would find any gas there. Not to mention the fact that the specter of a Bubonic Plague epidemic scared the hell out of her. She had thought that the problem in California couldn't be as bad as the media had made it out—the ghoulish glee they took in every dire situation had always annoyed the hell out of her—but the closure of I-80 and eerie emptiness of Nevada made her fear she was wrong.

When another hour had passed, with still no traffic, Nan decided to shoot off one of their flares. Elliott didn't say anything, but she could tell he thought it was futile. A half-hour later, however, she thought she spied a cloud of dust making its way across the barren wasteland behind them. She brought it to Elliott's attention and the three of them stood outside the van and watched it snake along until it apparently ran into the highway. Now that her flare seemed to have drawn someone's notice, Nan uncomfortably contemplated the possibility that whomever they had attracted might not be a person they wanted to meet.

It took a long time for the vehicle to become visible on

the road. As it came closer, Nan saw that it was a old, beat-up pick-up truck of an American make. It rattled as it came to a stop behind them, and the man who got out looked to her like a caricature of an old miner in a Humphrey Bogart movie. He wore a hat even more battered than his truck, his Adam's apple stuck out so much it looked like a growth, and his grizzled gray beard seemed to grow only on the bottom of his chin and jaw.

"You folks in trouble?" he asked.

"We've run out of gas," said Elliott, with a friendly nod. "I'm Elliott. Thanks for stopping."

The man nodded back and said, "Pleased to meet ya. My name's Joe." He checked out the van, rubbing his chin. "How big a tank you got?"

"I—I think about twenty gallons or so. Maybe a little more."

"Get good gas mileage?"

"Pretty good, for a van. About twenty miles to the gallon, usually."

Joe nodded again, then turned to his truck. "I've got saddlebags on this puppy," he told them, confusing Nan for a second until she realized he was talking about gas tanks. "Each one of 'em holds twenty gallons. So I can siphon one of 'em into your tank."

"Wow, that's really generous!" exclaimed Nan. "But what about you? There's no gas for miles and miles. We don't want to be responsible for getting you stranded."

He chuckled. "Can't happen. I got my own gas pump on my ranch."

"Ah," she replied.

He motioned them out of the way while he maneuvered his truck into position and then set up his siphoning device, a mechanized pump that swiftly and efficiently transferred the contents of his tank to theirs. When he finished, they thanked him profusely and Elliott tried to pay him for the gas, but he refused.

"I got all the money I can use and then some," he said. "I'm just happy to help you folks out. This should be plenty to get you to Reno."

He bent down to tousle Amber's hair, and she gave him an incredibly winning smile, which seemed literally to inflate him. His chest swelled as he stood up and he practically walked on his tiptoes to his truck. They giggled over this as they got back on the highway, themselves buoyed by his good Samaritanism. Nan reflected that one thing she had discovered on this trip was that the epidemic violence portrayed by the media had been exaggerated. Just about everyone they had encountered in a time of need had been helpful and kind.

The rest of the trip passed quickly, and even though it was late when they arrived in Reno, they decided to push on to California. They were too close to stop now, so they let Amber sleep snuggled down with her dolls and stuffed animals on the mattress while they gassed up and bought large coffees for the road. Nan viewed the Sierra that rose sharply and steeply before them with trepidation, not only fearing another storm, but fretting over what lay on the other side. A significant mountain range still, even in this day and age, represented an effective barrier for disease and all kinds of other things. I-80 was open into California, surprisingly, although it had check-points along the way, according to the cashier at the gas station. Californians didn't believe in quarantines, she had said with a sniff, although Nan couldn't tell whether she disapproved of Californians or quarantines. Perhaps, she thought, illness of so many kinds had become so pervasive, that they had given up. And the economy depended on some transit. On the other hand, perhaps they decided to rely entirely on people's desire to cooperate. She mentally rehearsed her spiel for any officers at checkpoints: They were public health workers pursuing a critical lead.

As they began their ascent into the mountains, Nan bolstered her spirits by telling herself that if California was allowing travel into the state, the situation couldn't be too horrendous. Still, even without The Plague to worry about, there were plenty of other concerns, such as the mystery e-mailer. Would they actually find the person? And if they did, what if he or she was insane, a dangerous, volatile sociopath capable of murder? The person had gone to great lengths to keep his identity secret. Surely he wouldn't be delighted to have her appear on his doorstep. Right now, she felt more relieved than ever that Elliott had insisted upon coming along. But what about Amber? How would they keep her safe if Elliott accompanied her to confront this person? Was confronting him even the best thing to do?

Nan briefly imagined breaking into this person's living quarters and rifling through his stuff, trying to get access to secret files stored on his computer. It wasn't exactly her style, and what if he had the place booby-trapped for just such an eventuality? Elliott was right, she wasn't some sort of hardboiled gumshoe. She had no skills to handle this situation properly.

She anxiously swallowed the last of her coffee. The fact that the pass they must cross, Donner Summit, was named after the ill-fated group of pioneers who had resorted to cannibalism in order to survive their encounter with these mountains didn't exactly comfort her. And in contemplating the enormity of the task she faced, Nan found herself becoming practically paralyzed with misgiving.

CHAPTER 20

The closer they drew to the Bay Area, the more
apprehensive Nan felt. They had managed to make it over
Donner Summit with no problems—just a few light snow
flurries—but if anything, California was feeling more deserted
than Nevada. When they drove past Sacramento, Nan received
the sense of a hugely sprawling city, but only a few lights
served as lonely beacons in the distance: a winking red light
atop a tower, a handful of scattered, dim house lights here and
there. Granted, it was late. They passed by close to midnight,
but still, not only did the blackness feel unnerving, the lack
of traffic seemed downright sinister. Normally, even at this
time of night, plenty of cars and trucks must traverse the I-80
corridor.

Was this what the East Coast had to look forward to? The
epidemic had started a bit earlier in the West. She and Elliott
had tried to get national news as they traveled, from the TV
sets in their motel rooms and from NPR stations as they
drove; but the national news infrastructure appeared to have
broken down since they left. Often they couldn't find the NPR
stations; perhaps they had gone off the air. The only news they
could find on television was local news, if that. Usually, they

were treated to canned programming, and several TV stations were also on the blink, both cable and network. Newspapers had shut down production overnight, it seemed. Nan hadn't seen a newspaper since they left home. She was beginning to comprehend how civilizations died, how they crumbled into ruins and memories, lost information and technology; she wondered how many ancient civilizations which disappeared mysteriously had disease to thank for their demise. Wars and battles had certainly been lost because of it, the course of history affected drastically and catastrophically time and time again.

When they crested the final hill that hid the Bay Area from view, the sight that confronted them looked both supernally beautiful and grotesquely unnatural: the entire Bay Area lay cloaked in an umbra of suffocating, lightless gloom, except for the lighted bridges, around which sinuous tentacles of fog had coiled. The glow illuminated both the bridges and the fog as they spanned the darkness, giving the impression that they led into the land of the fairies, a never-never land where sickness was an illusion and suffering only a dream.

Driving into Berkeley made it clear, however, that sickness was no illusion. As Nan and Elliott roamed the streets looking for an open hotel, they saw several bodies in tightly sealed bags carried out of houses by respirator-clad workers and carefully lifted into the backs of vans, trucks, and station wagons. These vehicles had some sort of logo stenciled onto the side, but it was difficult to see what it said without more illumination than just their headlights. After an hour went by and they hadn't found a single place to stay, they decided just to park on the street and spend the night in the van. They relieved themselves in an overgrown clump of tall bushes that separated two big houses and then crawled into bed with Amber.

Nan awoke early, feeling anxious and tense. She peered out the window at the street, expecting to see more activity in the light of day—an oddly gray, flat, shadowless dawn, she noted.

But instead, it was like a replay of the middle of the night: streets deserted and lifeless except for the respirator-outfitted workers who went into houses and sometimes emerged with a body in a bag, sometimes several bodies, then drove away to some unknown destination. Shivering, she pulled on a sweatshirt and then laced up her shoes, moving quietly so as not to wake Amber or Elliott. She eased herself out of the van onto the street, shutting the door silently behind her as she appraised their surroundings.

The neighborhood reminded her a little bit of New England, actually, with its grand old houses sporting dormer windows and circular towers, wide porches and gabled roofs. The flora, however, looked completely different. The tall, wind-ruffled palm trees that dotted the yards, as well as the riot of tangled, flowering vines and bushes, made her feel disoriented. Even the conifers looked foreign, Asian somehow, and they grew with a dense luxuriance that seemed unreal. Eucalyptus trees exuded pungent terpenes that mixed with the acrid scent of disinfectant.

Strolling to the end of the street, she came upon a telephone pole plastered with flyers, and although most of them had undoubtedly been placed there before the epidemic—advertisements for rock concerts, drumming circles, and poetry readings—one clearly related to the situation at hand. "BUBONIC PLAGUE!" trumpeted the headline, in scary, gothic lettering dripping with inky blood:

"Residents of Berkeley are hereby advised that following the influenza epidemic, we are in the grip of a deadly Bubonic Plague outbreak. Bubonic Plague is initially passed to humans by infected fleas, but once it is in the human population, it can be communicated through mucous droplets by coughing, sneezing, even talking. IT CAN BE PASSED THROUGH THE AIR AND BY CASUAL CONTACT!!!

"Therefore, we ask that you follow these precautions: Unless you have work directly pertaining to those activities that are involved in day-to-day survival, such as food production and distribution, medical care, maintenance of emergency communications networks, etc., PLEASE STAY IN YOUR HOME! If you have an emergency or are ill with either influenza or Bubonic Plague, call 911, 811, 711, or 611 and report your situation. Emergency workers will be dispatched to provide you with medical assistance, food and clean water, or body disposal.

"Keep all interaction with others to an absolute minimum. When you do go out, it is advised that you wear a mask and latex gloves. Keep pets outside. Periodic spraying for fleas will be conducted in all neighborhoods, and we ask that you not attempt to interfere with this activity. We understand your environmental concerns and we will do everything in our power to minimize the amount of toxic substances to which the citizens of Berkeley are exposed. We need everyone's cooperation to make it through this terrible scourge.

"Please report any activities that you feel might contribute to the spread of disease to this office." It was signed, "Citizens' Public Health Alliance, Berkeley."

Nan started shaking halfway through reading this announcement, and by the time she reached the end, she was trembling violently. She had to suppress the urge to run back to the van, paranoically imagining plague-infected fleas leaping, if not swarming onto her ankles and clothing. What the notice didn't say, but she knew from her conversations with Elliott, was that antibiotics were proving useless against this disease.

Returning to the van, she found both Elliott and Amber awake. She reported the contents of the flyer to them, trying to minimize the gravity of the situation so as not to frighten Amber. But she thought it made sense for all of them to apply insect repellent and she recommended that they don surgical masks and gloves when they went outside, both for protection and to avoid getting reported. After gulping down a quick bowl of granola, they started up the van to begin their search for the hacker. Nan's hopes that they might be able to purchase a street map of Berkeley began to fade as they drove down street after street without finding a single establishment open for business. Finally, however, they came upon a health food store called The Berkeley Bowl that had its doors open. Slipping on a mask and gloves, Nan went in to see if they had maps, which they didn't, but she couldn't resist picking up some tempting-looking groceries to supplement their dwindling stores. She asked the young man at the check-out stand whether he knew the street that she was looking for, and to her relief, he did have an idea. He gave her sketchy directions, which turned out to be good enough to locate the place after they wandered around a bit.

Finding parking near the address which afforded them a view of the house without putting them too close for comfort proved a bit of a challenge, too. No one seemed to be moving their cars. But at one point while they were circling the block, an emergency medical vehicle vacated a spot across the street, which they eased into.

"So, the address I have is 2243A," Nan remarked, squinting at the brass numbers that were tacked above the front door. "This address says 2243. No 'A.'"

"Maybe the house is divided up into apartments," suggested Elliott.

"Yeah, that's probably it. I wonder if they all use the same entrance."

"I suppose we could go up and look."

Nan bit her lip, considering. "I just don't want to scare the person off," she said. "If we start nosing around, won't that look suspicious?"

Elliott shot her an appraising glance. "Well, you're going to have to try to get in touch with this person sooner or later. We can go up to the front door, see if there's more than one apartment here, and if someone is listed as residing in 2243A, we can just ring the doorbell and see if they're home. Looks like there's a foyer that might serve as a lobby for several apartments."

"True," Nan replied tentatively. Now that the time had come, she was feeling extremely nervous.

"Ready?" asked Elliott.

Nan hugged her elbows. "Sure." She gazed at the house, a three-story edifice covered in wood shingles. "Wait—I think someone's coming out."

They watched as a young woman wearing a surgical mask opened the front door and trotted down the front steps. She continued down the sidewalk at a brisk pace. Nan and Elliott observed her until she disappeared from view.

"Now?" Elliott prodded.

"Sure." Nan swallowed, her stomach churning.

Elliott turned to Amber. "We're going up to that house to see if someone we need to find is living there, sweetie. You stay here in the van, okay?"

"No, I want to come!"

"Honey, it's not a good idea. You'll be safe here in the van."

Amber flounced down unhappily on the mattress.

"Lock all the doors after we leave, okay? And don't open them for anyone. We'll take our keys and let ourselves back in."

She nodded, her face crumpling as she struggled not to cry. Elliott put his arms around her and gave her a squeeze.

"Don't worry, sweetheart," he told her. "We'll only be a minute. You stay here with Bessie and take good care of her."

As they walked across the street, Nan couldn't shake the feeling that every single person on the block was watching them from the darkened windows, even though she saw nothing that would suggest such surveillance. When they got to the door of 2243 and peered inside the foyer, they did find a little lobby, so they tried the door, which turned out to be open. However, when they checked the half-dozen names posted next to individual doorbells, they didn't find 2243A.

They found 2243B, C, D, E, and F. But no A.

"Well, that's weird," said Nan.

"Must be a separate entrance."

"Oh, yeah."

"In back, maybe."

"Right."

They exited the foyer, walked up the driveway, and spotted the entrance to 2243A on the side of the house. Before Nan could say or do anything, Elliott had gone up to the door and pressed the buzzer. Nan waited in stricken silence, but no one responded. They waited a full five minutes, Elliott trying the buzzer once more. They could hear its vespish hum sounding faintly inside, but still no one came.

"What now?" asked Elliott.

"Let's go back to the van and wait. Maybe they're out."

They ensconced themselves once more in the van, watching as a handful of people left their homes here and there, all wearing masks and gloves. Most of them appeared to be getting around on foot or bikes, but a few got into cars and drove away. Emergency workers showed up occasionally, delivering food and medical supplies, carrying out bodies. It was all quite orderly and subdued, but Nan felt a growing sense of horror. What was going to happen to the world? she wondered. Was it going to turn into nothing but an increasingly futile effort to maintain the bare necessities of life, everyone avoiding contact with their neighbors and hiding in their homes?

Finally, after several hours during which Nan began to fear that their quarry had flown the coop, a young man came striding down the street. He had long, dark blond hair pulled back in a ponytail and he wore a black T shirt and ragged khaki-colored shorts. He walked with a peculiar bobbing bounce, and it appeared that he didn't bother with shoelaces; his dirty white canvas sneakers snapped to his feet with every bounce, like a pair of flip-flops. Despite the partial concealment of his face by his surgical mask, Nan had the odd feeling that she had seen this young man before somewhere. And when he turned at the driveway and headed for the entrance to 2243A, her heart began to pound.

Elliott took Amber's hands. "Okay, honey, same drill as before. You stay here, lock all the doors, and we'll be back as soon as we can, okay?"

She nodded mutely, her face wan and thin.

"We came right back last time, didn't we?"

"Uh-huh."

"Well, we might be a little bit longer this time, but don't worry. Nan and I will be fine."

When he took the gun out of the glove compartment and shoved it under the belt of his pants so that it was hidden by his jacket, however, Nan didn't feel so confident herself. She started to object but didn't want to draw any more attention to the gun than he already had. She glanced at Amber, who had wedged herself into the farthest corner of the van and held Bessie in a stranglehold.

When they got out of the van, she said. "Do you really think that's necessary? He's a kid."

"He's not a kid, Nan. He's a young man. And in case it hasn't escaped your notice, young men have a distinct propensity for violence in this country."

"Well, of course it hasn't escaped my notice. But he looked like a classic computer nerd. They're not known for their violent streak."

"Hackers are not exactly nonviolent. Nor are biological terrorists."

Nan shook her head, lowering her voice as they reached the driveway. "We don't know that he's either one of these things. For all we know, more than one person shares that apartment."

Elliott didn't reply.

"The weird thing is, he looks vaguely familiar to me."

Elliott half-turned his face to her but still didn't respond. He jabbed the doorbell as soon as they were in reach, startling Nan with his haste and intensity. This macho act was new to her. She knew that when he had served in Vietnam, he had needed to learn how to survive there the best he could; but he almost never spoke of that period of his life, and since then, he had gone to great lengths to live as easy-going a life as he could—one of the things she loved about him. That he was acting to protect her and his daughter wrenched her heart. She took his hand while they waited.

Her attention was diverted by a scuffling sound from inside, and then the youth opened the door, holding his mask to his face with one hand. His eyebrows —both pierced, Nan saw—scrunched together first in confusion, then flew apart in recognition when his gaze fell upon her.

Nan couldn't believe how much adrenalin was flooding through her body at this moment. To steady herself, she leaned against the door jamb. "You know me, don't you?" she said.

The youth seemed frozen. He looked from Nan to Elliott.

"Elliott Jenkins," said Elliott.

"And I'm Nan Schulte, professor of molecular biology. Can we please come in?" she asked. "We come in peace," she added lamely, not sure that she was speaking the truth.

Her comment, however, seemed to allow the young man to respond. He moved to let them in, almost falling over backwards. "C-come in," he stuttered.

The youth led them up a couple of flights of dark, narrow stairs, stairs put in as an afterthought, no doubt, when the house was converted into apartments. When they reached his apartment—a beautiful old sun porch that housed his futon, kitchenette, and desk, upon which sat a powerful-looking Sun computer—he pulled out two folding chairs for them to sit on, while he took the chair from his desk. The apartment smelled to Nan like miso.

"Mind if we dispense with the masks?" said Nan, taking

229

a seat. We can't be infectious with The Plague—we just got here—and if we don't get too close to one another, I would think we'll all be fine."

Elliott seemed somewhat reluctant to take off his mask, and he glanced around the apartment before taking it off. Fortunately, the boy favored a sleek, uncluttered Zen look in his dwelling, and the floors were polished wood, not carpet, which fleas adored. The youth lowered his mask right away.

Slipping hers off with relief, Nan took a couple of deep breaths. The guy looked even more familiar now, without his mask, but she still couldn't place him. "Can I ask you your name? I feel like I've seen you somewhere before, but ..."

He squirmed in his chair before answering. "Zach," he muttered.

Nan had to lean forward to hear him. "Did you ever sit in on one of my classes?" she asked.

He shook his head. "I saw you give some remarks at a CDC symposium."

"Do you know why we're here?" said Elliott.

Zach shrugged, not looking at either of them.

Nan and Elliott exchanged glances. Nan sat up straighter, crossed her legs. "Well, I'll tell you. We caught you hacking into my computer at my lab at the university. One of my graduate students traced you to this address."

Zach kept his gaze focused on the floor, reached up to tuck a stray tendril of hair behind his ear.

Annoyed by his unresponsiveness, Nan opened her bag and pulled out a wad of papers that had the triplet codes printed out on them. She got up and thrust the papers under his nose. "Recognize these?" she inquired flatly.

He took the papers and examined them, then folded them calmly in one fist. But Nan could see that his hands were shaking.

She waited. When he still didn't respond, she burst out, "Look, Zach, we need your help! People are dying out there!

Millions and millions of them! If you know anything at all about this global pandemic—and I'm pretty damned sure you do—and you're not a fucking sociopath, you need to help us!"

Zach's head jerked up and Nan could see that his eyes were filled with anguish, terror, and pain. His shoulders began to heave and tears dripped down his cheeks.

"Goddamn it!" he shouted; "All I ever wanted to do was save the frogs!" He buried his face in his hands, his body racked with sobs. "That's all I ever wanted to do!" he wept. "Save the frogs, goddamn it. I just wanted to save the frogs."

CHAPTER 21

Nan received this confession in mystified silence. She sought Elliott's eyes to see if what Zach just said made any more sense to him than it did her, but he seemed just as confused as she was.

"You were trying to save the frogs?" she said finally.

Zach nodded miserably, wiped his eyes.

"How do you get from trying to save the frogs to a global pandemic?" she asked.

His face twisted in pain. "Well, I—I'm not sure that this is what happened," he said. "That's—one of the reasons I was hacking into your computer. I was trying to figure out if there was a connection."

"Look, how about if we start at the beginning," said Elliott. "Just exactly how did you go about trying to save the frogs?"

Zach's gaze slid away. He tucked the errant lock of hair behind his ear once more and got up from his chair. "Anyone like a cup of herbal tea?" he asked.

"No thanks," said Nan. Elliott shook his head. They both waited while he filled up his tea kettle with water from a five gallon dispenser, then put it on to boil. He leaned against the sink and hugged his arms.

"Well, you know that frogs have been disappearing lately—dying out, right? All over the globe. Entire species."

They nodded.

"And nobody really knows why. I mean, there's lots of theories about different stuff, pollution, lack of habitat, whatever, but no one really knew why. So I started this independent research project at Berkeley to see what I could find out. I ... really like frogs," he said. "They're beautiful creatures—amazing creatures! And it's just a—a tragedy that they're dying wholesale like this, you know?"

"True," responded Nan.

The kettle began to chirp, so Zach turned off the flame and poured some of the hot water into a mug. He remained standing, gingerly poking at the tea bag in his mug with his finger. "Well, what I found out was that frogs—at least all of the ones I studied—have this bacterial symbiont in their skin that helps them breathe. It helps them to metabolize the oxygen in the air and gets it into their bodies more efficiently."

"That's interesting," commented Nan. "When did you find this out?"

"Two ... three years ago almost."

"Did you publish your results?" asked Elliott.

"Nah. I was only an undergraduate. And my advisor told me I'd need to do a lot more work first." Zach gave the tea bag a final poke, then dragged it out of the mug and dropped it in the trash. "But I found something else out, too." Blowing on his tea to cool it, he returned to his seat. "Healthy frogs from healthy populations had this symbiont. The ones that weren't doing so well didn't have it. And the longer I did my studies, the fewer frogs I found that had this symbiont."

"So ... something was killing the symbiont?" said Nan.

Zach nodded. "I figured it was antibiotics. I mean, they're everywhere. Not only are they fed to chickens and cows to improve yield, they've been overprescribed for humans for decades. Some studies in Europe found out that pharmaceutical drugs are in all of the water supplies over there, some of them in higher concentrations than pesticides and herbicides. More of a drug gets excreted out of a human body than stays in and gets used, did you know that?"

"Yeah," said Elliott slowly.

"Well, if they've got all kinds of drugs in the water in Europe, you know we've got them in our water. They must be in all the water all over the planet. And I mean, that's right where the frogs live. In the water. So, I figured that these antibiotics must be killing this bacterial symbiont. And that's what was killing the frogs." He stopped and began anxiously slurping his tea, gulping it down in big swallows.

A terrifying picture was starting to form in Nan's mind. "You decided you needed to save the bacteria, then, huh?"

Zach set his cup on his desk and stood up warily. "Look, if I tell you guys I did something that maybe turned out to be a bad idea, are you going to turn me in?"

Nan shook her head vigorously. "What good would that do?" she said.

He gave a sarcastic bark of a laugh. "You tell me. This society gets into punishment in a big way."

Elliott sighed. Nan responded, "Well, I don't really see that as a useful course of action under these circumstances. My only aim here is to find some way to curb the virulence and infectivity of the microbial population right now. I just want to know what you know. I'm guessing that at this point, you thought that the bacterial symbiont needed some help."

"Well—yeah! I mean, what else was I going to do? Take on the entire pharmaceutical industry? Tell them to stop making antibiotics because it was killing a bacterium? That would have gone over really big. People don't care about creatures like frogs."

"Not all people feel that way," Elliott remarked.

"Most of them do! They think human life is sacred, but no other life is! So what if entire families of organisms go extinct!

If we can't use them somehow or make money from them, what good are they, right!?" Zach set his cup on the counter and stood taut and trembling, his fists clenched.

"Look, your point of view is valid, Zach," Nan replied quietly. "No one here is judging you. So you decided you needed to help the frogs by helping their symbiont to survive. What, you ... engineered something to give them resistance to antibiotics?"

Zach nodded, began to pace. "I ... put together a bunch of resistance factors to the most common antibiotics. I strung them together in a plasmid."

Elliott whistled. Nan shot him a warning glance. "That must have been quite the independent project," she commented. "An awful lot of work for an undergraduate."

"Yeah, no kidding!" he said. "Then I had to replicate enough of them to go around."

"Go around where?" asked Elliott.

"The planet."

"The—planet?"

"Well, yeah. Frogs are dying all over the planet."

"You traveled around the entire world?" Nan gulped.

"Yeah."

"Doing what, exactly?"

Zach sank back into his chair, not bothering to push away the hair that fell into his face. He had gone from taut to completely limp. "Something that went really wrong is all I can think," he mumbled dejectedly.

"What was that?" Nan leaned forward as encouragingly and nonthreateningly as she could manage. What she wanted to do was grab him by the shoulders and shake the story out of him.

Zach scooched down in his seat, gazed up at the ceiling. "I made the plasmid," he recited mechanically. "Then I replicated enough for thirty vials. I knew I was coming into an inheritance when I turned twenty-one—from my grandparents—so I booked this round-the-world plane trip. I researched the best places to release my plasmids, places where frog populations were in danger but that would also be reasonably easy to get to from a major airport on my route. I couldn't hope to save all the frogs, of course. I just wanted to make a dent in the problem."

Elliott shifted in his seat, crossed his arms. "Um, when you say you released the plasmids, you …?"

Zach gnawed nervously at his lower lip before answering. "I went to ponds and other waterways. I captured some frogs. I smeared some innoculum on their skin."

"You just smeared it on their skins?"

"Well, that's where the symbiont was."

Both Elliott and Nan gaped at him. "It … didn't occur to you that some other kinds of bacteria might pick up this plasmid? Nan inquired tightly. "You know, that staph and strep and all kinds of other potentially lethal bacteria live literally everywhere?"

Zach gave her a desperate look. "Well, of course I thought about it! But you know, nucleotides are not all that stable outside of a cell! You know that! I figured any plasmids that didn't get picked up by the symbiont right away would get degraded."

"What about conjugation?" Elliott asked, clearly as flabbergasted as Nan felt.

"These symbionts didn't give any evidence of conjugation. I didn't think this species traded genetic information like that. And anyway, how can anyone be sure it was my plasmid? I mean, viruses are going nuts, too. I didn't design anything for viruses! I mean, maybe this whole thing is just one big, weird coincidence!"

When neither Nan nor Elliott responded, he added plaintively, "I—I have a really hard time believing that something so terrible could come out of something so well intended, you know?"

Nan suddenly felt exhausted. She stretched in her chair, met Elliott's gaze.

"I need to go check on Amber," he said.

"Who's Amber?" asked Zach.

Reluctantly, Elliott faced him. "My—daughter."

"Where is she?"

"In our van."

"Well, hey, bring her up."

"I'll see how she's doing in the van; she's pretty happy there. But thanks," he replied. He stood up, gave Nan a squeeze on the shoulder. "I'll be right back," he told her.

"Okay," she said, attempting a smile. When he left, she returned her attention to Zach, who was now fiddling with what looked to be some sort of climbing harness. Her emotions occupied such a muddle she didn't know what she felt. On the one hand, she felt ecstatic that they had finally located the mystery e-mailer and that he hadn't turned out to be any more sinister than this brilliant, geeky, confused boy. On the other hand, his appalling arrogance and short-sighted, goofy innocence had set in motion events that were killing millions of people and might even lead to the extinction of his own species. He was right about one thing, though; whatever he had released and whatever was now ravaging the human population were different. What had happened between the time he released his plasmids and now?

"So where did you start your, uh, tour?" she asked him.

"Great Britain."

"Why there?"

He set the harness down, his expression guarded. "You'll laugh," he said.

"I won't, I promise."

Zach sighed, got up once more. "You sure you don't want some tea?"

"I'm sure."

Rather than make more tea, Zach once again began to

pace. "Well, I thought of this as—as like, a holy quest or—a sacred act. That's what I wanted it to be. I knew there could be a downside to this—I'm not as stupid or naïve as you probably think I am." He unfastened his ponytail, then scooped his hair up and tied it back again, failing to capture the lock that kept falling into his face. "Have you ever heard of Findhorn?" he asked.

"Sure, it's that place in—where, England? Scotland? They grow enormous vegetables, right?"

He nodded eagerly. "Scotland. And the reason they're able to grow such enormous vegetables is because the people there are in communication with the devas. The devas that care for the plants."

Nan groaned inwardly. "Devas," she responded, trying to sound neutral. But Zach glanced at her suspiciously.

"I know, I know, scientists aren't supposed to believe in anything like devas. That's folklore, right?"

"Well—"

"But did you ever think that folklore was just a certain culture's way of describing physical phenomena so that they make sense to them?"

"Sure."

"So, like, maybe devas are some kind of subtle energy, some kind of energy entity that we haven't been able to measure yet or describe to our satisfaction. I mean, something is happening in the British Isles right now. Something is trying to get our attention. You've heard about the crop circles, right?"

Elliott returned, without Amber, Nan saw. He settled back into his chair. "Yeah," he replied. "Those two guys confessed to hoaxing those circles."

Zach regarded him with undisguised contempt. "Well, for one thing, there is no way in the world that those two guys could possibly be responsible for all the thousands of crop circles that have been created. And for another thing, it's pretty easy to tell the difference between a real crop circle and a fake one. Real crop circles have morphological changes in the nodes of the grains affected. There's also anomalous electromagnetic and radiation readings in real glyphs."

"Glyphs?" Nan echoed.

"Formations. In a real crop circle, you can't find any entrance or exit path leading to the glyph. People who've observed them being created see lights moving around. Just lights. No people. No bodies. No machines. Energy, pure and simple. And they create even the most complex patterns in a half-hour or less, sometimes in minutes."

Nan reflected. "Yeah, I think I heard some theory that they were created by some kind of plasma vortex or something."

"Whatever," Zach retorted. "Whatever you want to call them: Plasma Vortices. Interdimensional beings. Devas."

"Ah, the deva connection," Elliott mused.

Zach glared at him. "That's right. They care about living things. That's their job. They're the life force on this planet."

Nan prompted, "So, you wanted to start distributing your plasmids in England because you thought that ..."

"Well, I—I wanted to start it off right. With a ceremony and a blessing. Some place where I thought I would be heard and helped. So, I located a recent crop circle—a really beautiful one that formed a mandala from the air. And I took my plasmids with me so that I could bless them inside the energy of this crop circle. It felt really weird inside there, actually. I got kind of dizzy after a while so I had to leave." Zach returned to his chair, perched tensely on the edge. "But before that, I prayed for my actions to serve the greatest good. That's all I prayed for! These beings are not malicious! If they were, why would all they do is form crop circles? They don't hurt anyone, not like people do! I can't believe, I just can't believe, that they would betray me, that they would be responsible for something so purely intended to go so horribly wrong!"

Elliott ran his hand through his hair. "Uh, you think

that these ... these devas warped your work, is that what
you're saying? Because honestly, Zach, just stringing together
a smorgasbord of resistance factors to a whole bunch of
antibiotics and then slopping it around in every water hole you
find around the entire planet is enough right there. You don't
have to invoke divine intervention."

Zach leaped to his feet, his body practically convulsing.
"Fuck you, asshole!" he screamed.

Nan glared at Elliott now. "Would you back off a little?"
she demanded, exasperated.

"I'm sorry," he muttered. "I mean that, Zach. I'm sorry. I'm
just—we're all just—under a lot of pressure right now."

Zach turned his back to them and stalked over to the sink.
There he braced himself with both hands, leaning over as if to
vomit. But he didn't. He just stood there.

Nan cleared her throat. "Well," she said carefully, "I don't
know how much information you were able to glean from
my computer, but the fact is, whatever you engineered and
released is different from what's going around right now."

Zach spun back around, his face alight with desperate
hope. "So, maybe my plasmid isn't responsible!"

Nan shook her head. "No, the sequences are too close. Too
close to be a coincidence."

His face fell.

"They've obviously mutated, and in an amazingly short
time, too. But there's another interesting development. I need
to know: did you use a virus in your delivery system?"

"No. No way! I didn't want to screw around with viruses."

"And the timing of your trip to England when you first
released your plasmids?"

"A year ago last June."

Nan reflected. Mutations and unknown virus aside, this
plasmid had to be the first step in the sequence of events
leading up to the current pandemic. The timing and location
of the first deadly, resistant bacterial diseases—in addition

to the similarity of the gene sequences between what he concocted and what her lab was finding in organisms now—didn't leave much room for doubt. And as flaky as this kid was, it only made sense to have him working on the problem in her lab. He knew more about this resistance factor than just about anyone, herself and present lab staff included.

"Listen, Zach," she said. "What would you think about coming back East with us and working in my lab on this problem?"

He gave her a puzzled look while Elliott made a choking sound. He stood up, grasped Nan by the elbow.

"Excuse us for a minute," he said. He propelled Nan down the stairs and out onto the driveway below.

"Jesus, Elliott! Relax!" she exclaimed.

"Relax?" he exploded. "You invite a fucking sociopathic bioterrorist to ride back with us in our van and you want me to think this is a totally reasonable request? I'll ignore the fact that it's my van we're using and that you just sprung this on me in front of this joker without discussing it with me first. But did it occur to you in your rush not to judge this lunatic that he might be infected with Bubonic Plague and just not symptomatic yet? Did that even occur to you for a second?!"

Nan folded her arms, her lips mashed together tight. "Okay, first of all—he's not a bioterrorist. Bioterrorists are people who use biological organisms with the intent to do harm. He was trying to do something good, for Christ's sake! He was just … short-sighted is all."

Elliott rolled his eyes. "Try: incredibly stupid. Unbelievably arrogant. Completely and totally and sociopathically irresponsible!"

"A sociopath doesn't care about the hurt he causes," she replied tartly. "This kid cares! I admit, he acted stupidly and arrogantly. He's young—he didn't have the experience he needed to use good judgment. He's … too smart for his own good, too."

241

"Boy, that's for fucking sure," Elliott agreed, nodding up and down vehemently.

"But he knows stuff about this resistance factor that no one else does! And even though it's a travesty he was able to pull off creating that plasmid, that's a pretty impressive stunt from an undergraduate, you'll have to admit. He's good, Elliott. He's got tremendous talent in this area, talent that we need right now. It'll be better to have him on our side, where we can keep an eye on him. Who knows what he might do trying to remedy the situation on his own?"

Elliott massaged his jaw, closed his eyes briefly. "That is a fairly scary thought."

"I think so. This kid is the quintessential sorcerer's apprentice."

Elliott dropped down to squat on the stoop. He patted the space next to him and Nan joined him. "But what about The Plague?" he asked. "Honest to God, no matter how much we need him, we don't want him riding in close quarters with all of us if he's infectious."

"No, you're right. If he agrees to come, I thought we'd ask him if we could take a blood sample. I saw a scope on his desk. We could check his blood for *Yersinia pestis*. If he's clean, it should be okay."

"Right. Then we just pray that things work out for the greatest good, eh?"

Nan gave a feeble laugh. "That's right," she responded. "So—are we agreed? We'll offer Zach a ride back East and a place in my lab?"

Elliott rubbed the back of his neck wearily. "Sure. What the hell."

"Okay, good. You won't be sorry, Elliott," she reassured him. "I don't think," she added.

"Come on, let's go invite the twit." Elliott scrambled to his feet, offered his hand to Nan.

She followed him back up the stairs, a little nervous about

242

what they were about to embark upon, as a matter of fact. Elliott was right—Zach represented a loose cannon and there was no guarantee that he would end up being a help, not a hindrance. And despite her conviction that it made sense to keep an eye on him, she shared Elliott's incredulity over the boy's mind-boggling naïveté. How on earth could he have thought that conducting a "blessing" in a crop circle (of all things!) would ensure that an outrageously dangerous act would turn out just peachy?

Of course, she mused, Zach had prayed for the "greatest good," didn't he? He hadn't prayed for humans' greatest good . . . .

CHAPTER 22

Nan twiddled the knobs on Zach's scope, searching the slide she'd made up for any signs that he had contracted *Yersinia pestis*, the bacterium responsible for Bubonic Plague. Fortunately, the organism was transported intravascularly, so if he harbored it, it would show up in his blood; and it possessed a distinctive appearance when stained. It should be easy to spot. Additionally, his white blood cell count would be elevated, too, if he had unfriendly bacteria in his system. Much to her relief, she wasn't finding either of these indicators. She had made several slides using different stains, just to be extra careful, so when she scanned the final sample and didn't find any signs of bacterial infection, she leaned back in her chair with a grateful sigh. It had been difficult enough to persuade Zach even to consider coming back with them.

In fact, once it completely sank in that the current global pandemic had resulted from the plasmid he released, he had become morose and fatalistic to the point of feeling suicidal. While Elliott hung out with Amber in the van, Nan talked to him for a couple of hours, walking a fine line between stressing the responsibility he had to set things right and minimizing any blame for what happened.

"Look, if the human population hadn't been so promiscuous with antibiotics, the frog populations wouldn't have suffered and it never would have occurred to you to what you did, right?" she pointed out. "They're the canaries in the coal mine—something terrible was bound to happen sooner or later if we didn't change our behavior. Your actions were a trigger, not necessarily a cause. And clearly, the selection pressures were there to mutate your plasmid into something much more powerful and virulent than you ever dreamed. That didn't happen in a vacuum."

He didn't say much during the conversation, just mumbled a few incoherent comments about feeling like the fall guy, but she did finally get him to acquiesce to come back East with her. The idea of penance seemed to hold some meaning for him. She had to go to great lengths, however, to assure him that no authorities of any kind would be alerted to his existence or actions. He obviously possessed a paranoid fear of both authority and punishment, for reasons he didn't feel like divulging, apparently.

Zach was halfheartedly dragging together a few items to take on his trip while Nan checked his blood. He noticed her sigh, however, and regarded her questioningly when she took the last slide off the scope.

"You're right," she said. "You're clean."

"I've been really careful."

"What about the flu?" she asked. "Did you come down with that?"

Zach gave a humorless laugh. "Oh, yeah. Didn't everybody?"

"I haven't. So far."

He cocked his head. "Maybe we should be looking at your blood," he remarked.

"Maybe so," she replied with a smile. "But for now, let's get to the issue at hand. How soon can you be ready to go?"

He shrugged. "Well, I could be ready in a couple of hours,

probably. But it's getting kind of late in the day. Wouldn't it be better to get started in the morning?"

"Yeah, it probably would," Nan admitted. It could be tough finding open gas stations in the middle of the night, and there was no point in wearing herself and Elliott down any more than they were already. Amber would undoubtedly sleep better, too, if they weren't driving and having to make rest stops.

She decided to go out to the van and check with Elliott; she found him playing a board game with Amber, both comfortably ensconced on the mattress. The morning fog had cleared out, and the temperatures had warmed up, so they had the windows rolled down and the side door open. A pleasant breeze with a faint oceanic tang blew through the neighborhood, making the eerie stillness seem even more unnatural.

"How are you guys doing?" she asked.

"Great. Amber's beating the pants off me."

Amber giggled delightedly.

"Well, Zach checked out okay and he could be ready to go in a couple of hours. I suppose we could head out this evening, but don't you think it would be better to get a fresh start in the morning?"

Elliott nodded. "I do. It'll give us more time to plan our route for our return. If Zach's phone is working, I thought I'd make some phone calls."

Nan wanted to call her mother and her lab, too, so they locked up the van and brought Amber with them to meet Zach. The grave sweetness with which he greeted her touched Nan a great deal; Zach clearly liked children. He made her a glass of orange juice from frozen concentrate and dug through his closet until he produced a stuffed animal for her to play with: a bedraggled raccoon that looked so limp and worn it resembled a Davy Crockett hat more than an actual animal. Amber found it enchanting however, and retired to a corner of the room to play with it.

Elliott made his calls first as he needed to catch people before they left work for the day. Nan submerged her impatience while he phoned contacts across the country in an effort to piece together the safest route to take; it had only been a couple of days since she spoke with Joshua and Myra, but it felt like years. When Elliott handed her the phone, he looked grim.

"The influenza epidemic is hitting the Midwest really hard right now," he told her. "And get this: there's a diphtheria outbreak on the East Coast."

Zach took in this information with tense, white-faced silence, while Nan stifled a groan. No matter what she said to Zach or anyone else in her efforts to keep from giving up, the situation really did seem hopeless. It was like plugging one leak in a dyke, only to have three leaks spring some place else. Except that they hadn't even managed to plug one hole. She took the receiver, feeling anxious as she dialed the lab. Connor answered, sounding relatively chipper, which buoyed her spirits. She told him that they had located the mystery e-mailer and that he had turned out to be a student at U. C. Berkeley.

"He's coming back with us, in fact, to help us with our analyses," she said. "I'll give you the whole story when I get back, but for now, all you need to know that this resistance factor seems to have been an experiment that went tragically awry. The sequences have mutated since he engineered his plasmid, and we need to figure out how and why."

Connor clearly wanted to know more, but he stifled his curiosity and went on to tell her about what they'd found during the time she'd been away. The mysterious filovirus, he said, had made an occasional appearance here and there in older cell cultures, and they had managed to locate some that went even farther back than the ones Elliott had procured for them. There was still no sign, though, of the resistance factor that far back. "But the most interesting thing we've found," he told her, "has to do with that big weird protein that the mutated resistance factor codes for. Remember how Felix was having trouble crystallizing that protein?"

"Sure I do."

"Well, it turns out that the reason is because it can assume an unbelievable amount of structures. It's bizarre! It's like … Silly Putty or some damn thing! First we realized that it was taking on the crystal structure of the glassware it was in. Then a contaminant got in one batch, and it took on the shape of the contaminant. We started introducing different molecules into different batches of this protein, and every time we did that, it took on the shape of whatever molecule it encountered."

"You're right. That's very strange."

"It's like a prion in reverse!"

Studies had shown that the mode of infection of a prion was to get certain normal-shaped proteins that it encountered to assume the malformed, dysfunctional shape of the prion itself. What did the peculiar behavior on the part of this resistance factor protein signify? Nan suspected, as Connor clearly did, that the unusual chameleon-like behavior of this protein had some bearing on the current crisis. What on Earth could it be?

Nan congratulated Connor and the rest of the staff for this breakthrough, then inquired if anyone had come down with diphtheria. He told her that although cases had been reported in Boston, Hartford, and New York, it had yet to reach their neck of the woods. "It's probably only a matter of time, though," he said soberly. "How soon do you think you can make it back?"

"Four days from tomorrow, I hope. That's if everything goes smoothly," she told him. "You guys keep working on that protein, okay? I think you're on to something there."

After she hung up, she filled in Elliott and Zach on her lab's findings, then called her mother's number. Kristin answered, sounding rather distraught, and when she found out it was Nan who was calling, she told her worriedly that it seemed Myra had suffered a stroke during the night.

"When I went to get her up this morning, one side of her face was all droopy," she said. "And her speech was slurred. She's having a harder time moving her right leg, too. What should we do?"

Nan exhaled heavily. Continued strokes were only to be expected; it was part of the progression of her disease—if the various manifestations of old age and dying could be considered a disease. But that didn't make it any less difficult or distressing, for her mother or anyone who was caring for her. Taking her to the hospital, though, with everything else that was going on, didn't seem like a good idea. She asked Kristin to put her mother on the phone, and when she did, her mother sounded so bewildered and defeated that Nan felt like weeping. Instead, she assured her mother that everything was going to be okay and that she was on her way home.

"Kristin and the other students there will make sure you're well taken care of until I get there, Mom," she told her. "You're not in any pain, are you?"

"No," said her mother, in a funny little sing-song way she had developed.

"Well, that's good. I know this is frightening, Mom. I know. But it's going to be okay. Don't worry, all right?"

"I—I wasn't able to tell …" Nan waited for her mother to finish her sentence, but instead she repeated herself. "I wasn't able to tell …"

"You weren't able to tell what happened?" asked Nan.

"Wasn't able to tell what happened," she affirmed.

"It sounds like you had a little stroke. Like you've had before."

"Okay."

Nan bit her lip to keep her tears back. Her mother's helplessness grieved her terribly, especially since there wasn't a damn thing she could really do to help, either. Myra was going to keep having these little strokes until she finally died and they were going to continue damaging her brain, in tiny, cruel, relentless steps. All of the things that made someone distinctively human—standing upright, using one's hands, communicating—were slowly leaching away. Her condition left her isolated and trapped inside her mind, which, most cruelly of all perhaps, was still working, leaving her aware of what she had lost. As a biologist, Nan knew that her mother was simply dying very slowly and that this process was not an intentionally cruel or unnatural one, no matter how brutal it might seem to her or her mother. Still, it was agony. And no matter how much she tried to block the image, all she could think about when she considered her mother's mental deterioration was the ancient culinary practice in China of capturing a monkey, removing the top of its skull while it was still alive, and eating its brains spoonful by spoonful. In these terms, death from Bubonic Plague or influenza seemed almost merciful.

The conversation with her mother left her feeling drained and depressed, but Nan forced herself to put these feelings aside and concentrate on more pragmatic considerations. Elliott got out the road atlas and they pored over it, Elliott circling influenza hotspots with a pen. Those areas would be the least likely to have functioning services. They debated on whether to take Highway 50 again, this time taking extra gas cans full of gas, but with Zach joining them, they didn't really have room for an additional twenty gallons—not to mention the fact that it would be dangerous to travel with such flammable cargo. Elliott had been able to find out that as long as drivers stayed on I-80, they could go through.

"Fortunately—or unfortunately, however you want to look at it," he said, "they don't have enough personnel to cordon off very much of I-80." He frowned at the map, flipped the pages back to California and tapped the page with his pen. "The only other real option is to take I-5 all the way down to Bakersfield and then start east from there, but that would probably add an extra day to our trip. And if I'm not mistaken, we want to get back as soon as possible, right?"

Nan took the atlas and scanned the route he was proposing. The secondary highway that went from Nevada to Utah looked a little dicey, especially as it appeared to go through an extremely barren area that included a mountain range. She decided they should take the chance on I-80. They would avoid all of Colorado by taking this route, and even though they would be going further north, through Wyoming, the elevations that they would have to travel would be much lower, which should work in their favor.

"Sounds good," she said finally. Zach leaned over and glanced at the map but didn't say anything.

"Do you have any comments or suggestions, Zach?" asked Elliott.

"Nope," he said, shaking his head.

"Are we going to Disneyland?" Amber piped up.

"Sorry, sweetheart. Not this time," her father replied. Amber didn't look surprised, and Nan found herself wondering if Disneyland would ever operate again. Such an elaborate amusement park represented an extreme societal extravagance in energy, materials, and manpower; if they didn't get a handle on this resistance factor, and soon, the long term impact on technologically advanced human culture was going to be enormous.

When it became clear that they were going to put off their departure until the next morning, Zach offered to cook dinner for everyone. He had just stocked up on groceries before they arrived, and he enjoyed cooking, he said. Nan and Elliott offered to help, so he put them to work chopping vegetables. Nan wasn't surprised to find that Zach was a vegetarian, but she was amazed by the variety and quality of produce that he had on hand: bok choy, cilantro, broccoli, snow peas, chard, Napa cabbage, and jicama.

"Wow, I haven't seen produce like this since before the epidemic," she remarked, sneaking a juicy, crunchy bite of jicama. "Must be nice living in a warm temperate climate instead of a cold one."

"That's for sure," Zach agreed. "Let me guess, you're subsisting on root crops."

"If we're lucky," Elliott replied.

"Yeah, it's like the olden days. I'm going to have to clean out my root cellar," Nan laughed.

"Well, we've also got a pretty cool distribution network going out here," Zach told them. "People have come up with some creative ways to get stuff around, using all kinds of modes of transportation—mountain bikes, burros, horses, llamas …"

"Do tell," mused Elliott.

"Burros and llamas?" exclaimed Amber, looking up from her drawing. Elliott had brought in some of her things from the van to keep her occupied while they prepared dinner.

"Yup," said Zach.

"I have a lamb back home," she told him. "And a cat."

When all the vegetables were chopped, Zach put together a tasty Szechuan stir fry. He steamed some rice and added tofu to the veggies, flavoring them with miso, tamari, and sesame oil. For dessert, he had ice cream stashed in his freezer, three exotic flavors that involved tropical fruits and nuts. Nan preferred plain old vanilla herself, but enjoyed the pistachio-peanut-cashew-butter-rum-papaya concoction that she ended up with. Searching for a topic of conversation that didn't involve disease, she asked Zach where his parents lived.

"Mexico," he said. "Ixtapa."

"That sounds nice. Have they lived there long?"

"About five years, I guess."

"Do you go visit them there?"

"Yeah, I even went down there to live with them for a few months myself after I graduated from high school."

"They moved down there before you graduated?" Elliott asked.

"Yeah."

"But … you didn't? Where were you living?" Nan knew she was prying, but she couldn't help herself.

"With my foster parents."

"Oh."

Zach scraped the last bit of ice cream from his bowl and jumped up impatiently to put it in the sink with the rest of the dirty dishes. "Now you're going to want to know why I was in foster care, right?"

"Well, only if you want to tell us," said Nan.

"My parents were in jail, okay? For seven years. A fucking narc busted them for selling acid at a Dead concert."

"How awful!" said Nan, while Elliott barked, "Watch your language, Zach."

"No shit. I mean—sorry." Zach ducked his head, coloring. "Anybody want more ice cream?"

"I do," said Amber.

"I think you've had plenty, sweetheart," Elliott remarked.

"Yeah, too much sugar isn't good for you," Zach agreed. "You can have some more orange juice, though, if you want."

Amber shook her head, licked her spoon and then her bowl.

After dinner, they spent the rest of the evening packing up and planning for the trip back East. They pretty much cleaned out Zach's refrigerator, and those stores, along with the groceries Nan had bought at the Berkeley Bowl, gave them reasonably generous supplies, even given a few unforeseen circumstances. Their main concern revolved around gas, but there wasn't really anything they could do about that ahead of time. One of the advantages of taking I-80, according to Elliott, was that the country along that route had been less hard hit by the influenza epidemic than some other areas, so they hoped this would translate into a greater availability of fuel. When it came time to go to bed, they parked the van in the driveway and slept there.

As Nan lay on the mattress, cuddled up to Elliott and Amber, she had a hard time going to sleep. She couldn't stop thinking about the trip they had ahead of them, the implications of the findings Connor had given her, and the information she had gleaned from Zach. When she told Zach that the mutation in the resistance factor didn't happen in a vacuum, she had said this primarily to calm him down. But the more she thought about it, the more she believed it to be true. Everything had happened so quickly, in such a focused way. There really did seem to be some intelligence involved here, but whose or what kind she couldn't say.

It did seem that the microbial kingdom had mounted a counteroffensive against humans' war on disease, seizing upon Zach's ill-fated contribution with extreme alacrity. She knew that several recent experiments indicated that bacteria were able to mutate their genomes immediately when their survival was threatened, in ways that eerily suggested sentience—if not prescience. But she, like most scientists, had shrugged off these results, thinking that there had to be some other explanation. Now, she wasn't so sure. And if they were dealing with an intelligent entity, they needed to take this into account in any strategy they might devise. If we can't win a war against these microorganisms, we need to negotiate, she pondered groggily as she began to sink into unconsciousness; but how in the world would you communicate with a microbe?

CHAPTER 23

Nan gazed out across the empty expanse of Wyoming, resting her cheek against the cold glass of the van window. The thinly overcast sky created a strange pallor to the day and all the plants had died back in preparation for winter; so everything looked brownish gray for as far as she could see. Dust seemed to have settled over the entire landscape as well, giving the disturbing impression of a nuclear winter. Nan was growing used to the emptiness of the West, but at the same time, the blankness and somberness that derived from the epidemic created a disturbing subliminal effect, like a subsonic note too low for human hearing that nevertheless created a brooding uneasiness in the listener.

The trip through Nevada and Utah had passed uneventfully this time, although they had to stop more frequently for gas since fuel was now being rationed at every station. The drive through the salt flats had been eerie—miles and miles of sterile, glistening salt, stretching as far as she could see on both sides of the highway. Nothing grew there; travelers had used dark rocks on the blinding white surface to spell out their names here and there. Mountains lay in the distance. One bizarre peak rose up from the salt flats where a mirage around its base made the mountain look as if it were hovering above the horizon like a massive UFO or flying island.

Elliott and Zach were managing to get along pretty well; Nan had worried about the two occupying close quarters for the time it would take them to make the return trip. She suspected that Zach didn't quite trust Elliott and found him too "establishment," and she knew that Elliott was having a hard time not resenting the hell out of the boy for the disaster he had precipitated. Nan herself was taking a more pragmatic tack at this point; who started what and how had become irrelevant. All she cared about now was going back to her lab and getting to work, and every agonizing, incessant mile that they had to travel in order to get back home felt like torture. The happiest camper of all was Amber, who was enjoying the travel and having both Nan and Elliott around all the time, not to mention the friendship she had struck up with Zach.

"Do you have any brothers or sisters, Zach?" Nan asked him. He was seated next to Amber in the back, playing Gin Rummy with her.

He shook his head. "Well, no biological siblings. I had a foster sister, though, when I lived with my foster parents."

"Do you still see her?"

"Oh yeah. When I can. It's a little awkward, though. I didn't get along so hot with my foster dad."

"What was the problem?"

Zach frowned, kept his attention on his cards. "The guy is a complete and total control freak. I'm surprised he hasn't had a stroke by now, seriously. He hated my parents; he's this gung-ho, frothing-at-the-mouth, drugs-are-what's-destroying-this-great-country-of-ours Nazi fascist. He thought my mom and dad should have had their hands chopped off for dealing drugs."

Nan blinked in surprise. "Really."

Amber squirmed, kicked the bottom of the seat. "Ew," she said, grimacing.

"Yeah. He wanted me to hate them, too. He took me to all these 'Just Say No' meetings and rallies, with all these doofus losers. All he did was make me feel sorrier for my poor parents. I mean, sure they dealt acid, but they sold it to people who wanted it, who knew what they were getting into. They sold really clean stuff for a great price. They wouldn't sell it to anyone younger than eighteen," —Nan caught the sarcastic expression on Elliott's face when Zach said this, relieved that he held his tongue— "and whatever they did, they didn't go around saying people should have their hands chopped off. I mean, there's a great solution. If he wants them to get a job besides selling drugs, what're they going to do without hands?"

"Gin!" shouted Amber.

Zach shook his head in mock disbelief. "I think I've taken up with a card shark," he told her, reaching over to tap her on the nose. Amber giggled and scooped up the cards with an ingenuous, childish greed that tickled Nan. Settling back in her seat to return staring out the window, Nan spotted a station wagon parked up ahead on the shoulder, a couple of lit flares leading up to it.

"Looks like someone's in trouble," she said.

Elliott grunted, made no move to slow down.

Nan leaned forward to catch his eye. "Aren't you going to stop?" she asked.

"Not a good idea," he replied.

She regarded him in surprise. "Where would we have been if that nice old geezer hadn't helped us in Nevada?"

Elliott cleared his throat. "That nice old geezer didn't have a child to protect," he pointed out.

"I know, but still … these are desperate times, Elliott."

"Exactly."

"We need to help people, Dad," said Amber.

"I know we do, sweetie, but the highways are really dangerous right now," he told her.

"Oh, come on. Live a little," Zach prodded him. "Take a

risk."

Zach's needling aroused Nan's loyalty, so she retreated. "Well, you're probably right, Elliott," she said. But he had already put on his blinker and was slowing down to pull over, a grumpy expression on his face.

"Nobody but me gets out of the van until we're sure this is okay," he instructed as he coasted to a stop. Nan peeked out the window and saw a tired, shabby couple standing outside the car, a small boy holding onto the woman's hand. Seeing that it was a family, she relaxed. They'd probably run out of gas, or their car had broken down. It looked ancient.

Elliott left the engine running, put on the emergency brake and climbed out of the car. Nan rolled down her window, stuck out her head.

"Hi!" she called. The couple regarded her but didn't respond.

"What's the trouble?" asked Elliott.

The man mumbled something that Elliott obviously couldn't hear; he took a few steps closer, put his hand up to his ear. "Sorry," he said. "I didn't hear you."

Before Nan could even take a breath, the man's hand had shot out and he grabbed Elliott, pulling him roughly to his chest where he gripped his neck in a stranglehold. He drew an unbelievably huge, notched hunting knife from his belt and jabbed it up against Elliott's throat. It happened so quickly and unexpectedly that Nan remained frozen in her seat, unable to think, act, or move.

"Everyone get out of the car," the man rasped. "Slowly. One at a time."

Nan felt light-headed and faint. She struggled to gather her wits. "Zach, why don't you get out first?" she said. "Amber, stay put for right now."

Zach obeyed, slid open the cargo door and stepped outside.

Get out of the car, lady," ordered the man, tightening his

grip on Elliott.

She was forgetting something, she knew that—what was it? Nan had never felt so stupid or slow-witted. Suddenly, it dawned on her. A gun was in the glove compartment. Should she try to ease it out? Could he see her? Should she just grab it as quickly as she could? What should she do? The man's eyes narrowed as if he could read her mind. Abruptly, she punched the button on the glove compartment and the gun dropped into her lab. She seized it with both hands, shaking violently, and yanked off the safety. Thrusting the gun out the window, she aimed over everyone's heads and squeezed the trigger. The roar from the gun was deafening, the recoil knocked her back in the seat. She felt as if someone had just clobbered her on the hands with a crow bar. Elliott took advantage of the ensuing confusion to elbow the man savagely in the solar plexus. With a grunt, the man doubled over, loosing his hold. Elliott then whirled around and kicked him in the groin as hard as he could. The man fell moaning to the ground while his wife and child gaped.

"Get in the car, Zach!" Elliott yelled. Zach practically tripped over his own feet trying to scramble back into the van. Nan aimed the gun back out the window and trained it on the family, even though the barrel wobbled wildly in her grasp. Elliott ran to the van and sprinted into the driver's seat. He peeled out before Zach even got the side door closed; the cards that Zach and Amber had been playing with rose up from the wind and fluttered crazily around the interior of the van like a swarm of startled bats. Zach struggled to shut the door against the force of Elliott's wild acceleration and not tumble out of the van at the same time. Finally, he managed to slam it shut. He remained on the floor, breathing hard.

"Christ," he muttered.

No one else spoke, including Amber, who appeared to be in shock. Nan felt her heart beating madly in her chest, and she wouldn't have been surprised at all to see it pump visibly, cartoonishly, through her sweater and jacket. She made an effort to relax, and she observed Elliott doing the same thing. He loosened his grip on the steering wheel, leaned back in his seat. But the next moment, she looked up to see a nightmarish vision: a tractor trailer rig had careened out of control on the opposite side of highway and was rocketing across the median, heading straight for the van. This time Amber screamed. Elliott reacted instinctively, jerking the steering wheel to the right and stomping on the accelerator. The van began to fishtail, and still the semi bore down on them. The truck loomed so close Nan could see the driver slumped over the wheel through the windshield, apparently unconscious. She closed her eyes, expecting at any minute to feel either the truck smashing into them or the van rolling end-over-end down the highway.

Miraculously, Elliott managed to elude the truck. He also managed to get the van under control. When the expected impact didn't take place, Nan cautiously opened her eyes. She looked back to see the big rig tipped over on its side, sliding across the highway behind them with sparks shooting every which way. It was several minutes before she caught her breath, and for quite some time afterward, she felt as if the adrenalin in her body had scoured out the insides of her bones, leaving her with a brittle, quivering husk of a skeleton. Elliott slowed down to forty-five miles per hour, then he pulled over to the shoulder and stopped. He leaned over the steering wheel, breathing heavily. Then he turned around to grasp one of Amber's hands.

"You okay, honey?" he asked, his voice quaking.

She nodded, then burst into tears. Elliott reached back and unfastened her seat belt, then pulled her into his lap and stroked her back while she cried. Nan glanced back to see how Zach had fared during the ordeal. Fear had blanched his face white, making him look about sixteen years old. He still hadn't gotten up from the floor and he stayed there, wrapping his arms around his knees protectively.

"Somebody else is going to have to drive for a while," Elliott said.

"I'll be happy to," Nan responded automatically, then realized she actually couldn't drive until she calmed down a bit. She got out of the car and did some stretches, jumped up and down a few times, gulped in lungfuls of the sharp, cold air. When she felt ready, she walked around to the driver's side and opened the door. Elliott handed Amber to her and then got out himself. Nan hugged Amber close, smoothed her hair down. Then she included Elliott in the hug, too, and gave him a kiss.

"Some pretty fancy footwork back there, Dr. Jenkins," she told him.

He wagged his head dramatically. "I guess," he said. "I wasn't sure we were going to make it there for a minute."

"No kidding," she agreed. "Well, we're certainly living, aren't we?"

"Yeah, I wonder if this is enough risk for our adventure-some ward."

She laughed a bit humorlessly. "I don't think we're going to hear a peep out of him for a while."

"Break my heart, why don't you?"

When they climbed back into the van to resume their journey, it was a subdued and quiet group that hit the road. Zach appeared withdrawn to the point of catatonia, although Amber finally managed to coax him into playing another few rounds of Gin Rummy with her. This time, she seemed to be letting him win. He picked up on this and chided her, but Nan could tell that it touched him. He then roused himself for Amber's sake, and Nan found herself warming to him. She suspected that he might even be earning a few points with Elliott, too.

He's really not a bad person, she found herself musing; it was just so incredibly unfortunate that people had the power to precipitate such disastrous consequences from thoughtless, half-baked, short-sighted actions. She wondered if humans were ever going to attain the humility and wisdom they needed to avoid such catastrophes in the future. She also wondered, at this point, if they were even going to get the chance.

That tattered little desperate family behind them made her feel glum, too. Most of her life she had lived in such comfortable circumstances, with practically no exposure to hardship whatsoever. She believed that the majority of people lived that way in this country: most Americans had plenty to eat, clean water, energy galore, cars, televisions, decent clothing. But now, with the epidemics creating so much need and suffering for everyone—no one, rich or poor, was going to get out of this unscathed—hardship was becoming the rule, not the exception. As frightening as their confrontation with that family had been, she still felt sorry for them. What might she feel driven to do to protect or sustain her loved ones in dire straits? And if she didn't find some way to counter the resistance factor, things were just going to get worse. Unimaginably so, she suspected.

That night, they stopped in Kearney, Nebraska and found a small motel open for business where they spent the night. Most of the town looked deserted, however, even though Nan suspected that plenty of people lived there. They must be either at home sick or tending the sick. Or they were dying. Nan had begun to imagine that she could smell death in the air—a hoary, pungent smell like an infected wound or rotting, fermenting leaves. The psychological impact of the pandemic was beginning to feel as lethal as the diseases themselves. The young woman who checked them in at the motel behaved like a sleepwalker, her eyes red—from crying, no doubt—her demeanor listless and resigned. When hope was gone, the will to live faded with it. No one could understand why this was happening. It felt like a scourge from hell, like the wrath of God.

They avoided Chicago the next day—Elliott had heard

that in an effort to keep diphtheria from invading the city, officials had blocked off every single entrance to the city and were enforcing the quarantine vigorously. Elliott had heard reports of people getting shot who tried to sneak around the barricades. They decided to give the area a wide berth and spent the night a good deal south of Chicago, using farm roads and county highways to make their way back to I-80 in Indiana. The interstate turned into a toll road past the Illinois state line, but spookily, no one manned the toll booths, in either Indiana or Ohio.

They had enjoyed mild weather most of their journey, although they had run into rain here and there, but as they left the Toledo area and began to skirt the edge of Lake Erie, clouds began to gather overhead. Nan had heard of the "lake effect" and she knew that impressive snow storms regularly clobbered the areas south of the Great Lakes, but even the storm that they had encountered in Colorado didn't prepare her for the prodigious amount of snow that began to fall from the heavy, moisture-laden clouds as they approached Cleveland. Soon the snow began piling up so quickly and formidably that the few snowplows out trying to keep the roads clear couldn't keep up. After a while, they were driving in a tunnel through the snow, with drifts that towered over the top of the van.

When the snow fell so thick and furious that Nan couldn't see, even with the windshield wipers going full blast, she decided to take the next exit she could find to sit out the storm, well aware that the storm could last for quite some time. They searched for an open motel in Newton Falls, but the entire city seemed to have closed up shop. So they found a parking lot for a supermarket where the wind had swept a relatively clear spot on which to park the van and camped out for the night.

Elliott awoke periodically and started up the van so that they could run the heater; they had used up their Coleman fuel the day before and hadn't been able to replenish their supply. But he had to conserve their fuel; consequently, he wasn't able to keep the van all that warm throughout the night. Zach turned out to be a restless sleeper—tossing, turning, muttering, twitching—so between the activities of the two men, Nan didn't get much sleep that night.

When she awoke early the next morning, everyone else was sleeping rather heavily, especially Amber. Surprisingly, Amber felt warm even though the interior of the van felt freezing, despite Elliott's attempts to beat back the cold. Nan snugged Amber's jacket around her to keep her as toasty as possible, but as she did so, she realized that Amber was in fact burning up with fever. Alarmed, she shook Elliott awake and informed him anxiously of his daughter's condition.

"What do you think?" she asked, as he frantically felt her forehead, touched the back of his hand to her neck. "Do you think it might be a relapse of the flu? Or an ear infection?"

Elliott didn't reply. He seized his medical kit and scrabbled through it noisily to locate the otoscope he had brought along. Amber whimpered as he pulled her into position so that he could check her ears.

"Do your ears hurt, sweetie?" he asked her as he peered through the otoscope.

"Ow," she moaned plaintively.

Elliott shook his head as he withdrew the instrument and placed it back in its case. "Well, I don't know about the flu, but her ears are definitely infected."

"What do you want to do?" said Nan.

"I'll start up the van and get things warmed up in here." Elliott climbed over Zach to reach the driver's seat, jostling him awake.

"What's going on?" he mumbled. No one answered him.

"You do your thing with the lavender," Elliott instructed Nan, who moved to comply. Unfortunately, they didn't have any more Coleman fuel so that she could use their camping stove to heat up the carrier oil, but a cold treatment was better than no treatment at all.

The snow had stopped, but the sky still lowered threateningly in the early morning light. No snowplows had ventured out yet, either; the world was completely suffocated in snow for as far as they could see. As Nan massaged the lavender into Amber's cheek and prepared a sterile cotton plug saturated with the oil to tuck into her ears, she began to feel as though she were being buried alive, with adversity, hopelessness, and dread. Part of what kept her going was the belief that there were no malevolent forces at work here, that no matter how awful things might become, nature was neutral—no one had it out for them. But feeling Amber's scorching little body … watching her eyes glaze over with fever, she couldn't fight the feeling that someone or something was determined to break her spirit, to ensure that she didn't succeed, to see that no lucky breaks would come her way and aid her in her struggle.

When she accidentally caught Zach's eye as she cradled Amber in her arms and tried to will her to get better, the raw, bleak fear that she saw in his eyes pierced her heart like a jagged, splintered bone. And she felt at that moment that nothing could possibly save any of them—not Amber, not herself, not a single living soul.

CHAPTER 24

Nan tightened the belt on her raincoat, squashed her rain hat down firmly on her head as she eyed the freezing rain she was going to have to dash through to reach the garage.

"Ready, Zach?" she said.

He didn't reply, but Nan had already flown out the door, the icy raindrops pelting her noisily. They had arrived in town a couple of hours ago, leaving Newton Falls when the storm died down and the snow plows finally got moving, traveling nonstop through Pennsylvania, New York, and finally, Massachusetts. Amber had responded somewhat to Nan's essential oil treatment, but her ear infection hadn't cleared up entirely. It had settled into a persistent, low-grade infection. Nan hoped that once they got her stabilized at home and weren't traveling any more, her body could rally more vigorously, and she could shake the damn thing. Elliott was staying home to look after her.

This was a good thing, too, because when they stopped by the house where Myra was staying, the student at home tearfully informed Nan that they couldn't continue to care for her any more. Kristin and two of the other residents had suffered relapses from the flu, it seemed. And two more were planning on returning home.

"That leaves just me and Grady," Melinda told her. "And we can't do this by ourselves. Your mom's a total sweetheart but— she needs an awful lot of looking after."

Tell me about it, Nan had thought grimly, wondering what was going to happen to her generation when they reached her mother's age—if they reached it. Perhaps the current pandemic was Nature's way of ensuring that an enormous elderly population wouldn't be saddled upon a less populous younger generation, one that wouldn't physically be able to handle the care demands. The only problem with this theory was, the pandemic didn't seem to be sparing the young any more than the elderly.

So they had brought Myra home, where she didn't seem to be able to settle down. Her last stroke appeared to have programmed some weird, awful loop into her circuits where she kept trying to stand up without assistance, over and over again, just as soon as they got her comfortable in a chair or on the bed. The fact that one of her legs was in a cast didn't register with her brain; Nan found this both heart-rending and maddening. Elliott solved the immediate problem by saying that he would look after both Amber and Myra, and he moved Amber into Myra's bedroom on a portable cot, along with the television and a stack of videos, so that he could keep an eye on both of them at the same time.

Nan, however, couldn't bear to stay away from the lab for much longer; so once she felt certain that Elliott had everything under control, she told Zach they were heading over to the university. He looked extremely anxious, even hunted when she told him this, but she didn't have the time nor patience at this point to coddle him. She imagined that he must feel reluctant to meet her lab staff, given the fact that he represented the most responsible party for the current crisis, but she suspected that her graduate students would feel some sympathy for him.

Once they arrived at the university, they had no trouble finding a space in the faculty lot, and in fact, the emptiness of all the university lots gave her an odd, aching feeling. She hurried inside, Zach struggling to keep up with her, and burst into her lab, flinging droplets of water everywhere as she tore off her rain coat and hat, wadded them into a sopping ball and tossed them into her office.

"Hi, everybody!" she called. "I'm back!"

Two faces peered around the corner, giving her a start. One looked like a skull and the other a devil.

"Uh … am I missing something here?" she said.

"Halloween," Joshua and Teresa replied in unison.

"Oh. God. I'd forgotten," she admitted. Neither the mass media nor the popular culture had had the resources to play up Halloween this year, and she would be willing to bet money that no one, not a single person, possessed the energy to carve a jack-o-lantern or decorate a house. "Well. Wonderful gallows humor, guys. Anyone else here?"

Teresa shook her head, her plastic horns wobbling. "There seems to be some kind of relapse associated with this flu, or maybe a second wave of influenza," she said. "Janice is okay; she's just spending some time at home, taking care of one of her roommates who's got a bad case of bronchitis. But both Felix and Connor have gotten sick again."

"Not seriously, I hope?" Nan responded anxiously.

Joshua let out a heavy sigh. "I don't think so, but we haven't spoken to them since this morning," he told her. Both Teresa and Joshua had their attention fixed on Zach, however, not Nan.

"Oh, sorry!" she said. "This is Zach. He's going help us try to unravel the puzzle we have confronting us. Zach, these are two of my grad students, Teresa and Joshua."

"Pleased to meet you," said Joshua. Teresa gave him a brief, appraising nod.

Nan figured she might as well just get everything out in

the open right up front, so she filled them in on Zach's ill-fated crusade. An interesting mixture of emotions played over both Joshua's and Teresa's faces as she gave them the story: incredulity, horror, hope, hopelessness, pity, sorrow. Joshua, however, also looked quite animated. When Nan finished, he couldn't wait to impart some of his results.

"This is making sense," he said excitedly. "We were trying to figure out what the difference was between the gene sequences on the print-out and the sequences involved in the resistance factor that's circulating around now, like you said to do. That 'Ribbit ribbit' on the end of the e-mail sequence really nagged at me somehow, so I started doing some research on frog genes. And it turns out that several of the sequences are very similar to those found in frog DNA."

"Really," said Nan.

"But nothing corresponds exactly to any complete genes that have been sequenced in frogs. It's like something came along and copied bits and pieces, then strung them together."

"Do tell," she mused.

"Man," muttered Zach. "Could this be any creepier? I mean, Christ. Sounds like intelligence to me."

"What ... kind of intelligence?" asked Teresa.

Everyone fastened their gaze on Zach, but he shoved his hands in his pockets, clearly disinclined to elaborate.

"Zach has some unconventional private views," Nan informed them. But she had to admit, she agreed with him: Increasingly, these results did suggest intelligence of some kind.

Clearly, the spliced-together sequences meant something in the language of DNA and proteins, something powerful. They didn't end up expressing some kind of meaningless junk that didn't code for anything. Could that just be chance? Nan didn't believe in devas, necessarily, but she did believe in consciousness. With millions of molecules literally whirling about the cell, performing prodigiously complex biochemical reactions at dizzying speeds, maintaining the health of the cell as well as the organism, working elegantly, efficiently, consistently, adaptively … to her, such a miraculous system could only come into being through application of some sort of intelligence. She didn't believe in a cosmic puppet master directing the whole business from some lofty perch, but the more she studied life, the more she came to believe that every speck of it possessed sentience of some kind, from the gestalt assemblages known as organisms down to the very atoms and electrons.

"Any idea what these sequences might be doing in their new arrangement?" Nan asked Joshua.

He shook his head. "Well, not yet," he said. "I figure some of them have to be related to that big, weird protein that Felix has been working on."

Nan took a seat on a nearby lab table, gestured at everyone else to sit, too. "Okay, let's review what we know here," she said. "We know that a plasmid was released that contained several fairly standard resistance factors to specific antibiotics. We know that it mutated somehow into a more powerful, virulent, and infectious resistance factor. We know that there appears to be a filovirus associated with the new resistance factor, but as far as we can tell, there's no resistance factor associated with this virus in older cell cultures, right? Anybody find anything else different along those lines?"

Teresa and Joshua shook their heads. "Nope," said Josh.

"Okay, it appears that this virus has been around for a long time not doing anything destructive until this resistance factor showed up, right?"

"Looks that way," agreed Teresa.

"But we don't know that for sure."

"Right."

Nan bumped her heels absentmindedly against the table, pondering. "We also know that this new resistance factor codes for a large, anomalous protein that seems to behave like some kind of molecular mirror. It takes on whatever crystal shape it encounters."

"That's what we've found so far," Joshua concurred.

"We also know—or at least, we have some very strong indications—that the new resistance factor not only has gene sequences similar to Zach's plasmid, but some other genes, or at least portions of genes, have been incorporated from frogs," Nan observed. "But there seems to be some sort of selection involved in the fragments taken. They don't code for gibberish, and—if I'm reading you right, Josh—some skipping around the frog genome seems to have taken place."

Joshua gave a visible shudder. "I would have to say that's correct," he said. "The sequences are not all located next to one another the way you would expect if the virus just dragged along a couple of genes more or less by accident."

"God, this is weird," Nan sighed. "It's not looking very good for the home team."

"The home team?" echoed Zach.

"Humans."

Zach reacted defensively. "Well maybe it's time for humans to let some other species have a chance," he snapped. "I mean, as far as I'm concerned, we've really blown it. Blown it big time. We think that nature's laws don't apply to us, we're so fucking clever. But it turns out that they do. Big surprise."

Teresa looked angry, Joshua thoughtful. "Well, what are you doing here then, if that's the way you feel?" Teresa retorted. "Why don't you just go back to California and watch the demise of the human race from there, huh?"

"Come on, Teresa," said Joshua. "Give the guy a break."

Nan cleared her throat. "Look, I happen to know that's not your entire perspective, Zach," she told him. "And if he did feel that way and only that way, he wouldn't have come here," she said to Teresa and Joshua. "We're all terrified. We're all being pushed past our limits. And we're all doing the best we can." She fell silent, mulling over the information. Then she roused herself. "All right, I'm going to need everyone's notes, especially Felix's about this funky protein. It seems to me that it's the key here. We absolutely have to figure out what the hell it's doing."

Joshua and Teresa nodded, then set about gathering up all the notes from the various lab stations. Zach hung back awkwardly until Nan told him to take a look around the lab and familiarize himself with the set-up and equipment. She spent the greater part of the day reading everyone's notes and planning experiments.

Before she knew it, several hours had passed, and she realized she felt totally beat. She had dozed some in the van last night during their final push to get home, but she hadn't really gotten a decent night's sleep, and this was on top of the restless night they had spent in the parking lot. Leaving instructions with Joshua and Teresa on which experiments to tackle first, she headed out to her car with Zach in tow. She spied Ron in the faculty parking lot and tried to avoid him by hurrying to her car, but he called out to her.

"Nan! Wait!" he boomed with a false heartiness that set her teeth on edge.

She halted with her back to him, jamming the key in the car door. "Go ahead and get in the car, Zach," she said. "This'll only take a minute."

Ron hastened over to her with such eagerness that she figured he must have unwelcome news. She turned to face him with a fixed smile. "What's up, Ron?" she asked.

"Did you get my memo?" he inquired.

She shook her head. "No, I just got back in town. What's it about?"

He beamed. "Well, the president of the university has called an emergency meeting for all of the faculty involved with lab sciences tomorrow morning. As I'm sure you know, this crisis is getting worse by the day, and it's crucial that we devote lab space to those research projects that are actually generating results relating to the current pandemic."

"I see," she replied shortly.

"We haven't heard much coming out of your lab, you know, and since you were out of town for so long, I was afraid that the promising lead you had talked about earlier might have turned out to be a dead end."

Nan felt a rush of anger so intense that it took her by surprise. Why on Earth was he hounding her this way? Of all the times to engage in a pissing contest, this had to be the worst. "Well, it wasn't. It isn't. We've got some fairly dramatic results, in fact, but as you know, it's not a good idea to release this kind of information prematurely."

"Of course," he responded soothingly, infuriating her even more.

"What time is the meeting?" she asked.

"Ten o'clock. At the small auditorium."

"I'll be there. Thanks for letting me know, Ron."

"Anytime!" he told her, grinning so widely it made him look hideous. When she slid into the car, Zach wanted to know who the goon was, and she took great pleasure in telling him that the goon was just that: a goon.

Back home, things didn't appear to be going well. When Nan walked into her mother's bedroom, Myra was crawling about the floor with a wild and uncomprehending expression on her face while Elliott was trying to get her back in the bed. He glanced up when he heard Nan enter.

"Welcome to the monkey house," he said dispiritedly.

Myra pawed at the air, trying to speak. "The ... the ... the ..." she moaned.

"The what, Mom?" Nan prompted, squatting down to help Elliott haul her into bed.

"The ... the ..." she persisted, her eyes bulging, giving her a slightly amphibious look.

Nan bit her lip so hard she tasted blood. Her life seemed to be turning to a bizarre combination of some grotesque Kafka novel and a house of mirrors where suffering was reflected at every angle and in infinite directions. She called in Zach to help them, as even a petite body was heavy, and Myra's cast and her mindless agitation made her extremely awkward to handle. As they got her settled once more, Nan looked over at Amber, who lay listlessly in her cot while an animated Disney film played on the TV set. The contrast between Myra's compulsive thrashing and Amber's inert stillness seemed so wrong that Nan had to close her eyes before she started screaming.

When she opened them, Elliott was regarding her with concern, Zach with puzzlement. "How's Amber?" she asked.

Elliott shook his head dejectedly. "Her fever's been spiking all day," he said. "I've been using the lavender, but it's weird, it's like we're losing ground somehow. Little by little."

Nan exhaled heavily, exhaustion closing over her like a smothering shroud. "We can try rubbing her whole body down with the oil," she suggested. "Let me go see how much I have on hand." She started to leave the room but a sudden dizzy spell caused her to sink back down on Myra's bed.

"You okay?" Elliott asked anxiously.

"Oh yeah. I'm just tired," she said. "None of us got much sleep last night."

"That's for sure."

She stood up once again, but this time, her knees buckled and she collapsed onto the floor. Her head and limbs felt as heavy as neutron stars. She tried to lift them, but to no avail.

Elliott cried out in alarm and stooped down to gather her up in his arms. She felt as if she had no control over her muscles whatsoever, as if some invisible pygmy had shot her with a blow dart tipped in curare. She tried to speak, but even that seemed beyond her ability. She could do nothing while Elliott and Zach stretched her out on the ground and cushioned her head with a pillow. Elliott frenziedly chafed her cheeks and the backs of her hands, but soon she felt her eyes rolling back in her head and the darkness that rushed to greet her felt tangible, like water, like silk.

"Not now," she tried to mutter, but all she could hear was wind blowing past her ears. "Help!" she called. Or thought she did.

But the only response was still more darkness gathering, until a strange, dancing, piercing light glimmered in the distance. And out of the light slithered two enormous, garishly colored snakes who wrapped around her with terrifying tenderness and whispered insistently with their caressing, flickering tongues.

CHAPTER 25

Nan settled back in the couch, crossed her legs. A fire was raging in the fireplace facing her; in fact, the room felt too warm. The glow from the fire seemed to provide the only light, however; its writhing energy cast flaring, hollow shadows in an arc about the hearth. Against the mantel rested a broom with a gnarled, crooked tree limb for its handle, looking almost alive in the restless light. And she couldn't be sure, given the dimness, but she thought a lizard lay on the hearth, too, curled sinuously around the bristles of the broom. The room seemed familiar somehow, but she couldn't actually say where she was. She turned her gaze to her companion on the sofa, a beautiful young woman dressed in such dazzling hues of emerald, sapphire, and scarlet that her clothing resembled plumage.

"Can I get you anything to drink?" she asked, her voice carrying a tinkling, musical timbre, like ice shards clinking against the shore of a half-frozen pond.

"I am pretty thirsty," Nan admitted. And hot, too, she thought. Was a fire really necessary?

The woman got up and returned with a glass of cool water, which Nan drank gratefully in one long, gurgling swallow. She had a strange feeling that she was in the middle of a conversation with this woman, but she couldn't remember what they were talking about nor even how she had gotten here.

"As I was saying," said the woman, reaching over to touch Nan lightly on the knee.

"Right," Nan responded automatically. She racked her brain to remember what the topic of conversation had been.

"Normally, I don't take sides. The whole point of my work is to benefit everyone, to maintain balance."

Nan nodded. "Yes, I try to do the same thing in my work."

The woman smiled. "We know. That's why we invited you here."

We? thought Nan, perplexed; who's "we?" "Now, uh, remind me again—what's your work?"

"I move information."

An interesting way to put it, thought Nan. Did she run a courier service? Work on the Internet?

"Unfortunately, a lot of misinformation seems to have been generated lately. And I hate to say it, but it originated primarily from your side."

"M–my side?"

"Yes, and the really unfortunate thing is, misinformation begets misguided actions. I have to maintain balance above all, and if the balance becomes threatened seriously enough, everything is at risk. The entire system can go down."

Nan pondered this. The woman kept acting as if Nan knew what she was talking about, but for the life of her, she didn't seem to have a clue.

"Your side affected the balance so egregiously that I had to step in. It wasn't something I wanted to do, I hope you understand that. Drastic measures are never my first choice. And it's not too late to negotiate. However, the first gesture needs to come from your people. They're the ones who declared war in the first place."

She squinted at her companion, feeling hopelessly thick.

Was the woman Middle Eastern? Central American? She had an exotic cast to her features. And now that she thought about it, the woman had an intriguing accent that she found difficult to place, too.

"And quite frankly, it's not a war you can win. Even if you win, you lose. You of all people should understand that. Even more to the point, I can't allow you to win. My responsibility is to the whole, and the fact is, your people are more expendable. It's not the way I like to look at things, of course. But it happens to be the truth."

"I'm sorry," Nan told her. "I just don't know what you're talking about. You seem to think I do, but—"

The woman held up a silencing finger. "You're a little muddled right now, which is completely understandable. Take your time. Everything will become clear in time."

"But somehow … I don't feel like I have any time," Nan protested.

"I have to go now," said the woman, rising and offering her hand.

Nan stood, too, grasped her hand a little desperately. Now what? she thought. But before she could even blink, she found herself outside, walking the streets of an ancient village crowded with narrow stone buildings, their rooftops bristling with TV antennas. A turgid full moon floated in the sky, casting a deep orange light over every single surface like powder. And while Nan drank in its beauty, she found herself rising from the pavement. She drifted so leisurely, so languidly, it felt absolutely delicious, and she looked about as she rose. The roofs of the buildings were covered with a thick, lozenge-shaped terra cotta tile … every edge, every crease, every bump loomed sharp and clear and magnified.

It wasn't long before the village lay beneath her in miniature, a stubbled wrinkle in the earth's surface like a welt of coarse fabric. Soon, the continent lay sleeping below her in the syrupy golden-orange moonlight, and then before she knew it, the entire planet hung majestically before her in the utter blackness of space: a perfect, polished sphere, a living, brilliant, breathing orb, the most captivating creature she had ever beheld in her life.

Clouds swirled and snaked about the surface of the planet, but as she watched, the sphere began to glow from within, its outer husk to become transparent. She found herself staring at a beautiful, twinkling cell studded with precious gems on its surface, cytoplasm streaming about the interior with hypnotic, ceaseless grace. Mysterious lights flashed here and there, like lightning pulsing in a storm, and hauntingly familiar music oozed from every pore and prism.

She looked again and beheld a cathedral made entirely out of crystal. A gorgeous bird with brilliant plumage of emerald, sapphire, and scarlet swooped into the open door, carrying something in its beak. Nan followed the bird in through the entrance, and found before her a dazzling gold and ivory chapel, a private, sacred, inner sanctum. Into this chapel sailed the bird, and Nan followed it, shocked to discover what lay inside. Thousands upon thousands of snakes writhed within the interior, their movement ceaseless and hypnotic. The bird dropped its burden and Nan saw now that it had carried yet another snake, and when this creature fell into the writhing mass, a great boiling movement ensued.

As she watched, a cloud emerged from all of this activity, a silent, drifting, ominous cloud, whose very amorphousness gave her an odd chill. It drifted out of the chapel and she followed it. It drifted out of the cathedral and into the vastness, where Nan could see that an army of strange, menacing insects had gathered. The cloud floated towards them ever so gently, ever so slowly, but soon it had enveloped them—but only briefly. After a moment, it withdrew, gliding in its unhurried fashion back into the cathedral, back into the chapel, where Nan could see that the snakes boiled up in an even greater frenzy.

What happened next took her breath away. An entire army of vicious, angry hornets came speeding out of the cathedral, buzzing furiously as they rushed the approaching swarm, stinging and stinging and jabbing and stabbing their enemies. Dead insects began to litter the ground in grotesque and hideous surfeit. When enough of them had accumulated, their bodies began to putrefy and liquefy. The toxic stench that arose from the pool they created burned Nan's lungs and turned her stomach so violently that she vomited, over and over and over again.

She fell into a swoon, and when she awoke, she lay on a bier in a forest, where snow fell gently all around her, cooling her, soothing her. The stars burned brightly overhead, even though this made no sense, no sense at all as the snow fell ever more thickly and sensuously, brushed her lips and her eyelashes, flocked her hair and blanketed her body. She sank back into unknowingness, sank gratefully into the void, into the utter blankness and blackness that cradled her. She felt nothing, she felt everything, she felt as transparent as glass and as solid as the earth. She slept, deeply and endlessly. She slept until the beginning of time and the end of space. And all the while the snow fell, whispering its ageless secrets into her ears, singing to her very bones, kissing her lips and caressing her heart ... And she saw that her heart had turned into the earth and her bones into snakes, and everywhere lightning was flickering and flashing and darkness was gathering and smothering and she lay suspended in time and outside of space and she slept ... .

CHAPTER 26

When Nan awoke, she found herself surrounded by utter
silence. Pale shafts of chilly afternoon light filtered through the
windows of her bedroom; she lay in her bed dressed in a pair
of flannel pajamas she gradually came to realize were drenched
from her own perspiration. She threw back the covers to get
up and change, but just that movement alone exhausted her.
Feebly gathering the blankets around her, she began to shiver,
her teeth chattering.

"Elliott?" she croaked. "Anybody?"

She didn't hear a sound except for the grinding,
mechanized whir of the clock on her bedside table, which,
in the stillness, seemed amplified by a factor of a thousand.
Maybe everyone was out, she thought. How long had she been
sleeping? And what ... what had she been dreaming about?
It seemed important, whatever it was. She lay quietly, trying
to remember what had occupied her consciousness while she
slept. Suddenly it all came rushing back into her mind with
startling clarity. "My God," she whispered, compelled once
again to struggle out of the bed. Clinging to the furniture for
support, she staggered out to the hallway where she clutched
the bannister and called downstairs.

"Elliott? Zach? Anybody home?"

She heard a movement from the den and Elliott came to the bottom of the stairs and looked up. When he saw her, he came dashing up the stairs two at a time, his face contorted with such vast relief it looked like pain. He grabbed her up in an embrace when he reached her, hugging and hugging her.

"Thank God!" he choked, rocking back and forth with her in his arms until her knees began to buckle. He stooped to pick her up and deposited her back in the bed, exclaiming over how soaked she was and ransacking her drawers for an extra set of pajamas. When he found some, he carefully and tenderly helped her to change, brushing her damp hair out of her face and plumping her pillows up for her.

"You scared the holy shit out of me!" he scolded, once he got her settled and comfortable.

"Sorry," she said, reaching up to caress his cheek. "I don't know what happened."

"You got knocked unconscious by influenza would be my guess."

She nodded. "It was weird. I had some really strange dreams."

"Don't tell me. Snakes?"

"They were part of it." She paused, remembering. "How's Amber?"

Elliott's face fell. "She's ... still sick."

"Not getting any better?"

He shook his head, tears brimming his eyes. "No. Worse."

Nan sighed heavily. "What about Myra?"

Elliott got up, began to pace the room. He went over to Nan's dresser and picked up a vase, examining it for no reason that Nan could see. "She's been ... fairly out of control, I'm afraid. After you fell ill, she became so agitated that she was actually hurting herself, so we tried making some restraints out of bed sheets, but that seemed to make her go berserk."

Nan closed her eyes, trying unsuccessfully to block out the

mental images that this information evoked.

"So I gave her a sedative, which seemed to help a little, but then Zach came and sat by her bed and started doing these … guided meditations, I guess, and that calmed her down considerably."

"Really." Nan opened her eyes, intrigued. "Who would've thought?"

Elliott gave a short nod. "Indeed." He came back and sat down on the bed, tucking a lock of Nan's hair behind her ear. "She's been alternately wild and crazed and submissive and docile. Zach definitely seems to be the best with her. He's been tending to Amber, too, but unfortunately, nothing seems to be helping her." Elliott wiped away a tear. "I'm afraid—" he stopped.

Nan took both of his hands in her own. "We'll find a way, Elliott. We will."

Elliott regarded her without hope. "We'll need a miracle at this point," he responded dejectedly.

Nan bit her lip, blinking back her own tears. "Did you try rubbing her down with essential oils?"

"No, we weren't sure what to do. You became unconscious before we could try it."

"How long have I been out?"

"Two days."

"Two days?!" she exclaimed. "You've got to be kidding!"

"No, I'm afraid not."

Nan struck the bed with her fists. "Damn! Well, here's what you do: look in my kit for all the lavender oil you can find and rub it all over her. Just rub and rub. Make sure you get every square inch of her body. Keep her warm, of course, while you're doing this. You might want to build a fire in the fireplace and work on her in front of it."

Elliott was already on his feet, heading for the closet where Nan kept her first aid kit.

"And then I need to get to the lab," she said.

He halted, turned back around with an incredulous look. "You're joking, right?"

Nan gave a weak laugh. "I know I'm still sick, but Elliott—you're not going to believe the dreams I had while I was out."

Elliott groaned. "Jesus, Nan, you're delirious. Listen, whatever dreams you had—and I have no doubt they were compelling—"

Nan shook her head violently. "No, I know how this sounds. I do. But I—I think I have the key to this whole thing! I know what that weird new protein does. I know why this whole catastrophe happened!"

Elliott continued to regard her with a skeptical expression. "Okay, look—where's Zach?"

"Downstairs. Catching a little bit of sleep."

"Get him up here. You take care of Amber, and I'll start doing what I need to do."

Elliott heaved a sigh and fetched the first aid kit out of the closet. He brought it over to the bed to rummage through it. "Just promise me you won't try to get out of bed for a few days," he said, holding Nan's gaze.

She dropped her eyes and picked through the kit, looking for bottles of lavender. "I can't make that promise," she replied stubbornly. "But I promise I won't get out of bed today. Would that make you happy?"

He growled. "Marginally."

Nan gathered up the bottles she found and dropped them into Elliott's hand with a clink. "Here's three. That should be enough, I think. Get Zach for me, okay?"

Elliott left the room and headed downstairs; soon she heard Zach bounding up the steps. He looked tired, she noted, when he came into the room. Of course, these days, everyone looked tired.

She thanked him for being so kind to her mother and he shrugged as if it were nothing; but she could tell that he cared. She asked him to pull up a seat next to the bed, which he did, regarding her quizzically. She opened her mouth to speak but then realized she didn't know exactly what to say. The content of the dream remained sparklingly clear in her mind, but the significance of the content remained open to interpretation. She felt that she had communicated with some form of viral or microbial consciousness, but she had no way to prove that. And she knew that to say such a thing to anyone except, perhaps, Zach was to invite scorn, pity, and ridicule—even outright censure.

"You know those devas?" she said.

"Yeah," he replied suspiciously.

"Well, I think I encountered one while I was sick."

He didn't respond, just waited for what she was going to say next.

"Maybe not a deva," she amended. "But something like it." She picked absentmindedly at the quilt that covered the bed.

"What did it say?"

"She. She said that humans were more expendable than microbes. At least, that's how I interpret what she was telling me. And that we had picked a fight we couldn't win."

Zach gave a cynical laugh. "That's for damn sure."

"I think I even received a glimpse of how microbes are managing to defeat all of our defenses—or, actually, any of our defenses that are really offenses."

"You did?" Zach said cautiously.

"At any rate, I don't know exactly what to do yet, but I think if you and I and my grad students all put our heads together, we might be able to figure something out."

Zach nodded, beginning to look animated. "What do you want me to do?"

"Well, if you could call everybody from the lab and ask them to come over here, we could have a powwow, hash some stuff out. Then—oh, shit."

"What?"

"I missed that meeting that Ron told me about. Shit!"

Zach propped his foot on his knee, clasped his hands around his leg. "We went."

"We?" Nan inquired, confused.

"Me and your grad students. Most of 'em, anyway. I was going to tell you about this. The meeting was about the use of lab space to fight the pandemic. And that Ron dude was hoping to take over your lab space. You know that already, though. Anyway, the only way we were able to fend him off was to give the preliminary results about the resistance factor and the carrier virus. We've been given two weeks to come up with something to do with this information, or his biotech company gets your lab."

Nan gaped at him. "Two weeks?" she repeated, dumbfounded.

"Two weeks."

Nan writhed in frustration, bunched up the covers in her hands. "God, what an asshole," she muttered.

"No shit," Zach agreed.

She sat staring into space for a few moments. If only she didn't feel so damned feeble! "Okay, then," she said finally. "We need to get started right away. Tell everyone to get over here, okay? And let them know it's an emergency."

After Zach left to make his phone calls, Nan slumped back in the bed, exhausted from talking. Tears leaked from beneath her closed eyelids she felt so tired and frustrated. She couldn't believe that she had gotten sick now and that she had only two weeks to come up with some tangible results. Of course, if Amber didn't respond to the essential oil treatment, two weeks from now might be too late for her. Nan had never in her life wanted to work so much as she did now; but she had to be realistic about her physical condition. She was, quite simply, too ill to work right now. She didn't need Elliott to tell her that.

She drowsed for a little while, awakening when she heard voices floating up the stairs. As the group filed into the room, she felt relieved to see that everyone had come: Janice, Joshua,

Felix, Teresa, and Connor. Zach hovered in the doorway, too, nervous and fidgety. Elliott came up shortly with some folding chairs and saw to it that everyone was seated, then took Zach's post at the door to listen for Amber or Myra. The sharp, woodsy tang of the lavender oil clung to him and filled up the room. Nan enjoyed the fragrance, feeling that it cleared her fuzzy head somewhat.

"Okay," she announced, once everyone had quieted down. "I have some information that I think might help us. That weird amorphous protein—it's like a molecular copying machine, or a camera, or molding clay. I believe it to be a microbial equivalent of our immune system, except that it works on a molecular level, rather than a cellular one. Somehow—and just how is a matter of extremely interesting speculation—these microbes, including viruses that are ensconced inside our cells, are able to sense a threat coming at them. The threat triggers the production of our mystery protein. It is transported outside the cell where it encounters the threat and takes some kind of snapshot. I can only think that it must receive an electromagnetic imprint of the molecule. Then the imprinted protein returns to the nucleus where it stimulates the production of whatever molecule or molecules are needed to neutralize the threat. It's the by-product of the neutralized molecular complex, I believe, that is so toxic and virulent in the majority of cases." She paused. "Any questions so far?"

No one moved or spoke. The group looked both fascinated and stricken.

Nan cleared her throat and continued. "Now, why this has happened is another question altogether. I believe that human activities have tipped the balance of power in the biosphere to a dangerous state of disequilibrium. By eradicating so many species, we're seriously eroding the sum total of genetic diversity on this planet. As everyone in this room knows, genetic diversity is absolutely essential for the long term survival of life on Earth. And as everyone in this room is also aware, half of the cells in our bodies are bacteria performing essential biological functions. If we kill them, we kill ourselves.

"I believe that the earth is an organism in her own right—capable of sensing and responding to threats." Nan swallowed, her tongue clicking dryly in her mouth. "This intelligence extends to every single living entity, including microbes. Including viruses. As incredible as this might seem, the defense system that the microbes have evolved, by seizing upon Zach's plasmid and then selectively assembling all the other genes it needed, can only suggest intelligence or consciousness of some kind. The short time frame in which this all happened suggests the same thing. We are dealing with an intelligent force here, gang. And we need to proceed with that assumption."

She looked around the room but was met with perplexed blankness.

"What do you suggest?" asked Elliott.

Nan exhaled heavily. "Well, that's where we all need to put our heads together. All I can suggest at the moment is what we refrain from doing. It would probably be the easiest approach to find some way to knock out the imprintable protein—lock it into a fixed configuration with a covalent bond of some sort so that it can't take information back to the microbial genome. But I'm afraid if we do that, this will be interpreted as a hostile act that once again threatens the survival of the microbial kingdom. Given the fact that we're dealing with an intelligent opponent here, I don't think it's too far-fetched to believe that microbes will just come up with some way around such an attempt. I think we need to, uh, well—negotiate."

"Negotiate?" Elliott burst out. "Just how, exactly, does one negotiate with a microbe?"

Teresa nodded in agreement. "Yes, I have to admit—that does sound a bit, um, well, you know ..."

"Insane?" Nan suggested.

"Very, very difficult, at the least," Joshua observed.

"Where did you get all this information, Nan?" asked Connor.

Nan caught Zach's amused gaze. "I—I've just been putting this all together while I've been sick," she said. "I'll admit, I'm relying heavily upon intuition. But honestly, I think that's what is needed right now. Intuition is where flashes of insight come from and quantum leaps in understanding take place. No one likes to say so, but science would be nowhere at all if we ignored our intuition. I'm asking all of you to start tuning into your own in coming up with a solution here. What about you, Zach? Any thoughts on this?"

He shifted uneasily in his seat. "Well, you know that I agree with you about the intelligence part. If you're right about the virulence being mostly associated with the neutralized molecular complex, then it would make sense to stop using drugs and antibiotics, for one thing."

Elliott coughed. "As a matter of fact, public health has some results that support this idea," he confirmed. "But that's not going to address our bodies' own defenses. If I understand your theory correctly, Nan, any kind of threat to these microbes is dealt with the same way. That would include antibodies and killer cells and the like. We can't exactly get our bodies to stop producing them. And if we did, then just the usual effects of the microbes would kill us."

"I know, I know," she responded glumly. "That's why I think what we need is cooperation. We need the microbes to cooperate with us on this—they have to want to help us out here. I know this sounds completely and totally crazy. But our other approaches certainly aren't working at the moment."

The room fell silent while everyone digested this information. Elliott cocked his head, evidently thought he heard something, and hurried downstairs to check on Amber and Myra. Nan sank back against her pillow, her brain in a feverish state of overstimulation while her body seemed as if it weighed so much she almost couldn't feel it at all.

"Well," Janice said finally, "if what you think is happening is really happening, then it seems to me the responsible thing is to let people know that they might want to refrain from trying to treat diseases with drugs and antibiotics for the time being. We can at least post the information we have on the Internet and people can make their own decisions about what to do."

Nan nodded. "I was thinking about that."

"I can do that, Nan," Joshua offered.

"Okay. Thanks, Josh." She waited for other comments, but everyone seemed a bit stymied. "All right, look—let's break for the day. I'm exhausted and I don't think I'm good for much at the moment. I should probably get some rest."

The students jumped to their feet, telling her to get plenty of rest and take care of herself. "Hell," said Felix, "if you can get this much done while you're practically comatose, you probably should go back to sleep."

Nan laughed and thanked them for their support. They all headed out except for Zach, who hung around after they left.

"Are you doing okay?" he mumbled, eyes downcast.

"I won't lie to you—I've certainly felt better. But … I'll be fine." She smiled at him, touched by his awkward solicitude. "So much for my supposed invincibility to illness, huh? I guess we won't need to study my blood after all."

Zach shook his head, briefly met her gaze. "I'll tell you who we should be studying, though, and that's Myra. Has she gotten sick at all during this whole pandemic?"

Nan frowned, considering. "No, she hasn't. I mean, apparently, people with dementia often have extremely robust immune systems—or something. They rarely seem to become ill with infectious diseases. At least, it's less common than in the general elder population. But actually, she's always been pretty amazing in this regard. I don't believe I ever remember her getting sick when I was growing up. And she certainly hasn't been ill lately. Not since she's come to live with me."

Zach slouched against the wall, folded his arms. "What do you think? Would it be okay to get some blood from her and do a few tests?"

"I can't see how that would hurt," she said, intrigued. Why hadn't she thought of this herself? She had, in fact, always been impressed with her mother's physical resilience. Perhaps the dementia so overwhelmed every other aspect of Myra's being these days that it had blocked out all of Nan's other perceptions of her. She thought of her mother as ill, not well.

"Okay, then," Zach replied. "Do you and Elliott have syringes and stuff? And, uh, would he mind drawing the samples, do you think? I don't have a lot of experience drawing blood from people."

"No, I don't think he would mind. And yes, I believe he does have the necessary supplies to get the samples."

"Cool. I'll get started."

"Thanks, Zach."

"No problem," he said, then ducked out of the room.

Nan closed her eyes after he left, trying to calm her mind so that it was in synch with her body. Fever often did this, she had noticed over the years—took her brain out of gear and then revved up the engine. What was it about Myra's immune system that made it so she never got sick? Thinking about it now, she realized that she had always unconsciously assumed that her mother must have a very aggressive immune system, that invaders didn't get a chance to secure a foothold. But perhaps that wasn't it at all. Hosts and reservoirs of a disease harbored the infectious microbe but didn't express symptoms of illness. The microbe and the host had established some sort of harmonious balance, some happy medium. What was it Lewis Thomas had said? Disease usually resulted from inconclusive negotiations for symbiosis. Perhaps Myra's immune system was not only clever, it was accommodating.

Before long, however, drowsiness overtook her, and she fell

into a deep, dark fathomless sleep. This time, she didn't dream. But she healed ... .

CHAPTER 27

Nan set aside the legal pad on which she'd been scribbling notes all morning. She was starting to feel better enough that she thought she could probably go into the lab this afternoon—for a couple of hours, anyway. The past three days had been psychologically agonizing and she felt desperate to get out of the house.

Amber had rallied a bit after the essential oil treatment, but then she sank back into a feverish torpor, while Myra had bordered on the hysterical. Like a child who acts out when her parents were stressed to the maximum, Myra had begun to obsess over things she couldn't articulate, or couldn't remember, or couldn't remember how to articulate—it wasn't clear which. Then her right arm would shake violently and she would emit tortured, plaintive cries that turned into howls and screeches. Zach was spending most of his time in the lab analyzing the blood samples he had obtained from her and Nan was trying to stay in bed, so it was usually Elliott to whom the task fell of trying to calm her.

As much as Nan pitied her mother's frenzied state, when she heard her howling and screeching, it was all she could do not to start screaming herself and she found herself, to her

horror and exasperation, fantasizing about taping her mouth
shut and strapping her to her bed. Myra's agitation was so
seemingly mindless and so irritating and so exhausting for
everyone around her that Nan felt stripped of all patience.
Amber was sick and needed quiet; Nan was recuperating and
needed rest. But Myra was thrashing around and squealing like
a banshee.

Thankfully, she was quiet at the moment. Nan heard
Elliott moving around downstairs, washing dishes in the
kitchen. She decided that now might be a good time to call
Marjory in England and let her know what she and her team
had found out about the pandemic, as she had promised
she would do. It could be helpful, too, to see if Marjory had
any information or insights to offer. She experienced a great
deal of difficulty getting through, even though, according
to Elliott, the government had currently established a state
of national emergency which required everyone working
in a nonessential sector to suspend their regular activities
and devote their efforts to what were deemed essential
endeavors: food production and distribution, energy
production and distribution, medical care and research, and
communications. Only one radio station aired now: NPR.
And only one television station was broadcasting: PBS. All of
the programming revolved around information that people
needed to survive.

Despite these efforts, things were running anything but
smoothly. Hoarding had become a serious problem, and food
was getting scarce. For the last three dinners in a row, Nan and
everyone in her household had eaten rice and acorn squash.
Heating oil supplies had become tight, with practically no
new deliveries taking place. Elliott had turned the thermostat
in the house down to the mandated 63 degrees, but this had
increased his worry and concern about Amber. Not only
that, the first cases of diphtheria had been identified locally,
and water needed to be boiled for twenty minutes before

drinking. Conventional water treatment wasn't working any more. In fact, some scary reports of fatal reactions to the usual microbes present on raw food was prompting everyone to cook all vegetables and even fruits before eating them. If someone didn't come up with a solution soon, the human race wasn't going to survive. Their war upon disease had taken a frightening, ruinous, nightmarish turn.

She finally managed to put her call through to Marjory's home, as it was evening in England, and Nan felt so glad when she answered that tears crowded into her eyes. Marjory sounded brisk and calm, which bolstered Nan's spirits considerably; she sounded glad to hear from Nan as well. She asked after Nan's own health, and Nan told her that she was recuperating from the flu but that she was calling to fill her in on what her research team had come up with in the past six weeks since she left England. Nan told her about Zach's plasmid, how it had mutated, and the role of the amorphous protein in providing microbes with the means to thwart any conceivable defense. Marjory didn't say much while Nan explained what she had found, and when Nan finished, there was nothing but silence on her end.

"M–Marjory?" Nan prompted, fearing they'd been cut off.

Marjory sighed. "I'm here, pet," she said. "My goodness, what a frightful development."

"No kidding."

"Well, I have to say that this explains a great deal. We've been finding the same patterns over here that you have in the States—that patients who use drugs and antibiotics to treat their illnesses have been faring worse than those who haven't. But I've also been noticing an interesting positive correlation between fatalities and patients who suffer from allergies, with their overly aggressive immune systems."

"Really," Nan responded, intrigued.

"So ... you've identified the problem. Have you come up with any solutions?"

"Not yet," Nan told her. "We're working on it, though. It seems to me we need to somehow find a way to, well—declare a truce of some kind. In a way that the microbes understand. I know that sounds sort of nuts, but—"

"Not at all," Marjory replied firmly. "I've thought for a long time that we've been conditioning our immune systems with a certain paranoid flavor. I privately believe that the increase in asthma and allergies might be at least partially explained by a certain germ phobic stance programmed into the system, along with a corresponding lack of challenges to the immune system. Up until now, we've managed to do a good job of avoiding exposure to infectious organisms. All dressed up in full war regalia with nowhere to go, aren't we?"

"Until now," Nan pointed out grimly.

"Indeed!" Marjory concurred. "And now it appears that our defenses have turned into Trojan horses."

"That's … about it." Nan picked absentmindedly at the coverlet that she had drawn around her knees. She hadn't mentioned anything about her dream, so she was rather startled when Marjory said softly, "She's protecting her own."

"Excuse me?" Nan blurted.

"Earth, dear. We're the disease, unfortunately."

"Yes, it seems that way."

They both fell silent.

"Well," Marjory finally said. "I'll be sure to give this some thought, and if I come up with anything I'll let you know. You've done some excellent work, Nan. Keep trying, won't you?"

When she hung up, Nan spent several minutes thinking over Marjory's comments about conditioning the immune system. Recent experiments had determined that an immune system could be programmed, in much the same way as Pavlov's dogs. Researchers would pair a strong, distinctive taste or scent with the application of a powerful drug to sufferers of autoimmune disorders and soon just the taste or scent alone would provoke the same response in the individual's immune system as the drug. In addition, countless experiments had demonstrated the link between a person's thoughts and moods and the state of his or her immune system, in the activity of macrophages and so forth. It didn't sound so far-fetched to think that a widespread and deeply entrenched fear of microbes could put the human immune system on a DEFCON 1 alert when in fact most of the time all it had to contend with was a band of ragtag bandits armed with tire irons and kitchen knives.

Nan also pondered the fact that the cells of the immune system were capable of using intracellular mutation processes in a directed way to produce the antibodies and T cells necessary to grapple with the ever-changing microbial population that bodies encountered. This was how the human immune system was able to produce millions of antibodies without having to carry around millions of genes, a clumsy strategy which would make the genome far too big to be practical. Obviously, the microbes were able to mutate intelligently as well; in a healthy, well-adapted system, the mutations on both sides proceeded in a balanced way. Fascinating, amazing stuff, but ... how could she use this information?

An answer seemed tantalizingly close, but for the life of her, she could not wrap her mind around it. Impatiently, she threw back the covers and climbed out of bed, clutching at the bedside table when she found herself swaying with dizziness. She waited until the dizzy spell passed and then began, slowly and laboriously, to get dressed. She felt as if she were ninety years old. Fifteen exhausting minutes later, she bumped down the stairs holding onto the bannister for support as she went, feeling as if her head was filled with gelatin and she was wearing someone else's prescription eyeglasses.

She slipped into the kitchen first and sidled up behind Elliott as he stood at the sink, rinsing plates and silverware.

She entwined her arms around him and gave him a long, heartfelt hug, beaming love and gratitude into his back as she held him. She could tell the poor guy was utterly exhausted—physically and emotionally. But he kept plugging away at caring for everyone as best he could, sweet, good man that he was. She had noticed, too, that he and Zach seemed to have worked out a truce, even a grudging mutual respect.

"I hope you're not getting ready to do what I think you are," he said, glancing back at her.

"I'm just going in for a couple of hours. I want to talk to everyone and see how they're doing, find out what kind of results they're coming up with."

Elliott shook his head. "You're a hard woman, Dr. Schulte. Hard-headed, that is."

"You wanna make something of it?" she teased.

He dried his hands on the towel he had slung over his shoulder, then turned around to face her, rested his hands on her waist. "Yeah," he told her.

"Okay then."

He kissed her on the nose, pulled her closer. "I am so glad you're on the mend," he said.

"Me, too." She snuggled into his embrace for a moment, then jumped when she heard a thud and a crash from Myra's room. They both hastened to her aid and found her lying on the floor, along with lamp from her bedside table, a small wisp of smoke curling up from the broken bulb, the lamp shade torn and bent. Myra wore a nonplused expression that Nan didn't quite know how to interpret.

"Are you okay, Mom?" she exclaimed.

"You okay?" Myra echoed, her lips flat, her eyes bulging.

Nan stooped down beside her, searching for signs of trauma to any part of her body. "Did you hurt anything?"

"Hurt anything?" Nan waited for her to answer the question, but Myra just looked at her.

"Yeah, did you bonk anything, hit anything?"

"Yes!" she burst out.

Nan sighed. "Can you show me where? Point to it?" She waited while her mother slowly and gracefully raised one arm and pointed to her back, reminding her of an actress in one of Robert Wilson's glacially slow-motion stage productions. Nan sighed again. "Let's see if we can get her back in the bed, Elliott."

He nodded, grabbed Myra under her arms. Nan picked up her mother's legs and then they heaved her into the bed. Nan took the Arnica ointment that she kept in Myra's bedside table and smoothed it over her dry, bony back, feeling an awful, complex mixture of emotions. She felt so sorry for her poor old mom, falling and hurting herself and unable to care for herself or even talk. She felt angry and frustrated that her mother was having to go through this, and that she was having to go through it with her. She felt guilty for feeling angry; she felt trapped, and guilty about that, too. She felt fiercely protective toward her brave, vulnerable mother, but she also desperately wanted to get away from her.

Nan told her that she was going to the lab for a while and that she would be back soon. She cautioned her once again not to try to get up without someone there to help her, but she did this more out of habit than any belief that Myra would be able to comply. Then she tiptoed into the den to check on Amber, Elliott following after he'd made sure that Myra was comfortably arranged in bed. Amber slept, her breathing shallow and somewhat labored, tiny whistling sounds coming from her stopped-up nose. Her color had turned sallow and her hair had become limp, as if all the bounce and bloom of her being was slowly seeping away. Nan's heart ached so much as she stood and gazed at Amber, she turned to Elliott and grabbed him for support. He tightened his arms around her, his body rigid with despair and fear.

Reluctant to disturb the child, Nan finally disengaged herself from Elliott and turned away. "I'll be home in a couple of hours," she told him. "I promise I won't leave you alone for very long."

She walked light-headedly out to her car, well aware that she wasn't in the best state to be driving. She took her time and headed slowly over to the University, drenched in perspiration by the time she got there. She rested for several minutes in her car before getting out, relieved when she looked around the faculty parking lot and didn't see Ron's car. Then she plodded to the lab, feeling as if her brain floated above her skull.

When she arrived at the lab, she found the group gathered in a tense little knot, engaged in a discussion of some kind. Everyone glanced up, startled, when Nan opened the door. They all greeted her, appearing uneasy. Teresa's face was streaked with tears, and Connor looked angry.

"What's ... up?" Nan asked.

No one answered right away; they all regarded one another hesitantly, evidently hoping that someone else would speak up first.

When no one volunteered, Nan touched Teresa on the shoulder. "Have you been crying, Teresa?"

Teresa nodded stiffly, pulling away from her.

"What about?" she asked, surprised and a little hurt.

Teresa threw her hands in the air. "I just can't do this! I can't work on trying to ... negotiate with these stupid microbes!" she shouted, tears starting up afresh. "They killed my sister! And my favorite cousin, and my favorite uncle, goddamn it! They killed my brother's fiancée, and they killed a friend of mine I've known since I was six years old! I hate them!"

Nan blinked, unsure what to say.

Connor remarked, "I feel the same way, Nan. My folks are having a real hard time, both of them sick with pneumonia. I've lost some family and friends, too. I don't mind working on ways to combat disease, but I just don't have it in me to try to cooperate with it. I don't think the microbes will cooperate, frankly. I mean, why should they? It's survival of the fittest. We need them, but they don't need us. In fact, we're in their way right now."

Nan groped for the nearest chair and sat down heavily, wishing she didn't feel so muddled. "I understand how you must feel," she told them. "Does everyone else feel the same way?" The rest of the group shook their heads. "I see. Okay. Well, no one has to do any work they don't want to, all right?"

"But Nan," Felix burst out, "this is a crisis! There is so much work to do—we need them! We need everyone who can work!"

She closed her eyes wearily. "I know that, believe me. I feel awful that I haven't been more help."

"You've been sick!" Janice exclaimed indignantly.

"I know. Still." Nan gazed bleakly at the floor, trying to muster her strength and thoughts. "Look, I realize that we're at an extreme disadvantage here in terms of competitive natural selection. If that were all that was going on right now, I might agree with you, Connor. But the fact is, I don't think that is the whole story. We've neglected cooperation in nature for so long that we can't see anything except competition. But the counterweight for competition is cooperation. And biology, if it strives for anything, strives for balance."

She stopped, sought Connor's and Teresa's gaze. "'Survival of the fittest' doesn't just refer to competition, you know—it doesn't just mean the biggest, baddest guy on the block. It refers to the ones who survive because they are fit in the most successful way, whatever way that is. And right now, I believe the ones who will survive will be the ones who cooperate. I'm not asking anyone to agree with me or to work on something they don't believe in. But out of all the mass of confusion and devastation and horror of the past couple of months, this is the one thing that I feel I can say with some confidence: We have to cooperate. We either cooperate or we perish. And anyone who wants to help me with this strategy is welcome to do so."

301

Teresa kept wiping her eyes, and Connor walked away from the group. Nan got up and put her arm around Teresa. "Please don't think I'm going to feel let down if you can't do this," she said. "You've suffered an awful lot. I'm not expecting you to work, not with all you've been through."

Teresa gave a small sob. "I just need to go home and think about this for a while," she said, her voice wobbling.

"You do that, sweetie," Nan replied. Teresa gave Nan's hand a squeeze and then gathered up her coat and purse. Connor watched her, giving her a smile and a wave as she left the room, but he made no move to go. Nan turned her attention back to the remaining group. "So ... does anyone have any results they want to share?" she asked hopefully.

Zach cleared his throat. "Yeah, I do," he said.

Nan brightened. "What have you got?"

"Well, your mom has a very interesting constitution. She actually harbors quite a few bugs. But nothing is overrunning her system, the way an infection would. All her resident flora seem to be kept in check. She's not eradicating anything completely, but at the same time, she's not allowing anything to take over, either. It's very intriguing."

Nan pondered this. She knew that most people thought a prerequisite of health was to be germ-free, but in fact, most humans were infected with such critters as herpes virus and cytomegalovirus; they just never experienced any symptoms from them. Those people who did experience symptoms had outbreaks and "infections" only when their immune system was stressed or impaired in some way.

"The immune system of the future?" Joshua mused.

"Perhaps," murmured Nan. "What about the current flu virus? Does she show any signs of harboring that?"

"Oh yeah. She hasn't been sick, though, has she?" Zach chafed his arms; the lab felt quite chilly, Nan realized.

"No. Not from flu." Nan tugged at her lower lip with her fingers, mulling over the implications of this information. "If only we could give everyone in the world my mother's immune system."

"That would be nice," Janice agreed.

"Hmmmm." Nan felt it out there—the solution shimmering somewhere just beyond her reach. "You know, the carrier virus that spread the resistance factor ... from everything that we can determine, didn't it pick and choose the genes it wanted from the frog genome to come up with its mutations?"

Felix nodded soberly. "Well, that's the only way we could explain the data."

"What if we were somehow able to get it to select some information from Myra's immune system?"

Zach's eyes lit up. "Yes!" he exclaimed. Everyone else perked up, too. Then Connor said, "How do you propose to do that? What—you plan on having a little chat with the virus?"

Nan reflected on her dream, thinking that perhaps a chat wasn't such a bad idea. She didn't feel like sharing this perspective with her lab staff, however. "Not per se," she began; but then Joshua jumped in eagerly.

"Not a bad idea, Connor!" he exclaimed.

"Excuse me?" said Janice.

"Well, not a chat in the usual way, of course. We send a telegram!"

"A telegram?" echoed Felix, confused. Nan saw where he was going, however.

"A genetic telegram," she said. "We construct another plasmid. We decide upon a message that we want to convey and then we figure out the best way to say it—in genetic code. One the microbial world will understand."

"Precisely!" Joshua beamed. "The language of microbes and cells is molecular. That's how they communicate."

"Whoa, wait a minute!" Connor protested. "We're going to come up with some way to say, 'Pretty please, Mr. Virus, will you help us design our immune systems so that we can withstand your onslaught?'"

Nan, Zach, and Joshua exchanged glances. "Basically, yes," said Nan.

Connor squeezed his eyes shut in disbelief, then opened them again as he burst out, "Look, no offense, guys. I know that this has been an awfully long haul—and that you're still suffering from the effects of the flu, Nan—but that just sounds …well… unbelievably stupid and naïve, if you ask me! I mean, forget about how you're going to express that in some sort of 'molecular language!' Why on Earth would the virus do that, even if we could somehow communicate that request?"

"In the spirit of cooperation," Zach responded. "Viruses need higher organisms to replicate and exist."

Connor rolled his eyes. "Yeah, it's sure given a lot of evidence that it's willing to cooperate with the human race."

"Well, we've never attempted any sort of cooperation with this virus," Nan observed. "Have we?"

"No, but—Jesus, I can't even believe we're having this conversation!" he exploded. "Have you all gone completely nuts? Viruses don't have minds, okay? They don't reason! They don't think. They do what they do just because they do it! They're nucleic acids wrapped in protein coats. That's all they are!"

"Basically, that's all we are," Zach retorted. "And if you ask me, we behave a lot more mindlessly than microbes do!"

"Okay, let's move on," Nan interjected. "I realize that not everyone is going to agree with me; but I believe that the microbial population of this planet possesses a collective consciousness in just the same way as humans do. Biological wisdom exists that every single organism and cell seems to be able to tap into. It's how electrons know how to spin, DNA repair enzymes know how to fix chromosomal damage, and embryos know how to develop. We don't understand it, it's true. We don't know where it comes from. But it's there, and if we refuse to acknowledge it and work with it, then we are being willfully blind. And that, in my opinion, is how we got ourselves into this mess to begin with. No one's expecting you to help us on this, Connor. But I am following through on this."

Everyone in the room was so caught up in the debate that no one noticed someone else had stepped quietly into the lab. They looked up in dismay, however, when Ron came forward, laughing so loudly it hurt Nan's ears. "I can't believe what I'm hearing!" he guffawed. "This is my competition? Excuse me for saying so, Dr. Doolittle, but talking to viruses seems just a little loony tunes, even for you!" Zach and Joshua glared at him, while Nan sagged in her chair and Janice and Felix looked chastened. He turned to Connor. "Listen, if you want to do real science, come work in my lab. We can use a bright young scientist like you."

Connor clenched his fists. "I'm going home for the day," he announced. "Thanks for your offer, Dr. Holt, but I'm not sure what I want to do right now. Sorry, Nan. I'll talk to you later, okay?"

Nan nodded, hating Ron so much at this moment she wanted to punch him in the face. She knew it wasn't highly evolved to consider resorting to physical violence, but she couldn't help herself. "Did you have some actual business to conduct here, Ron?" she snapped. "Or did you just come in to insult me?"

"I just wanted to remind you and your staff that you have ten more days to wrap things up. After that, we'll be using this lab to tackle this problem the way it should be handled."

"Your reminder is duly noted. For the next ten days, however, this is my lab, and we'll be conducting whatever experiments we want. So, unless you want to be thrown out, I suggest you leave."

Zach, Joshua, and Felix took a step forward to lend weight to Nan's words. Ron gave another hearty laugh. "Pathetic," he pronounced, then turned on his heel and strolled out of the lab, taking his time.

After she was sure he was gone, Nan took a few deep breaths and gathered her remaining staff in a huddle. "Okay, this is what we're going to do," she told them. "Zach, you start getting some nucleotides ready. Janice, you work on isolating a batch of the carrier virus. Make as much as you can. And Joshua, you start working on a code, all right? I'll compose the message."

Everyone nodded eagerly. If anything, Nan noted to her satisfaction, Ron's bullying had galvanized them into action. A wave of fatigue washed over her, however, and she realized that she had probably accomplished all she could for today. She needed to go back home and get into bed.

Janice noticed her dragging and offered to drive her home, but Nan didn't want to distract anyone from their tasks. She assured her that she could make it home okay.

And if she was on the right track at all, perhaps going home and sleeping was the best thing she could possibly do in trying to figure out how on Earth to negotiate with a virus.

CHAPTER 28

Nan lay on the couch in the den with Amber snuggled up against her stomach. Glaring up at the ceiling, she tried to will more energy into her body, frustrated to find herself feeling tired and viremic after her visit to the lab. Her fever had risen back to 101, which was not enough to knock her into a visionary stupor, but definitely enough to make her feel lousy and listless. The heat from Amber's toasty little body wasn't really helping, but she felt the need to cuddle her, maintain physical contact.

Elliott reappeared, carrying a couple of glasses of clinking ice water, Amber's sporting a fancy straw with a plastic Tweetie Bird on it, which looked a bit like a bow tie. Amber sat up long enough to suck her water glass dry, then sank back against Nan with a bubbly, congested-sounding cough.

"How're you feeling?" he asked Nan.

She shrugged. "Shitty," she said.

He nodded, perched himself on the edge of the sofa, offering her the ice water. She drank it gratefully, knowing how much effort he had put into making it: boiling the water even for the ice cubes, sealing up the sterilized ice cube trays in plastic bags and setting them outside overnight so they would freeze. The freezer was stuffed with emergency food rations so there wasn't any room for ice trays.

"Now, go over this plan with me again," he told her. "I'm not sure I understand what you're hoping to do."

Nan bunched her pillow under her head, shifted around to get comfortable and still have one of her hands resting on Amber's shoulder. "Well, we thought we would compose a message out of nucleic acids, use triplet codons to try to communicate with the virus that's spreading the resistance factor."

Elliott pursed his lips. "But … using what language? You don't speak Virus, do you?"

"No, not exactly. I thought we would code the message in English. I know that sounds totally idiotic. But I felt that the virus communicated with me in my language in that dream I had." She could feel Amber dozing off again, her body sagging slackly against Nan in a way that made her heart catch. "It's like … there's a language of cells and molecules, and you can interpret it however you need to so that it makes sense to you. I feel like the cells and molecules of my body translated the microbes' information to my brain—through neurotransmitters, maybe, or something like them." She frowned, frustrated in trying to put her ideas and feelings into words. "It's almost as if intent exists in a universal language of probabilities, and when you fashion a molecule around it, it becomes a reality, one that other atoms recognize. Everything living is made of atoms, you know. They're obviously communicating with each other constantly. Perhaps our intent, once we set it in the form of a molecule—no matter what human language we choose for our code—will be recognized by the virus." She closed her eyes. What she said didn't make any sense, she knew that.

Elliott folded his arms and pondered. "Well," he said finally, "I'm just glad you're not having to submit a grant proposal on this idea."

Nan chuckled. "Why? You don't think I'd get a grant for this idea?"

He snorted, threw her an amused glance. "In fact, I have to be honest with you, Nan. It sounds like a completely irrational plan born out of nothing but desperation."

"You won't get any argument out of me," she replied, leaning her head against him bleakly. "I'm flying by the seat of my pants. I just refuse to give up until I've tried every single thing that occurs to me."

Elliott twisted around so that he could stroke her hair and gave her a kiss on the top of the head. "My girlfriend, the pit bull."

Nan tried to smile, but she shared all his doubts and then some. Not only that, she hadn't told him that she planned on obtaining the information from her mother. It had sounded like a good idea in the lab, but now that she thought about it more carefully, it seemed vampiric and Frankenstein-esque. And was Myra really in any condition to understand what she would be agreeing to if she let them inject her with virus carrying their truce factor? What might happen to her if she did? The virus and its resistance factor didn't seem to have impacted her in any negative way— certainly no more than her own body was doing to her at this point—but the truce factor represented a wild card. No one could have any idea how it might interact with her immune system until they inoculated her with it. Nan would be more than happy to act as the guinea pig, but Zach was right, Myra was the one with the well-adapted immune system. Their best chance lay with trying to access it.

They heard a rustle and a clunk coming from Myra's room, and Elliott arose with a sigh to go check on her. She had a bell right by her bed that she was supposed to ring when she needed something, but she rarely used it. After a few moments, Elliott came into the room pushing Myra in her wheelchair. After her last stroke, Myra's facial expressions had become both more blank and more tortured. Nan could barely stand to look at her, it had become so painful.

"She wanted to be part of the conversation," Elliott explained, and Nan forced herself to smile at her mother.

"Hi, Mom. We were just talking about the strategy we're thinking about using to achieve a healthier balance with the microbial kingdom."

Myra didn't reply, just bored her gaze into Nan as if she were trying to communicate telepathically.

"In fact, uh, when I was at the lab earlier, we were commenting on the fact that you have such a resilient immune system. You never seem to get sick."

"Never seem to get sick …" Myra echoed. Her face drooped sadly.

"Right." Nan swallowed, wondering if she should or could just go ahead and lay out her proposal, see what her mother's reaction would be. "You know, we—we were talking about the possibility that we might be able to use a virus to collect information from your genome that we could then give to other people."

Myra's eyebrows arched into two perfect U's, the way they did when something interested her. "Give to other people?" she queried, sounding hopeful.

"Yes, I know that might sound a little weird," Nan caught Elliott gazing at her with consternation out of the corner of her eye, "but we're kind of desperate right now and we need to try everything we can think of."

"I don't believe I've heard this part of the plan," Elliott interrupted.

Nan turned to face him, feeling shaky. It was one thing to offer yourself as an experimental animal; it was quite another to ask this of someone else—especially your mother, for God's sake. "I know. I hadn't gotten around to it yet." Nan once again sought out her mother's gaze. "We … would need to inject you with the virus that's currently making the rounds with

the resistance factor, the one that's made all the microbes
so resistant to antibiotics and drugs; but this one would be
carrying a truce factor. You've already been exposed to this
virus, and it doesn't seem to have hurt you in any way. But I
have to be honest and tell you that there's no way to know what
the virus with the truce factor would do. It would be a big risk."

"A big risk," Myra repeated.

"Look, Nan, I don't know that this is such a good
idea," Elliott burst out nervously. "I mean, like you say, you
don't have a clue how it might act with this new genetic
information."

"You're right," she agreed mournfully. "Elliott's right, Mom.
I just wanted to bring it up so you would know what we were
thinking about. No one is expecting you to agree to this."

Myra didn't reply for a while. She continued to stare
intently at Nan. Then her arm began to shake.

"You know what, Mom?" Nan said. "Just forget I said
anything. It was a hare-brained idea to begin with."

Her mother screwed up her face and bellowed, "NO!!"

Nan drew back, surprised. "'No' what, Mom? No, you don't
want to do this?"

"Absolutely, positively," she mewed plaintively.

"That's fine, Myra," Elliott told her. "No one is going to
make you do anything you don't want to do."

"NO!!!" she shrieked once again, her arm wobbling
violently. Elliott tried to grasp her hand to quiet it, but she
jiggled his arm along with hers. "I—" she gasped, her face
contorted with effort, "I—I—I—" Nan could barely stand it.
She didn't know what to do or say. "I want to do things!" she
finally cried.

"I know, Mom," Nan replied, tears crowding into her eyes.

"No! I want to do things! I want—I want—I want to—to—
help!" she howled.

Elliott and Nan exchanged stricken glances. Elliott rested
his hands on Myra's shoulders. "This is a very generous offer

you're making. But … quite honestly, Myra—there's the chance that this could kill you. Do you understand that?"

She craned her head around so that she could look at him. "Absolutely!" she gasped. "Absolutely. Positively."

Tears began to stream down Nan's cheeks. "Are you sure, Mom?" she asked. She gently disentangled herself from Amber and knelt down next to her mother's wheelchair, taking her hand.

Myra began to keen. "I—don't want to be here!" she lamented. "Absolutely, positively! Absolutely, I want to do things! I want to do things!!!"

Nan's squeezed her eyes shut, her heart aching. "Okay, Mom," she choked. "We'll see what we can do."

She had to get up and leave the room then; she rushed upstairs to her bedroom where she crawled into bed and sobbed and sobbed. Nothing might happen, she kept telling herself; she might come through the whole process perfectly fine. But then, was death the worst thing that could befall her mother? She had said she didn't want to live any longer, that life was no fun for her any more. Nan didn't know which was sadder, the fear that her mother might die, or the possibility that she might not. And the fact that her mother wanted to die was the saddest thing of all. Why not give her a chance to be a hero?

Elliott came up after a while and sat beside her, stroking her back and shoulders. He didn't say anything, he just held her hand and caressed her. Nan felt so thankful to have him in her life, she started crying again, and she felt so afraid that Amber might succumb to her infection, this made her cry all the harder. She couldn't believe how painful life had become at this time in human history; she knew that everyone was going through what she was experiencing. This plague had devastated the human race so universally, she would be willing to bet that there wasn't a person alive who hadn't been personally touched by it.

Soon she sank into sleep and didn't even move until the next day. She awoke with a clear idea of what she wanted her message to be: something simple and direct. She called Joshua and discussed the wording with him; she was pleased to find that he had already constructed a code, using the triplet codons for the amino acids to stand for letters in the English alphabet. There were twenty-six letters to the alphabet and twenty amino acids, but the genetic code was redundant in that more than one triplet codon coded for a particular amino acid. He just used some of the extra codons for the extra letters, spaces, and punctuation marks.

"What's interesting to think about," he told her, "is that both the language and the genetic code are nondeterministic—you know, the correspondence between the elements is arbitrary. There's no way to predict that the word "door" will derive from what it looks like or does, in the same way that there's no reason any particular triplet codon should, through some sort of selective chemical law or advantage, code for the amino acid it represents. Makes you kind of wonder how the genetic code got selected for in the first place, doesn't it?"

Nan did find this to be a rather interesting aspect to the genetic code, particularly in light of what they were about to attempt. She gave Joshua her message, which said, "The human species seeks a truce with the microbial kingdom. Please help us to achieve a mutually desirable balance with the microflora of the planet." They both agreed that the message should be short and sweet and that the protein this sequence generated, according to Joshua's code, should not translate into any known proteins, even though most proteins were much larger than their brief message would generate. He said he would call her back when he'd finished all his tweaking, and he told her that everything else had been going smoothly: Janice's proliferation of the carrier virus and Zach's construction of the nucleotide library they would need for the plasmid carrying the white flag.

Nan got dressed and headed downstairs where she found Elliott boiling water while Myra sat in her wheelchair with her eyes closed, dozing. Zach had left for the lab already, and Amber was still asleep on the sofa in the den. Elliott told Nan worriedly that she seemed to be sleeping more and more, and that it was becoming increasingly difficult to rouse her.

"Her fever's not all that high," he said, his face drawn with fatigue. "It's just not going away. And she seems to get weaker every day."

Nan went into the den and spent a little time consulting her Touch for Health manual, then did a treatment on Amber. She seemed to relax a little after Nan worked on her, but Elliott was right—her color looked frighteningly pale, and Nan could swear she could watch Amber's life force ebbing away, bit by bit.

Nan believed that death was a natural and necessary part of life, and that those who died did not get snuffed out when their bodies ceased to function, even though she had no clear idea of what an afterlife might consist of, nor what a soul might be. She believed that in the case of someone like Myra, death could even be a blessing. But for those left behind, the death of a loved one could inflict a wound that never healed. She didn't even want to imagine life without Amber in it; and she shuddered to think what the child's death might do to Elliott. She recalled the young couple she'd interviewed in England, who had lost their son and daughter to killer bacteria, and how difficult it had been for them to take pleasure in life, to smile, and to laugh. The entire world was going to have a hard time with this, she realized with a sorrowful shock, even if they did manage to stem the pandemic. The world had already changed irrevocably, and healing would have to go much deeper than simply turning the tide of infection.

Nan decided not to wait for Joshua's phone call; she grabbed up her hat and coat and headed for the lab, after stopping in the kitchen to kiss Elliott and tell him where she was going. She was feeling a little better and she didn't want to waste any time when she had enough energy to work. She spent the morning working with Joshua and Zach to assemble the plasmid; in the afternoon, they ran tests to make sure that it had come together properly. Then they set about reproducing enough plasmids to offer to the carrier virus. Nan felt so anxious about performing this next step—and seeing whether her idea possessed any merit whatsoever—she hated to go home; but she could feel the toll her day's work was taking on her. She needed to rest. So she tore herself away, taking Zach with her, promising Janice and Joshua that she would see them first thing in the morning.

Zach seemed to sense that Nan wasn't in the mood to talk, so he remained quiet for most of the drive. Before they arrived at the house, however, he asked Nan if she had talked to Myra about their plan. Nan nodded, her throat closing up at the mention of her mother. Zach shot her an appraising glance, twisted a lock of hair around his finger while he thought. "If I know Myra," he finally said, "she probably loved the idea. She's a total hot shit."

Nan started crying at these words, wiping her tears away with the back of her hand. "That she is," she agreed.

Zach scrunched himself down in the space between the door and the seat, hugged his knees to his chest. "You know," he said softly, "I am so sorry about what I did. I know an apology doesn't exactly cut it at this point, but I ... I really am sorry. If I could take it back—" his face twisted and he fell silent.

Nan reached over and squeezed his shoulder. "I know, Zach. I know." She sighed heavily. "Well, if it's any consolation, I really do think something was bound to happen, sooner or later. It was already happening. If the microbes hadn't seized upon your plasmid, they would have found something else."

"I guess," he muttered.

When they arrived home, Zach took a shower, then came

down to the den and read to Amber out of *Winnie the Pooh*.
Zach apparently possessed quite a fondness for the Pooh
stories, and he had funny little voices for each one of the
characters. Amber didn't respond much, but that didn't seem
to dampen Zach's enthusiasm. Myra continued to doze on and
off during dinner, and Nan realized that her mother could
no longer feed herself, that she couldn't get anything to stay
on a utensil long enough to make it to her mouth. So she and
Elliott took turns feeding her while Amber picked at her food.
Nan wished she could put together a fruit smoothie for her,
something which had always tempted her in the past; but they
hadn't been able to buy yogurt for quite some time, and fruit
had also disappeared from market shelves, even canned and
frozen fruit.

After dinner, they turned off all the lights—another
request from the utility company, in an effort to conserve
energy—and they all sat in the den with a few candles lit.
Nan found that darkness tended to subdue conversation and
this evening was no exception. Everyone sat lost in thought,
motionless in the weighty darkness.

In the lab, Nan knew, her truce message was also sitting
in the dark—a hopeful probability, an intention phrased in
biological language, a molecular letter waiting to be delivered.
In the shadowy, ambiguous candlelight, Nan imagined that
she could see a shimmering lattice that pervaded everything, a
cosmic ocean of energy and particles that comprised biological
consciousness, one that connected, bathed, and supported
every living thing. Help us to achieve harmony, she prayed,
casting her prayer into the fathomless, dark unknown; help us
to survive.

CHAPTER 29

Nan unwrapped the rubber tourniquet from her mother's arm, withdrew the syringe, and mashed a sterile cotton ball against the puncture that the syringe left. Bending her mother's forearm back so that the cotton would be held securely in the crook of her elbow, Nan emptied the contents of the syringe into a stoppered test tube. Then she placed the test tube in a cooler to keep it fresh until she could get it into the lab.

"Thanks, Mom," she said, giving her a smile, which Myra returned. Lifting the cotton ball so that she could take a peek at the small wound underneath, however, Nan felt disconcerted to see that it didn't appear to be clotting. The last couple of times she'd drawn blood from her mother, she'd had trouble getting the bleeding to stop. She had discontinued the aspirin a day that her mother had been taking as a preventative against strokes, but perhaps it was too soon to see any results in terms of how quickly her blood would clot. Nan wound some gauze around her mother's arm and pressed down hard on the puncture to staunch the flow. Five minutes later, it had finally stopped bleeding, and Nan sat back with a sigh of relief.

She glanced over at her mother, whose eyes were now closed, giving the false impression that she was either asleep or resting. Nan knew that the minute she made a move to get up, her mother's eyes would fly open and she would start thrashing around. A shadow beneath Myra's nose caught her eye and she bent forward to examine it more carefully. She had just realized that the dark smudge was blood when all of the sudden a bright red stream began pouring out of both nostrils.

"Oh my God!" Nan cried, snatching some tissues out of the dispenser on Myra's bedside table and pinching down hard on her nose. She managed to get Myra to scoot down farther so that her head was level with the rest of her body, and after she had applied pressure for another five minutes, she grabbed some ice out of the cooler and packed it against the tissues. Zach came into the room and stood watching them.

"Nose bleed?" he asked.

"Yeah," Nan muttered. "Her blood doesn't seem to be clotting that well."

Zach nodded. "I've been noticing the same thing. I ran some tests in the lab this morning, and it seems that her platelet count is awfully low. That could be why her blood isn't clotting."

"That's weird. I wonder what's going on with her platelets?"

"Beats me. Maybe Elliott would know. Is he at work?"

"He went in a couple of hours ago." She swallowed, trying to ease the lump in her throat. Amber had lapsed into delirium last night. Bacteria had spread throughout her body, causing a raging systemic infection. If Nan had to guess, she would say that Amber would be able to hold on only a few more days, at the most. Her fever had risen to 103 and stayed there, and nothing that they could do had helped bring it down. In a panic, Elliott had rushed off to work with some quixotic notion that he could come up with a solution in the time they had left, but Nan knew it was hopeless. Everything looked hopeless. They had inoculated Myra with the carrier virus bearing the truce factor a week ago, and they had been drawing blood from her and testing it twice daily since then.

But no new gene sequences had shown up in any of the samples. The only thing they had noticed was that the number of carrier viruses in Myra's system seemed to be multiplying, and given the information about her platelets, Nan had a terrible feeling that this was the reason behind her mother's reduced ability to clot her blood, not the aspirin.

Zach ran his hand through his hair awkwardly, then hugged his elbows, his hunched shoulders making him look even skinnier than usual. "If you want to go to the lab for a while, I'll watch Myra and Amber," he offered.

"Thanks, Zach," she told him, wiping away a tear. She bent over and gave her mother a kiss on the forehead. "I'm going to the lab, Mom. Zach's going to stay here and look after you, okay?"

"Okay," mumbled Myra through the wad of tissues and ice.

"Leave the ice on here for ten minutes or so," she told Zach. "I shouldn't be too long. I'm just going to drop this sample off and see how everybody's doing."

He nodded and sat down on the edge of the bed, holding Myra's ice pack in place. Nan gathered up the cooler and stopped by the den to see how Amber was doing. She hadn't moved since the last time Nan checked on her, and if she didn't awaken soon, she and Elliott were going to need to rig up some sort of IV in order to get fluids into her. She tried calling him on her way out, but there was no answer; either he was on his way home or he was too busy to pick up.

As she drove over to the university, she tried to shake the feeling that everyone on the planet had already died. It felt like an immense mausoleum, with practically no activity whatsoever on the streets and a heavy sense of mourning pervading every single aspect of the landscape—from the bare branches that looked scraped raw to the drooping houses with their darkened windows that bore no sign of inhabitants within. One yard she passed had a pink-and-white tricycle lying on its side in a patch of dirt, looking so forlorn and unused that she found herself fighting tears back once again.

She parked in the faculty lot, not even bothering to see if Ron's car was there, and plodded glumly to the lab. When she entered, Felix, Janice, and Joshua glanced up at her from their various stations, but she could tell from their expressions that they had nothing new to report.

"Another sample, guys," she announced, setting the cooler down on one of the lab benches. Janice came over and opened it, removed the test tube and began to work up the blood. "Any news?" she asked, without much hope.

"Well, some bad news, I'm afraid," said Felix.

"Oh great. I'm starting to think there isn't any other kind. What is it?"

"Teresa has diphtheria."

Nan twisted as if someone had stuck her with a knife. "Oh man," she breathed. "Christ." She slumped down on the lab bench and lost it. She began crying so hard, she gave herself the hiccups. Her students crowded around her and patted her back and shoulders, but nothing could comfort her. The human race was expiring right before her very eyes, and despite the anger and frustration she had sometimes felt toward her species—with their ecological stupidity and biological myopia—she realized that she loved humanity more than she had ever thought she did, even in her most idealistic moments. What other creature would have ever come up with a pogo stick or an Empire State Building or a violin? She couldn't believe that they weren't going to have a second chance to get things right. She couldn't believe that this was happening in her lifetime.

Despite her promise to Zach, she found that she couldn't bear to go back home right away. She helped perform tests on the blood samples from Myra, her heart sinking the whole time she worked. She had a feeling that Myra was starting to lose her tenacious hold on life, and Nan felt terrified that she might slip away from them before they could obtain the genetic information from her that they needed. Assuming it was ever going to happen. She was starting to think that Elliott was right. Her plan had been borne out of nothing but fever-induced delusion and desperation. How could she have ever imagined that her truce factor would work, anyway? It was a totally insane idea, she could see that now.

Still, she worked doggedly through the afternoon, ignoring the weariness that crept into her bones and muscles. Everyone worked without speaking, almost as if they were in a trance; so when Joshua exclaimed that he had found something, it took a while for his words to sink in. Everyone gazed at him blankly.

"What is it?" Nan finally asked.

"The virus in yesterday's sample seems to have a different molecular weight than the others."

"Really?" Nan hurried over to his side to inspect his results. "How different?"

"Quite a bit, I would say." They exchanged glances, a tiny, minuscule flare of hope beginning to bloom.

"Double-check that, okay?" she said. "It could be a contaminant."

"Right," he concurred, trying to sound neutral; but Nan could hear the excitement in his voice.

She returned to her experiments in which she was using enzymes to break the viruses from Myra into fragments that she could then match up with and compare to the old viruses. She told herself that she couldn't really expect to find anything, but Joshua's results had galvanized her, and she found herself fidgeting with impatience while she waited for some of the slower parts of the process to take place. When she finally obtained her first results, she felt so keyed-up, she had a hard time taking in what she was looking at. The longer she stared at her print-out, however, the more the significance began to sink in.

"Hey, guys!" she shouted. "This virus is different! It has new sequences! It has a lot of new sequences! Something has happened!!"

Everyone dropped what they were doing and rushed over to see for themselves. When they saw what she was talking about, Joshua gave a whoop and they all grabbed each other in a group embrace and hugged each other hard, dancing and jumping up and down.

"Now, we don't know what these new sequences code for," Nan cautioned, once they quieted down a bit. "They could code for anything."

"Right," they responded in a chorus. But no one looked any less excited.

Nan asked everyone to quit whatever task they were working on and start cloning more of the virus with the new gene sequences while she set up a battery of tests to start analyzing and translating the new genes. She didn't feel tired at all now. When the phone rang a couple of hours later, she considering letting it ring, but it could be Elliott or Zach calling from home. She ran into her office and snatched up the receiver.

"Nan Schulte," she said.

"Nan, it's Elliott."

"Elliott, I've got some outstanding news!" she told him.

There was a pause. "Well, that's great. Because I've got some bad news."

Fear clutched Nan's heart. "What?"

"Amber's in a coma." His voice caught and then he began to sob. "We've lost her, Nan. She's not coming out of this."

Nan sat down, feeling light-headed and breathless. "Oh God," she murmured. Were they too late? "Look," she said quickly. "We've managed a breakthrough here. One of the samples from Myra is carrying a whole slew of new gene sequences. Now, obviously we don't know what these genes do, but if we don't have any other choice left ... if we're going to lose Amber if we don't do something drastic ..." She stopped, unsure how to finish her sentence.

Elliott didn't reply for a moment. "What are you suggesting?" he asked finally.

"Well, that we try inoculating her with the new virus. I know it's risky—riskier, even, than what we've done to Myra, but—"

"That's the other thing," Elliott replied grimly. "Myra's not doing well at all. Zach noticed that her skin is covered with more than bruises—she's developing petechiae. She seems to be bleeding around her gums, too."

Nan sank forward onto her desk, propped herself up with her elbows. "Jesus."

"I don't know that it would do much good to save Amber from an infection only to have her bleed to death."

"No, that's true. But—we're talking about a different entity," she said. "The virus we injected into Myra was carrying only the truce factor; what's coming out now is different."

"Right, and the problems with Myra didn't start showing up until a couple of days ago. Probably right around the time that the new viruses were being released into her system."

Nan exhaled heavily, her feelings of hopelessness returning. "Yeah, that's probably correct," she muttered.

Neither of them spoke.

"Oh hell," Elliott exclaimed. "She's going to die anyway if we don't do something. Try it."

"Are—are you sure?"

"Yeah, what have we got to lose?" he said dispiritedly.

"Okay, I'll get a dose together and come home immediately."

"Okay," he responded, hanging up without saying good-bye.

Nan raced around the lab to prepare a dose of the new virus for Amber. She felt unwilling to tell anyone what she was going to do with it, although she figured that everyone could probably guess. No one said anything to her, just gave her a hug before she left.

The drive home passed by in a blur. Nan felt so anxious about what she was about to do, she felt sick to her stomach. What if the new virus wasn't benign? What if it was killing Myra and would do the same to Amber? They didn't know how the virus would interpret the truce factor on a genetic and molecular basis; they couldn't count on its cooperation even if it did understand the message. On the other hand, Elliott was right about one thing: if they didn't do something radical, they were going to lose Amber anyway.

Nan charged into the house, afraid that every second might count. She hastened into the den, where Elliott sat on the sofa next to Amber, massaging her arms and legs. He looked up when he heard her step, and the anguished expression on his face hit her like a spray of glass shards. Before either one of them could lose their nerve or change their mind, Nan took out the syringe which contained the new virus. Holding her breath, Nan eased the needle into Amber's limp, burning arm, shaking her head sorrowfully when the child didn't even flinch. After her task was completed, she sat back on her heels and met Elliott's gaze. He stretched out his arms and grabbed her up in bone-crushing embrace, his tears trickling down the side of her face.

After a moment, Nan gently extricated herself and took both of Elliott's hands. "We've done everything we can do at this point, sweetheart," she told him. "All we can do now is hope and pray."

Elliott nodded, his face so haggard, he looked ten years older than he had even a month ago. Nan then went into check on Myra, where she found Zach reading to her out of *The Hobbit*. Nan knew that her mother had never been a big fantasy fan, but her face looked peaceful as Zach read. She saw right away the petechiae that Elliott had mentioned over the phone; they freckled her face with blue-and-purple dots, tattooed her arms and hands with spidery splotches. If grief could kill, Nan thought, she herself would be dying right now.

She couldn't rule out the possibility that infecting her mother with the carrier virus and its accompanying "truce" factor was causing her lowered platelet count. In fact, all the evidence pointed to the fact that this was the case. It didn't matter that Myra had insisted; Nan was her protector. She shouldn't have listened to her, shouldn't have let her put herself in harm's way.

On the other hand, she reflected, easing herself quietly into a chair so as not to disturb Zach's reading, one of the things she had always liked about her upbringing was that her parents allowed Nan to make her own mistakes. They didn't try to shield her from every bad thing that might happen to her as many of her friends' parents did. As hurt as she had sometimes felt by her mother's emotional distance, she had noticed that many of her friends who were over-protected ended up fearful and insecure about their own abilities. Myra had often said that life was all about making efforts and along with those efforts, mistakes. Mistakes were not bad or sinful; they were the result of trying, stretching limits, and venturing into unknown territory. In her mother's opinion, Nan knew, a life spent trying to avoid mistakes was a life not fully lived. Nan also knew that "mistakes" in the genetic code lent flexibility and adaptivity, effectively made it possible for life to exist. Letting Myra take this chance was at least not infantilizing her, Nan told herself, grasping at any straw she could; it at least gave her some power at a time in her life when she virtually had none.

After a while, Zach ceased reading, closed the book, and leaned back in the chair, observing Myra. She did seem to be sleeping at this point, so he signaled to Nan and they left the room.

"I take it you talked to Elliott," he said, once they were in the hallway.

"Yeah," she sighed. She filled him in about the new developments with the virus and the chance they were taking with Amber. His eyes teared up when she brought up Amber;

she gave his shoulder a squeeze and told him not to lose hope, although her words sounded hollow even to her.

It was a grim and gloomy dinner that Nan, Zach, and Elliott shared: baked carrots and plain noodles. Nan found an old bottle of cooking sherry in the pantry and they all drank a glass afterward. Nan tried to feed Myra, but after two bites, she said she wasn't hungry, so Nan let her be. After dinner, they turned out all the lights and sat silently in the den with Amber. Zach disappeared after a while to go to bed, but both Elliott and Nan wanted to stay up, to keep an eye on Amber and Myra.

It wasn't easy to stay awake in the close darkness, especially as tired as she was from her day's efforts; so somewhere in the wee hours of the morning, Nan finally dozed off in her chair. She awoke with a start when the room began to lighten from the wintry dawn, crestfallen when she looked over at Amber and saw that she still hadn't moved from last night. She glanced over at Elliott and saw that he, too, had fallen asleep. He snored softly in the rocking chair, an afghan wrapped around him for warmth.

Tiptoeing soundlessly into her mother's room, Nan's heart practically stopped at the scene that greeted her. Obviously Myra's nose had bled again during the night; dark, coagulated blood led from there and fanned out onto the blankets, which were positively soaked in blood, covering Myra in deep, dark scarlet. She had died sometime during the night while Nan slept; rigor mortis had already begun and her limbs were frozen in a contorted position that they had often assumed while she lived. Nan sank down on the bed and wept. She tried to arrange her mother in a more comfortable-looking pose but couldn't. She knew she couldn't before she tried, but she couldn't stop herself. She grabbed up tissues and dabbed uselessly at the blood that was everywhere, keening and crying and rocking herself back and forth. Elliott came in then and joined her on the bed, holding her close and murmuring comfort.

"I killed her, Elliott," she moaned.

"She was dying, sweetie," he told her.

"I know, but still …" She buried her face in his chest, her shoulders heaving from silent sobs.

"It's okay, sweetheart. Shhhhh."

Suddenly Nan jumped up. "What about Amber?" she exclaimed. "Did you check her when you woke up? I mean, Myra died and we didn't even know it! Is—is Amber okay, do you think?"

"She hasn't budged, if that's what you mean."

Nan headed for the den in a panic. "Did you check her breathing, though? Her pulse?"

"Not yet. I heard you crying, so—" Elliott hurried behind her.

When they burst into the den, fearing the worst, they couldn't believe their eyes. Amber was sitting on the sofa, pushing the covers out of the way. She glanced up at them, frowning, her eyebrows crinkled in a way that suggested she needed something.

"I'm thirsty," she said plaintively. "Can I have a glass of water?"

CHAPTER 30

Nan waited while Elliott pounded on the door, then stamped her feet and breathed on her hands to warm them as they waited for a response from inside. Her breath left small frozen droplets clinging to the wool of her mittens; the air even smelled cold. After several long minutes, the door opened a crack.

"Yes?" said a quavering voice.

"My name is Elliott Jenkins, ma'am. I'm with public health. Do you mind if we step inside for a moment?"

"I wouldn't come in here if I were you. Two of us have diphtheria. I've got bronchitis."

"That's okay. We're both immune."

Silence.

"We'd like to know if there's anything we can do to help you folks. We're going door to door checking to see if people have needs that relate to public health."

"We don't have any bodies, if that's what you mean," the woman replied wearily.

"Well, I'm glad to hear that. But that's not all we can help you with. We've got food, clean water, medical supplies, extra blankets …"

The door opened wider to reveal a gaunt, middle-aged woman dressed in slacks and an overcoat, a scarf wound around her head for warmth. "Food?" she asked hopefully.

"That's right. May we give you some?"

Tears welled up in the woman's eyes as she opened the door all the way and beckoned for them to enter. "We'd be awfully grateful," she choked.

Elliott held up a gloved finger. "We'll be right back with the food."

Nan followed him back to the van where they had stashed their supplies. In the past couple of weeks, they had been busy collecting food in a food drive—the ghoulish reality was that a number of households had no survivors yet the larders were relatively well-stocked—and now they were delivering it. People needed and welcomed the supplies they brought, of course, and Nan felt only too glad to be able to distribute them; but the food deliveries were really a cover for a more important activity: spreading the new virus bearing the genes it had collected from Myra.

For a week they had remained closed up in the house, not going outside for any reason whatsoever, making do with whatever they had on hand and burying Myra in the cellar after a simple ceremony. They had watched Amber closely for any signs of unusual bleeding or bruising, but not only had she continued to recover from her bacterial infection, she had shown no symptoms related to any other health problems. Her blood clotted quickly and well. She was getting stronger and rosier by the day. Her energy levels appeared to be soaring. So they finally risked taking a blood sample to Elliott's office to check her platelet count, which turned out to be well within normal levels.

Ron had made good on his threat to take over Nan's lab space, since she and her staff had decided that they couldn't risk letting the world know what they had done. With all the fear and hysteria surrounding the pandemic, telling everyone that they had engineered a virus to solve the world's health problems would undoubtedly be met with disbelief and resistance. They might even get locked up in the slammer, a Level Four containment facility which would keep them from spreading the new bug. But by the time he took over, it didn't matter. They had their cure. After Amber, they had treated Teresa, who was dying from diphtheria. Much to their relief, she had recovered as well. Then Elliott took a chance on recruiting a group of gravely ill members of the community for what he termed an "experimental treatment," implying that it was a vaccine, but in actuality, the injection carried the new virus. Forty-six of Elliott's volunteers made full recoveries from their illnesses; the other five had been too far gone to benefit from the treatment. At this point, though, he and Nan and everyone they came into contact with were spreading it through their breath and touch.

By delivering food and other supplies door-to-door, they gained access to people's homes, where they would talk, handle this and that, breathe into the closed-up air, and shed viruses around them. Their efforts had already begun to have an impact. Reported recovery rates over the past two weeks had begun to climb, slowly at first, but momentum was building. It was encouraging enough that they had started thinking about what they wanted their next step to be.

Nan waited while Elliott opened the van's cargo door, then selected a box which held an assortment of items: canned pumpkin and pineapple, tins of sardines and tuna, jars of baby corn and strawberry jam, a wedge of cheddar, a couple of loaves of Russian brown bread, and some chocolate bars. Elliott hefted a box packed with gallon jugs of boiled water since people would still be vulnerable to the microorganisms in the water until the helper virus kicked in. One of the exciting prospects of the dawning new immunologic era was that drinking water might not have to be so heavily treated in the future, which could reduce the risk of cancer for lots and lots of people.

Nan placed a couple of blankets on top of her box, too, in case the family could use them. Heating oil deliveries were still few and far between, and the weather had turned bitterly cold. When they returned to the house, the woman held the door open, holding her scarf over her mouth as Elliott and Nan walked past her, whether because of the cold air or to minimize their exposure to her bronchitis, Nan couldn't be sure. Such shielding had become automatic over the last few months. Inside, the rooms were dark, as the curtains were drawn shut to conserve warmth. The house smelled stale and fetid, heavy with sickness and rank with the lingering flatulent odor of boiled root vegetables. Nan didn't see the other two people the woman referred to but figured they must be in bed.

"Do you mind if we just look in on your other family members?" she asked, setting her supplies down on the floor.

The woman hesitated. "They're awfully sick," she said. "Are you sure you're immune?"

They nodded.

"Well ... okay. I suppose that would be all right." She led them reluctantly up the stairs and led them first to the master bedroom where her husband lay gasping for air, his color appallingly gray. Elliott approached the bed and knelt down beside him, picked up his hand and pretended to take his pulse. Nan knew that he was doing this simply to increase his exposure to the man. She hoped that the man wasn't too ill to recover once the virus became established in his system. It didn't look good, but on the other hand, she'd been amazed at some of the recoveries they had witnessed recently. After a few minutes, Elliott got up.

"What ... do you think?" the woman asked anxiously.

Elliott laid his hand on the woman's shoulder. "He's very sick," he said. "But he has a chance to recover."

Tears glistened in the woman's eyes once more as she turned and led them to her teen-aged son's room. He was asleep, his breathing labored and ragged, but he didn't look nearly as gray as his father. Elliott bent over him and murmured a few words into his ear, snugged the blankets closer around him. Then he straightened up. "He should be okay," he told the woman. " Just keep him hydrated. Your husband, too."

She nodded, hope suffusing her features for the first time. "I can't thank you enough," she said. "You said you're from public health?"

Elliott and Nan nodded, although they were hoping that no one would actually check with the public health department to see if their activities were officially sanctioned. They found that the words "public health" had a reassuring effect on people, but what they were doing was nothing more than a grass roots effort, and they didn't want to attract too much attention. Someone somewhere might think that what they were doing was contributing to the spread of disease.

They made a few more stops before they called it a day and headed for home where Zach was babysitting Amber. Zach was starting to feel like a member of the family, although Nan had noticed a certain restlessness in him lately. She imagined, being a California boy, he didn't care much for the New England winter. He had mentioned wanting to go to Mexico and see his parents.

When they drove up to the house, they were surprised to find several cars parked out front. She recognized them as her graduate students' cars, and she almost expected to be greeted with a surprise party when they entered the house. Everyone was sitting casually around the table in the kitchen, however, where the mouthwatering aroma of hot spiced cider filled the air.

"Man oh man does that ever smell good!" she exclaimed. "Where on Earth did the cider come from?"

She noticed Connor sitting at the table along with everyone else, looking pleased with himself. "I traded some thermal socks to a farmer for it," he told her. "I have two more gallons, in fact."

"Well, aren't you the high roller!" she teased, sitting down to join them. Janice handed her and Elliott a cup, while Amber wriggled out of Zach's lap and climbed into her dad's.

"How did it go?" asked Felix.

"Good," Elliott replied. "We gave away a lot of food and didn't find one deserted household today."

"Great!" said Janice.

Nan nodded, inhaling the sweet steam rising off her cider. "So ... to what do we owe this festive gathering?" she inquired.

Everyone exchanged glances, obviously wondering who should speak first. The group ended up with their gaze fastened on Joshua, so he cleared his throat. "Well, we've been talking about where we should go next with this thing," he said. "I mean, it's great to help out in our own back yard, so to speak, but people all over the world are suffering. We were thinking that we might want to pull a 'Zach.'"

Zach winced at his choice of words. "Thanks, man," he grumbled.

"No offense intended!" he added hastily. "What I meant was, we should scatter. We should travel all over the world. We should breathe on and drool on and paw as many people as we possibly can. We need to spread this thing, and quick."

Nan smiled; in fact, it wasn't too different from a notion she had begun to entertain. Trying to ship "vaccines" around the world would pose a problem. Someone might want to analyze the contents and find that a live virus resided inside. There could be oceans of red tape to wade through in each different country. Shipments could get lost, delayed, and waylaid. Spreading the virus personally carried a risk, of course. The world was undoubtedly a much trickier place to travel around in these days as several governments had collapsed during the pandemic, the majority of airlines had gone bankrupt, and chaos ruled in hot spots all over the globe. Renting vehicles might be impossible in certain locales and reports from the Internet indicated that a number of developing nations were now operating as a collection of city states without much communication taking place between them. Still, delivering the virus personally would improve the chance that it would get circulating soon enough to save the billions of people who needed it.

"What were you thinking about specifically?" she asked.

"Well, basically the same thing that Zach did," Joshua replied. "Fly around to different cities, fan out from there and travel around the countryside a bit. Each of us could go to a different part of the world to maximize the distribution."

Elliott nodded thoughtfully. "We could pose as relief workers. We could go help out in places that were hard hit."

"Hey, we could even make up some sort of bogus organization that we're from. Things are so disorganized now, nobody's going to know whether we're official or not," Janice said.

"Sure!" Teresa exclaimed. "We could be the Global Pandemic Health Initiative or something."

"We could get hats and T shirts made up," Felix laughed. "At least badges, anyway."

Nan nodded, her enthusiasm growing. "I received a little inheritance from my mom. I'd be happy to use that money for travel expenses."

"I've still got some left from my grandparents," said Zach.

"And Elliott and I are only going to need one house since we're getting married," Nan added, glancing over at Elliott to see how her statement would affect him. He looked startled.

"What?" he sputtered.

"You heard me," she replied, reaching over and slipping her arm inside his.

"Yay!" squealed Amber. Elliott grinned so widely Nan began to laugh. Everyone lifted up their mugs in a toast while Joshua shouted, "Hear hear!" and Teresa burst into tears. Nan grabbed Amber and Elliott in a three-way embrace, crushing them to her so tightly she expected them to protest; but they didn't.

Thank you, she thought, hoping the virus could hear her, that the planet could hear her, that every single organism in the biosphere could hear her. This human-microbe detente was the first step in a new way of interacting with the earth's other inhabitants; she only hoped that once this cooperative venture took root, it would encourage and sustain even more efforts at cooperation.

"'We have seen the enemy and they is us,'" she quoted softly, so softly that no one could hear her, not even Elliott. She sat back, snatched up her cup and held it aloft. "Here's to peace," she said. "Here's to life."

ABOUT THE AUTHOR

Celeste White, M.S., holds degrees in Biology from Wellesley College and the University of Massachusetts, Amherst, where she studied epigenetics, microbiology, and cell biology. She graduated a Wellesley Scholar, and she was awarded a University Fellowship at U. Mass. She is the author of two theoretical papers on gene regulation: one on the effects of the three-dimensional structure of the interphase genome, and one on a biophysical mechanism that could affect gene regulation.